About

With a background of [...]
and a love of the rom[...]
Sue MacKay writes [...]
wrote her first story a[...]
since. She lives in New Zealand's Marlborough Sounds
where she indulges her passions for cycling, walking
and kayaking. When she isn't writing she also loves
cooking and entertaining guests with sumptuous meals
that include locally caught fish.

Marion Lennox is a country girl, born on an Australian
dairy farm. She moved on, because the cows just
weren't interested in her stories! Married to a 'very
special doctor', she has also written under the name
Trisha David. She's now stepped back from her 'other'
career teaching statistics. Finally, she's figured what's
important and discovered the joys of baths, romance
and chocolate. Preferably all at the same time! Marion
is an international award winning author.

USA TODAY bestselling author **Jules Bennett** has
penned more than fifty novels during her short career.
She's married to her high school sweetheart, has two
active girls, and is a former salon owner. Jules can be
found on Twitter, Facebook (Fan Page), and her website
julesbennett.com. She holds contests via these three
outlets with each release and loves to hear from readers!

Island Escapes

Island Escapes:
Tropical Trysts

SUE MacKay

MARION LENNOX

JULES BENNETT

MILLS & BOON

First Published in Great Britain 2021
by Mills & Boon, an imprint of HarperCollins*Publishers* Ltd,
1 London Bridge Street, London, SE1 9GF

www.harpercollins.co.uk

HarperCollins*Publishers*
1st Floor, Watermarque Building,
Ringsend Road, Dublin 4, Ireland

ISLAND ESCAPES: TROPICAL TRYSTS © 2021 Harlequin Books S.A.

Breaking All Their Rules © 2016 Sue MacKay
A Child to Open Their Hearts © 2016 Marion Lennox
A Royal Amnesia Scandal © 2015 Jules Bennett

ISBN: 978-0-263-30059-8

MIX
Paper from
responsible sources
FSC™ C007454

This book is produced from independently certified FSC™ paper to ensure responsible forest management.

For more information visit: www.harpercollins.co.uk/green

Printed and bound in Spain
by CPI, Barcelona

BREAKING ALL
THEIR RULES

SUE MacKay

Dear Lyn, I am going to miss your laugh and those good times we yakked in your sewing room. Thank you for dragging me out to find my other passions that I'd forgotten all about until I met you. You read every book and this one is definitely for you.

CHAPTER ONE

OLIVIA COATES-CLARK STRAIGHTENED up and indicated to a nurse to wipe her forehead in an attempt to get rid of an annoying tickle that had been irritating her for some minutes. 'Is it me, or is Theatre hotter than usual this morning?'

'I haven't noticed,' Kay, the anaesthetist, answered as she kept an eye on the monitors in front of her. 'Sure you're not stressing about tonight, Olivia?'

'Me? Stress?' Olivia grimaced behind her mask. She was a control freak; of course she stressed. 'Okay, let's get this second implant inserted so we can bring our girl round.'

'So everything's good to go for the gala fundraiser?' Kay persisted.

'Fingers crossed,' Olivia muttered, refusing to think about what could go wrong. Her list of requirements and tasks was complete, neat little ticks beside every job and supplier and by the name of every attendee, including the seeing eye dog coming.

'I bumped into Zac yesterday. He's looking forward to catching up with everyone.' Kay's forced nonchalance didn't fool her.

'I'm sure everyone feels the same.' The anaesthetist *had* hit on the reason for Olivia feeling unnaturally hot. Zachary Wright. Just knowing he'd be at the function she'd spent weeks organising made her toes curl with unwanted anticipation. Not to mention the alien nervousness. 'Zac,' she sighed into her mask. The one man she'd never been able to delete from her mind. And, boy, had she tried.

'You need more mopping?' the nurse asked.

'No, thanks.' That particular irritation had gone, and she'd ignore the other—Zac—by concentrating on supervising the plastic surgery registrar opposite her as he placed the tissue expander beneath the pocket under Anna Seddon's pectoralis major muscle on the left side of her chest wall.

The registrar had supported Olivia as she'd done the first insertion of an expander on the right side, watching every move she made, listening to every word she said, as though his life depended on it. Which it did. One mistake and she'd be on him like a ton of bricks. So far he was doing an excellent job of the second breast implant. 'Remember to make sure this one's placed exactly the same as the first one. No woman is going to thank you for lopsided breasts.' This might only be the first stage in a series of surgeries to reconstruct Anna's breasts but it had to be done well. There was no other way.

The guy didn't look up as he said, 'I get it. This is as much about appearances and confidence as preventing cancer.'

'Making a person feel better about themselves is our job description.' Her career had evolved along a path of repairing people who'd had misadventures or deforming surgeries. But she didn't knock those specialists working to make people happier in less traumatic circumstances. Everyone was entitled to feel good about themselves, for whatever reasons; to hide behind a perfect facade if they needed to.

For Olivia, looking her absolute best was imperative: a confident shield that hid the messy, messed-up teenager from the critical world waiting to pounce. Making the most of her appearance hadn't been about attracting males and friends since she was twelve and the night her father had left home for the last time, taking his clothes and car, and her heart. Leaving her to deal with her mother's problems alone.

Kay glanced down at the table. 'This isn't the first time I've seen a perfectly healthy woman deliberately have her breasts removed, but I still can't get my head round it. I don't know if I'd have the guts to have the procedure done if I didn't already have cancer.'

Olivia understood all too well, but... 'If you'd lost your grandmother and one sister to the disease, and your mother had had breast cancer you might think differently.' Bad luck came in all forms.

'I'd do whatever it took to be around to watch my kids grow up,' one of the nurses said.

'You're right, and so would I.' Kay shivered. 'Still, it's a huge decision. You'd want your man on side, for sure.'

'Anna's husband's been brilliant. I'd go so far as to call him a hero. He's backing her all the way.' A hero? If she wasn't in Theatre she'd have to ask herself what she was on. Heroes were found in romance stories, not real life—not often anyhow, and not in her real life. Not that she'd ever let one in if one was on offer.

As Olivia swabbed the incision a clear picture of Zac spilled into her mind, sent a tremor down her arm, had her imagining his scent. *Oh, get over yourself.* Zac wasn't her hero. Wasn't her *anything*. Hadn't been since she'd walked away from their affair eighteen months ago. But—she sighed again—what would've happened if she'd found the courage to push the affair beyond the sex and into a relationship where they talked and shared and had been there for each other? Eventually Zac would've left her. At least by getting in first she'd saved herself from being hurt. Tonight she'd see quite a bit of him, which didn't sit easily with her. The day his registration for the gala had arrived in her inbox she'd rung him for a donation for the fundraising auction. Since then she hadn't been able to erase him from her mind. *Come on. He's always been lurking in the back of your head, reminding you how good you were together.*

'So there are good guys out there.' Kay's tone was acerbic.

Zac might be one of the good guys. She hadn't hung round long enough to find out. She'd got too intense about him too quickly and pulling the plug on their fling had been all about staying in control and not setting herself up to be abandoned. Going through that at twelve had been bad enough; to happen again when she was an adult would be ridiculous. So she'd run. Cowardly for sure, but the only way to look out for herself. And now she had an op to finish and a gala to start. 'Let's get this tidied up and the saline started.' She had places to be and hopefully not many things to do.

An hour later she was beginning to wish she'd stayed in Theatre for the rest of the day. The number of texts on her phone gave the first warning that not everything was going to plan at the hotel where the gala evening would be held; that her list was in serious disarray.

As she ran for her car, the deluge that all but drowned her and destroyed her carefully styled hair, which she'd spent the evening before having coloured and tidied, was the second warning. At least her thick woollen coat had saved her silk blouse from ruin. But rain had not been on her schedule, which put her further out of sorts. *Everything* about tonight had to be perfect.

Slamming the car door, she glared out at the black sky through the wet windscreen. 'Get a move on. I want you gone before my show starts tonight.'

The third suggestion that things were turning belly up was immediate and infuriating. One turn of the ignition key and the flat clicking sound told a story of its own. The battery was kaput. Because? Olivia slapped the dashboard with her palm. The lights had been left on. There was no one to blame except herself.

Olivia knew the exact moment Zac walked through the entrance of the plush hotel, and it had nothing to do with the sudden change in noise as the doors opened, letting in sounds of rain and car horns. She might've been facing the receptionist but she knew. Her skin prickled, her belly tightened, and the air around her snapped. Worse, she forgot whatever it was she'd been talking about to the young woman on the other side of the polished oak counter.

So nothing had changed. He still rattled her chain, made her feel hot and sexy and out of control—and he hadn't even said a word to her. Probably hadn't recognised her back view.

'Hello, Olivia. It's been a while.'

That particular husky, sexy voice belonged to only one man. 'Since what, Zac?' she asked, as she lifted her head and turned to face him, fighting the adrenaline rush threatening to turn her into a blithering wreck. This was why she'd left him. Zac undermined her self-control. How had she found the strength to walk away? Not that there'd been anything more to their relationship than sex. Nothing that should be making her blood fizz and her heart dance a tango just because he stood a few feet from her. No way did she want to jump his bones within seconds of seeing him. She shouldn't want to at all. But no denying it—she did. Urgently.

Black-coffee-coloured eyes bored into her, jolting her deep inside. 'Since we last spent the night together, enjoying each other's company.'

'Go for the jugular, why don't you?' she gasped, knowing how wrong it was to even wish he'd give her a hug and say he'd missed her.

Zac instantly looked contrite. 'Sorry, Olivia. I didn't mean to upset you.'

'You didn't,' she lied. Behind her physical reaction her heart was sitting up, like it had something to say. Like what? Not going there. 'The bedroom scene was the grounds of our relationship.' That last night she'd got up at three in the morning, said she couldn't do it any more, and had walked out without explaining why. To tell him her fears would've meant exposing herself, and that was something she never did.

'So? How's things? Keeping busy?' Inane, safe, and so not what she really wanted to ask. *Got a new woman in your life? Do you ever miss me? Even a teeny, weeny bit? Or are you grateful I pulled the plug when I did?* Right now all her muscles felt like they were reaching for him, wanting him touching them, rubbing them, turning her on even more. Had she done the right thing in leaving? Of course she had. Rule number one: stay in control. She'd been losing it back then. Fast.

Zac had the audacity to laugh. 'What? You haven't kept tabs on me?' His grin was lazy, and wide, and cut into her with the sexiness of it. There was no animosity there whatsoever, just a deliberate, self-mocking gleam in his beautiful eyes. He was as good as her at hiding emotions.

Shaking her head at him, Olivia leaned back, her hands pressed against the counter at her sides, the designer-jeans-clad legs Zac had sworn were the best he'd ever had anything to do with posed so that one was in front of the other and bent slightly at the knee, tightening the already tight, annoyingly damp denim over her not-so-well-toned thigh. 'My turn to apologise. I haven't kept up with any gossip.'

'Dull as dishwater, that's my life.' Unfortunately that twinkle she'd always melted for was very apparent, belying his statement.

'Right.' She rolled her eyes at him, unable to imagine Zac not being involved in and with people, especially feminine, good-looking, sexy people. Was she jealous? Couldn't be. She'd done the dumping, not him. But Zac with another woman? Pain lodged in the region of her heart.

'Never could fool you.' It was inordinately satisfying to see his gaze drop to the line on the front of her thigh where the mulberry three-quarter-length coat cut across her jeans. Even more gratifying when his tongue lapped that grin, which rapidly started fading. And downright exciting to see Zachary blink not once but twice.

She didn't need exciting in her life right now, and Zac and exciting were one and the same. 'I keep to myself a lot these days too,' she muttered, not really sure what she was talking about any more with the distracting package standing right in front of her.

'Now I'm shocked.' The grin was back in place,

lion-like in its power to knock her off her feet and set her quaking.

'Why? It's not as though I've ever been a social butterfly.'

'There's never been anything butterfly-like about you, Olivia.'

Confidence oozed from Zac that didn't bode well for the coming evening when they'd be in the same crowd, the same venue. At the same table. Of all the things she'd organised she should've been able to arrange that he sat on the opposite side of the room. It had proved impossible as they were the only two people attending the gala who were on their own. All the others were in pairs.

'You're saying I'm not a flapper?' They were toying with each other. Reality slammed into her, made her gasp aloud. They'd teased each other mercilessly the first night they'd gone to bed together, and had never stopped. Well, she was stopping now. Time to put distance between them. She needed to get on with what she was supposed to be doing. 'I've got a lot to do so I'll see you later. I hope you have a great evening.'

Disappointment flicked through his eyes, quickly followed by something much like hurt but couldn't be. Not hurt. She hadn't done anything more than push him aside, though that'd probably spiked his pride. He had a reputation of loving and leaving.

It had taken the death of a small child in Theatre to throw them into each other's arms for the first time. Desperate to obliterate the anguished parents from her mind, Olivia had found temporary comfort with Zac. She'd also found sex like she'd never known before. How they'd spent years rubbing shoulders at med school and not felt anything for each other until that day was one of life's mysteries. From then on all it took had been one look and they'd be tearing each other's clothes off, falling into bed, onto the couch, over the table. They'd done little talking and a lot of action.

Tonight, if they were stuck together for any length of time, she'd talk and keep her hands to herself. That had been the plan, but so far it wasn't working out. Not that she'd touched Zac yet. Yet? With her mouth watering and her fingers twitching, it would take very little to change that. She had to get serious and focus on what had to be done. 'I'll leave you to check in.' Her voice was pitched high—definitely no control going on there.

'I'm not checking in.'

She should've remembered that. She knew all the names of the people who'd elected to stay the night here instead of driving home afterwards. 'Do you live nearby?'

'Over the road.'

'In that amazing apartment building designed to look like a cruise ship, overlooking the super yachts and high-end restaurants?' Oh, wow. He had done all right for himself. Of course, he came from a moneyed background, but she recalled him saying he'd paid his own way through med school. She had never told him she also came from money or that her mother had used it to bribe her to keep her onside until she was old enough to work out that hiding bottles of alcohol from her father wasn't a joke at all.

'Are you staying here?' he asked casually, making her wonder if he might have plans to pay her a visit if she was.

'Yes.' The house she'd bought last summer was less than twenty minutes away in upmarket Parnell. 'I'm going to be busy here right up to kick-off, and going home to get ready for the evening would use up time I might not have if things go wrong.' Which plenty had done already. She looked over at the receptionist, suddenly remembering she'd been in the middle of another conversation before Zac had walked up. 'Can you let me know when Dr Brookes and his family check in, please?'

The girl nodded. 'Certainly, Dr Coates-Clark.'

'I'll be in the banquet room,' Olivia told the girl needlessly. The hotel staff had her cell number, but right now she wasn't doing so well on remembering anything she should. Better get a grip before the evening got under way.

Zac shrugged those impressive shoulders that she'd kissed many times. 'I'll give you a hand.'

'Thanks, but that won't be necessary. I'm getting everything sorted.' As much as having someone to help her would be a benefit, Zac would probably get her into a bigger pickle just by being in the same room. Turning on her heel, Olivia headed to the elevator that'd take her up to the room where tonight's dinner, auction, and dance would be held. The evening was due to get under way in a little over three hours and she wanted to check that everything was in place and see if the flowers had finally arrived. Something about bad weather causing a shortage of flowers at the markets that morning had been the harried florist's excuse. But bad weather didn't explain why the place name cards were yet to arrive from the copy centre.

Unbelievable how she'd softened on the inside when she'd first looked at Zac, despite the heat and turmoil he instantly ramped up within her. Like she'd missed him. But she hadn't known Zac beyond work and bed so not a lot to miss apart from that mind-blowing sex.

Odd she felt there was more to him she wanted to learn about when she hadn't been interested before. Not interested? Of course she had been. That's what had frightened her into ending the affair.

A large palm pressed the button to summon the elevator. 'It's out there on the surgeons' loop that you need some help with running the auction tonight. I'm stepping up. Starting now.' Zac looked down his long straight nose at her, his mouth firm, his gaze determined. 'No argument.'

Why would he want to do that? It meant being in her company for hours. She'd have sworn he would've planned on keeping well away from her, and that the last five minutes had been five too many in her company. 'Thanks, but no thanks, Zac. I've got it covered.' Second lie in minutes. She doubted she could spend too much time with him without dredging up all the reasons why she'd been a fool to drop him—instead of remembering why it had been a very sane move. No one was going to walk away from her ever again.

She made the mistake of looking at Zac and her tongue instantly felt too big for her mouth. Zac was so good looking, his face a work of art, designed to send any female who came near him into a lather. Including her. Olivia closed her eyes briefly, but his face followed her, seared on the insides of her eyelids. Zachary Wright. If ever there was a man she might fall for, it was Zac. That was a big 'if'. Painful lessons growing up were a harsh reminder that there was only one person who'd look out for her—herself.

But one touch and Zac had always been able to do anything he liked with her. Not that he'd taken advantage in a bad way. He wasn't that kind of man. See? She did know something about him. Hopefully he hadn't known how close she'd come to being totally his, as in willing to do absolutely anything to keep him.

'You all right?' He touched her upper arm, and despite her layers of clothing the heat she associated with him shot through her, consumed her.

'F-fine,' was all Olivia could manage as she stared at him, pushing down hard on the urge to touch him back, to run her hand over his cheek, and to feel that stubble beginning to darken his chin.

Taking her elbow, Zac propelled her forward, into the elevator. 'Third floor?'

'Yes,' she croaked. *Go away, leave me alone, take your sexy body and those eyes that were always my undoing, and take a flying leap off a tall building. I don't need this heat and need crawling along my veins. Go away.*

'I'm not going anywhere for the rest of the day, so get used to the idea, Olivia.'

Ouch. Had she said that out loud? What else had she put out there? One glance at him and she relaxed. He hadn't heard anything about jumping off a building. But she couldn't relax fully until tonight was put to bed.

Olivia groaned. 'Bed' was so not a safe word when she was around this man. It brought all sorts of images screaming into her head. Images she refused to see or acknowledge. They were her past, not her future. Or her present.

CHAPTER TWO

WHO'S TAKEN ALL the air out of this box? Zac stared
around the elevator car, looking for a culprit. His eyes
latched onto Olivia. He had his answer. It was *her* fault
he couldn't breathe, couldn't keep his heart beating in
a normal, steady rhythm. Olivia Coates-Clark. CC for
short. CC *was* short. Delicate looking—not delicate of
mind. Tiny, yet big on personality. Filled out in all the
right places—as he well knew. Fiery when pushed too
far, sweet when everything was going her way. An itch.

An itch he would never scratch again. He absolutely
had to ignore it.

She'd dumped *him*. Hard and fast. Slapped at his
pride. *He* did the leaving, when he was good and ready,
not the other way round. He should've been grateful,
was grateful. Having more than his usual three or four
dates with Olivia had got him starting to look out for
her. On the rare unguarded moments when something
like deep pain had crept into her gaze he'd wanted to
protect her; and that was plain dumb. Given his past,
that made him a danger to her. He hurt people; did not
protect them. He also didn't feel like having his heart
cut and cauterised again when she learned of his inad-
equacies. No, thanks.

Hang on. Had she found out? Was that why Olivia

had pulled the plug on their affair? Because she'd found him to be flawed? No. She still looked at him as she always had—hot and hungry, not disgusted or aloof.

Breathing was impossible. Not only was Olivia using up the oxygen, she was filling the resulting vacuum with the scent of flowers and fruit and everything he remembered about her. *Hell, let me out of this thing. Fast.* He took a step towards the doors, stopped, glanced at the control panel. They were moving between floors. *Get a hold of yourself.*

Yeah, sure. This is what Olivia always did to him. Tipped him upside down with a look, sent his brain to the dump with a finger touch, and cranked up his libido so fast and high just by being in the same air as him. Exactly what was happening now. His crotch was tight, achingly tight. As was his gut. Nothing new there. Eighteen months without setting eyes on her, with only once talking on the phone about the auction, and he was back to square one. Back to lusting after her. Unbelievable. How could a grown man with a successful career as an orthopaedic surgeon, presumably an intelligent and sane man dedicated to remaining uninvolved with women, lose all control because of this one?

Olivia Coates-Clark. She was why he felt three sheets to the wind—and he hadn't touched a drop of alcohol all week. He'd been too busy with scheduled surgeries and two emergencies involving major operations to have any time to enjoy a drink and take in the ever-changing view from his apartment living room. But within minutes of being with CC he felt as though he'd downed a whole bottle of whiskey. This was shaping up to be a big night in a way he didn't need.

A phone buzzed discreetly. As nothing vibrated on

his hip it had to be Olivia's. He listened with interest as she answered, totally unabashed about eavesdropping.

'Olivia Coates-Clark speaking.' Her gaze scanned the ceiling as she listened to her caller. Then, 'Thank you so much. Your efforts are really appreciated.' Her finger flicked across the screen and the phone was shoved back into her pocket. 'One problem sorted.' She smiled directly at him.

'Had a few?' he asked, trying to ignore the jolt of need banging into his groin as his gaze locked on those lush lips.

'I guess it would be too much to expect arranging something as big as this has become to go off without some hitches. It hasn't been too bad, though.' Had she just crossed her fingers?

'Whose idea was it to raise money for Andy Brookes? Yours?'

Olivia nodded, and her copper-blonde hair brushed her cheek, adding further to his physical discomfort. 'I'll put my hand up, but from the moment I started talking to surgeons at Auckland Surgical Hospital it went viral. Everyone wants to be a part of supporting Andy. I imagine tonight's going to raise a fair whack of dosh. People have been unbelievably generous with offering art, holidays, and other amazing things to auction.' She smiled again, her mouth curving softly, reminding him of how he used to like lying beside her in his bed, watching her as she dozed after sex. All sweet and cute, and vastly different from the tigress who could sex him into oblivion. 'Thank you for your generous gift,' she was saying.

He'd put in a weekend for a family of four on his luxury yacht, with all the bells and whistles, and he'd be at the helm. 'Andy was the most popular guy in our

senior registrar years. He never failed to help someone
out when they were down.'

'You forget the practical jokes.' Again she smiled,
making those full lips impossible to ignore.

So he didn't; studied them instead. Covered in a deep
pink sheen, he could almost feel them on his skin as she
kissed his neck just below his ear, or touched his chest,
his belly, his… He groaned inwardly and leaned away
from her, concentrating on having a polite conversation with his ex-lover. 'I have vivid memories of some
of the things Andy did to various people.' He sighed as
he tried to ease his need. Memories. There were far too
many of Olivia stacked up in his mind. He should've
heeded them and replied no to the invitation to join his
colleagues tonight. He could've said he was doing the
laundry or cleaning his car. But he'd wanted—make
that needed—to get her out of his system once and for
all, and had thought joining her tonight would be the
ticket. Now he'd like nothing more than the gala to be
over so he could head across the road to his quiet, cold
apartment and forget Olivia.

'Have you met Andy's wife?'

'Kitty was at a conference with Andy that we attended in Christchurch last year.' *The conference you
were supposed to speak at and cancelled the day after
you walked out of my life.*

Olivia must've recalled that too because a shadow
fell over those big eyes, darkening the hyacinth blue
shade to the colour of ashes. Why did he always think
of flowers when he was around her?

'I had an emergency. At home.' She spoke softly,
warily.

'You lived on your own.' She didn't have kids. Not

that he knew of. Hell, he didn't even know if she had siblings.

'My mother was unwell.' She straightened her already straight spine and said, 'Andy was going places back then. Hard to believe he's now facing the fight of his life to remain alive, instead of continuing his work with paraplegics.'

What had been the problem with her mother? If he asked he doubted she'd tell him, and if she did then he'd know things about her that would make him feel connected with her. The last thing he wanted. Feeling responsible for her was not on his agenda. So, 'Andy's got a chance if he has the radical treatment they're offering him in California.'

'It must be hard for Kitty too.'

'Unimaginable.' Zac took a step closer to CC, ready to hug away that sadness glittering out at him. Sadness for their friend? Or her mother? Something had disturbed her cool facade.

Zac understood confronting situations that threatened to destroy a person. He'd been eighteen when the accident had happened that had left his brother, Mark, a paraplegic. Two years older than Mark, he was supposed to have been the sensible one. *Try being sensible with an out-of-control, aggressive younger brother intent on riling him beyond reason.* Nearly twenty years later the guilt could still swamp Zac, despite Mark having got on with his life, albeit a different one from what he'd intended before the accident.

The guilt was crippling. Being ostracised by his family because he'd been driving the car when it had slammed over the wall into the sea was as gutting. That's what put the shields over his heart. If his parents couldn't love him, who could? If he wasn't to be trusted to be responsible then he had no right to think any woman would be safe with him. Or any children he might have. So he had to keep from letting anyone near enough to undermine his determination to remain single, even when it went against all he believed in.

Olivia shuffled sideways, putting space between them. 'Here's hoping we raise a fortune tonight.'

Zac swallowed his disappointment, tried to find it in himself to be grateful Olivia had the sense to keep their relationship on an impersonal footing. It didn't come easily. He'd prefer to hug her, which wouldn't have helped either of them get past this tension that had gripped them from the instant he'd sauntered into the hotel. He wanted her, and suspected—no, he knew— she wanted him just as much. The one thing they'd been very good at had been reading each other's sexual needs. There hadn't been much else. Shallow maybe, but that's how they'd liked it. Their lives had been busy enough with work and study. Their careers had been taking off, leaving little time for much else.

But right now hugging Olivia would be wonderful. Why? He had no idea, but being this close to her he felt alive in a way he hadn't for months. Eighteen months, to be exact. This feeling wasn't about sex—though no denying he'd struggle to refuse if it was offered—but more about friendship and closeness. No, not close- ness. That would be dangerous. He hauled the armour back in place over his heart. One evening and the itch would be gone.

The elevator doors slid open quietly. Zac straight- ened from leaning against the wall, held his hand out to indicate to Olivia go first. 'After you.'

Following her, his gaze was firmly set on the backs of those wonderful legs and the sexy knee-length black boots highlighting them to perfection. Was it wrong to long for what they used to have? Probably not, but needing the closeness with her? That was different from anything he'd experienced, made him vulnerable. Earlier, seeing Olivia standing in Reception, looking like she had everything in hand, he'd felt the biggest lurch of his heart since the day his world had imploded as that car had sunk into the sea and his brother had screamed at him, 'I hate you.'

'Zac.' Olivia stopped, waited for him to come alongside her.

That slim neck he remembered so well was exposed where her coat fell open at her shoulders. 'CC.' If he used the nickname he might stop wanting something he couldn't have. This woman had already shown she could toss him aside as and when it suited her.

He watched as the tightness at the corners of her mouth softened into another heart-wrenching smile. 'Funny, I haven't been called CC for a while. I used to like having a nickname. More than anything else it made me feel I belonged to our group.'

'You never felt you belonged? Olivia, without you we wouldn't have had so many social excursions or parties. You held our year together.' She'd worked hard at organising fun times for them, sometimes taking hours away from her studies and having to make up for it with all-night sessions at her desk. But to feel she hadn't been an integral part of the group? How had he missed that?

Her smile turned wry. 'I've always taken charge. That way I'm not left out, and I get to call the shots. No one's going to ignore the leader, are they?'

His heart lurched again, this time for the little girl blinking out from those eyes staring at some spot behind him. He certainly didn't know this Olivia. 'I guess

you're right.' With his family he'd learned what it felt
like to be on the outside, looking in, but at university
he'd made sure no one had seen that guy by working
hard at friendships. A lot like Olivia apparently. Everyone at med school had adored her. She could be extro-
verted and fun, crazy at times, but never out of control.
It was like she'd walked a tightrope between letting go
completely and keeping a dampener on her feelings.

Except in bed—with him.

Damn, he'd like nothing more than to take Olivia to
bed again. But it wouldn't happen. Too many consequences for both of them. The vulnerability in Olivia's
eyes, her face, told him he could hurt her badly without
even trying. That blew him apart. He wanted to protect
her, not unravel her. *He cared about her.*

Trying to get away from Zac and her monumental error,
Olivia rushed through the magnificent double doors
opening into the banquet room now decorated in blue
and white ribbons, table linen, chair covers. Since when
did she go about telling people about her insecurities?
Not even Zac—especially not Zac—had heard the faint-
est hint of how she didn't trust people not to trash her.
She did things like this fundraiser so that people thought
the best of her. That was the underlying reason she
could not fail, would not have tonight be less than perfect. The same reason everything she did was done to
her absolute best and then some. She must not be found
lacking. Or stupid. Or needy.

Coming to a sudden halt, Olivia stared around the
function room, which had been made enormous by
sliding back a temporary wall. The sky-blue shade of
Andy's favourite Auckland rugby team dominated. In
the corner countless buckets of blue and white irises had

finally been delivered and were waiting for the florist to arrange them in the clear glass bowls that were to go in the centre of each table. Everything was coming together as she'd planned it.

She was aware of Zac even before he said, 'Looking fantastic.'

Zac. Those few minutes in the elevator had been torture. Her nostrils had taken in his spicy aftershave, while her body had leaned towards his without any input from her brain. When he'd looked like he'd been about to hug her she'd at least had the good sense to move away, even when internally she'd been crying out to have those strong arms wound around her. Now she stamped a big smile on her face and acknowledged, 'It is.' Too bad if the smile didn't reach her eyes; hopefully Zac wouldn't notice.

'You're not happy about something.' He locked that formidable gaze onto her. 'Give.'

Once again she'd got it wrong when it came to second-guessing him. 'The florist's running late, the wineglasses haven't been set out, the band assured me they'd be set up by four and…' she glanced at her watch '…it's now three twenty-five.' *And you're distracting me badly. I want you. In my bed. Making out like we used to. Actually, I'd settle for that hug.*

'We can do this. Tell me what you want done first.' His eyes lightened with amusement, as if he'd read her mind.

He probably had. How well did she know him? Really? They hadn't been big on swapping notes on family or growing up or the things they were passionate about. Only the bedroom stuff. Shoving her phone at him, she said, 'Try the band. Their number's in there. Eziboys.'

'You've got the Eziboys coming to this shindig?'

Admiration gleamed out at her. 'What did you have to do? Bribe them with free plastic surgery for the rest of their lives?'

With a light punch to his bicep she allowed, 'One of them went to school with Andy's younger brother. They want to help the family.'

'Not your formidable charm, then?' He grinned a full-blown Zachary Wright grin, one that was famous for dropping women to their knees in a begging position.

Click, click. Her knees locked and she stayed upright. Just. 'Phone them, please.' Begging didn't count if she remained standing. Anyway, she wanted the band at the moment, not sex with this hunk in front of her looking like he'd stepped off the cover of a surfing magazine. Another lie.

Zac was already scrolling through her contact list. 'Got a dance card? I want the first one with you. And the second, third, and fourth. Oh, I know, I'll put those in your diary for tonight.'

Dance card, my butt. How out of date could he get? 'You'll be inundated with offers.' Did he really want to dance with her? She'd never survive. What little control she might exercise on her need would sink without trace if he so much as held her in his arms, let alone danced with her. Anyway, he wasn't making sense. He'd been peed off when she dumped him, so he wouldn't want to get close to her on the dance floor. Or did he have other plans? Plans that involved payback? Tease and tempt her, then say bye-bye?

As Zac put the phone to his ear he shook his head. 'If you didn't want dancing tonight you should've gone to the retirement village to find a group of old guys with their tin whistles to play for us.'

'I enjoy dancing.' *Just don't intend doing it with you.*

'I didn't know that. Looking forward to it. Looks like your florist has arrived.' He nodded in the direction of the doors, then went back to the phone. 'Jake, is that you, man? How're you doing?'

Olivia stared at Zac. He knew Jake Hamblin, the band's lead guitarist? That could be good for getting the band to actually turn up. Zac was full of surprises. Hadn't he said something about the florist too? Spinning around, she came face-to-face with a neat and tidy woman dressed in black tailored trousers and an angora jersey under her jacket. Nothing flower-like about her. 'You're the florist? I'm Olivia Coates-Clark.'

The woman nodded, sent Zac a grin. 'That's me. I see the flowers finally turned up. Show me exactly where you want these arrangements and I'll get on with it.'

Zac was handing the phone back to Olivia. 'How's things, Mrs Flower?' That really was her name. 'Your hip still working fine?'

'You were the surgeon. What do you think?'

Zac's laughter was loud and deep, and sent pangs of want kicking up a storm in Olivia's stomach. 'Good answer,' he said.

So he knew this woman too. Probably used her for sending beautiful flowers to all his women. Ouch. He'd sent her flowers when she'd dumped him. A stunning, colourful bouquet of peonies, not thorns or black roses, as well he might've.

'Do we have a band?' she asked in her best let's-get-on-with-things voice.

'Filling the service elevator with gear as we speak,' Zac said. 'What's next? Want those buckets of flowers moved somewhere?'

The band was on its way; the flowers were about

to be fixed. Olivia shook her head in amazement. Two more ticks on her mental list of outstanding things to get finished. Things just happened around Zac. Somehow it had all got easier with him here. 'We need two long tables up against that far wall for the auction. The hotel liaison officer went to find them an hour ago.' She needed to display the gifts that'd been donated.

'Not a problem.' Did he have to sound so relaxed?

The clock was ticking. That long soak she'd planned on in the big tub in her room upstairs before putting on her new dress, also from the shop where she'd got her coat, might just be a possibility. 'Easy for you to say,' she snapped.

Zac took her arm and led her across to where the florist was already wiring irises into clever bunches that were going to look exquisite. 'You explain where you want everything and try to relax. We'll get this baby up and running on time. That's a promise.'

'I am relaxed.'

'About as relaxed as a mouse facing down a cat. A big cat.' He grinned and strolled away before she could come up with a suitable rejoinder.

Very unlike her. She always had an answer to smart-ass comments. Watching Zac's casual saunter, she noted the way those wide shoulders filled his leather jacket to perfection. Her tongue moistened her lips. No wonder she wasn't thinking clearly—the distractions were huge and all came in one package. Zachary Wright.

CHAPTER THREE

AN HOUR LATER, Zac handed Olivia a champagne flute filled with bubbly heaven. 'Here, get that into you. It might help you unwind.'

'I can't drink now. I've got to finish in here, then get myself ready.' Her taste buds curled up in annoyance at being deprived of their favourite taste. But she had a big night ahead of her so having a drink before it had even begun was not a good idea.

With the proffered glass Zac nudged her hand—which seemed to have a life of its own as it reached towards him. 'One small drink will relax you, Olivia.' He wrapped her fingers around the cool stem. 'Go on.' There was a dare in his eyes as he raised his own glass to his lips.

Zac knew she never turned down a dare. But she'd have to. Tonight's success rested on her being one hundred and ten per cent on her game. Her mother had taught her well—go easy on the alcohol or make a fool of herself. Not going to happen tonight when everyone's eyes would be on her.

Zac's throat worked as he tasted the champagne. Appreciation lit up his eyes. His tongue licked his bottom lip.

And Olivia melted; deep inside where she'd stored all

her Zac memories there was a pool of hot, simmering need. The glass clinked against her teeth as the divine liquid spilled across her tongue. And while her shoulders lightened, tension of a different kind wound into a ball in her tummy and down to her core. 'Delicious,' she whispered. Zac or the wine?

He nodded. 'Yes, Olivia, it is. Now, take that glass upstairs to your room and have a soak in the hot tub before getting all glammed up. I'll see to anything else that needs to be done here before I go across to change.'

She went from relaxed to controlled in an instant. 'No. Thank you. I need to check on those flowers and—'

'All sorted.' From the table he handed her an iris that been tidied and then tied with a light blue ribbon. 'Take this up with you.'

Even as she hesitated, her hand was again accepting his gift. What was it with her limbs that they took no notice of her brain? 'My favourite flower.'

'That particular shade matches your eyes perfectly.'

'Wedgwood. That's the variety's name.' She stared at it, seeing things that had absolutely nothing to do with this weekend. Or Zac. All to do with her past.

When she made to hand it back he took her hand and held it between them, his fingers firm. His thumb caressed the inside of her wrist. 'Who does it remind you of?' Very perceptive of him.

How had she walked away from this man? She must've been incredibly strong that day, or very stupid. 'My father used to grow irises.' Before he'd left because he'd been unable to cope with his wife's drunken antics. *And I could? I was only twelve, Dad.*

Tugging free from Zac's hand, she stepped back a pace. 'Why are you helping me?' He hadn't decided to target her for sex, had he? Or was that her ego taking a hit? Zac never had trouble getting a woman; he didn't need her. Even if what they'd had between them had been off the planet.

Zac's eyes held something suspiciously like sympathy. She hated that. She didn't need it, had finally learned how to deal with her mother by controlling her own emotions, not her mother's antics. The same tactic kept men at a distance. Except for Zac, she'd managed very well. When she'd shocked herself one day by realising she cared about him more than she should she'd immediately called the whole thing off. No one would ever leave her again. No one could ever accuse her of being a slow learner.

'I'm here because you needed help.' Zac tapped the back of her hand to get her attention. 'I'm alone, as in no partner, so doing stuff behind the scenes isn't going to get anyone's back up. I figured you'd be pleased, not trying to get rid of me.'

I've already done that once.

The words hung in the air between them, as though she'd said them out loud. She hadn't, but her cheeks heated, as if she was blushing. Not something she was known for. 'I'm sorry for being an ungrateful cow.' She sipped from her glass while she gathered her scattered brain cells into one unit. 'It's great you're here. I'd still be trying to persuade that florist into doing things my way if you hadn't worked your magic on her.' She'd felt a tad ill at the ease with which he'd managed to convince the florist that her way was right. 'You also got that kid behind the bar to arrange the glasses in a much more spectacular pyramid than he'd intended.'

'While you charmed the floor manager into putting a dog basket in the corner for the seeing eye dog. It's against all the rules apparently.' Zac's smile was beautiful when he wasn't trying to win a favour. Too damned gorgeous for his own good. And hers.

'A blind person is allowed to take their dog anywhere.'

'But not necessarily have a bed for the night in the banquet room.' That smile just got bigger and better, and ripped through her like a storm unleashed.

She needed to get away before she did something as stupid as suggesting he give her a massage before she got dressed for the night. Zac's hands used to be dynamite when he worked on her muscles. He'd done a massage course sometime during his surgical training and was more than happy to share his ability with anyone needing a muscle or two unknotted. He'd done a lot more than that with her at times, but tonight she'd settle for a regular massage to get the strain and ache out of her shoulders.

Another lie. She gulped her drink, but forgot to savour the taste as the bubbles crossed her tongue. Lying wasn't something she normally did, not even to herself, as far as she knew.

'Here.' Zac held the champagne bottle in front of her, and leaned in to top up her glass. 'Take that up to your room.'

'You're repeating yourself.'

'Didn't think you'd got the message the first time.' Taking her elbow, he began marching her towards the elevators where he pressed the up button, and when the doors whooshed open he nudged her in. 'See you at pre-dinner drinkies.'

'I'll be down well before six.' As the doors closed quietly Oliva drew in his scent and along with it a whole heap more memories. The night ahead was stretching out ever further. She'd tried again to change the seating arrangement at the tables, but couldn't without up-setting someone else. She sighed. Have to swallow that one and hope she'd be too busy to sit down.

Olivia tapped the toe of her boot until the elevator eased to a halt on her floor. Surprisingly she had nearly an hour to herself, thanks to Zac's help. Plenty of time to wrestle into submission the strong emotions she'd never expected to feel for him again. Then she could carry on as planned: friendly yet aloof. So far her ap-proach had been a big fail.

Inside her room she began shedding clothes as she headed for the bathroom and the tub she wanted full, steaming and bubbling.

After turning the taps on full, she poured in a hefty dose of bubble bath and shucked out of the rest of her clothes. Removing her make-up, she saw a goofy smile and happier eyes in the mirror than she'd seen in a very long time.

Hey, be careful.

Why was she excited? She didn't want another affair with the man. It had been hard enough walking away from the first one; to do that again would kill her. Even though their affair had had little to do with anything other than sex, she'd stumbled through the following weeks trying to get back on track. It had her wondering for the millionth time how her father had walked out on her and her mother without a backward glance. He'd had more to lose, yet every communication from him—not many—had come through a lawyer. No birthday cards, Christmas phone calls. Nothing. Her dad had vanished from her life. And that was that.

Slipping into the warm water and feeling the bubbles tickle her chin eased every last knot of tension from her taut body. Sure, it'd make a comeback, but for the

next twenty minutes she'd enjoy the lightness now in
her muscles, her tummy, her everywhere. That might
help with facing Zac tonight.

Olivia knew she had to be on her best form because
their friends wouldn't be able to refrain from watching her and Zac, looking for any hints of dissension or,
worse, any sign they might be interested in each other
again. Not a chance, folks.

Lying back, her eyes drifted shut and she watched the
movie crossing her mind. Zac looking good enough to
devour in one sitting. That well-honed body still moved
like a panther's, wary yet smooth, the same as the expression in his eyes. Unbelievable how much she'd
missed that body. Missed everything about Zac. There'd
been the odd occasion they'd shared a meal, because
when anyone had had as much exercise as they'd had
together they'd got hungry and what had gone best with
after-match lethargy had been great food. Ordered in
from some of Auckland's best restaurants, of course.
The only way to go.

What she'd never seen in his eyes before was that
concern that had shown when he'd moved her towards
the elevator. Concern for her well-being, and then there
had been the flower, the champagne—which had shown
he'd remembered she only drank wine, and then usually
this nectar. Yes, she pampered herself, but there was
no one else to. Except her mother, and she got her fair
share of being looked after.

Was it possible Zac had missed her an incy-wincy
bit? She'd never ask. That would be like setting a match
to petrol. Anyway, he'd never admit it, even if it came
close to being true.

Hah, like you'd admit it either.

* * *

Zac prowled the small crowd pouring into the banquet room, and for the tenth time glanced at his watch. Six o'clock had been and gone twenty minutes ago and there was no sign of Olivia. So unlike her. If anything, she'd have been back down here, ready to get things cranking up, almost an hour before it was supposed to start.

'Hey, Zac, good to see you.' Paul Entwhistle stepped in front of him. 'How have you been?'

'Paul.' Zac shook his old mentor's hand. 'I'm doing fine. What about you? Still creating merry hell down there at Waikato?' The older man had taken over as director of the orthopaedic unit two years ago, citing family reasons for leaving the successful private practice he'd set up here in Auckland.

Paul gave him an easy smile. 'I've semiretired to spend more time with the family. What about you? I couldn't believe it when I heard you and Olivia had parted. Thought you'd never be able to untangle yourselves long enough to go in different directions.'

Zac swallowed a flare of annoyance. This was only the first of what he had no doubt would be many digs tonight about his past with Olivia. 'Aren't we full of surprises, then?' Instantly he wished his words back. Paul had been a friend to him as well as teaching him complex surgical procedures that he now used regularly. The man certainly didn't deserve his temper. He tried again. 'There was so much going on at the time something had to give.'

That was one way of looking at it. He knew from friends that Olivia ran with the crowd these days and never with another man. He didn't get it. She'd been fun, and always hungry for a good time. But apparently not since *them*. Did that make him responsible for her change? Had he done something he was completely unaware of to cause her to dump him and become a solo act? He'd always been honest in that he'd had no intention of having anything more than a fling with her. She'd been of the same sentiment. Neither of them had been interested in commitment. Yet it still sucked big time that she'd pulled out. He hadn't thought he could feel so vulnerable. Why would he? He'd spent his life guarding against that.

'I get that, but never thought it would be your relationship that would stop.' Paul unwittingly repeated Zac's thoughts as he looked around the room. 'Where is Olivia anyway?'

Twenty-five past six. 'I have no idea. I'll give her a call.' Walking away to find somewhere quieter, he dialled her cell. Yes, he still had her numbers, just never used them. Deleting them should've been simple, but he hadn't been able to, even when he'd been angry with her for walking away.

'Hey, Zac, I fell asleep.' So she still had him on caller ID. Interesting. 'Is everything okay? I'll be right down.' Olivia sounded breathless.

He knew the breathless version, had heard it often as they'd made love. 'Breathe deep and count to ten. Everything's going according to your plan.'

'Yes, but I need to be there, welcoming everyone. Oh, damn.' He heard a clatter in the background. 'Damn, damn, triple damn.'

'Olivia, are you all right?'

'I knocked my glass off the side of the tub. Now there are shards of glass all over the floor.'

'Call Housekeeping.'

'Haven't got time. I'm meant to be down there before everyone arrives, not after, as though I don't care.' Panic mixed with anger reached his ear. 'How could I be so stupid as to fall asleep in the tub?'

'Listen to me.' Zac stared up at the high ceiling, trying hard not to visualise *that* picture. Olivia in a hot tub with soapy bubbles framing her pert chin, covering her full breasts. *Aw, shucks.*

'I worked every hour there was to get this gala happening and I'm tired, but I only had to hang on for a few more hours.' She was on a roll, and Zac knew it would take a bomb to shut her up.

He delivered. 'I'm coming up to help you get ready.' Like Olivia would let him in. She hated being out of control over any damned thing and would be wound up tighter than a gnat's backside.

'You can't come up here,' she spluttered. 'I'm not dressed.'

So his words *had* hit the bull's-eye. She'd heard him. He found himself smiling, and not just externally. Warmth was expanding, turning him all gooey. Bonkers. This was all wrong.

Zac told her, 'Take your time getting ready, then make a grand entrance. Everyone will be here and you can wow them as you walk to the podium to make the opening announcements.'

There was utter silence at the other end of the phone. No more spluttering. No glasses smashing on the tiled floor. Not even Olivia breathing. Then his smile spread into a grin. He could almost hear her mind working.

'Love it,' she said, and hung up on him.

Zac slid his phone back in the pocket of his evening suit trousers. He guessed he'd see her shortly. Heading back into the room, he hesitated as the elevator doors opened. Seeing the pale, thin man who stepped out, he crossed over to shake his hand. 'Hey, Andy, great to see you.' The guy looked dreadful. Leukaemia was making short work of his health.

'Isn't this something? I couldn't believe it when Olivia told me how many people were coming and all the amazing things that have been donated for the auction.' Andy wiped a hand down his face. 'Enough to make a bloke cry.'

'Can't have that, man.' Zac dredged up a grin for him, feeling a lump rising in his own throat. 'You'll have all the females copying you.'

Andy laughed, surprising Zac. 'Damn right there. What sort of dinner party would that be? They'd be handing round tissues, not champagne.'

'Guess you're off the drink at the moment.' Zac glanced behind, and saw Kitty and their three small boys waiting calmly. 'Great to see you.' He wrapped the woman in his arms and when he felt her shivering he knew it was from trepidation about tonight. 'You're doing fine,' he said quietly, so only she heard.

Kitty nodded. 'Thanks to CC. She's arranged a table for us and the boys, a babysitter for when it's time to send the little tykes to our suite, and basically anything we could possibly want.'

'That's our CC.' *Damn you, Olivia. A man could fall in love with you—if he hadn't locked his heart in a cage. You've done the most amazing and generous thing, arranging this evening.* 'Come on, I'll show you to your table.' Andy looked ready to collapse and they hadn't started.

It took time to move through the throng of people wishing the family all the best for the auction. Zac knew everyone meant well and most were shocked at Andy's appearance, but he wanted to snarl at them to back off and give the man time to settle at his table. He held onto his sudden burst of temper, wondering where it had come from in the first place.

As he finally pulled out a chair for Kitty a collective gasp went up around the large room. Olivia had arrived. He hadn't seen her but he knew. She had that effect on people, on him. Like lightning she zapped the atmosphere, flashed that dazzling smile left, right and centre. Everyone felt her pull; fell under her spell. Which was why they were here, and why many had willingly donated such spectacular gifts for the auction. She was the reason these same people would soon be putting their hands in their pockets and paying the earth for those things. Sure, this was all about Andy, a man everyone liked and respected, but it was Olivia who'd got them all together.

Looking towards the podium, Zac thought he'd died and gone to heaven. Never, ever, in those crazy weeks he and Olivia had been getting down and dirty had he seen her look like she did right this moment. If he had he'd have hauled her back to his bedroom that last night and tied her to the bed so she couldn't dump him. He'd have taken a punt on her not breaking his heart even when it was obvious she would've. Stunning didn't begin to describe her. And that dress? Had to be illegal. Didn't it? She shouldn't be allowed to wear it in public. It appeared painted on, except for where the soft, weightless fabric floated across her thighs. Everywhere her body was highlighted with the gold material shimmering over her luscious curves.

And he'd thought he could handle this evening, being around Olivia. He hadn't a hope in Hades. Not a one.

CHAPTER FOUR

'WELCOME, EVERYONE, TO what is going to be a wonderful night.' Olivia stood behind the podium, the mic in
her hand, and let some of the tension slide across her
lips on a low breath. She'd done it. Andy and his family were here, the colleagues who'd said they'd come
were here, and the noise level already spoke of people
having fun. Phew.

Zac's here. So? She knew that already.

Olivia could see him standing by Andy, staring over
at her, his mouth hanging a little loosely. He looked
stunned. What had put that expression on his face? Not
her, surely? She stepped out from behind the podium,
shifted her hips so that her dress shimmied over her
thighs, and watched Zac. Forget stunned. Try knocked
out. She bet a whole team of cheerleaders could be leaping up and down naked in front of him right now and he
wouldn't notice. His gaze was intense and totally fixed
on her. Or, rather, on her thighs.

Despite being like nothing else she'd worn since
she'd been a teen, she'd loved this dress from the moment she'd seen it; now she thought it was the best outfit
ever created. That sex thing she and Zac had once had
going? It was still there, alive and well, already fired
up and ready to burn.

Then the silence reached her and she stared around at the gathering of friends and colleagues, the reason she was standing up here finally returning to her bemused brain. She was supposed to be wowing them, not getting slam-dunked by Zac's comatose expression. Slapping her forehead in front of everyone wasn't a good idea, but she did it anyway. 'Sorry, everyone, I forgot where I was for a moment. Thought I was back at med school and about to give you all a demo on how to drink beer while standing on my head.' Like she'd ever done anything close.

But it got her a laugh and she could relax. As long as she didn't look in Zac's direction she should be able to continue with her brief outline of how the evening would unfold.

'I hope you've all got your bank managers' phone numbers handy because we are going to have the auction of all auctions. It will be loads of fun, but just to get you loosened up there are limitless numbers of champagne flutes filled with the best drop of nectar doing the rounds of the room. Stop any of those handsome young men carrying trays and help yourself.'

She paused, and immediately her eyes sought Zac. He hadn't moved, still stood watching her, but at least he'd stopped looking like a possum caught in headlights. His eyes were hooded now, hiding whatever had been eating him, and that delicious mouth had tightened a little. Then he winked, slowly with a nod at the room in general.

She got the message. *Get on with it. Everyone's waiting for you.*

Again she looked around the room filled with people she knew, admired and in a lot of cases really liked. 'Just to keep us all well behaved and lasting the distance, there will be platters of canapés arriving over the next hour. We will have the auction before dinner so take a look at all the wonderful gifts set out on the tables over by the entrance. Most importantly, enjoy yourselves, but not until I've kept hotel management happy by telling you what to do in case of fire, earthquake, or the need to use a bathroom.'

After giving those details, she wrapped up. 'Let's have a darned good time. If there's anything that you feel you're missing out on talk to...' she looked around the room and of course her gaze fell on Zac '...Zachary Wright. He's volunteered to help with any problems and we'd hate to see him sitting around with nothing to do, wouldn't we?' She grinned over at the man who'd got her stomach in a riot. Not only her stomach, she conceded, while trying to ignore the smug smile coming back at her. Not easy to do when her heart rate was erratic. The noise levels were rising fast as she stepped away from the podium to go in search of a distraction that didn't begin with a Z.

Paul Entwhistle stepped in front of her. 'Olivia, you're a marvel, girl. There's as many people here as you'd find at Eden Park watching an international rugby match.' He wrapped her into a bear hug. 'Well done.'

'Still prone to exaggerating, I see.' She laughed as she extricated herself. 'Are you going to be bidding at the auction? There are some wonderful prizes—if I can call them that.'

'I've got my eye on one or two.' There was a cunning glint in Paul's eyes.

'What?'

Paul went with a complete change of subject. 'I see you still like to give Zac a bit of stick. It saddened me when you two broke up. Thought you had what it took.'

Her stomach sucked in against her backbone. *Not in this lifetime, we don't.* But even as she thought it her eyes were tracking the crowd for a dark head. Not hard to find when Zac towered above most people, even the tall ones. He was heading in her direction, an amused tilt to his mouth. 'I beg to differ,' she told Paul. 'Neither of us are the settling-down type.' *If only that weren't true.* 'Now, if you'll excuse me…'

'I think you're wrong.' Paul glanced in the direction she'd seen Zac. The cunning expression had changed to something more whimsical, which didn't make her feel any more comfortable.

'I need to circulate.' *Before Zac reaches us.* 'I'm sure Zac will be happy to chat with you.'

'Thanks a bundle, Olivia,' Zac breathed into her ear.

Too late. She plastered on a smile and faced him, wondering why just talking to him got her all in a twist. 'Thought you'd be pleased. You're flying solo, remember?'

He actually laughed. 'Touché.'

Paul was watching them with interest. She really needed to stop this; whatever the man was thinking didn't have a part in the evening's plans.

'I have to see the auctioneer about a few details,' Olivia put out there, and began walking away.

'Are we going to be holding up the various items as they're auctioned?' Zac was right beside her.

She was regretting giving in to his offer of help—if she had actually given in. He hadn't exactly left it open to negotiation. 'I'm doing it.'

'Then we're doing it.' His hand on her arm brought her to a stop. When he turned her to face him his eyes were full of genuine concern. For her? Or did he think she was going to make a mess of the evening? 'I know you've done everything so far and by rights this is your show, but I'd like to help. And I'm not the only one. Andy's been a good mate to a lot of people.'

'That's a valid point.' Didn't mean she'd hand over the reins, though. When she set out to do something she did the whole thing, from first phone call to seeing the last couple leave at the end of the night. That would give her a deep sense of accomplishment, something she never achieved with trying to keep her mother on the straight and narrow.

Zac's bowed upper lip curved into a heart-squeezing smile. 'Let's grab a drink and go talk to your auctioneer.'

For some reason Zac made her feel desirable on a different level from the hot need she usually found in his gaze. That was there, burning low and deep, but right now she could have curled up on a couch with him and just chatted about things. Not something they'd ever done before. Had never wanted to do. Shaking her head, she gave him a return smile. 'I'll stick to water until I've packed up this baby.'

Without looking away from her, he raised his hand and suddenly there was a waiter with a tray of full glasses standing beside them. Zac lifted two flutes of sparkling water and handed her one. Tapping his glass against hers, he gave her another of those to-die-for smiles. 'To making a load of money for our friend.'

'Lots and lots.' She sipped the water, and tried not to sneeze when bubbles somehow went up her nose. The bubbles won, and she bent her head to brazen out the sneezes.

Her glass was gently removed from her hand as Zac's firm, warm hand touched her between her shoulder blades, warm skin on warm skin, softly rubbing until she regained control. Straightening up, she reached for her glass and locked eyes with Zac. 'Th-thanks,' she stuttered.

How could she speak clearly with so much laughter and fun beaming out at her from a pair of eyes the shade of her first coffee of the day? Those eyes had always got her attention, had had her melting with one glance. For some strange reason tonight they had her fantasising about other, homier things. Like that couch and talking, or sharing a meal over the table in her kitchen, or going for a stroll along the beach. *A bit cosy, Olivia. What happened to forgoing doing things like that with someone special?* 'You ever think of settling down?' she asked, before she'd thought the question through.

His expression instantly became guarded. 'Thought about it? Yes. Followed through? No.'

Oh. Disappointment flared, which didn't make sense when she never intended putting her size five shoes under someone's bed. Not permanently anyway. 'That's sad.' For Zac. He'd make a wonderful husband and father.

'Not at all. I'm happy.' So why the sadness lurking in the back of those dark eyes?

'You sound very sure.' Her blood slowed as her heart slipped up on its pumping habit. Strange that here, surrounded by friends and colleagues, Zac was admitting to not wanting happy-ever-after.

'I am,' he muttered, as he took her elbow and led them in the direction of the auction table and the man standing behind it. 'Just as I'm sure I'm enjoying playing catch-up with you.'

Okay. Hadn't seen that coming. 'We could've done that any time.' What? Since when? She'd been ruthless in avoiding Zac, turning down invitations to any functions she'd thought he might be attending. The air in her lungs trickled out over her bottom lip. Now he stood beside her she couldn't keep her eyes off him. He warmed her through and through, touching her deeply, like a close friend. Except friends didn't do what they'd done, and sex-crazed lovers like they'd been didn't sit around discussing fashion or trips to the supermarket. But she told him anyway. 'I've sort of settled, bought a nineteen-twenties villa in Parnell that I'm slowly doing up.' *My own house, all mine.*

Zac's eyes widened. 'Are you working the do-up yourself?'

'I've got a very good builder for most of it, while I do the painting and wallpapering. Seems I've got a bit of a flair for home decorating.' She felt a glow of pride when she thought of her new kitchen and dining alcove.

'Go, you.'

'Hi, Olivia.' The auctioneer, Gary, held out his hand. 'You've got an amazing array of donations. We should be able to pull off a major coup.'

'That's the plan.' Shaking Gary's hand, she introduced Zac. 'Anything we can do for you?'

'You can take a break and leave this to me and my partner over there. He's come along to help.' Gary nodded at a man sorting through the donations and placing numbers under each one. 'Just keep our glasses full and we'll be happy.'

Zac's hand was back on her elbow. 'Come on, let's mingle.'

She could do that on her own. Yet she went with him as if that was the most important thing she had to do tonight.

Zac groaned inwardly. He should be running for the exit and not looking back. Standing beside Olivia as she charmed everyone within sight was sending him bonkers with need. Every time she moved even a single muscle he'd swear he inhaled her scent. She moved almost nonstop, even when standing in one spot, her face alive, with those lips constantly forming belly-tightening smiles while her eyes sparkled. Her free hand flipped up and down, then out between her and her audience, and back in against her gorgeous body, expressive at every turn.

While one of his hands was shoved deep into his pocket to keep from touching her, the other gripped a glass tight. His feet were glued to the carpet, and his face hopefully impassive. Letting anyone, especially CC, know what he was thinking and feeling would be catastrophic. He'd never hear the end of it from Paul either. The guy stood with them, his gaze flitting between him and Olivia with a crafty glint that made Zac uncomfortable.

A waiter was approaching with a tray laden with glasses. Zac drained his sparkling water and replaced it with champagne. To hell with not drinking. He needed something stronger than H2O, bubbles or not. 'Thanks.' He nodded at the waiter, which was a waste of time.

The guy was too busy gaping at Olivia, the tray on his outstretched fingers getting quite a tilt. 'Ma'am,' the young man croaked.

Totally understanding the poor guy's reaction, Zac tapped the tray. 'Hey, buddy, watch those glasses.'

Olivia swapped her empty glass for a full one, nodded at the waiter, and looked around the room as she gulped a mouthful of water.

Zac saw some of the tension in her neck ease off a notch. Being a perfectionist, CC didn't do relaxing very well, and tonight she was coiled tighter than a snake about to strike.

'Time to start the auction,' Olivia said in a sudden gap of the conversation. 'I think everyone must be here by now.'

'Good idea,' Paul said. 'Make the most of this amazing atmosphere.' He nodded at the crowd talking and laughing.

'Why don't we hold up the articles being auctioned while Gary's man deals with the financial side?' Zac led the way through the throng to the podium.

Olivia nodded, picked up the mic. 'Okay, everyone, can I have your attention?'

Nope. Not happening. If anything, the noise level seemed to increase. Zac reached for the mic, touching the back of her hand as he did so. Soft, warm, different Olivia. His mouth dried. It wasn't too late. He could still run away. And then what? Spend the night thinking about Olivia and coming up with a hundred questions about her?

Clearing his throat, he spoke loudly and clearly into the mic. 'Quiet, please.' The conversations petered out as everyone turned to face him. He wanted to crack a joke but doubted he could pull it off with this tight band strangling his throat. If only Olivia would move away and let him breathe. Finally he started talking and slowly got his voice back to normal. 'We are about to start the auction so take a seat. Gary is our auctioneer and we want him to be able see each and every one of you, so even if you scratch your knee he can take it as a bid.'

As the bidding got under way Olivia's tension climbed back up. 'Relax,' he told her. 'This is going to be amazing, you'll see.'

She turned worried eyes on him. 'How can you be so certain? What if we barely raise enough money to get Andy a one-way ticket to the States?' Her teeth nibbled her bottom lip.

Olivia didn't do nibbling. Taking her hand in his, he squeezed gently. 'I believe in you, that's how.'

Her eyes widened, her chin tipped forward. 'Truly?' she squeaked.

'Truly.' He did. He realised that through the years they'd been training to become surgeons he mightn't have noticed how sexy she was but he had known of her determination never to fail. Perhaps he hadn't learned much more about her during their affair but this was still Olivia, the same woman who'd qualified as an excellent plastic surgeon. Only now he saw how much she cared for their friends. Olivia was a big marshmallow, really, and he liked marshmallows.

'Thanks.'

'Olivia? So do all the people in this room. That's why they're here.'

He felt a responding squeeze where her hand was wound around his. 'You say the nicest things,' she whispered, before pulling free and turning to face the now-quiet room.

She'd been flip in her tone and yet it didn't bother him. That was Olivia covering her real feelings. He was beginning to see she was an expert at doing that. Come to think about it, she'd always shut him up with a kiss whenever he'd started to talk about anything personal. What was she hiding? Who was Olivia Coates-Clark? The real CC?

As Zac picked up the envelope to be auctioned, which contained a week in a timeshare bure in Fiji, he knew he was getting into trouble. Forget quietening the itch. Now he had to fight the need to get to know all about Olivia, right from when she'd lost her first tooth to what her idea was of a dream holiday.

The bidding was fast and furious, with plenty of people vying to buy the first offering. In the end Paul outbid everyone, paying enough to send a dozen folks to Fiji rather than the two that the deal covered.

'That's auctions for you,' Zac whispered to Olivia as at last she began smiling.

'It's not about what they're bidding for, is it?'

'Nope. It's all about the man sitting at that table with his wife and kids, looking like hell and pretending otherwise.' Andy looked shocked, actually. Probably because of the ridiculous amount Paul had bid.

Olivia nudged him. 'We're not a bad bunch, are we?'

'Apart from opinionated, hardworking, and overly comfortable with our lot, you mean?' He grinned at her.

'I'd like to think more along the lines of caring, hardworking, and overly focused on helping others.' She grinned back.

His stomach clenched. That grin, that mouth…oh, man. *I've missed her so much.* Not just the sex. He'd liked being with her too, even if only while they'd ridden the elevator to the apartment she'd rented then, and before they'd fallen into bed.

'What are we auctioning next?' he growled, needing to get back on an even keel.

'The weekend on your luxury yacht. If you're at the helm that should attract a lot of female bidders.' Her grin only grew.

'The ladies here are all taken.' *Except you.* Zac sighed when one of the partners in the surgical practice where he worked bought the weekend excursion.

The man wasn't easy to get along with, and now he'd have to spend two days holed up in a yacht with him and his whole family.

'You're being uncharitable,' Olivia whispered beside his ear.

'I didn't say a word.'

'There was a brief wincing and tightening of your mouth when the hammer hit the podium.' She laughed. 'That man paid a small fortune for the pleasure of going sailing with you.'

'He did, and I'll make sure he has a fantastic time.'

Gary had the crowd in the palm of his hand now, and the bidding went through the roof for everything from a painting of a seagull hovering over a beach to a meal at a restaurant down at the Viaduct Harbour.

Zac watched Olivia every time the gavel hit the podium. Her eyes were getting brighter and brighter. 'We're killing it,' she whispered at one point.

'Says the woman who was worried this wouldn't work,' he retorted. The more she smiled the more she relaxed, and the more beautiful she was. Zac felt his heart soften even further towards her. So he sucked in his stomach and hardened himself against her. Mentally, that was.

'That's me. Control freak with no control over the outcome of the auction. Of course I was going to be concerned.'

Was that why she'd ended their affair? So she could keep control and not wait until he decided to call it quits? Since the morning he'd woken to hear Olivia say she was walking away from their affair he'd felt bruised and let down. He hadn't known why, except it had reminded him of the day his family had cut him off. But with Olivia he'd had nothing to feel guilty about.

'That's it, folks. We've sold everything,' Gary called out.

Olivia crossed to stand behind the podium, a piece of paper in her hand, tears in her eyes. 'You're an amazing group of people. This auction went way beyond even my dreams.' She read out the amount they'd raised and had to wait a long time for the applause to die down. 'You are all so generous it's humbling.'

Zac glanced across to Andy's table, and felt emotion tug at his heart. Kitty was crying and Andy slashed his arm across his face as he slowly stood up. Carefully negotiating his way around tables to reach Olivia, Andy gave her a long hug before gripping Zac's shoulder.

'Hey.' Zac could think of nothing else to say. The success of the auction said everything that needed to be said about the love he felt for this man.

Taking the mic, Andy stumbled to the podium. 'What can I say? Olivia's right. You're awesome.' His voice cracked. 'Tonight means so much to Kitty and me, and our boys. You have given us a chance.' He stopped and looked down. Everyone waited quietly until he raised his head and said, 'CC, I can't thank you enough. I know so many people contributed to tonight and I thank each and every one of them, but without you, CC, none of this would've happened.'

Zac clapped and instantly everyone leapt to their feet to join him. He reached for Olivia's hand and raised it high. 'Our CC.'

Tears were streaming down her cheeks. 'Stop it,' she hissed. 'You're embarrassing me.'

Zac retrieved the mic from Andy and when the clapping died down said, 'In case you missed that, CC says we're embarrassing her. When did that ever happen?'

Laughter and more clapping broke out. Olivia shook her head at him. 'You'll keep.'

There was the problem. He shouldn't want to be kept for Olivia. Or any woman. He wouldn't be able to deliver what she wanted, needed.

CHAPTER FIVE

'DID YOU JUST YAWN?' Zac asked as they danced to the Eziboys' music.

Olivia shook her head. 'Just doing mouth stretches.' Did there have to be a smile in his eyes? It was devastating in its intensity. Made her happy to be with him, when she shouldn't be. Exhaustion had returned as dessert had come to an end, yet somehow she'd still found the energy to shake her hips to the beat of the music.

Zac's eyes widened, and the tip of his tongue appeared at the corner of his delectable mouth. 'Right,' he drawled.

She mentally slapped her head. Mouth stretches. She used to trail kisses all over his body, starting below his ear and tracking down, down, down. The memories were vivid now, in full technicolour, and heating up her cheeks. Hopefully he wouldn't notice her heightened colour in the semidarkness of the dance floor.

It would take very little to fall in against that wide chest and let him be her strength for a while. She'd never known what it was like to let someone be strong for her. If she ever loosened up enough to try it, Zac might be her man.

How had she managed to leave him that morning? Fear. Always a powerful motivator. For her it had been fear of losing control, of never knowing which way was up. As an adult she had no intention of reliving the turbulent life she'd known growing up. Not for anyone.

'Feel like taking a break, having a drink?' Zac asked.

Definitely. Anything to put some space between them. 'Good idea.' She immediately turned for their table.

Waving at a waiter, Zac pulled out a chair. 'Take the weight off.'

When he sat down beside her his chair was way too close, but she was reluctant to make a show of moving away. Anyway, she didn't have the strength to resist him at the moment. Glancing at her watch, she sighed. The band was booked for at least another hour. Sneaking off to her room and that huge comfortable-looking bed was not yet an option.

The champagne was cool and delicious. 'Perfect.' She settled further into her chair. 'You keep dancing, if you want. I don't need babysitting.'

Zac chuckled. 'Dancing has never been one of my favourite pastimes.'

'But you're good at it. You've got the moves.' *Ouch.* Shouldn't have said that.

That devastating smile returned briefly. 'I'd say thanks except you seemed to nearly fall asleep while we were shaking our hips.'

'I can't believe how tired I am. Probably won't go to sleep for hours when I finally make it to my room. My muscles feel like they're pulled tighter than a tourniquet.'

'What you need is a few days away somewhere where no one can reach you to talk about work, or fundraising, or anything more stressful than what you'd like for dinner.' Zac sipped his drink. 'When did you last take time off?'

She thought about it. Glanced at him. Remembered. 'It was a while ago.'

'A little over eighteen months ago maybe?'

'Maybe.' Zac had booked three nights at a retreat on Waiheke Island. They'd only managed one night before he'd returned home after his brother had been admitted to hospital with a collapsed lung.

While accepting he had to go, Olivia had been disappointed he'd not returned to the resort later. She sometimes wondered—if they'd had the whole time together would they have got to know each other a little better outside the bedroom?

'I might as well have stayed with you,' Zac muttered, as if reading her mind.

Olivia's stomach flipped. 'What? Your family needed you.' So had she, but not as much.

'No, they didn't.'

'But they phoned you.'

He shook his head. 'My grandfather called to let me know about Mark. Not my parents.'

She wanted to say that made sense if his parents had rushed to be with his brother, but something in his eyes stopped her, told her she was wrong. 'You don't get along—'

'Mind if I join you both for a moment?' Paul plonked himself down without waiting for an answer.

Relief flicked across Zac's face. 'Can I get you a drink, Paul?'

'No, thanks. I won't take up much of your time.' Leaning back in the chair, he studied first Zac then her so thoroughly she began to think she had chocolate mousse on her chin.

The band stopped for a short break and most people were making their way to the tables. And Paul still wasn't saying anything. She ran her fingers across her chin, came up clean. She glanced at Zac, who shrugged his shoulders.

Finally, Paul pulled an envelope from the inside pocket of his jacket and Olivia instantly recognised it as an item that had been auctioned earlier. A trip somewhere. There'd been a few trips auctioned tonight but she thought Paul's one had been to Fiji.

As he laid the envelope on the table between her and Zac she felt a flutter of trepidation in her stomach. She couldn't keep her eyes off that large white envelope or the finger tapping it, as though it was beating out her fate.

'This is for the two of you. Five nights at Tokoriki Island Resort on the west side of Fiji's mainland.'

No. No, please, no. Tell me Paul didn't say that. I can't go anywhere with Zac, and certainly not somewhere as intimate as a resort in Fiji.

Olivia slowly raised her gaze to Zac and saw him looking as stunned as she felt. 'It's kind of you, Paul, but I have to say no.'

'Zac? What do you think?' Paul looked a little smug.

It didn't matter what Zac thought. She wasn't going.

A few days far away from everything and everyone with only Zac for company held a certain appeal. White beaches, warm sea, palm trees bending in the breeze, and... And Zac.

'It's a no from me too. Thank you, though.'

Paul wasn't easily fobbed off. 'Think before rejecting my offer out of hand, both of you.'

Olivia shook her head. One evening with Zac had her

in a state of longing and wonder. She would never cope with being stuck on a tiny island with him for a week.

'What's this about?' Zac asked in a surprisingly level tone, his eyes fixed on the man issuing the challenge.

'Look at you. You're exhausted. I know you haven't had a break all year. You need a holiday. So does Olivia. Why not someplace exotic? This timeshare bure is on an island catering for approximately twenty couples at any one time. No children allowed. All meals provided, massages as well.' Paul smiled.

Any other time she'd be drooling at the thought of going. But never with the man sitting beside her, looking as perplexed as she felt.

'It sounds wonderful, but you're expecting Zac and me to go together?' Olivia shook her head. *Not going to happen.* Looking at Zac, she could see the lines at the edges of his mouth. He *was* tired. It had taken Paul pointing it out for her to notice.

'You have two weeks to choose between, both in July, so you'll need to get your heads together quickly.'

Which part of 'I'm not going' doesn't Paul understand? 'July's two weeks away. I can't just pack my bag and leave my patients in the lurch.'

'Neither can I,' Zac growled.

Paul hadn't finished. 'I'll cover for you, Zac, and I'm sure we can find someone to pick up the reins in your department for five days, CC.'

'You still haven't said why you're doing this. Us needing a holiday doesn't cover such generosity.' Zac sipped his drink, a thoughtful expression on his handsome face.

An expression that worried Olivia. He'd better not be considering this crazy idea. She snapped, 'It doesn't matter why. It's not going to happen.' Knowing how ungrateful that sounded, and yet annoyed that Paul thought he could manipulate them, she added, 'It's a lovely offer, Paul, but I'm turning you down.'

The moment the words left her mouth she was regretting the lost opportunity. A holiday would be fabulous right now. Keeping up her usual number of patients and working on this gala fundraiser had finally caught up with her. Throw in her mum's latest crisis, and heading offshore to somewhere she'd be pampered sounded better and better. A sideways glance at Zac and she couldn't deny that going away with him didn't have appeal. Her head snapped up. *She was not going anywhere with Zac.*

Someone coughed. 'I'll cover for you, Olivia.' A colleague at Auckland Surgical Hospital sat on the other side of the table, looking completely relaxed about the whole scenario. 'You know you've been wanting to get away for a while now. The timing couldn't be better. Leave it another couple of months and I'll be on maternity leave.'

Thanks a million. You obviously haven't heard the whole conversation, especially the bit about Zac going too. But as Olivia glared at the woman she felt herself wavering. This might be working out too easily, but did that mean she shouldn't be considering it? Should she be grabbing that envelope and rushing home to pack, or was it wiser to continue refusing Paul's kindness?

Zac was watching her with something akin to an annoying challenge in his eyes. 'What about it, CC? It could be fun.'

'It could be a nightmare.' How would she remain aloof when they were sharing accommodation on an island with very few people around for distraction? How would she be able to control herself with that hot bod so close for days on end?

Pulling her gaze from that infuriating taunt in Zac's eyes, she looked around the now-crowded table and found everyone watching, waiting for her answer, almost as though they were all challenging her.

You never turn down a dare, remember?

She'd never had one quite like this, though. She could not go on holiday with the man she'd had to walk away from once already. Not when he'd got her in a tangle of emotions within minutes of turning up in the hotel earlier that afternoon. She'd never survive with her heart and her brain functioning normally if she spent five days and nights in the same space as Zac.

You'd have a lot of great sex.

Not necessarily. They could avoid that. It wasn't as though they were going *together*-together, right?

Tell that to someone who'll believe you.

The little gremlin that had flattened her car battery and made her fall asleep in the hot tub now had her saying, 'It would have to be the first week of July.'

Zac shoved his hands deep into his trouser pockets as he strolled along the Viaduct beside Olivia. At one-thirty in the morning, in the middle of winter, they were the only ones crazy enough to be out here, but he knew he wouldn't be able to sleep. Why the hell had he agreed to go to Fiji? His brain had to be fried from too many hours in Olivia's company. No other explanation popped up. Accepting he wanted time out with her went against everything he strived for. His hands clenched at his sides. What if he liked Olivia even more by the end of the trip? He liked her too much already. Her beauty, her wit, her sense of fun, and her concern for others. He'd pushed her to go away to a place that was all about romance. Romance. A subject he knew nothing about. And didn't want to. That would be like rubbing salt into the wound.

Olivia would be regretting her acceptance of Paul's generous gift. But she would never back down. Not now that others had heard her accept.

Zac sighed unhappily. He was as bad as Olivia. Paul had challenged them both, and he'd fallen for it. Given in to the emotions that had been battering him since he'd arrived at the hotel. To have spent his entire adult life avoiding commitment only to find himself well and truly hooked didn't bear thinking about.

A gust of rain-laden wind slapped them. Olivia pulled her jacket tight across her breasts and folded her arms under them. Her face looked pinched—from cold or from anger at herself for agreeing, he wasn't sure.

Taking her elbow, Zac turned them around. She was shivering. 'Come on. We'll go to my apartment. The weather's about to dump a load of wet stuff and getting soaked doesn't appeal.'

'I should go back to the hotel.' She didn't sound convinced.

'We need to talk about what we've got ourselves into.' Then he might feel happier. Might. 'I've got wine in the chiller. Or there's tea, if you'd prefer.' He also had a huge bed, but doubted he'd get a hug for mentioning that.

'Why didn't you tell Paul no?' she asked when they were in the elevator, heading up to his apartment.

Initially he had. 'Maybe I want to go.'

'Do you? Really?'

While I'm standing here breathing in the floral scent that's you, yes, really. When I see that uncertainty flick through your eyes, yes, I want to spend time with you. When I think about actually scratching my itch, defi-

nitely, yes, but if I remember why I have to move on from you, then a resounding no.

The elevator shook to a halt and the doors glided open. He took her elbow again. 'The idea of going to Fiji, it's growing on me.' His parent's fortieth wedding anniversary was in the first week of July and they were having a party to beat all parties at one of Auckland's top restaurants. Of course he wanted to celebrate with them. Of course he was not invited. 'Yep, getting away has appeal.' He tried to ignore the surprised look on her face and opened the door to his penthouse. 'After you.'

Olivia slipped past him, and walked through to the lounge with its floor-to-ceiling glass wall that allowed an extensive view of Auckland Harbour, the bridge, and closer in the wharves with a collection of large and small sea craft tied up.

He followed, stood next to her, stared out seeing nothing. Why did Olivia unsettle him when no other woman ever had?

'I've never been to the islands,' she said, without looking his way. 'Haven't been anywhere since I was ten, and then it was to Australia with my parents. Mum hates flying.'

'Makes for an uncomfortable trip, I imagine. You haven't inherited that fear?'

Her head moved slowly from side to side. 'Not at all. In fact, I'd like to learn to fly one day.'

'What's holding you back?' It wouldn't be lack of brains or money.

'I have a feeling it would become a passion and what with work and doing up my house there isn't enough spare time to spend hours in the air.' Her reflection in the window showed she was nibbling her lip again.

He didn't like it when she did that. It indicated distress, and he didn't want her to feel distressed. 'Ever thought of cutting back a few hours so you can do some of the things you like?'

Olivia finally looked at him. 'I spent so much time training and working my way to the top that I think I've forgotten there's a whole world out there waiting to be explored, whether through travel or doing things like learning to fly.'

'You're right.' Apart from going sailing whenever he could get a weekend away, he spent most of his time working. 'You said you're enjoying doing up your house. I bought this apartment because the idea of renovations and painting and all the things required to turn a house into a home seemed too huge. It's not a job for one weekend, is it?'

'No, it's a project. But, then, most things I've ever done have been projects.' She frowned. 'That's how I stay in control. Take the house. Next month is bathroom month. The builder's going to gut it and then everything I've chosen goes in and I get to go shopping for all the little bits and pieces, matching the towels with the tile colour, the fittings with the rest of the house.'

Sounded too organised for him. He liked a little disorder, certainly didn't have perfectly matched towels or even dinner sets. Not that he'd gone to the second-hand shop for anything, but he hadn't been hell-bent on getting everything looking like a show home. 'What was last month?'

'My bedroom.' She turned away, and her voice was low as she told him, 'It's cream and rose pink. Very girlie, but I wasn't allowed that when I was growing up so I'm having it now.'

Wow, she'd just mentioned her childhood twice in a short amount of time. Very briefly, sure, but there it was. She hadn't been allowed to pick the colours for her room. Not a big deal maybe, but it could mean there was nothing she'd been allowed to choose. 'I've never seen you wear pink.'

'Rose pink.' Her smile was unexpectedly shy. 'There's a difference. And, no, I can't imagine what patients would think if their surgeon turned up dressed in pink.'

'They'd probably love it.' Taking a step back before he walked into that smile filling him with a longing for something special, he brought everything back to reality. 'Tea or champagne?'

'Have you got camomile?' Her smile had widened into that of a cheeky girl.

He told her, 'Yes, I have,' and laughed at her surprise. 'My mother drinks it.' *On the rare times she's visited.*

'For some reason I didn't think you were close.' She followed him to the kitchen, where she perched on a bar stool at the counter. Crossing her legs showed off a length of thigh where that golden creation that was supposedly a dress rode high.

'We're not.' Mum at least tried to accept he was still her son, while Dad… Forget it.

'You mentioned one brother.' Was that longing in her voice? Hard to tell from her face.

'Mark. He's married with two kids. I only get to see them at Christmas and birthdays.'

Olivia picked at an invisible spot on the counter. 'That's incredibly sad.'

'Yep.' He made himself busy getting mugs from the cupboard and teabags from the pantry.

She lifted her head and locked her blue eyes on him, suddenly back to being in control. 'Think I'll head back to the hotel. I don't really want tea. Or anything.' She slipped off the stool and turned towards the doorway. 'Good night, Zac.'

With little thought he reached for her, caught her wrist and gently tugged her close. With a finger under her chin he tilted her head back so he could gaze down into her eyes. And felt his head spinning with wanting her.

Olivia's eyes widened and her chin rose further as her mouth opened slightly.

Zac was lost. Any resistance or logical thinking disappeared as he leaned closer to place his mouth over hers. As he tasted her, the heat and need he'd kept tamped down most of the night exploded into a rainbow of hot colours. Olivia. She was in his arms, her mouth on his, her tongue dancing with his. Olivia.

Slim arms wound around his neck, pulling his body closer to hers. He felt her rise onto tiptoe, knew the moment when her hips pressed against his obvious desire. Those breasts he'd been fantasising about all night flattened against his chest, turning him into a molten pool of need. His hands spread around her waist to lift her onto the stool, where she immediately wrapped her legs around his thighs.

This is what I've missed so damned much. We are fire on fire. Feeding each other. Consuming the oxygen.

She tasted wonderful, bringing more erotic memories back to him. Making new ones.

Lifting his mouth, he began trailing kisses over her jaw, down her neckline, on towards her deep cleavage. When she whimpered he continued while lifting his gaze to her face, where he recognised the same fiery awakening racing along his veins.

Her fingers kneaded his scalp as she pushed her breasts higher to give him more access with his tongue.

She wasn't wearing a bra. Of course she wasn't. That dress had clung to every curve and outlined her shape perfectly; including her breasts, those peaks now hard against his mouth and hand.

Zac growled as he licked her, tasted her skin, her nipple. A gentle bite had her arching her back and tipping her head so that her hair fell like a waterfall behind her. And he lost himself, tasting, touching, rubbing.

'It's been so long,' she murmured in a low voice that spelt sex. Her hands fumbled with the buttons of his shirt, finally pushed it open, and then her palms were on his skin, smoothing and teasing as only Olivia could do.

The memories that he'd lived on for all those long months apart rapidly became reality. He hadn't enhanced any of them. This was how it had been between them. Then his belt was loose, the zip being tugged downward, and... *Oh, hell.* Her soft hand was wrapped around him, sliding down, up, and down again. *Oh, hell.* There was nothing quite like making out with this woman. She knew the buttons to push, remembered what he most enjoyed, and if she wasn't careful would have him coming long before he'd pleasured her.

That wasn't happening. Zac wrapped his arms around her and carried her quickly down the hall to his bedroom and the super-king-sized bed she had yet to try out. Toeing his shoes off, he knelt on the bed and leaned forward with Olivia still in his arms so that he was covering her before she could move. 'Your turn.'

'I'm ready,' she croaked.

'I haven't touched you yet.' But, then, often he hadn't had to. All part of that explosiveness that had been them.

'Don't, if you want this to last more than the next three seconds.'

Now, there was a challenge. Pushing her dress up over her thighs, Zac slipped down to find her core with his tongue. The moment he tasted her she jolted like she'd been zapped with an electrical current.

Her hands gripped his head, holding him there. Not that he'd been going anywhere else until he had her rocking against him.

'Zac!' she cried when he licked her. 'Zachary...' As he pushed a finger inside.

Her hips lifted, her fingers pressed into his scalp, and she was crying out his name. Over and over as her body convulsed under him.

Reaching for the top drawer of his bedside table, he grabbed a condom and tore the packet open with his teeth. A small, warm hand whipped the condom from his fingers. 'Let me.'

Then he was lying on his back, unsure how she'd managed to flip him so effortlessly. She straddled his thighs and, achingly slowly, slid the condom onto his erection.

Placing his hands on her waist, he lifted her over him and lowered her to cover him, took him inside to her moist, hot centre.

'Zac!' She screamed his name.

He hadn't forgotten she was a screamer but it still hit him hard, stirred him and had him pushing further into her.

It was never going to take long, he was that hot for her, had been wanting this from the moment he'd seen her leaning against that counter in the hotel reception. When she put her hand behind to squeeze him he was gone. Over. Finished. One final thrust and Olivia cried out and fell over his chest, gasping for air, her skin slick with sweat and her body trembling against his.

As she lay sprawled across him, he spread his hands across her back, stared up at the barely illuminated ceiling and smiled. Everything was in place in his world. Olivia was in his bed. They'd shared the mind-blowing sex he knew only with her. Everything was perfect. His itch was being appeased.

Or would be when they did it again, just as soon as he got his breath back.

CHAPTER SIX

Zac had no idea what the time was when he rolled over and reached out for Olivia, only to come up empty-handed. 'Olivia?' He sat up and stared around. His heart thumped hard. Not again.

'I'm here.' Her voice came from the en suite bathroom.

Phew. He dropped back. Something clattered in the hand basin, and Olivia swore. 'You okay in there?' he called.

Silence.

'Olivia? Are you all right?' His gut started to tighten.

'I'm making sure I can walk past the hotel receptionist without looking like I've been...um, doing what I've been doing.'

'You're heading over the road?' Now he was on full alert. Swinging his legs over the side of the bed, he stood. 'What's wrong with staying the rest of the night? You and I don't usually settle for once.'

'Don't do this, Zac.' She stepped into the room, but kept her distance. 'We've got to stop before we get carried away.'

As the cold reality of her words hit him he pulled his head back, glared down at her. 'Why? We are willing, consenting adults, not two teenagers who have to go home to Mum and Dad looking guilty.' Hopefully she didn't hear the anger her rejection made him feel. Again. And the pain because she was right.

'I'm sorry.' Her eyes were brimming with tears. 'I shouldn't have got so carried away.'

A gut-buster, that statement. 'We got carried away, sweetheart. We.' He shoved a hand through his hair, trying to figure out what had happened to cause her to haul on the brakes. He should be grateful. He'd hoped to sooth his need, not crank it wide-open. How wrong could a bloke be?

'Exactly. We didn't stop to think about what we were doing. Not for a moment.' Her back was straight, her shoulders tight, but her chin wobbled as she said, 'Which is why I can't go to Fiji with you.'

'You're changing your mind?' Of course she was. For some reason he didn't feel happy. He'd enjoyed being with her tonight. It had been like finding something precious after a long search. He could barely look at her and not reach for her again. She might've put the brakes on but it would take a tank of icy water to cool his ardour and return his out-of-whack heart rate to normal.

In the doorway she hesitated, turned around to look at him, sorrow leaking out of those baby blues. 'Yes, Zac, I am. Going on holiday together would only exacerbate the situation. I can't have another affair with you. It's too casual, and anything more is impossible for me.'

He stood rooted to the floor, unable to ignore the sharp pain her statement caused yet knowing she was stronger than him. The itch had gone beyond scratchy, was now an open wound that needed healing. Olivia was the cure but, as she'd so clearly pointed out, that wasn't about to happen.

Moments later his main door clicked shut, presumably behind her, and still he stood transfixed. For a moment earlier on, when they'd been sated with sex, he thought he'd found that untouchable thing he'd been looking for in his dreams and pushing away when he was wide-awake. Hell, he'd felt as though he'd connected with Olivia in a way he'd never connected with another human being in his life. Sure, they'd had sex without any preamble, as they'd always done, but there'd been more depth to their liaison. He'd made love to the woman of his dreams. Literally.

Which made Olivia heading back to her hotel room absolutely right. Unlike him, she had a handle on their situation. Where was his gratitude?

Zac's phone vibrated its way across the bedside table. 'Hello?' Had Olivia had a change of heart?

'It's North Shore Emergency Unit, Dr Wright. We've got a situation.'

Not Olivia. Guess it wasn't his night. 'Tell me,' he sighed.

'A bus full of rowers returning to Whangarei went off the road an hour out of the city. There are many casualties so we're ringing round everyone. Can you come in?'

'On my way.' It wasn't as though he'd been sleeping. A certain woman had taken up residence in his skull, refusing to let him drop off to sleep even when his body was craving rest.

'Kelly Devlin, nineteen-year-old rower, fractured tibia,' the ED registrar told Zac within moments of him striding into the chaotic department.

Zac studied the X-rays on the light box. 'She needs a rod insertion,' he decided, and went to talk to his patient.

Kelly glared at him. 'I'm a national rowing champion, Doctor. I can't have a broken leg.'

Zac's heart went out to her. 'You have. I'm sorry.'

'Does that mean the end of my career?'

'First I'll explain what I'm going to do to help you.' He sat on the edge of her bed. 'I've seen the X-rays and your left tibia is fractured in two places. To allow the bone to heal without too much added stress I'm going to put a titanium rod down the centre of the bone. There will be screws to hold it in place while you heal.' He kept the details scant. He knew from experience that too much information at this stage usually confused the patient and added to their distress.

'Will I be competitive again?' the girl demanded.

'That will take a lot of work on your part, but I don't see why not.' When disbelief stared him in the eye, he added, 'You're a champion rower so you know what it's like to work your butt off to get where you want to be. This will be harder. Your muscles will need strengthening and the bone will require time to knit.' He hoped he wasn't misleading Kelly. 'You may have to compensate in some way for the damaged leg, but we won't know for sure until further down the track.'

Tears slid down her cheeks. 'You're honest, but I don't have to like what you're telling me. It's going to be painful for a while, isn't it?'

'You'll have painkillers.' Bone pain. Not good. 'A physiotherapist will have you working on that leg when I think you're ready.'

'When are you operating?'

'As soon as I get things sorted a nurse will come and get you ready for Theatre.' He stood up. 'I'll see you in there. Have your family been told about the accident?'

'Mum and Dad are on their way from Whangarei,

but I don't want to wait. If I've had surgery before they arrive it'll be easier on them.' She shifted on the bed and cried out as pain jagged her.

'Take it easy. Try to stay as still as possible. You'll soon be given a pre-anaesthetic drug that will make you feel drowsy and dull your senses a little.' Zac nodded at the nurse on the other side of the bed. 'I'll talk to the anaesthetist now, get everything under way.'

As he headed out of the ED to arrange everything Zac rubbed the back of his neck. What a night.

'Morning, everyone. Sorry I'm late. Forgot to set my alarm.' Olivia slid into the only vacant chair at the table in the hotel dining room where she was having a late brunch with Andy and his family, Maxine and Brent Sutherland, who were Andy's close friends, and Zac.

'Have a late night?' Zac asked.

She scowled at him. 'Something like that.'

He told her, 'I've been in surgery.'

'Already? Were you on call?' He'd have mentioned it, wouldn't he?

'A bus went over the bank near Waiwera. The hospital needed orthopaedic surgeons in a hurry.'

'Why was a bus travelling through the night?' she asked.

'Taking rowers home from the nationals down south.'

'Coffee or tea?' A waitress hovered with the brunch menu.

'We've all ordered,' Zac informed her.

'The kitchen will make sure your meal comes out with the others,' the waitress said. 'Drink?'

Yes, yes, yes. Give me a moment. Olivia took the proffered menu. 'A pot of English Breakfast tea, thank you.'

A quick read of the list of tasty dishes on offer. 'Pancakes with bacon and banana, and lots of maple syrup.'

When she turned to find Zac watching her with a soft smile on those adorable lips she snapped, 'What?'

'Pancakes and syrup? I thought you'd be a muesli and fruit girl.'

She was. Always. But this morning her usually strict control over her diet had gone the same place any control seemed to go when Zac was around—out west somewhere beyond the hills. 'Thought I'd spoil myself.' She looked around the table at her friends. Zac's friends too, don't forget. 'Did everyone enjoy last night?'

'You have to ask?' Maxine asked with a grin. 'The band kept playing until one and only stopped because the hotel management asked them to.'

'The dinner was amazing,' Brent added.

Olivia looked at the boys sitting quietly opposite her. 'Did you all have fun too?'

'Yeah. But Mum made us go to our room early. I liked dancing,' the oldest said.

'Your mum's mean.' Andy grinned tiredly. Now that the excitement of the night before had worn off he looked as though he had little energy left.

'It's part of the job description,' Zac added.

'That was a generous gift from Paul,' Maxine chipped in. 'I'm assuming you're both going to take it up. I mean, who wouldn't go to a luxury island in Fiji, all expenses paid? I know I would.'

'Does everyone know?' Olivia shivered. No way would she go after how things had played out last night in Zac's apartment. Nearly a week sharing a bure with Zac would make a joke of her self-control. Remaining impervious to Zac's charm would be impossible. As she'd already proved. 'I don't think I'll be going.'

Unfortunately her eyes drifted to the right and locked with Zac's.

'If that's what you want.'

She wasn't sure about it being what she wanted, but she knew it was how it had to be for her sanity. Amidst exclamations from just about everyone else at the table Olivia told Zac quietly, for his ears only, 'It's for the best.'

'Yours, or mine?' Why the disappointment? Surely he hadn't thought they'd be having a five-day sex fest? Though, if she was being truthful with herself, he had good reason to think that, given how quickly they'd leapt into each other's arms last night.

'Ours.' A picture of blue sea and coconut palms crossed her mind. Going to Fiji would be marvellous. That lump at the bottom of her stomach was her disappointment. It was a great opportunity and she was reneging on it.

'Last night you accepted.' Zac's words arrowed to the core of her concern.

'I did.' She'd be letting Paul down after he'd done something so generous. She wasn't used to people doing things like that for her. She had a feeling she'd also let Zac down. Would he want to go alone? Or could he take someone else with him? Jealousy raised its ugly head. She didn't want Zac going to the tropical island with another woman. If he was going she wanted to be the one at his side. In his arms. Gulp. *Make up your mind. What do you want with Zac?*

She wanted Zac in her life. But to follow up on that would be dangerous. What if they did get close; moved in together? How long would that last? When her mother acted once too often with the mess Olivia was used to dealing with, would Zac walk? If she had a month like she'd had in February, when she'd had so much work she'd all but lived in the hospital for four weeks, would he begrudge the time he didn't have with her and leave? There'd only been one man in her life she'd loved unconditionally—her father—and he'd deserted her. She doubted her ability to cope with anyone else doing that to her.

Her tea arrived and she concentrated on pouring, tried hard to ignore the dilemma going on in her head.

But Zac didn't seem to have any problem continuing the conversation. 'I take it this is because of what happened in my apartment?' He leaned closer so only she could hear him.

Unfortunately his movement brought that heady smell that defined him closer to her nostrils. There was no avoiding the scent, or the challenge in his eyes. 'We wouldn't be able to go the distance without touching each other.'

'Is that what you want?' Disbelief darkened his eyes, deepened his voice. Who could blame him? Last night she hadn't mucked around about getting into the sack with him. He asked, 'Seriously?

No, she wanted to spend the whole time in bed with him. That was the problem. 'It's what I need.'

Zac sat back, leaning away from her, his gaze fixed on her as though he hoped to see inside her skull and read her mind. 'I should be glad you're saying no, but there's one fabulous holiday going begging. Until Paul pointed it out I hadn't realised how much I could do with a break. Fiji would be perfect.'

Olivia said, 'You can still go.'

'Not much fun alone,' he said softly.

'Apply the pressure, why don't you?'

'Yep.'

'Not happening,' she muttered. Lifting her cup, Olivia tried to concentrate on what the others were talking about. When the meals arrived she joined in the conversation, relieved that the subject of Fiji had been dropped. But all the while that picture of the sea and coconut palms remained at the forefront of her mind, with Zac firmly in the middle.

Her phone rang just as everyone was getting up from the table to go their separate ways.

'Olivia, it's Hugo. I'm sorry to disturb your weekend when I said I'd cover for you, but I'm concerned about Anna Seddon.'

Alarm made her voice sharp. 'What's up?' Anna was a healthy woman who shouldn't be having any post-op complications.

'Medically she's fine. Her obs couldn't be better, she slept well until four this morning. But she's having a meltdown about the operation. I've tried talking to her but I'm a mere male and have no idea what it's like to have my breasts removed.' Hugo sighed. 'She's right, of course.'

'Of all the people I've done that procedure for I'd never have thought Anna would break up about it. She's been so pragmatic.' Olivia echoed Hugo's sigh. 'Is her husband with her?'

'Yes, and looking lost. She keeps yelling at him to go away. He doesn't know how to help her either.'

And I can? She had to try. She'd told Anna she'd be there for her throughout this difficult time, and she had meant it. 'I'll come over now.' She dropped her phone into her handbag and turned to face everyone. 'Thanks for the catch-up, guys. I've got to go.'

Maxine stepped up to give her a hug. 'Don't take

so long next time. I want to hear all the details about your trip to Fiji.'

'There won't be any. I'm not going.' She tried to free herself from Maxine's arms and failed.

'Go. It would be good for you.'

Maxine dropped her arms to her sides and Olivia stepped back.

'You might be surprised.'

Olivia couldn't help herself: she glanced across at the man in question. His familiar face snatched at her heart. Talking animatedly with the others, he appeared relaxed and comfortable in his own skin. Then he looked over at her and winked. Caught. He'd been aware of her scrutiny all along. Like they were in tune with each other, which was nonsense. They'd never been like that. Except when it came to sex. But there was nothing sexual about that wink. It had been more a 'Hey, girl' gesture. Friendly and caring, not deep and loving or hot and demanding. But it had been…? Nice? Yes, nice.

Turning back to Maxine, she said, 'I'd better run. A patient needs me.'

'You have to be somewhere in a hurry?' Zac strode alongside her as she raced for the lobby and the elevators, keen to get away before anyone else brought up the subject of that trip away with Zac.

'The hospital. I did a double mastectomy and implant yesterday morning and apparently my patient is losing it big time this morning.'

'That's a biggie for any woman to deal with.'

'She's been so brave all the way through discussions about the operation and what size implants she'd like. She's dealt with her family's history of breast cancer matter-of-factly, and accepted she didn't have a lot of choice if she wanted longevity. Guess it had to catch up with her some time.'

'Has she got good support from her family?' Zac asked as he pressed the up button for the elevator.

'Yes, very good.' Olivia drew a breath. Only yesterday she'd been saying to the Theatre staff how Anna's husband was a hero in her book. Yep, and she'd had thoughts about the man next to her being a hero too.

'You want me to get your car out of the basement? Save you some minutes?'

She stared at Zac. 'I forgot. I need to order a taxi. My car's in the hospital car park with a flat battery. I didn't have time to phone a service man yesterday.' She made to head for the concierge only to be stopped by Zac's hand on her arm.

'I'll be waiting in my car out the front when you're ready.' He nudged her forward into the elevator. 'It'll only take a couple of minutes to get it.'

But I don't want to sit in a car with you, breathing your smell, feeling your heat, wishing I could go away with you. 'A taxi will be fine.' She was talking to the closing doors, Zac already halfway across the lobby. She'd lost that round. There'd been determination in the set of his shoulders and the length of his quick strides taking him out of the hotel. He'd be ready for her the moment she emerged from the revolving door of the hotel.

Nice.

Leaning back against the wall, Olivia smiled despite her misgivings. She'd have to come up with a better word than 'nice'. Zac was more than nice, and his gestures were kind and caring. All good, all sounding bland for a man who was anything but. 'Hot' used to be her word for him and, yes, he was still that.

But now? Now he was a mixed bag of emotions and characteristics she hadn't taken the time to notice before. This Zac was intriguing. She wanted to know more about him. Hell, she wanted to know everything.

As the elevator pinged at her floor she knew she had to walk away from him, because the more she learned about Zac the harder it became to remain aloof. Her emotions were getting involved, putting her heart in turmoil, and that was a no-go zone.

CHAPTER SEVEN

'I AM SO SORRY.' Anna Seddon sniffed, and snatched up a handful of tissues to blow her nose. 'I know it's your weekend off. Hugo shouldn't have called you.'

Olivia sat on the edge of the bed and shook her head at her patient. 'It's not a problem. I'd have been annoyed if he hadn't. What started this off? What's distressed you this morning?'

'I took a look under the gown and saw where my breasts used to be. It's horrible there. The new ones don't look right even wrapped in bandages. I know you said to wait, but I had to see.' Anna slashed at fresh tears spilling down her cheeks. 'Nothing looks normal. The implants are different, ugly, not me, and the scars are bright red. I shouldn't have done this. I should've taken a chance I wouldn't get cancer.'

Olivia waited until Anna ran out of steam, then took her hand. 'You've had a shock. No amount of explaining could've prepared you.' Which was why she asked patients to wait until she was there before they looked at the results of their surgery. 'Remember, I said that your breast implants were going to look and feel strange. They're not natural, like your real breasts were, and we have yet to bring them up to full size. This will take time as we can't pump them full of saline instantly. It's a gradual process, giving your skin time to stretch and accommodate the implants.'

'You told me that, but I saw them and freaked out,' Anna whispered. 'You must think I'm a total head case.'

'Not at all. You've just had your breasts removed when as far as we know there's nothing wrong with them. You're not dealing with the fear of knowing you've already got cancer. Instead, breast cancer is a real possibility for you, so you're working ahead of things. Of course it's a shock and very different from other situations.'

'I know you went over this more than once. I thought I understood how I'd feel, and that the fact I was doing it to be there for my kids and Duncan would override every other emotion. I was wrong.' At the mention of her husband tears began pouring down her face again.

'You're a woman, first and foremost. Our breasts help define us. When we're young we can't wait for them to start growing and then it's what size will they be? Will they be sexy? They're also about nurturing our babies. You've done something very brave. Don't ever think you're not as feminine as you were before yesterday because you are. You've got a lovely figure, a pretty face and a heart of gold. Not to mention a family who adores you. Especially that husband of yours.'

A shadow of a smile lightened Anna's mouth through the deluge of tears. 'Duncan's something, isn't he?'

'He's a hero.' There, she'd said it again. What was it with her that she kept coming up with that word? It wasn't as though she believed in heroes. *But you want to. You want one of your own.*

'You think?' Anna asked, a twinkle slowly lightening her sad eyes and easing her tears.

'I know.' She stood up. 'In fact, there's a hero out

in the waiting room. I'll go tell him you're busting to see him.'

'What will he say when he sees my false breasts?' There was a hitch in Anna's voice and fear in her eyes.

'I bet he tells you he loves you.' Lucky woman. *What was it like to have a man to love you, to say those precious three words to you?* Olivia had never known and wondered if she ever would. It must be the most precious thing—love, unconditional and everlasting. When she walked into the waiting room she found Zac talking rugby to Anna Seddon's husband as though he'd known him for ever.

Her heart did a funny little jig. Zac. Sexy Zac was doing nothing more than yakking to a stranger who was trying to cope with his wife's unenviable situation, and yet he looked…like everything she'd thought she might want in a man, in her man. Her hero.

Get out of here. Where had that come from? Yeah, sure, yesterday when she'd called Duncan a hero it had been Zac's face flitting across her mind, but Zac? Hero? Why would she even think that? What had he done for her to think so?

She'd dumped him and he'd sent her beautiful flowers.

He'd driven her here this morning and taken her keys to get her car battery sorted.

He'd turned up to help yesterday afternoon when everything had been turning to custard.

He'd never once been rude to her, or made fun of her need to keep herself to herself, or told her to stop being so much in control of just about everything she touched.

Did any or all of those things make a man a hero? Didn't heroes slay dragons? She still had dragons, but Zac didn't know about them because she'd never shown that weakness to him. It wasn't as though he could make everything right for her, even if he was aware of her screwed-up family life.

'CC, you're daydreaming.' Zac was smiling at her, his head at an angle that suggested he wanted to know exactly what was on her mind.

Thank goodness she wasn't the type to blush. The absolute last thing Zac needed to know was what she'd been thinking. 'I don't daydream.'

'Then you're missing out on a lot of fun.'

'How's Anna?' There was a load of worry in Duncan's short question.

'Wanting to see her man.' Olivia moved closer. 'She's got past that little meltdown but, Duncan, you need to be prepared for more episodes. I'm not saying Anna's going to fall apart on you long term, but she's facing reality now, whereas before surgery it was still an unknown. It's scary for her.' She continued, 'She's afraid you won't be able to cope when you see her breasts. It's natural to feel that way, but it's how you handle the situation that's going to make the difference.'

'I'll tell you this for nothing. I don't care about scars and a change in her shape. I love that woman and think she's the bravest person I've ever met.' Duncan touched the corner of one eye with a forefinger.

'I think Anna's a lucky woman.' Olivia swallowed the sudden lump in her throat. 'Go tell her exactly what you just said.'

'She's not going to throw her water bottle at me or tell me to go away for ever?' Duncan was deadly serious.

'I doubt it, unless it's because you've taken so long to get along to her room since I said I was coming to find you.' Anna shouldn't have thrown anything—it would hurt her wounds and might pull some stitches. Something to check up on when she examined her later. She hadn't wanted to have Anna expose herself for an exam when she'd been so upset, and had figured that as all the obs were fine it didn't matter if they waited before doing that.

Dropping into the seat Duncan had vacated, she stared at the toes of her boots. And yawned.

Zac chuckled. 'Want to grab a coffee while we wait for the battery man? He's about twenty minutes away and we could both do with something to keep us awake.'

'Hospital coffee will be a comedown after that fabulous brunch.'

'Nothing like a reality check.'

Reality. Of course. 'You don't need to hang around. You've got a perfectly good vehicle downstairs. I can visit patients while I wait.'

'You don't want to share crap coffee with me?' His grin set butterflies flapping in her tummy. 'Anyway, the guy's got my number, not yours.'

'I hate it when you gloat.' She laughed tiredly. 'Disgusting coffee it is.' Along with great company. All in all, not a bad way to continue her morning.

Olivia's bubble burst quickly.

Zac directed her to a corner table as far away as possible from the few staff and visitors using the cafeteria, ordered long blacks for them both, and dropped onto the chair opposite her. 'I've talked to my practice manager so she can arrange for my days off when we go to Fiji. The hospital roster is easy to fix, with Paul offering to cover for me.'

The man didn't muck about. He must've been on the phone the moment she'd clambered out of his four-wheel drive in the hospital garage; ordering a battery, sorting his week off.

She sighed. 'I thought I said I wasn't going.' He had to be deaf as well as organised.

'You did.'

'So you *are* planning on going alone.'

'Nope.' Zac leaned back as a girl placed two over-full coffee cups on the table and took away their order number. 'I want you to come with me.'

So do I. 'No.'

Those eyes that matched the coffee in colour locked onto her. 'Are you telling *me* no? Or yourself, Olivia?'

'We'd probably end up hating each other.'

'Somehow I don't think so.' Shock widened his eyes. So he hadn't thought it through. 'But we won't know if we don't try.'

What was this about? Zac had made it clear he'd only been interested in sex last time round. Her hands were back in her lap, her fingers aching with the tightness of her grip. 'Is this so you can then walk away with no regrets? Did I finish it too soon last time?'

Now his gaze dropped away. He leaned far back and draped one arm over the top of the chair next to him. His eyes cruised the cafeteria before returning to her, a guarded expression covering his face. 'I've learned more about you in the last twenty-four hours than I ever did in those eight weeks last year.'

'Then you're probably up to speed and there's nothing more to find out.'

Zac stared at her. 'You're selling yourself short.'

To hell with the coffee. Pushing up from the table, she aimed for a moderate tone. 'No, I am not. What you see is what you get, and as for Fiji, you get nothing. I'm not going.' *But I want to. Really, really want to.*

Of course he followed her. He was persistent if nothing else. Unlike last time. 'Rethink that, Olivia. We don't have to live in each other's pockets while we're there, but it would be fun to lie in the sun together, to share a meal under the stars.'

The problem was that if she lay on the beach in her bikini beside Zac in his swimming shorts they would end up having sex. Not that doing so didn't appeal. Of course it did. Her mouth watered, thinking about it. But she'd made up her mind the day she'd walked out on him that they weren't going anywhere with their relationship because she couldn't afford to get her heart broken. Neither had she wanted to break his—if it was even up for grabs.

Zac pulled his phone from his pocket and read a message. 'Your battery's nearly here.'

'Good. Thanks for arranging it.' She didn't know why she felt small and mean, only knew she was floundering, fighting between going with him on that trip and staying away from temptation. She was looking out for herself, something she'd always done. Her mother had never put her daughter before herself, never would. She gasped. That meant she was the same as her mother. Putting her determination to remain alone before anyone, anything else. *But... But I'm doing it for a good reason. Dad left Mum because she'd worn him down, tossed his love back in his face again and again. I'm not doing that to a man I might fall in love with.*

A hand on her elbow directed her to the elevator. Seemed that Zac was always taking her to the lift. 'Five

days of sunshine and no patients. Sounds wonderful
to me.'

Ain't that the truth?

At least Olivia hadn't questioned why he was so adamant they should go to Fiji together. He should be grateful she was refusing to go, but the thought of being
alone when he should be celebrating with his family
grated. A distraction was needed and Olivia would certainly be that.

But, more than that, it was time to start changing
from being reactive to his family's attitude to becoming
proactive in sorting out what he wanted for his future—
starting with taking time off from his heavy work schedule to have some fun. Hell. When was the last time he'd
done that? Nothing came to mind except the hours he'd
snatched to be with Olivia eighteen months ago.

The sound of squealing tyres filled the basement garage as they exited the elevator on the way to the outside car park. The smell of burning rubber filled his
nostrils. 'What the hell?'

A nearly new, upmarket car raced past them. At the
end of the lane it spun left, the rear wheels sliding out of
control. Just when impact with parked vehicles seemed
imminent the driver got the car under control.

Zac pushed Olivia back against the now closed el-
evator doors, tugged his phone from his pocket to call
Security, and cursed. There was no signal down here.
'The driver looked very young. How'd he get in?'

The garage and car park were reserved for medical personnel and accessed with a swipe card. The car
flew past them again as Zac looked around for a wall
phone. Spying one by the stairwell door, he changed
direction, only to spin around when he heard an al-

mighty thump, followed by a metallic crashing sound. Then ominous silence.

'He's hit someone and then slammed into a vehicle!' Olivia began running in the direction of the crashed car.

Zac raced alongside her. 'We need someone down here, taking charge of that kid.' A boy looking about fifteen staggered out of the car, looking shocked and bewildered.

'Where did she come from?' he squawked as they reached him.

Zac's hands clenched as he saw a woman in blue scrubs sprawled across the concrete, a pool of blood already beginning to form by her head. 'What the hell were you doing?' Zac shouted at the kid as he dropped down to his knees beside the unmoving woman.

'Hey, steady.' Olivia reached across from the other side of the woman to grip his arm. Shaking her head at him, she said, 'This nurse needs our undivided attention.'

'You're right,' he ground through gritted teeth. 'Kid, get on that phone by the elevator and get help down here fast.'

Without a word the youth was gone, and Zac could only hope he was running for the phone.

Zac felt for a pulse, and sighed with relief.

Olivia was carefully feeling the nurse's head. 'Amelia, can you hear me?'

A low groan was the only answer she got.

'Amelia, you've been in an accident. There are two doctors with you and we're going to check your injuries.'

'How much do you think she's heard?' Zac wondered aloud.

Olivia shrugged. 'We can't be sure anything we say registers.'

'You know her?' Zac noted the odd angle of the

nurse's legs and checked for bleeding in case a blood vessel had been torn. 'No major swelling indicating internal bleeding.'

'I can read,' Olivia muttered.

The name badge. Duh. Left his brain behind this morning, had he? With gentle movements he began assessing her hips and thighs for fractures. 'Broken femur for starters. This knee has taken a thump too.' His fingers worked over the kneecap. 'Smashed, I'd say.'

Their patient groaned again and lifted an arm a small way off the ground.

Zac quickly caught her, and gently pressed her arm down by her side. 'Amelia, try not to move.'

One eye opened, shut again.

'At least she's responding,' he said.

'Oh, my God. What's happened?' A man loomed over them.

Zac told him, 'An out-of-control car hit her.'

The newcomer said, 'I'm in Admin, but I can get help if you tell me what you need.'

'Get us the emergency equipment and a bed. I told the driver to ring upstairs but you're part of this hospital, you'll know exactly who to speak to,' Zac told him. Who knew if the boy had done as he'd said or taken a hike before everyone turned up and started pointing fingers?

Olivia was speaking quietly. 'We've got a soft cranial injury, probably from impacting with the concrete. Left ear's torn.'

Zac added to the list of injuries. 'At least her chest appears to have dodged a bullet.' His fingers were gently working over Amelia's ribs. 'The car would've hit her in the lower body.' What had that kid been thinking, doing wheelies in here? He hadn't looked old enough to know how to drive. *Who are you to ask? You were eighteen and still got it wrong.*

'On my way.' The admin man nodded at the vehicle parked with its nose caught in the side panel of a sedan. 'That the car? It's Maxine Sutherland's.'

Olivia's head shot up, horror in her eyes, but all she said was, 'Can you run? This woman needs urgent help.'

With the man gone, Zac said, 'Maxine must've left the car unlocked, unless...' Had it been Maxine and Brent's son driving? Shock rocked through Zac. No parent ever wanted to deal with something like this. He knew. He'd done it to his brother and parents, with dire consequences. They'd never forgiven him, blaming him for not looking out for his younger brother. Like they'd ever been there for either of their sons. But every time Zac saw his brother and that blasted wheelchair the guilt crunched his insides. Zac's remorse would never go away, and was stronger than anything anyone else could lay on him.

'Zac? You okay?' A gentle hand touched his cheek.

His chest rose as he dragged in a lungful of air. 'Yes.' *No.* Now wasn't the time to explain. If ever there was a right time. He tried to straighten Amelia's right leg. 'Her knee is also dislocated.' He had to know. 'Do you think the kid is Maxine and Brent's boy?'

Distress blinked out at him from Olivia's hyacinth eyes. 'No. Couldn't be.' Her bottom lip trembled even as the truth pushed aside her automatic denial. 'How dreadful for them if he is.'

'He was in here, and only card holders have access.'

They were interrupted by the sound of people running and an emergency trolley laden with everything they needed being pushed at a fast pace between the cars. Guess the kid had fronted up for help.

As Olivia explained to the ED staff what had happened and her assessment of Amelia's injuries, the anger Zac had put on the back burner roared to life. 'That boy really has made a mess of things for her.' Zac was equally worried for the lad. *His* life had changed for ever. 'Where is he, anyway?'

'Probably safer away from you.' Olivia came to stand beside him and reached for his hand. 'Calm down, Zac. You're not helping an already tricky situation. I know he's done wrong but let's leave that to others while we help with the medical side of things.'

The last thing Zac wanted was Olivia telling him what to do. It took a moment for it to register in the red haze of his brain that he had an excuse to put distance between them. 'The battery guy. I'll go and wait for him at the gate.' He needed to get away from what had happened before he blew a gasket. Amelia was getting all the attention she needed from Olivia and the ED doctor, while his attitude wasn't helping anyone. He stomped off before Olivia could say anything more.

But not before he saw the shock in those beautiful eyes. Yes, he had his secrets, just as he suspected she had hers. Secrets neither of them wanted to share. His definitely held him back from having a complete and fulfilling life. Was it the same with Olivia? Could that be why she'd walked out on their affair? She hadn't wanted to keep going in case they grew close?

There was nothing for it. They had to take that trip. Time together, talking, relaxing, getting to know each other on a whole new level, was becoming imperative.

Which really meant he should sign up for every orthopaedic surgery coming up at his clinic for the next six months.

CHAPTER EIGHT

OLIVIA POURED BOILING water over the tea leaves. Earl Grey Blue Star. 'Bliss.' She sniffed the air.

Every bone in her body ached with weariness. Her head pounded, her muscles drooped, and it felt as if there was grit in her eyes. The long soak in a very hot shower probably hadn't woken her up at all. Seven o'clock on Saturday night and she couldn't wait to crawl into bed. How pathetic could she get?

Her stomach was crying out to be fed. She hadn't eaten since brunch—the incident in the hospital garage and the resulting investigation by the traffic police had taken up a lot of the day. The pizza she'd ordered would arrive at the front door within the hour. She licked her lips in anticipation and tasted tea.

Her sitting room felt cosy, and lounging in pyjamas and a baggy sweatshirt in front of the fire she'd lit earlier felt decadent. A rare treat to be so sloppily dressed, and she'd die if anyone but the pizza delivery girl saw her in this state.

Right now a holiday would be perfect. *There's one on offer.* Had she been too hasty turning it down? *Not going to think about it.*

Picking up the remote, she turned on the TV, volume low, and flicked through the channels. Nothing interested her, not even the spunky guy showing how to swing a golf club. Not that sport of any kind interested her. It required energy she didn't like expending getting sweaty.

At the moment the most energetic she wanted to be was lying on a beach, getting a tan. Fiji would do that every time. She sighed. Fiji with Zac? What was wrong with her? She should be grabbing those tickets and packing her bag.

The doorbell rang loud in the quiet house. Someone out there must be looking out for her because that pizza was early. She went to get her dinner.

'Hi, Olivia. I hope you don't mind me dropping by.'

'Zac.' Her stomach growled while her heart lifted.

'Is that a good "Zac", or a go away "Zac"?'

'Take your pick.' She stepped back, opening the door wide.

Zac walked in quickly, as though afraid she'd change her mind.

She probably would've if she'd had the energy to think about the consequences of letting him into her home. 'Along here.' She led him into the sitting room.

When his gaze landed on her tea he asked, 'Got anything stronger? Scotch on the rocks?' He sank onto the couch and stared into the fire.

'Sure.' That was one spirit she did have, kept for her delightful elderly neighbour who liked an occasional tipple when he dropped in after a lonely day at home.

Returning with a glass, ice and whisky, Olivia placed everything on the coffee table she'd spent weeks sanding and varnishing to make it beautiful. Taking her mug to the other end of the couch, she sat with her feet tucked under her bottom and flicked glances at her visitor.

Something was going on. He'd been furious when

Amelia had been knocked down by that car. No, as he'd told her angrily, it had been the boy who'd banged the car into Amelia. The car was not at fault. Couldn't argue with that.

His anger had been more than she'd have expected, but there hadn't been an opportunity to talk to him about it. When they'd realised it might've been their colleagues' son doing wheelies in the garage Zac had turned pale and charged outside to let the battery guy into the car park. Later she'd seen him standing beside her car, hands on hips, staring up at the rain-laden sky, impervious to everything going on around him. When he'd joined her and the police, he'd gained some control over his emotions but hadn't been able to look her in the eye. After they'd finished telling the cops what little they'd seen Zac had been quick to drive away, leaving her none the wiser about what had been going on. Now here he was, looking badly in need of some quiet time and a big hug.

She'd give him the quiet time by waiting until he was ready to talk, but she'd hold back on the hug in case she'd read him wrong and he took it as more than she intended.

Zac reached for the bottle, slopped more whisky into the glass, and leaned back, his head on the top of the couch, his eyes closed.

It was far too tempting. Placing her glass on the coffee table, she leaned over, pulled him against her, and wrapped her arms right around him. Zac didn't resist, instead shuffling closer to lay his head on her breast.

She was starting to get pins and needles in one leg by the time Zac moved to sit up. Broaching the subject she thought was bothering him, she said, 'Amelia's going to be a mess for a while.'

'That boy will be a mess for the rest of his life.'

'It's going to take patience and counselling, yes, but his parents will be there for him all the way. He'll make it. Hopefully he learned a huge lesson today.' Though what the kid had been thinking, taking the car for a spin in a packed garage, was beyond her.

Zac leaned forward, his elbows on his knees, the glass between his hands turning back and forth. 'You don't know what you're talking about. I do.'

Olivia leaned closer to place her hand on his thigh, her shoulder against his upper arm. 'Tell me.'

She said it so quietly that at first she didn't think he'd heard, but as she was about to repeat herself he said, 'I've been there.'

'Oh, Zac.' Her heart broke for the sadness and despair in those words.

'My brother's in a wheelchair. Because of me.'

She closed her eyes. The pain in Zac's face was too much. He hurt big-time. The load of guilt he carried must crush him at times. Tonight was one of those times. Today's event had brought back the memories in full colour. She opened her eyes and tried to eyeball him. 'Zac, I'm sorry.'

'Don't give me any platitudes, CC. I couldn't stand that.'

'You've heard them all before, huh?'

'Every last one.' He stared into his glass, the liquid golden in the light thrown by the fire. 'I prefer honesty and you've never given me anything else so please don't change tonight. No "Mark's doing fine, it's okay". No "You're forgiven so get on with your life as though it didn't happen".' The warning was issued softly, which made it all the more real.

What the heck was she supposed to say if he didn't

want to talk about it? Or did he want to say what had happened to cause his brother's injuries but couldn't get the words out? Had he changed his mind about telling her anything more? Her mind was a jumble of questions and emotions. She wanted to help him, but Zac wasn't one to ask for help. Or was that what he'd done by turning up on her doorstep?

The doorbell ringing was a welcome interruption while she tried to work out where to go with this. Grabbing the money she'd put out earlier, she went to get dinner.

Zac stood up as she returned to the sitting room. 'I'll head away and leave you in peace.'

'You're welcome to share this. I never eat more than half.' Though tonight she might've, considering the state her stomach was in. 'Sit down, Zac. I'll get some napkins and plates.'

'You want anything stronger than tea to drink?'

Was that a *Yes, I'll stay*? 'No, thanks.'

'You're cautious with your drinks, aren't you?' Zac smiled half-heartedly. 'Afraid of making an idiot of yourself?'

'Absolutely.' Rejoining him on the couch, she sighed. 'Life when I was younger was chaotic and messy. I learned to be rigid in my dealings with my mum, school, everything. Too controlled maybe, but that's how I manage.'

Taking her hand, Zac locked eyes with hers. 'Yet you're completely off the radar when it comes to sex.'

She spluttered over the mouthful she'd just bitten off her pizza.

Zac wiped her mouth with his napkin. 'I wasn't complaining.' The smile he gave her was tender, turning her inside out.

'Maybe sex is my one outlet,' she managed, holding back from explaining it hadn't been like that with the few other men she'd slept with.

He was very quiet for a few minutes, then blew her away with, 'Would you come to Fiji with me if we agreed to no sex for the whole trip?'

'What?' she asked.

'Think you—we—can do that?'

Talk about a challenge she couldn't resist. Especially as she was struggling to keep refusing to go in the first place. And now that she'd heard more about what made Zac tick she wanted to spend more time with him.

Zac grimaced. The need to go away with Olivia just got stronger and stronger, no matter how often he told himself he was making a mistake. When he'd told her about Mark he'd very nearly continued with the whole sordid story of how his life had changed for ever but a modicum of common sense had prevailed. Fear of seeing disgust in her eyes had locked his tongue to the roof of his mouth.

But if only she'd agree to go to that resort island with him. Go and have some good, honest fun. Even if she agreed to the bizarre suggestion he'd just put out there, he'd be happy. He wouldn't mind someone to talk to, to relax with.

He saw Olivia open her mouth, heard her say as though in slow motion, 'I'll go. I won't change my mind again. I'm sorry I've been vacillating.'

Excitement zipped through him, temporarily drowning out the horrors of that morning's disaster. They were going to spend time together without the pressures of work; with time to talk, to be themselves, and maybe learn more about each other. 'Good.'

'That's it?' She laughed, a tinkling sound that lightened his mood.

'Yes.' Relief softened him. 'You know what? I think it'll be great. Just the two of us.'

Olivia smiled.

It was a big, soft smile that caused him to take a risk. 'I was driving Dad's car.' Swallowing hard, he continued. 'It was late. We'd been out all day at the rugby, and stopped at a friend's on the way home.' His gut churned. 'Mark was being a pain in the arse, winding me up as only he knew how, and when we drove away from that house he said one thing too many and I lost it. Slammed my foot on the accelerator. The car spun into the stone wall along the waterfront and flipped into the water. Mark's back was broken.' That was all there was to it.

Her expression showed no condemnation. 'How awful for your family. Especially you. You've taken the blame ever since, right?'

Air huffed out of his lungs. 'Of course. I *was* at fault. I lost my temper.' *Damn, but it still hurt so badly.* If he never made another mistake in his life it wouldn't be good enough.

'You haven't forgiven yourself. Does your brother blame you?' When he nodded once, she continued. 'What about your parents? Surely they don't?'

He went for broke. 'My parents put me in charge of my brother from very early on. They were both busy with their careers as CEOs of big businesses. We were the children to be trotted out at functions or for family photos, and they were proud of us as long as we didn't stuff up. Which I did—monumentally.' At least now she'd understand why he wasn't looking for a woman to love and settle down with, that he'd always fly solo.

One holiday in Fiji being the exception. 'Of course they haven't forgiven me. I was in charge of Mark that night.'

Olivia wanted to cry for him. How could parents do that? Then again, her father had left her with Mum, hadn't he? Zac shouldn't, mustn't take all the blame, but he'd obviously made a lifelong habit of shouldering it. 'So you and Mark don't get along even now?'

'Hardly.' His mouth flattened. 'He's a successful architect, which is something to be grateful for.'

'More than something. It says he's moved on, hasn't let his spinal injury hold him back.' If only she could remove Zac's pain. But there was only one person who could do that. Zac.

'My parents pretty much disowned me after the accident.' Zac's face was bleak. 'I continued living with them for the rest of that year but it was as though I was a stranger. Come the last day of school I was gone. I got a job in a supermarket and went to live with my grandfather. Dad gave me a generous allowance but I turned him down and paid my university fees myself. I never went back home.'

And she'd thought her life had been bad. No wonder she and Zac both balked at commitment. 'That's harsh.' Actually, it was lousy. How could any parent do that? Did Zac think if he moved on, let himself stop feeling guilt, then he'd be setting himself up for another fall? Zac was a very responsible person. That had been abundantly clear when they'd been training to become surgeons. Had that come from this accident? Or had he always been a responsible person who'd made one mistake? Now she understood his outburst over the boy who'd knocked down Amelia that morning. 'I'm glad you have your grandfather.'

He cocked an eyebrow at her. 'So am I. Except he died last Christmas.' That sadness had returned to his eyes, tightened his face, more deeply, more strongly than ever.

Olivia wanted to banish it—if only for a few hours. And she only knew one way. They weren't in Fiji yet. Standing up, she put her hand out to him. 'Come with me.'

His hand was warm and firm as his fingers laced through hers. He didn't say a word as she led him down the hall to her bedroom. Or when she began unbuttoning his shirt.

Running her hands over that wide expanse of muscular chest, her blood began to thrum along her veins. Her lips surrounded his nipple, her tongue caressed slowly. Then Zac's hands were lifting her head so he could kiss her.

A long, slow kiss that had none of the urgent fire of any of their previous kisses and all the quietness of giving and sharing. It was heady stuff.

'Olivia,' Zac groaned against her mouth.

Without breaking the kiss, she pushed his shirt off his shoulders and down his arms, then found the stud and zip of his jeans. When Zac moved to lift her top she took his hands and placed them at his sides, and continued removing his jeans.

When she had him naked she gently shoved him backwards to sprawl across her bed. Her tummy quivered at the beautiful sight. His well-honed muscles accentuated his masculinity. Slowly she raised her top, exposing her bra-covered breasts. Next she slid her hands under the waistband of her shapeless trackies and began pushing them, oh, so slowly down to her hips, her thighs, her knees.

Zac's gaze followed her actions, his eyes kissing her skin. Shivers of excitement touched all the exposed places of her body. Standing in her panties and bra, she suddenly felt uncomfortable. What was she doing? Then Zac's tongue lapped his bottom lip and she relaxed. It wasn't as though he hadn't seen her naked, and while she mightn't be a strip dancer she could undress seductively.

Zac put his hands behind his head and kept watching her.

Placing one foot on the bed, she undid her bra and let it fall into her hands to be twirled across the room.

Zac's eyes widened and his tongue did another lick of his lips.

With one forefinger she began lowering her panties, never taking her eyes off his. She saw when they widened, when his chest began rising and falling faster, when his erection strained tight. Swinging a leg over his body, she hovered above him, moving so that her centre barely touched the tip of his shaft.

'Oh, sweetheart, let me touch you.' Those firm hands she craved on her skin covered her breasts, lifting them, caressing and gently squeezing them. His thumbs teased her nipples into hard, tight peaks.

Heat spread throughout her body like a slow burn, sending lazy flames of desire to every corner, warming her skin, drying her mouth. She began to lower herself over him, taking him deep inside.

Zac moved his hands to her buttocks, and he held her still. 'Not yet.'

Suddenly Olivia was on her back with Zac above her, kissing every inch of her heated skin, drowning her in need and longing. Taking his time to work down her body. They'd never made love like this.

This felt like lovemaking; not hot, frantic sex.

And when Zac moved over her, claimed her, they moved in unison, a slow rhythm that built and built till finally they reached a crescendo that stole the breath out of her lungs and sent her spinning out of control.

Olivia woke slowly. A heavy weight lay over her waist. Zac's arm. His breaths were soft on the back of her neck. His knees tucked in behind hers, and his stomach pushed against her lower back. Wow. This was amazing. Comfortable and cosy, warm and sexy. But mostly wonderful. Something she'd never experienced before. She snuggled nearer, closing her eyes to absorb every sensation moving through her. Warmth from that splayed hand on her stomach, from those thigh muscles behind her.

'Morning, beautiful,' Zac whispered against her neck.

'Wow,' she said. Hard to believe what she'd been missing out on. A small laugh escaped her. Slipping her fingers through Zac's on her stomach, she admitted, 'I've never had a man stay the night.'

Warm lips laid a soft kiss on her shoulder. 'Glad I'm the chosen one.' Another kiss. 'It's not something I normally do either.'

It was as though her whole body smiled. She and Zac had slept together, as in 'closed their eyes and gone to sleep' slept. She'd heard women talk about how good it was to sleep, spooned with their partner, and had thought they were exaggerating. Now she got it.

Careful. This was starting to feel like a relationship, as in not just about sex. Olivia tensed. Really? Damn. Just when she was beginning to enjoy things reality raised its annoying head to remind her she knew nothing about a good, solid, loving relationship between a man and a woman. Neither did Zac.

'Hey, relax. I'm not going to bite.' Zac's voice sounded sleep-laden.

No, but was he going to hurt her? Not today, or next month maybe, but eventually would he realise he didn't want to spend time with her, and walk? She had to protect herself. Wriggling free, she sat up. 'I'm going to take a shower.'

Zac reached for her, pulled her down. 'Come here. Let's stay tucked up for a little longer.'

'But...'

'Do you have to be somewhere in a hurry?' he asked reasonably.

'No.' Neither could she deny that lying in Zac's strong arms gave her a sense of belonging. Something that had been missing most of her life. Tension began tripping up her spine. Not good. Belonging went hand in hand with a serious relationship. Squeezing her eyes shut tight, she worked at banishing the negative feeling. She'd make the most of this moment; give herself something to remember later.

'I can't believe that in less than two weeks we'll be lying under palm trees.' Excitement warmed Olivia as she talked to Zac on the phone the following Thursday night. 'I'm going on holiday.'

'Says the woman who went out of her way to avoid it.' Zac's laughter rolled down the phone.

'Yeah, well, I'm glad I came to my senses. A holiday is definitely what I need. How are you getting on with sorting your surgical list?'

'Not too bad. Because Paul's taking over my private list I haven't had to change too many appointments.

Most patients I've talked to have been understanding about the change.'

Olivia grimaced. 'I wish mine were as accepting. There've been a few tears and tantrums, but I think I've got it sorted. I'll be working some long days leading up to our departure and will be busier than rush hour on the motorway.'

'Wonderful,' he groaned. 'Are you going to sleep the whole time we're away?'

'Absolutely not.' Somehow she doubted she'd sleep much at all, knowing Zac was in the same room and out of bounds. Why had he suggested that? Getting to know each other was one thing, but seriously? No sex? This would be a very interesting holiday. 'I'm going shopping for bikinis at the weekend.'

'Can I come?'

'I don't think so.' She grinned. That so wasn't happening.

'What if I waited outside the shop and took you to lunch afterwards?'

'What sort of lunch?'

'You'd have to wait and see.' Zac laughed again.

'Sorry, not happening.'

'So where do you go shopping for beach gear in the middle of winter?'

'My favourite fashion shop has an accessories section all year round. Apparently bikinis are holiday accessories. Who'd have thought it? But, then, I haven't owned a bikini in more years than I care to count.' Or gone on a holiday.

'Don't you go to the beach?' Zac asked.

'Going to the beach is a family thing, or a teen group party.' Which had been the last time she'd gone with a crowd.

'I think it's time you started getting out there and living, CC. All work and no play is not healthy.'

'Didn't you tell me how little you do outside work?' They were a right messed-up pair. 'We'll make up for it in Fiji.'

'Can't wait.' A sigh filtered down the line. 'I mean that. You have no idea how much I'm looking forward to this now that it's real.'

'Oh, but I do. After at first refusing to accept the trip, I now find I'm often daydreaming about being on the beach or swimming with the fishes. I don't remember being this excited about anything since... Well, I don't remember.'

'We are going to have a blast.' Now he was sounding like an excited schoolboy.

'Sure are.'

Another voice interrupted the moment. 'Olivia, sweetheart, where's the tonic water?' Her mother's wheedling voice grated more than usual.

'Zac, I've got to go. Talk to you again.'

'Something up? Your tone changed. Is your mother there?' He missed nothing, damn him.

'Yes, she is.' Sometimes her mother could be demanding and unrelenting in her quest for whatever today's greatest need was, and other times she'd be all sweetness and light. 'I've got to go.'

'Hey, I'm here for you.' The excitement had gone, replaced with concern. 'We can still have that lunch.'

'I'm good, Zac. Truly.'

'Olivia, tonic water. Where have you hidden it?' Mum stood in front of her, her eyes bloodshot and her tomato-red lipstick smudged on her upper lip.

'Talk to me, CC.' Zac was in her ear.

'It's complicated.' And ugly.

'Try me,' he persisted.

'Not now, Zac.' Her mother was in her face. 'Talk later. Bye.' Olivia pressed the off button, dug deep for patience. No surprise. She was all out of it. 'There's no tonic in this house.' There hadn't been any gin either until her mother had arrived with a bottle an hour ago.

'Darling, that's no way to treat your mother.'

Air hissed over Olivia's lips. 'Keeping an endless supply of gin and tonic isn't either.' She rubbed her thumbs over her eyes. 'You said there was something you wanted to talk about.'

'I think I should sell the house. It's time to move on with my life. But you're going to say no to anything I suggest.' Petulant as well.

Being one of the trustees for her mother's property and banking details came with its own set of difficulties. But if left to her own resources her mother would've gone broke long ago. 'Mum, we've discussed this so often I can't believe you'd bring the subject up again.'

'You are so unfair. About everything.'

Yep, a right old cold fish with a bank account tighter than a fish's backside. That's me. 'Where would you live if you sold? Another house? Or an apartment somewhere?'

'I could move in with you. There're more rooms here than you know what to do with.'

That was never going to happen.

Never say never.

Olivia shuddered. She did love her mother, but for sanity's sake preferred to keep her at a distance. To share the same house day in, day out would send her climbing the harbour bridge and leaping off.

CHAPTER NINE

'TOKORIKI.' THE HELICOPTER pilot pointed to an island ahead of them.

Olivia gasped. 'Oh, wow, it's tiny.'

Zac grinned. 'Perfect. You won't be able to get away from me.'

She elbowed him. 'Want to spend the night outside in a hammock? Alone?'

Zac just laughed. Damn it. 'A night in a hammock would be a novelty. I wonder if there's room for two.'

She did an exaggerated eye roll. 'Not to mention mosquitoes.'

Zac stared down at the bright blue sea as the pilot brought the helicopter around to line up with the landing pad on the resort's lawn. 'Isn't it stunning?'

Olivia leaned over Zac to get a good look at the island. 'Pretty as a picture.'

'Yes.' Zac's head was right beside hers, his scent tickling her nostrils.

Pulling sideways so that she no longer touched him, she tried to ignore the buzz of excitement fizzing along her veins. Not easy in the confined space with the smell of aftershave and hot-blooded male teasing her. How was she going to remain immune to him when they'd be sharing a bure? The photos on the internet had been a reality check, like a dousing under cold water. The one large room containing an enormous bed towards the back and lounge furniture at the front looked so romantic and had set her heart racing—and that had been back at home. Couples didn't come here to sleep in separate beds. Not unless they were Zac and her.

The helicopter touched down with a bump and Olivia snapped open the clasp on her safety belt. A big, strapping Fijian man opened the door and held out his hand to help her out. Feet firmly on the ground, she looked around and was greeted by two young girls.

'*Bula,*' they said in unison, before placing leis made of pink and yellow hibiscus flowers around her and Zac's necks.

'*Bula,*' she replied.

Zac took her hand. 'Welcome to paradise.'

The bure was gorgeous, made from dark wood and covered with thatch. Wide doors and large open windows let the sea breeze through. An overhead fan spun slowly. A perfect spot for a couple to enjoy themselves and each other. Even with the sex ban? A second shower stall, outside and without a roof, made her smile. 'All the better to stargaze.'

'Come here.' Zac still held her hand and now he tugged her over the lawn to stand on the beach twenty metres from what was to be their home for five nights.

'It's going to be dark shortly,' she sighed. The day had sped by getting here.

'Let's pop the cork on that bottle of champagne I saw in an ice bucket on the coffee table. We can sit out on our front porch and pretend we do this every night after a hard day at work.'

Olivia started walking backwards so she could watch Zac. 'You're as excited as a kid on his first holiday, aren't you?' His eyes shone, his mouth the most relaxed she could ever remember it.

'I reckon. This is like my first holiday, only way better.'

'We've barely started.' She stopped so that his next step brought him right up close. Close enough to lean in and kiss that happy mouth, which she did. But when his hands spanned her waist she reluctantly pulled back. 'Sorry, I shouldn't have done that.'

'Did the rule state no kissing?' He was shaking his head at her, his smile only increasing. Was nothing going to mar his enjoyment? 'I must've missed that.'

'Maybe you didn't put it in.' She hoped not. Kissing Zac was too much fun not to be able to do it whenever she wanted. But then there'd be consequences. Looking around for something else to talk about, she spied two hammocks slung between nearby trees. 'There's your bed. You even get a choice.'

'I am not spending my nights slapping at the mozzies, thank you very much.' Zac caught her hand, laced his fingers through hers, then swung their joined hands up to his lips and kissed her knuckles.

Careful. That might start a fire I can't put out. And we have rules. She slipped her hand out of Zac's. 'Where's that champagne?'

He tried not to look disappointed, but she saw it and felt a heel. He'd only been having fun, and she *had* instigated the kiss.

Inside, Zac picked up the card leaning against the bucket in which the ice was rapidly turning to liquid. 'Compliments of Andy and Kitty. They say thanks for the gala night and hope we have a wonderful time.'

'That's lovely. It's not as though they haven't got enough to think about at the moment.'

Minutes later they sat in front of their bure and watched the sun turning the sky red and yellow. 'That's an abrupt change from day to night,' Zac commented.

'Guess that's the tropics for you. Hard to believe we left winter behind.' The warm, heavy air made her clothes stick to her skin. She wouldn't be wearing much for the next few days.

'What's your favourite season?' Zac asked.

'Summer, followed by summer. I hate being cold.'

'Yet you bought an old villa that must be freezing in winter. Though, come to think of it, I didn't notice a chill when I was there.'

'First thing I did was improve the insulation in the roof and some of the walls. Then I had that firebox installed to replace the open fire. There's also a heat pump in the hall.'

Zac chuckled. 'I bought a very modern apartment and you went for the opposite.'

'I love old villas. There's something magical about them. Yes, they come with loads of problems, but get them sorted and there's an amazing home waiting to be loved.' She sipped her champagne. 'There's history in the boards. When I bought the place the vendors passed on to me a book written about the family who originally built it. The man had been an excise officer and his wife a nurse in the First World War.'

'So you're a history buff.'

'Only when it comes to my property, but it's neat knowing about the original owners.' She laughed softly. 'It was also a surprise finding I enjoy working on the redecorating. In spring I'm going to start putting in a garden to grow a few salad vegetables.'

'I saw your pot plants in your hallway. Just go to the markets. That way you won't starve.'

'Thanks, pal.' He was right. She always forgot to water the plants until they were drooping over the edges of their pots.

'You grew up in Auckland, right?'

She nodded. 'Remuera.' One of Auckland's most sought-after areas, where many of the city's wealthy lived. On a street where fences were metres high, hiding a multitude of sins. 'I went to a private school for girls, played the cello and joined the debating team.' That was after the in-crowd had worked their number on her because her mother had followed her around dressed in identical outfits to hers, trying to look way younger than she was.

'Was your childhood home another old house?'

She blinked, got back on track. Her mother wasn't welcome on this holiday. 'Yes. A massive, six-bedroom edifice with half an acre of gardens, a tennis court and a swimming pool.'

'You played tennis?' He didn't hide his astonishment.

'Me run around chasing a ball to bang it back over a net? Not likely.'

They were getting close to things she didn't want to talk about when she was sitting in paradise. 'I can't wait to go snorkelling amongst the fishes.'

Zac went with her change as easily as butter melted on warm toast. 'We should take a boat trip to Treasure Island and the marine reserve where the best array of fish is supposed to be.'

Zac had done some research before they'd left Auckland. She hadn't had the time. 'Five days might not be enough.'

How was he going to cope with not getting up close and naked? Zac grimaced. This magical setting was work-

ing mischief on his libido. What had he been thinking when he'd come up with that brainwave? Hadn't
been thinking, that was the trouble. Now his body was
screaming out for Olivia's, and he had no one to blame
but himself.

'Want a top-up?' was the only lame excuse he could
come up with in a hurry for getting out of the cane
chair and putting some air between them for a moment.

'Of course.' When she handed him her glass she
seemed to take desperate measures to prevent her fingers touching his.

Phew. Damn. Hell. He dragged his hand down over
his hair. Less than an hour and he was a cot case. Cer-
tifiable. Had he been so desperate to come here with
Olivia he'd have bargained with the devil if it had meant
she'd agree? Seems like it. Didn't make any sense,
though.

Back on the porch he passed over a full glass. 'Drink
up. That ice bucket is now a water receptacle and the
fridge is warmer than my toaster on full.'

'Do we get dinner brought over? I'm kind of relaxed
and comfortable now.'

*And I'm in need of space and people around to break
the grip you have on me. I am so not ready to spend
all evening alone with you when I can't touch you.* 'I'm
thinking dining on the restaurant deck with candles
under those palm trees would be special.'

'I guess you're right.' When Olivia yawned there was
nothing ladylike about her.

He grinned. 'That's it? No argument?' Then she must
be very tired.

'If I stay here I'll be asleep by seven, and probably awake again by midnight.' Her throat worked as
she swallowed.

'CC? You all right?'

Olivia stood up and took a step to the edge of the porch. 'Yeah,' she huffed out over the lawn. 'Good and dandy.' Her voice sounded anything but.

Moving quietly, Zac stepped up beside her, rubbed his shoulder lightly against hers. Gave her a moment to regroup her thoughts. But *his* brain wasn't quiet as it tossed up questions about this sudden mood swing. Was Olivia regretting the trip already? His stomach plummeted. Please, not that. No matter what happened after they left the island, he wanted this time with Olivia. Wanted them to have fun and be relaxed, to enjoy each other's company. He felt rather than heard her soft sigh. A gentle lifting of her shoulder against his.

'I'm afraid.'

Or that's what he thought she'd whispered. Olivia afraid? Of what? Him? The urge rose to rant at her, to tell her he'd never hurt her. But reason caught him in time. If she'd ever believed he'd hurt her she wouldn't have come near him, certainly wouldn't be on this island with him. 'Want to talk about it?'

'No.' She spoke to the dark space in front of them. Then after a minute, in a stronger tone, 'Let's go eat.' Back in control of her emotions.

Which bugged the hell out of Zac. How was he supposed to get behind the walls she put up when she kept doing this? He wanted to shake her, shake out her story, then begin to help her move past whatever locked her up so tight. But one look at that jutting chin said that now wasn't the moment. Though when would be the right time was a mystery to him. Olivia had made self-control an art form.

The only place he'd seen her enjoy herself completely, without thought for anything else, was in the sack. Light-bulb moment. Because when she'd finished she could, and did, put on her corporate-style clothes again and the control they represented.

For which he should be glad, but wasn't.

A vision of Olivia in track pants and a sweatshirt. That night she'd started making love to him and it had been as different from any other time as north was to south. Slow and tender, giving and sharing.

For him it had been a game changer. Waking up in her bed in the morning had been a first. Lying tucked up against her back, his arm over her waist, holding her close, had been another first, and absolutely wonderful, like nothing he'd experienced before. So wonderful he'd settle for cuddling Olivia all night to wake up like that again.

Okay, he'd try, but it wouldn't be easy. But he'd try really hard. *Hard is the wrong word, buddy.*

'You plan on daydreaming all night?' the woman causing these thoughts called from the door.

'Why is it called daydreaming when I'm doing it at night?'

As they strolled along the lantern-lit path Zac found himself wondering for the first time ever if he was wrong to stick to his guns and deliberately deny himself a future that involved a beautiful, loving woman and maybe equally beautiful and loving children.

No, he couldn't be wrong. How else did he justify keeping Olivia at arm's length?

Later, Olivia slid beneath the bedcovers and tucked the sheet under her neck like a prissy girl from the convent.

Zac laughed. Long and loud. His eyes twinkled and his gorgeous mouth looked good enough to devour.

'It's not that funny.' She tried not to laugh too, and
only succeeded in making hysterical squawking noises
instead.

'Yeah, it is, when you think what we've got up to in
beds before.'

That dampened down her mirth. 'You want to change
the rules.'

'Damn right I do. I'd be lying if I said otherwise.'
He came and sat on the edge of the bed, on his side; no
sign of laughter in his face now. 'But I'm enjoying our
time together. It's like nothing we've ever done before
and it's…' He waved his hand in the air between them.
'Does fun sound boring?'

'Fun is good.'

'I want to get to learn more about you, what makes
you tick, the things that you'd choose to do first if time
was running out. Hell, I want to know everything about
you. Before the gala night I didn't know anything about
you despite having spent many hours in your company.'

Wow. Really? Of course, he didn't know what he
was asking for. 'We trained together. You can't do that
without learning some things.' But she was ducking
for cover, and that wasn't fair. 'Doctor things, I guess.
Like how much you care about your patients, how intelligent you are, oh, and how pig-headed you can be.'

'Thanks a bunch.' Zac smiled. 'Okay, random question. Do you still play the cello?' He leaned back against
the headboard and stretched his legs all the way down
the bed.

She laughed. 'No way. I sold my cello to buy an
amazing pair of leather boots that were the envy of
every girl at school.' Which was why she'd wanted
them. Now she bought the most amazing pairs of boots

any time because she could, and loved them without needing any acknowledgement from others.

'I bet you were good at music.'

'Try very average on a good day. I think the music teacher only persisted with my lessons because he needed a cello in the school orchestra and no one else wanted to be hauling such a large instrument on and off the bus.'

'Why are you doing that?'

'What?'

'Putting yourself down again. You're a highly skilled surgeon, yet right now you're sounding like you don't believe in yourself.'

'I'm not perfect, can't excel at everything I do. For example, the pot plants in my house. But I am honest.' Most of the time.

Zac reached for her hand and held it between both of his. 'I know.'

Warm fuzzies uncurled inside her. It would be all too easy to lean her head against his chest and pretend they were a couple, a real couple with a history and a future that involved more than bedroom antics. The couple that woke up in the morning in each other's arms.

Pulling her hand free, she shuffled further down the bed. 'Time to get some sleep. Sunrise is early around these parts.' As if she'd fall asleep with Zac barely inches away from her. Those pillows she'd stuffed down the middle as a barrier were a joke, and would take two seconds to get shot of. She could only hope his mental barrier was stronger. Hers was weakening.

'Good night, Olivia.' Zac leaned over and dropped the softest, sweetest kiss of her life on her forehead. 'I'll sit out on the porch for a while.'

If he was cross at her abrupt withdrawal he wasn't

showing it. But, then, he was good at hiding his feelings behind a smile or laughter. This time the smile was stretched a little too tight, and his eyes held a tinge of sadness.

'Zac,' she called as he reached the door leading outside. 'Thanks.'

His eyebrow rose in query. 'For?'

'Being you, caring and understanding.'

Understanding? Zac growled under his breath. *Newsflash, CC, I don't understand a thing. Whatever's going on between us is a complete mystery. What I want is no longer clear. I feel like I'm walking in deep mud and every now and then stepping onto a dry patch. A brief moment of hope before sliding back into the mire.*

His right foot pushed against the ground to set the hammock swinging. Stretched full length, he linked his hands together behind his head. The dark sky twinkled with so many stars it was as though a kid had lit up a whole pack of sparklers. The hammock was unbelievably comfortable. So far the mosquitoes hadn't found him. Hopefully when they did, he'd put enough insect repellent on what little skin was exposed to deter them.

His heart was back in the bure, lying next to Olivia. His mind was seeing the despair and fear that sometimes altered her expression and briefly filled those eyes that usually reminded him of flowers. Whatever had caused her grief, she wasn't prepared to talk about it. Yet.

Come on. Why should she choose to bare her soul to him?

Because they were connected. They mightn't have known it before but the threads were becoming more obvious by the day. They both had issues holding them back from getting into a serious relationship. What Olivia's troubles were he had no idea, but they were there. He recognised his own stock standard coping mechanisms in her now that he'd started looking for them.

He wanted to hold her, protect her for ever.

Kind of strange for a guy who had no plans to commit to settling down. Yet all the reasons for why he shouldn't were slipping away, one by one dropping off the edge, leaving him exposed and cautious yet strangely ready to try for the rainbow.

Was Olivia the pot of gold at the end of his rainbow?

No. There wasn't any rainbow. The hardest lesson of his life had been that night of the accident when he'd learned his parents didn't love him unconditionally. Didn't love him enough to support and help him through the trauma of what he'd done. Sometimes he wondered if they'd loved him and Mark at all; as in deep, for ever, parent kind of love. Their careers had been their priority, taking all their time and concentration, with nothing left over for their sons. *Why did they have children?* They clearly hadn't wanted to be with their sons. Zac had asked his grandfather about it on numerous occasions but Grampy hadn't been able to come up with a satisfactory answer. Not one he was prepared to tell his grandson anyway.

Zac swallowed the usual bile that came from thinking about his parents. Coming from a dysfunctional family, the odds were he'd be bad at parenting too. Another reason not to settle down with a wonderful woman and contemplate the picket-fence scenario.

Zac's sigh was long and slow. Around him everything had gone quiet, and lights were being turned off. With nothing to do after dinner most people would be settled in their bures. He pushed with his foot again, swinging the hammock high, sighing as the movement slowed and the arc became less and less. Beyond the edge of the lawn the waves rolled up the sand, then pulled away, rolled in, pulled away.

'Zac, come inside.'

Someone was shaking his arm gently.

'Come on. Wake up. You're getting wet from the dew.'

Hauling his eyelids up, he saw her leaning over him, her long hair framing her face. 'Olivia.' His Olivia.

'The one and only.' She tugged at him. 'You can't spend the whole night out here.'

Swinging his legs over the side, he awkwardly pushed out of the hammock. 'What time is it?'

'One o'clock.' She took his hand and led him inside to that damned bed with its row of pillows down the middle.

Zac shucked out of his shirt and trousers, jerked the bedcover back and threw the pillows on the floor. Dropping into bed, he reached for Olivia where she now lay on her side, facing him. 'Roll over,' he whispered. 'I want to hold you all night.'

If only it were that easy.

CHAPTER TEN

AT THE END of the next day Zac stretched his legs out and laced his fingers behind his head. He would not think about night number two and lying beside Olivia again. Nope, he'd have a drink and watch the sunset. 'Come on, woman, bring me that beer you promised.'

'Sack the last slave, did you?'

'Hell, no. She's good for bed gymnastics.' So much for not thinking about bed.

'For that you're going to have to wait. Or, novel idea, get your own drink.' Olivia laughed. 'I'm changing out of my bikini.'

Phew. Those two narrow strips of red fabric had kept his head in a spin all day. Had had him swimming in the sea four times, and in the pool once. Then there'd been the cold shower half an hour ago. He'd even taken a kayak out to paddle around the island. Anything to keep busy and the need strumming through his veins under control. Huh. As if. One look at Olivia and his blood was boiling and his crotch tightening. This sex ban would be his undoing. Who knew what state he'd be in by the time he got back to Auckland? Ruined for ever, probably.

'Here.'

An icy bottle appeared before his eyes. 'Thank you,

and whoever's responsible for these things.' Then he made the mistake of looking at Olivia and pressed the bottom of the bottle over his manhood. The bikini would've been preferable.

'You're staring.' She sank onto the deckchair beside him. 'You don't like my dress?'

While the skimpy piece of floral material did cover more of that exquisite body than the bikini had, the way the fabric draped was plain punishing. Mouth-watering, muscle-tightening, hormone-fizzing, blood-heating cruel. 'You call that a dress?' he hissed over dry lips.

She laughed, low and sexy. 'Well, it's not a T-shirt.'

How in hell was he to sit here drinking beer and not choke? Then he had to take her to dinner where every male on the island was going to gag, and their women would beat them around the head. 'You're a danger to mankind.'

'I'll change before dinner. Put a T-shirt on.'

'Does that come with trousers?' The beer was cold in his over-hot mouth; cool as it slid past the lump in his throat. One bottle wasn't enough. Holding out his empty one, he growled in a mock bossy tone, 'Another one, as soon as possible.' His eyes were fixed on the horizon, glazed over for all he could see. His imagination was so busy dealing with pictures of Olivia's hot bod and that handkerchief that was apparently a dress, nothing else about him seemed to be in good working order. Except the one muscle he wasn't allowed to use.

'Here you go, sir.' A bottle held around the neck by slim fingers waved in front of his face.

He was going insane. Had to be. Grabbing the bottle, he raised it to his lips and gulped. *Do something. Talk about anything, just get your brain working.* Glancing around, he came up with, 'So you're not into spiders.'

Olivia shuddered. 'Not at all, but until today I thought one the size of my thumbnail was a problem. But those things hanging over the path in webs wider than our bed?' Another shudder. 'Ugh. You were my hero, clearing those monsters out of the way.'

Our bed? This wasn't helping. He tried again. 'The outlook from the top of the hill showed how small the island is.' Not exactly scintillating conversation. 'It's hard to imagine living on such a tiny spot in the ocean. I'd go stir-crazy if this was home for me.'

'I guess if you're born here it's what you're used to.'

'Have you ever thought how lucky we are just because of where we were born?' Deep, Zac, boy. And diverting. 'Imagine how different our lives would be if we'd been born in the Sahara, or on the Indian continent.'

'I'd have five kids and look ready to retire, except that wouldn't be an option.' Olivia grinned. 'You're right. It does come down to luck.'

'I'm going to give that fishing a crack tomorrow. Donny—he's the gardener—is lending me a hand line.'

The guy had strolled up to him as he'd watched the local men work the sudden rush of fish churning up the water at the shoreline and told him, 'Trevally chase the Pacific sardines into the beach in a feeding frenzy. It happens about twice a day at this time of year.'

'Do the men catch many?' Zac had asked.

'Good days and bad days. No one relies on trevallies as a regular supply of food for the family.'

'I've never seen anyone use a hand line and no rod. The skin on those men's hands must be tough.' Zac had introduced himself and before he'd known it he'd had a fishing date for tomorrow. 'I haven't fished since I was a kid and Grampy took me out.'

Olivia was chuckling. 'This I have to see. The immaculate surgeon getting his hands stinky from fish.'

'I'm taking that as a positive sign. You obviously think I'll catch one.'

'And if you do? What will you do with it?'

He hadn't thought that far ahead. 'Ask the chef to cook it for us? Other people must've caught fish and taken them to the kitchen.'

'Talking of kitchens, shall we stroll across to the outdoor lounge for a cocktail before dinner? I've never had one but this seems the place to give it a try.'

'Good idea.' Hopefully there'd be some diversions from that dress. 'You'll get one of those tacky little umbrellas to keep as a souvenir.' He grinned.

'Thought I'd start with a mimosa.' She returned his grin.

'Start? Are we in for a session?'

She shook her head, that shiny mane sliding over her shoulders. 'You want me off my face and losing my mind?'

If it meant forgetting their promise—then, yes. But if he was being a gentleman—then, no.

'I've caught one,' Zac shouted triumphantly early the next morning as he wound the hand line in as fast as possible.

'What? A sardine?' Olivia teased. She'd strolled down the beach to join him, after opting for a leisurely start to the day by reading in bed after Donny had knocked on the door to tell Zac the fish were running.

'A damned big trevally,' Zac scowled. 'This nylon's hard on the hands.'

'Toughen up. You don't see the locals complaining.' Looking along the beach, she could see two Fijian men also winding in taut lines. 'You've got to get in the water and use your foot to scoop the fish up onto the sand.'

'Glad I've got an expert telling me what to do.' He started walking backwards up the beach, hauling his catch out of the water. 'Look at that beauty.'

Trying not to laugh, she bent down to admire Zac's fish. 'Should keep a toddler from starving.'

'Any time you want to go read your book again feel free. This is man stuff. Where's Donny?'

'Donny,' Olivia called to the man standing further up the beach. 'Zac's caught something.'

As he wandered close Donny nodded. 'Not bad for a first time.'

'I guess that means I'm going to release it back into the water.' Zac sighed, and carefully removed the hook.

'Wait, photo opportunity.' Olivia snapped a quick shot as Zac ignored the camera.

'Wait till I get a proper fish.' He held the fish in the water until it swam away, then threw the line as far beyond the churning water as possible so he could draw the hook through the seething trevally.

Olivia sat down, her elbows on her knees, and watched him. Never had she seen him so relaxed. He was concentrating so much he didn't notice her snap a couple more photos. This holiday was showing her a different Zac. She particularly liked the one who'd tossed those pillows aside to hold her against him while they'd tried to go to sleep.

The climate had done a line on them, spoiling that hug, though probably saving her from having to haul the brakes on the raw need that had begun filling her. The humidity had made her skin slick and her body uncomfortably hot in a way that had had nothing to do with sex. They'd rolled apart after twenty minutes. Unbelievably, she'd fallen into a deep sleep not long after. Had to be because she'd felt so secure with this Zac who could take a night off the passion. She'd never spent a night just sleeping with a man. That spoke of intimacies too close for comfort, yet now she craved it with Zac more than anything.

A shudder ripped through her, disturbing in its intensity. Was she seriously in danger of falling for him? Unlikely. She only had to think of her parents' marriage to knock those ideas into place.

Zac tossed a fist in the air. 'Got another one.'

Olivia jumped up and went to stand beside him, eager to enjoy the moment and drop the past for a while. If only it was that easy to dump for ever.

Zac was focused intently on getting his catch on shore. 'Want fish for breakfast?'

'Breakfast of any kind would be good.'

Zac wound furiously. 'This one's definitely bigger than the last baby.'

'That's a good trevally,' Donny agreed minutes later.

'Will the chef cook it for me?' Zac asked.

'Yes, or my wife could use it to make you a traditional Fijian meal to have at our house tonight.'

'Really? Your family would join us?' When Donny nodded, he continued, 'That would be fantastic.'

Olivia asked, 'What do we bring?'

'Nothing. We eat at five thirty because our grandson goes to bed early.'

'You have a grandchild living with you? Bet you love that.'

'His mother's our daughter. She does the massages in the spa.'

Olivia smiled. 'Then I'll meet her this afternoon. I'm booked in for a full body massage at two o'clock.'

Zac laughed. 'Think she'll be better than me?'

She looked away to hide the sudden flush creeping up her cheeks. 'No comment.'

Donny and his wife, Lauan, greeted Olivia and Zac warmly, welcoming them into the small thatch bungalow crowded with relatives. It felt as if half the island's population was there. The fish hadn't been that big, Olivia thought as she sat down on the woven flax mat in front of a larger one with plates stacked at one end.

Zac was soon chatting with the men and Olivia tried to look around without appearing nosey. Apart from her, all the other females were seated behind the circle enclosing that mat. 'Lauan,' she said quietly. 'I can sit with you.'

Lauan shook her head. 'You're a visitor.'

Yes, but I'd love to be with the women. Unfortunately it would be rude to protest. 'I've been looking forward to coming here all day. How do you cook the fish?'

'I wrap it in banana leaves to steam over the open fire. There is coconut milk added, and potatoes. Thank your husband for the fish.'

Husband? To the locals they probably did appear to be a married couple. 'I will.'

Lauan squatted beside her. 'I've also made a chicken stew with carrots, potatoes, and broccoli.' She rolled her eyes softly. 'Too many people for one fish. But they all wanted to meet you.'

Thinking of the scrawny chickens she'd seen pecking around the base of the trees behind the resort, Olivia wondered if one chook would go any further than the fish. All part of the adventure. 'I'm happy to meet you all.' She nodded to the women.

Two of them disappeared into another room and

soon large plates of steaming food were being placed
on the mat.

'That smells delicious,' Olivia said.

'Doesn't it,' Zac agreed. Leaning closer, he asked,
'You okay?'

'Absolutely. I'm glad you caught that sucker, or we
might never have had this opportunity.' She took the
plate of food handed to her and looked for cutlery, feeling silly when there wasn't any. When in Fiji do as the
Fijians do. But as she placed a piece of fish in her mouth
a fork appeared in front of her.

'For you.'

Zac got one too. 'Thanks, but I'll use my fingers.'

The food was simple and tasty, the vegetables so
fresh they must've been picked only hours ago. 'Sometimes I think we forget the pleasure of plain food.' Olivia noticed a child peeking around at her from behind
Donny.

'Hello. What's your name?'

The child ducked back.

Remembering Donny's earlier conversation on the
beach, she asked Lauan, 'Your grandson?'

'Yes. Josaia. He's shy.'

'I hope he comes over to say hello while we're here.'

'After dinner.'

But it seemed Josaia couldn't wait to take another
peek, and Olivia winked at him.

When he winked back she felt she'd won a prize. Her
mouth widened into a smile and she was rewarded with
one in return. When dinner was finished she did get
to see the boy properly when he came close to pick up
the empty plates at his grandmother's bidding. Olivia's
heart rolled. One of his arms was stiff and awkward,
and his left cheek marred by terrible scarring.

Josaia knew she'd seen and his smile vanished as he twisted his head away from her. When he reached out for her plate she picked it up and placed it in his hand. 'Thank you,' she said. 'Where do you go to school?'

Donny was watching her guardedly. 'The kids go to the mainland for school.'

That didn't answer her specific question but she knew when to mind her own business.

Josaia disappeared with his load of plates, and she suspected she wouldn't be seeing him again tonight.

Donny tugged his shoulders back. 'He doesn't go to school because other children tease him. I try to teach him, but he's missing out on so much.'

What had happened to cause that disfiguring scar? She felt sure he hadn't seen a plastic surgeon. That wound had been too crudely sutured. Maybe she could help in some way. But was it her place to ask? It might be better coming from Zac. Man-to-man stuff. Leaning sideways, she gave him a wee nudge and got the slightest of nods.

He asked, 'Did Josaia have an accident here on the island?'

The older man nodded, his eyes so sad Olivia felt her heart slow. *He's broken-hearted for his grandson.* 'Last year Josaia was swimming with a group of his mates when a tourist joined them, asking about the fish and where he should go to try out his spear gun.'

Zac asked softly, 'Josaia was shot with a spear gun?'

Olivia stifled a gasp. *Josaia is lucky to be alive.* She slipped her hand between Zac's arm and his side, wrapped her fingers around his elbow.

Zac continued in the same low, calm voice. 'Where was Josaia treated?'

'On the mainland. In the hospital. It's a good hospital, but no one knew what to do for my grandson. I begged the doctors send him to Australia or New Zealand. They said it wasn't possible, and Josaia would be all right once they stitched him up and set his broken bones.' Tears streamed down the proud man's face. 'I begged them to rethink. He's only seven.'

'There's nothing wrong with him.' Lauan's voice was sharp and angry. 'But you'd think he was a leper from the way boys who used to be his friends laugh at him now.'

'That's so hard for anyone, but especially a child.'

'He was always so popular until the accident.' Donny stared at a spot on the dining mat. 'His mother works hard to raise money to take him away for help. His father works in Australia to make money.'

'When was the last time Josaia saw his dad?' Olivia asked, her heart thudding.

'Christmas.'

Seven months ago. What sort of life was that for a young boy? Not to have his dad there had to be hard. Olivia knew about that. She wanted to slap the floor and say she'd see that Josaia got whatever he needed and as soon as possible, but despite the urgent need to help this boy she held her tongue. She'd talk this through with Zac first.

Zac knew Olivia was barely holding herself together for the remainder of their time with Donny's family. He could see the sadness in her face, feel the need for her to do something to rectify what had happened with Josaia. But most of all he understood how much she was struggling to hold it all in so that she didn't make rash promises she mightn't be able keep and thereby hurt the family further.

The meal was over early by their standards. As they walked away from their hosts Zac draped an arm over Olivia's shoulders. 'I'd like a drink.'

'I could go a cup of tea.'

'We can discuss what you're desperate to do for Josaia.'

'That poor kid. I bet the worst part of the whole deal is the way his old friends are now treating him. Children are cruel.' She shuddered.

'Insecurities, jealousy, wanting to be popular with the in-crowd. Anything and everything. Even plain old nastiness.' The sudden tension in her fingers suggested she'd had her share of being on the outside. But of course. She'd said she'd worked hard to be liked and be a part of the group at med school. 'This is why you want to help Josaia? Apart from the medical point of view?'

They'd reached the outdoor lounge at the main building by the time she answered. 'That boy is surrounded by people who love him, but they're all adults. There don't appear to be any children in his life. At first I thought that was because it was the end of the day and everyone would be at home, except when we walked to Donny's house there were kids playing behind the huts.'

'Then we saw his face and heard the despair in his grandparents' voices.'

'You're onto it.'

Zac pulled out a chair for Olivia at an outside table. 'What are you having?'

A wicked twinkle lit up her eyes, banishing that sadness for a boy she'd barely met. 'You know what? Forget tea. Make that a cocktail.' She looked around. 'Where's a menu?'

'What about PS I...' His voice trailed off at the realisation of what he'd been about to say. It was only the name of a drink, but the import of the words he hadn't finished were slowly sinking in, one by one, adding up to a frightening whole.

'Zac? What's up? Are you all right?'

The concern in her tone wound around him, added to his confusion. Had he really been going to say 'PS I love you'? Shaking his head, he sank onto a chair, putting a gap between them. But her eyes followed, as did that floral scent she wore. Or was that the smell of the frangipani growing a metre away?

'Zac.' Her eyes widened. 'You're worrying me.'

'I'm fine.' *Really? This palpitating heart thing is fine? The knot in your gut is A-okay? The sweat on your palms due to the humidity?* 'Sorry. There's a cocktail made with amaretto, Kahlúa, and Irish cream that's perfect for after dinner. Very creamy and sweet, like a dessert, which you've missed out on tonight.' Blah, blah, blah. Shoving up onto his feet, he asked, 'Will that do?' Ordering drinks would give him the space he needed right now.

'Sounds good.' Olivia nodded, looking perplexed. As well she should. Did she know she was with a lunatic?

Moving through the tables full of happy diners, Zac tried to ignore the questions battering his brain. He'd been enjoying getting to know Olivia better, happy being with her, wanted more time together. So why the hell hadn't he ever considered he might be falling for her?

Because love spelt commitment. *Commitment isn't the problem.* No. It wasn't. *It's the responsibility.* That went with any relationship, whether the other person was his best friend, his lover, or his brother. He loved Mark, had done from the day his tiny, wriggly body had been placed in his arms. Yet he'd still managed to screw up in a very big way, changing Mark's life for ever.

'Yes, sir. What would you like?'

Zac shook his head and stared across the bar at the woman waiting patiently for him to tell her what drinks he wanted. 'A whisky on the rocks. Make it a double. And do you know a cocktail called PS I Love You?'

She frowned. 'Not sure, but we've got a book describing most cocktails.'

When Zac told her the ingredients she smiled. 'We call it Love on the Wind. I'll bring the drinks across to you.'

He wasn't ready to return to Olivia. 'I'll have that whisky now.' And ordered a second to take with him.

Olivia watched him placing her glass on the table, returning to his seat. He waited for her to ask why he'd taken so long, and was grateful when she didn't.

'Where do we start with Josaia's case? Talk to his family, or go to the mainland to check out the hospital and see if I can do a surgery there?'

'Why not take him back to Auckland for the operation? If there's going to be one. You've only seen that horrendous scar from across the room in dim light. There might be nothing you can do.'

She sipped her Love on the Wind—he would not think of it as PS I Love You—and smiled. Her tongue did a lap of her lips. 'That's amazing.'

So was the way his heart squeezed and his insides softened. Of course his libido sat up to attention. That was a given around this woman. What was extraordinary was that she didn't know about this new effect she was having on him. He'd have sworn there were signs written all over his face. 'Glad you like it. About Josaia and what to do first.' He had to talk, about anything except them, and talk lots.

Olivia said, 'Operating back home might be preferable so we get the best people on side for Josaia. It's going to involve huge expense for the family, though. Hospital costs, accommodation, flights, and other incidentals I can't think of right now.'

'I doubt there's a lot of spare money in that household.' He locked his eyes on hers. 'You're going to throw in your time for free.'

'Of course.'

'I want to look at that shoulder. There might be something I can do there.' See, he could move on from those other thoughts that had swamped his brain. 'First we'll talk to Donny. If he's willing to take this further, we'll decide how to go about it.'

Olivia's hand covered his, and her fingers curled around his. 'We have a plan.'

'You like plans, don't you?'

'They keep me centred.'

So what was her plan for the rest of the night? It wouldn't be what he hoped for. She'd be keeping to the other plan. Zac drained his glass, trying not to bemoan the fact he'd set the rule in the first place.

CHAPTER ELEVEN

THE ARRAY OF fish in every colour imaginable stole Olivia's breath away when she sank beneath the sea's surface off Treasure Island. She automatically reached out for Zac's hand and tugged him down beside her. 'Unbelievable,' she spluttered in her mouthpiece, even though he couldn't hear her.

When Zac looked her way she saw the same amazement in his face. When he started stroking through the water, heading further out from the shore, she followed. She'd never seen anything like this. When Zac paused she swam up beside him to lean in against his body. Skin to skin underwater. Delicious and exciting. And then there were the fish. One big, fat, enjoyable picture.

Olivia kicked her flippers slowly so as not to disturb the dainty creatures too much and followed a group of yellow and blue fish. Then a larger orange one swam through the middle, scattering the others. Yellow and blue fish. Orange fish. She grinned. Very technicolour. Down here it was like a moving painting: sharp colours, delicate manoeuvres, majestic shapes—and innocence. As though these creatures had no enemies. Which was probably far from the truth, though at least they were safe from mankind. This was a sanctuary, and the results were stunning. The numbers and varieties of fish were unbelievable.

'That's magic down there.' Zac echoed her thoughts when they finally crawled out of the water and flopped onto the sand.

'I've been missing out on so much by not travelling.' She lay on her back, arms and legs spread in the sun. 'It's one of those things on my to-do-one-day list. Think it's time to make that a do-it-now list.'

'Shame your mother hated flying.'

'Didn't matter.' Olivia sat up and started brushing off the sand, which was scratchy on her skin. 'Dad left when I was twelve.'

'That's tough.'

She swallowed hard. 'Mum was—is—an alcoholic.' Swallow. She couldn't look at Zac. 'As in often totally crazy, uncontrollable, off-the-rails alcoholic. Dad ran out of patience.'

'How the hell did you cope?' Zac's hand covered hers.

'Not sure I did, really.' Spill the rest. 'I tried becoming a part of the school in-crowd so that I could forget what went on at home. Failed big-time because of Mum. Everyone knew what she was.'

'Where did the cello fit in?' Zac was giving her breathing space.

'When I didn't make it as an in-person I went for the nerd brigade.' She huffed out a tight laugh. 'That probably saved me, considering where some of the girls I'd desperately wanted to befriend ended up while I was at med school.'

'Why medicine?'

She shrugged. 'No idea. It was just something I

wanted to do. As a little girl my dolls were always covered in plasters and bandages.'

'At least you'd have been sure of your choice, then.'

'You weren't?'

Zac grimaced. 'I started university intending to become an engineer.'

'What changed your mind?'

'Seeing my brother going through rehab and getting no end of help from doctors along the way made me think I'd be happier doing medicine.'

'Your parents didn't sway you?'

'Put it this way, Dad's an engineer at the top of his game, being the CEO for one of the country's largest steelworks.'

'You wanted to follow him into the business?'

'No, I wanted to gain acknowledgement that I was his son.'

Reaching for his hand, Olivia said, 'That's the wrong reason to choose a career.'

'I was desperate.'

She shuddered. 'I understand.' Seemed she wasn't the only one with difficult parents. 'Being an only child, I was never really treated as a kid even before Dad left.' Not wanting to spoil a wonderful day with talk of her childhood, she said, 'Let's go eat lunch by the pool. All that fish-gazing has made me hungry.'

Zac scrambled to his feet and held out his hand, hauling her upright with one easy, fluid movement. 'I could murder a beer. Think I've swallowed a litre of salt water.'

'Yuk.' Around at the front of the resort Olivia dived into the pool, eager to get rid of the salt and sand on her skin. When she hauled herself up over the side Zac was sitting at a nearby table, beer in hand, and his gaze fixed on her. Suddenly her bikini felt non-existent. A pool attendant handed her a towel and she quickly dried off before pulling on a sleeveless shirt and shorts and joining Zac under the coconut palms. 'Food and water, I think.'

Zac pushed a bottle and glass towards her. 'Sparkling water, as requested.'

Turning her hand over, she slipped her fingers between his and enjoyed the moment. This was something she hadn't known before. She had never spent time just holding a man's hand without sex being the ultimate goal. Unbelievable how wonderful it felt. Full of promise without any expectations.

A group of children was leaping into the deep end of the pool, splashing half the contents over the side while shrieking their heads off.

'They're fun but I'm glad glad we're not staying here on Treasure Island when Tokoriki is a no-go zone for kids,' Zac commented. 'I don't mean anything nasty by that, but as a childless adult I don't really want to share my rare break with other people's offspring.'

'I get it.' She took a risk. 'You think you'll ever have children? Once you find a life partner, I mean.'

Zac's eyes widened, and his mouth alternated between a smile and a grimace. 'Now, there's a loaded question. Or two.'

'It wasn't meant as such.' *Wasn't it?* 'Just wondering if you were planning on having a family and a house in the burbs.' Geez, what would she answer if he turned the question back at her?

The level in his beer glass dropped as he drank and stared at the kids in the pool. 'You know what? I'd love to have children of my own.' The surprise in his voice told her plenty.

'Isn't that a natural thing for most people to want?'

'Yeah, but after Mark's accident I decided I wasn't having a family. Too easy to hurt them.' Again he raised his glass to his lips and sipped the beer thoughtfully. 'I think I've been wrong. I do want children.' His head jerked backwards as though he couldn't quite get his mind around this revelation.

Little Zacs. Olivia let the breath that had stalled in her lungs dribble over her lips, and tried to ignore the band of longing winding around her heart. *Pick me for their mother.* She spluttered and almost spat water down her shirt. Where had that little gem come from? Having children meant getting married and *that* would never happen. 'Where's that waitress? I want to order lunch.'

Zac shook his head and looked around. He must've spotted someone who could help because he raised a hand and waved, before doing what she'd hoped he wouldn't. 'What about you? Obviously you'd want more than one child if you felt you'd missed out not having a sibling.'

She went for her standard reply, not prepared to reveal her deep but well-hidden longing that she barely acknowledged to herself. 'I've worked too hard to get where I am with my career to be taking time out for babies. Women I've talked to say that has set them back on the career pathway, and I'm not prepared to do that.'

Zac watched her, while behind those eyes she knew his brain would be working overtime. 'I don't buy it. That's the press-release version. What's the real story behind answering the same question you threw at me?'

He had a valid point. She hadn't minded asking him where he was headed on the subject of family, so she should be able to take it in return. Except she couldn't. They'd moved beyond the couple that used to have crazy sex all the time with no stopping for conversations. Now there was more between them they were learning about each other and she definitely liked the man she was getting to know. More than liked. But to reveal everything about her sorry upbringing was going too far. From years of learning to shut up those memories, they were now firmly locked away and she doubted the words were there. 'I—'

'Excuse me.' The waitress chose to arrive right then.

Phew. Not a reprieve but a few minutes to consider how to get around this without upsetting Zac and the easy way that had grown between them. Because *that* was important. She did not want to lose any ground they'd gained.

'Another water?' Zac asked.

'Yes, and I'll have the red snapper with salad.'

The waitress hadn't even turned away before Zac was saying, 'There's a question on the table, CC.'

Might as well get this over. 'I got Mum's undivided attention. She put all her love onto me. Except it was conditional and ugly.' Her sigh was bitter and very out of place in such a wonderful setting. 'Parenting takes special people and I'm not one of them.'

'Am I allowed to argue that point with you?' His voice was soft, gentle, almost a caress that said, *I'm here for you*.

'Afraid not. It's pointless.'

His mouth tightened. She'd hurt him.

Reaching for his hand, she said, 'I need to drop this, Zac. Seriously. I'm sorry if you think I don't trust you enough to talk about it. It's me I don't trust. My judgement about everything that happened in my family is warped and I'm just not ready to dissect it. I probably never will be, okay?'

His chin dipped in acknowledgement, though his eyes said he was still there for her if she changed her mind.

Squeezing those strong fingers that were curled around her hand, Olivia asked, 'Can we relax and make the most of sitting next to a sparkling pool on a tropical island? Leave the other stuff out of the picture?' She'd get down on her knees if that would help.

Zac leaned forward and placed his lips on her mouth. 'Yes,' he breathed as he kissed her.

As far as kisses went this one was tame, but it wound through her like a silky ribbon, touching, comforting, telling her that she wasn't alone with those deep fears any more. Had this Zac always been there? Should she have scratched the surface of him right back at the beginning, on that very first night they'd fallen into his bed, exhausted after making out in his lounge and still eager for more? No, she didn't think so. They would never have revealed anything about themselves back then. Talking hadn't fit the mix of what had made their affair so exciting. 'Thank you,' she murmured into his kiss.

They were interrupted with cutlery being placed on the table and the waitress asking if she could get them anything else while they waited for their meals.

'No, thanks.' Zac sat back, a smile tipping that gorgeous mouth upwards. His eyes locked on Olivia's. 'We've got everything we need.'

'The trevally are here,' Olivia called from the edge of the lawn in front of their bure an hour after they returned to Tokoriki.

Zac grabbed the fishing line and raced down to the

beach, calling at Olivia as he passed her, 'Watch this. I'm going to catch dinner.'

'You sure you weren't a caveman in a previous life?' She laughed.

'Weren't we all?' He unravelled the line and threw it as far as possible.

'I don't know. This whole "me man, me like hunting-gathering thing"—it's like men are born that way. I prefer going to a supermarket.'

Winding the line in as Donny had taught him, he grinned. 'The urge lurks below the skin, waiting for opportunities to show our women what wonderful providers and protectors we are.'

'So when women fish or hunt, what are they proving?'

'You've just flipped the argument. If I said that women are trying to prove they're as good as us I'd get my head knocked off, right?'

'I'll go and get my club.'

'Before you do, I admit that there are females who love all that outdoor activity as much as their menfolk, and some of them are very good at shooting deer or pig and catching a fish.'

A soft punch was delivered to his bicep. Olivia nodded along the beach. 'The score so far is locals three, visitor none.'

Zac tapped his chest with his fist. 'She wounds so easily.' He loved it when she was being cheeky and not considering every word before uttering it.

'If you can feel anything on the end of your line it's probably a pebble. There's your hook.' She peered at the water's edge, her grin wicked, making his toes curl with longing.

'This time.' He hurled the line out once more and began winding it back in.

'I don't think so,' Olivia said beside him.

'How do you know?'

Throw it out, bring it in. There was a timeless rhythm to this and, yes, he was enjoying fishing with the men.

'You've got another pebble.'

It took a second but he finally remembered where he was and what he was doing. 'This time,' he assured the disbelieving woman.

'Hey, Donny,' Olivia called. 'Zac's last fish must've been beginner's luck.'

Glancing over his shoulder, Zac nodded to the Fijian. 'Donny, don't listen to a word she says. I've got this.'

He was relieved the man had shown up. He and Olivia had agreed this might be the best place to talk to Donny about Josaia. Olivia had also suggested that he do the talking at first, man to man, so to speak.

Zac heard Olivia say, 'Hello, Josaia,' and his disappointment rose. They could not talk about surgery in front of the boy. Damn.

But Olivia had her ways. 'Josaia, can you help me find a shell to take home? One of those small conches would be good.' She waited for Josaia's reply, looking at him as she would any other child.

'I know where the best shells are.' He spoke hesitantly, as though expecting Olivia to withdraw from him any second.

'Cool. Let's go. Hopefully, by the time we get back Zac will have finally caught a fish.'

'Granddad catches them all the time.' Josaia bounced along beside Olivia, looking up at her so often he tripped over his own feet.

Donny watched them walk away. 'She's kind.'

'She is. She's also genuine.'

'I can see that. So can Josaia. He wouldn't have gone with her otherwise. He's learned to be wary of people's empty gestures.' Sadness lined Donny's statement.

Flicking the line out again, Zac said without preamble, 'You know we're doctors?'

'I wondered. Neither of you flinched when you saw Josaia, like you're used to seeing disfiguring scars.'

Zac was relieved. He'd thought he might've shown his feelings for the kid's predicament far too much. 'Olivia's a plastic surgeon.'

Donny turned to stare after his grandson again. 'What about you? Do you work in the same field?'

'I'm an orthopaedic surgeon.'

The man spun around to stare at him. 'Are you pulling my leg? Because if you are and my grandson learns…' He spluttered to a stop, unable to voice his anger.

Placing a hand on Donny's arm, Zac said, 'I am speaking the truth. We want to help Josaia.'

Donny gasped a few deep breaths, rubbed his forearm across his face. 'We don't have enough money. That's why our son-in-law works in Australia. He's trying to save for an operation for Josaia but…' Donny shook his head.

The line was getting into a tangle since Zac had stopped winding. Concentrating on sorting it out, he told the proud man, 'Let's start at the beginning and work from there. If it's okay with you, we'd like to look at Josaia's injuries and request copies of his medical records.'

His statement was met with silence. Could he have approached Donny differently? Might as well lay it all out. If he'd got it wrong then he had nothing to lose. 'We think it's probably best if Josaia has surgery in Auckland, where both of us practise.'

'You make it sound so easy.'

'I do know a thing or two about the New Zealand health system.'

Donny gripped Zac's hand. 'Thank you. I am glad you caught that trevally. It has brought my family much good luck.'

Zac grinned. 'Maybe that's why I haven't caught one today. There's only so much luck out there and we've used up our share for a while.'

Once Donny had talked with his wife and daughter, and explained everything to Josaia, he brought the lad to the bure.

'At the time of the accident we were told by a visiting doctor that plastic surgery would make the scar less visible and the lumps could be removed.'

'Has Josaia seen anyone else about this?'

'There aren't any plastic surgeons in Fiji. But, please, you can look today. Josaia likes you, he won't be a problem.'

'He found me a shell to take home.' She'd treasure it, as long as she could take it through quarantine at Auckland Airport. 'Hey, Josaia, can I touch your cheek?'

The boy nodded solemnly.

The muscle was tight and knobbly under her fingers. 'Open your mouth wide,' she instructed Josaia. Inside there was further scarring. 'I can do something to improve this.' She stepped back to allow Zac space.

'Josaia, show me how far you can move your arm,' Zac instructed.

Donny talked as his grandson moved his arm back and forth. 'It's tight. He can't move it far. Tendons were severed by the arrow of the gun and sewn back together shorter than before.'

'Will you make me better?' Josaia asked them, his eyes wide with hope.

Olivia answered, 'Would you like us to try?'

He nodded. 'Yes, please.'

'You would have to go to hospital again.'

'Will it hurt?'

Zac nodded. 'Yes, I'm sorry, but we'll give you something to stop most of the pain.'

Donny spoke quietly. 'I would like to accept your help, but how do we pay for this?'

Olivia wanted to wrap him in her arms and say *Don't worry, everything will be all right*, except she didn't want to trample on this family's pride. So she dodged some of the question. 'If we go ahead, would it be all right with you if we did the operations as a gift to Josaia?'

Donny blinked, ran a hand over his face. 'Why would you do that?'

'Part of what I like about being a doctor is helping people, giving them second chances, and Josaia deserves one.' Goodness, she'd be crying next.

Zac must've sensed her problem because he leaned closer so that his arm touched hers, and told Donny, 'Children shouldn't be disadvantaged because of someone else's mistake.'

'What can I say?' Donny asked in such a strangled voice Olivia smiled.

'You gave us a beautiful meal in your home. You might think there's no comparison but being welcomed into your house, meeting all your family, sharing that dinner with you was an experience we'll both remember for ever.' Now a tear did leak from the corner of Olivia's eye and trek down her face.

Donny reached for her hands, gripped them tight. 'Thank you so much. It's been hard, you know, watching my Josaia turn into a quiet, withdrawn version of himself. I will ring his father and tell him the good news. He'll be so happy.'

No pressure.

CHAPTER TWELVE

'THERE'S A BAND playing tonight,' Zac called from the outdoor shower box, where he was towelling himself dry.

'What sort of band?' Olivia asked from the bathroom, where she was apparently putting on her face.

Why she did that when her skin was clear and her face naturally beautiful he did not understand. But he knew not to say a word. 'It's a surprise.'

'Which means you have no idea.' She chuckled.

That sound, relaxed and happy, did things to him. Made him wish for more with Olivia: for a future, to be able to wake up every morning with her lying beside him, if not tangled around him. To know she'd be there for him, day in day out, and that he'd have her back all the time would be amazing. Right. Not that he didn't have her back already, but sometimes he didn't know what he was protecting her from.

'Something like that,' he agreed, as he wrapped the towel around his waist and headed into the main room. 'Anything from locals to visiting rock stars. I heard a whisper about two guys and their guitars.'

Olivia leaned around the corner, her hair swinging over her arm, her face lit up with a big smile. 'That narrows the options.'

'Better than bongo drums at any rate.'

She just laughed and disappeared back into the bathroom.

If only they weren't going to dinner but staying here, checking out that enormous bed for what it was intended. He was done playing Mr Nice Guy on the far side. While wonderful, the spooning hadn't been enough, more a teaser of what could have been. Pulling on a shirt, he sighed. One more night. Tomorrow they would fly out of here in a float plane, headed for the airport. This had been a fabulous few days. Continuing to get to know each other seemed the way forward.

'I heard that there's going to be lobster on the menu tonight.' Olivia bounced into the room, her hands busy slipping earrings into her lobes.

His hands faltered, stopped, buttons ignored. 'You look stunning.'

The red dress she'd somehow squeezed into accentuated all those lovely curves to perfection.

'You think?' She spun around on her tiptoes. 'Not my usual style.'

Her cleavage had never been so—so... His mouth dried. The back of the dress—there wasn't any. Nothing worth mentioning anyway. Was it really a dress when there was hardly any more fabric than in the blue and lime-green bikini she'd lounged around in all day? The hemline barely made it onto her thighs. 'So not you.'

Her smile dipped. 'Should I change?'

Zac's heart stopped. He stepped across the gap between them, caught her hands in his, and tugged her close. Not so close that they were touching. Then they'd never go to dinner. But close enough that he could breathe in her scent. 'I have never seen you look so, so beautiful. Ravishing. And before you go thinking you're not beautiful all the time, you absolutely are. I'm going to order you more dresses like that.'

'You say the nicest things.' Her smile was back. 'I've always wanted to go all out and wear something like this but don't often have the courage. That creation I wore on the night of the gala was the first in a long time. You make me feel it's okay, so for a moment there I got a bit worried.'

'I'm a bloke. Clear and concise speech isn't one of my strong points.' He dropped her hands. He needed to finish dressing if they were ever going to head to the restaurant.

But one button done up and Olivia was laughing at him. 'Let me.' She undid the button, realigned his shirt front and started over. Her fingers were light as they worked down his shirt. Over his chest. Down to his abs—which were sucking in on themselves and just about touching his spine.

Zac gritted his teeth, and his hands clenched at his sides. She was killing him. Cell by damned cell.

'Relax,' she said in a low, throaty growl.

Oh, right. Sure. Easy as. He took an unsteady step back and snatched up his trousers from the bed, and muttered, 'Relax, she says.'

Olivia did wicked without even trying. Her mouth curved into a sumptuous smile, her eyes widened with promise as she slapped her hands on those slim hips. 'How soon can you get me those new dresses? I never knew wearing something so simple could have this effect on a man.' Her eyes widened even further, her smile grew bigger. 'Not just any man either.'

'There is nothing simple about you or your damned dress.'

'Damned dress, huh?' Her gaze cruised down his

body, pausing at his obvious reaction to that piece of fabric that was in danger of being torn off her. 'This is our last night.'

Squeezing his eyes shut, he counted to ten, slowly. Nothing changed. He continued to twenty. His blood still pulsed throughout his body, heating every cell it touched. Finally he drew a shaky breath and locked eyes with her before growling, 'Last night, last cocktail and final dinner under the palms, last of everything to do with our holiday.'

Last of that stupid ban on sex. Whoa, did that mean they could get up close and personal tomorrow? As soon as they landed back in Auckland could they go straight to his apartment? Or her house? He didn't care which as long as he could scratch this itch.

Olivia just laughed and picked up a pair of red shoes with heels that would be lethal if flung at a guy. 'Let's go enjoy ourselves.'

At least she had the sense not to hold his hand or slip her arm through his as they walked along the path to the restaurant. If she had Zac doubted his ability not to swing her up into his arms and run back to their bure. Last evening or not.

'We've been given the best table.' Olivia glanced around the outdoor dining area as she sank onto the chair being held out for her by their waiter. The table was set well back from everyone else with hibiscus growing on three sides, soft light from lanterns making it feel as though they were in a bubble. A very cosy bubble.

Zac blinked. Was he still trying to get his libido under control? 'Maybe it's our turn.'

Every other night honeymooners had sat here. She and Zac didn't have that qualification. 'I feel special.'

'What can I get you to drink?' the waiter asked.

Zac didn't ask her what she preferred, instead rattled off the name of the best champagne on the wine list. 'We're celebrating,' he told her when the young man had gone.

'Celebrating?'

'Anything and everything.' He leaned forward, those dark eyes suddenly serious. 'I haven't had such a wonderful holiday, ever. Thank you.'

Her eyes filled with unexpected tears. 'I didn't do anything.' *Except tease the hell out of you back in the bure.*

'Exactly. You were just you, and I'd never met that you before.'

A tear escaped. Then another. She quickly lifted her glass of water to her lips. What was with this crying stuff? She was usually stronger than that.

'You're supposed to reciprocate, tell me how you've discovered a superman.'

Then the champagne arrived. 'Compliments of management,' the waitress told them.

'This isn't anything to do with Josaia?' Zac asked.

A huge smile split the woman's face. 'Enjoy your evening.'

When Olivia had a glass in her hand she raised it to Zac. 'To us and our fabulous holiday.' This experience had loosened a lot of permanent knots inside her. She and Zac had gelled so well she was even wondering if it might be possible to have a life together in some way. She wanted to ask if they might continue seeing each other back in Auckland, but the old warning bells rattled in her skull, putting a dampener on that. *Just enjoy tonight and wait for tomorrow to unfold.* But she didn't do waiting to see what happened. That meant no control.

Zac tapped his glass on hers. 'We haven't finished yet. Our plane doesn't leave until ten in the morning.'

'Okay, to the rest of our stay in paradise.' Excitement shimmied down her spine. One more night. Dinner under the stars, maybe some dancing if the band of two turned out to be halfway decent, a stroll on the beach after ditching her heels, and then... Then she planned on seducing Zac into using that enormous bed for something other than spooning.

Those picks Olivia called shoes swung from one of her hands while she held onto him firmly with the other. 'There's something about walking on sand at night.' Her voice was a murmur, drifting on the warm, still air, encasing Zac in tenderness.

The need he'd barely been holding onto spilled through him, hissed out between them. It would not be contained any more. After days of bikinis and figure-hugging dresses, laughter and fun, he had to have Olivia—in his arms, under his body. He ached to fill her, to kiss her senseless. But there was that damned rule. He would not be the one to break it. He'd given his word. Never again was he going to make a promise. About anything. Tugging his hand free, Zac went for flippant. Only way to go. 'Who wouldn't love damp sand between their toes, scratchy and irritating? Wonderful stuff.'

Olivia's laughter was so carefree it tugged at his heart. She glanced down at their bare feet and dropped her shoes. 'Come on, then. Let's wash the sand off.' And in a flash her dress was being flung onto the sand beside those red picks. 'Coming?'

'You're such a tease, Olivia Coates-Clark,' Zac growled, even as he tore his shirt over his head. Talk about upping the ante. His failing self-control would never cope, and yet he followed her towards the sea, nearly falling flat on his face as he ran down the beach while trying to step out of his trousers at the same time.

Plunging into the warm water, he swam towards Olivia, who seemed to be treading water too far out. 'Hey,' he growled. 'Stop right there.'

'Or what?' She laughed and began swimming away.

Zac poured on the speed and quickly caught her, catching her around the waist and pulling her to him. 'Or I'll have to kiss you senseless.' She felt good. That compact, smooth body slip-sliding against his. Cranking up his lust. As if that was hard to do.

Salty lips covered his, and her tongue exploded into his mouth. Her hands gripped his head, holding him to her. This was no soft, sweet kiss. This was CC giving her all. This was what he needed. His hands were on her butt, lifting her higher up his body, across his reaction to her. Without breaking the kiss, she wound her legs around his waist and hovered over his throbbing need.

Twisting his mouth away from those lips, he croaked, 'No sex, babe.'

'Stupid rule. I'm breaking it.' Low and sexy laughter highlighted her intent.

Relief nearly dumped him underwater. Words dried in his mouth. So he went back to kissing while trying to hold Olivia and shove his boxers down his thighs all at once.

Suddenly a small hand pressed between them, her fingers splayed on his chest. 'Wait.'

'Wait?' His voice was hoarse with longing. If she'd changed her mind he'd lose his permanently.

'That massive bed. The bure. The Fijian experience. I want that.'

This time relief had Zac sinking into the water, taking Olivia with him, so that she sat over his point of desire. 'Since when have we been one-act-per-night types?'

Her answer was to slide over him, taking him deep within her, her head tipped back, her body quivering as she came fast. Four nights of restraining himself exploded in one deep thrust into her heat.

Dragging themselves up the beach, they scooped up their clothes and, holding hands, raced to the bure. *Except I'm not running.* Olivia grinned. *I'm skipping. I am over the moon with happiness.* 'What a goddamned waste. Four nights and we didn't do it. Are we idiots or what?'

Zac swung their hands high. 'There are plenty of words out there we could use, but I'd rather concentrate on getting you to beg me to make love to you in that bed we've been pretending we haven't shared.'

'Good answer.' Her shoes and dress slipped out of her hand at the doors leading inside. 'Let's hit the shower first. I don't usually season my sex with salt.'

'The outside shower.'

'Is there any other?' A quick sluice off and she dried Zac as he fumbled with a towel to do the same with her. Impatient, she tossed the towels aside and grabbed his hand, pulled him into the main room and leapt into the bed, taking him with her so that they tumbled into a heap of arms and legs. Not that Zac had needed any persuasion. He was already showing interest in her, in the way only men could.

Goddamn. She grinned and shook herself. This had to be the most wonderful, magical, fabulous way to end their stay on the island. Maybe waiting those long, tension-filled nights had been the way to go, had added to the tension and wound up the orgasmic relief. 'Zac,' she whispered. 'Long and slow.' As she trailed kisses over his chest she continued, 'We've got all night.'

'Yeah, babe, not leaving until ten tomorrow.'

Some time after four in the morning, as the sun began to lighten the bure around the edges, Olivia snuggled her exhausted body against Zac's and traced a line across his chest with a fingertip.

'This is unlike other times for us.'

'Yeah, you're talking too much, for one thing.'

'I feel different. I guess lying in bed together afterwards has something to do with that.' In fact, she was shocked at how much she was enjoying lying here with Zac, knowing neither of them would shortly leap out of bed and head home, or to work, or anywhere. 'This is taking it to a whole new level.' As if there was a depth to making out with Zac she'd never known before. She should be scared. She wasn't. Not right this moment, with Zac's body wrapped around hers and her muscles feeling deliciously sated.

The hands that had been working their magic on her back stopped moving. 'Regret not zapping that rule earlier?'

Locking gazes with him, her heart pounded at a ridiculous rate. He didn't look unhappy about what she'd said, more cautious. 'Not at all.' Having fun doing other things together had added more to their relationship. 'I have had the most amazing holiday with you.' *I want to have more of them.*

'Aw, shucks.' He pulled the sheet up to their necks. 'You say the nicest things. In case you're wondering, I've had a wonderful time doing some great things with you too. Now let's fall asleep in each other's arms for the last few hours of our holiday.'

Yep, soon reality would return in the form of Auckland, work and her mother. And in thinking where to go with this new relationship with Zac. Her eyelids drooped shut. She would not think about that now. Not when his strong arms held her as though she was delicate. Not when she could breathe in the scent of their lovemaking and Zac's aftershave. Not when... She drifted into a dream-laden sleep filled with images of the man sharing the bed.

Josaia and all his family were standing on the beach when Zac and Olivia turned up to board their float plane.

Olivia hugged Lauan. 'I'm so glad we met you and your family.'

Lauan was crying openly and shaking her head. 'No, it is us who are glad.'

'We'll be in touch very soon, I promise.' Leaving these wonderful people wasn't as easy as she'd expected. Zac nudged her out of the way to have his turn hugging Lauan. 'We'll schedule Josaia's surgeries as soon as possible.' He was repeating what they'd all discussed yesterday afternoon.

Donny stepped up and said, 'Josaia has something for you both.'

'Dr Zac, this is for you.' The boy handed over a bright blue *sulu* with all the gravity of a ceremony for royalty.

Zac took the carefully folded cotton cloth that Fijian men traditionally wore tied around their waists at special times.

Josaia stepped in front of Olivia. 'This is yours.'

She dropped to her knees and wrapped her arms around Josaia, a yellow *sulu* that could be wrapped around her body like a strapless dress in her hand. 'Thank you so much. I'll look after it, I promise.'

Once inside the plane Olivia leaned forward to wave goodbye. Suddenly the plane was racing and bumping across the sea and finally lifting into the sky.

She'd had the most amazing five days, and now she didn't know what was ahead. Hope rose, hope for a future they could share. The hope backed off. She couldn't make a full commitment to Zac. Her mother made sure of that. There just wasn't enough of herself to go round. She wasn't going to try to spread herself too thin. That's how people got hurt.

Zac lifted her hand and kissed her knuckles. 'Stop overthinking things.'

Did he know what was going on in her mind? Of course not. He didn't know the half of what went on in her life.

She gripped his hand and turned to stare outside, absorbing every last moment of Fiji.

Olivia shivered as she clambered out of the taxi outside her house. 'Why does the weather have to be wet and cold tonight of all nights?' she grumbled.

Zac only laughed. 'Bringing us back to earth with a thump, isn't it?'

Grabbing her case, she ran for the shelter of her covered veranda. That's when she noticed lights on inside. Then the steady beat of music reached her. And her stomach dived. *No. Not tonight. Not when I'm so happy.*

'You going to open that door?' Zac asked.

Not while you're here. She waved frantically at the taxi driver. He had to take Zac away. Now. Not after that coffee she'd suggested when they'd turned into her street. 'Wait,' she yelled.

'Too late,' Zac muttered. 'You don't want me coming in after all?'

'I've got a headache.'

Zac dropped his case and reached for her. 'That sudden? I'm picking it's because there's someone inside you don't want me to meet.' His hands were gentle on her upper arms, his thumbs rubbing back and forth in a coaxing manner. 'I thought we were better than that, had moved on from the quick visits to something more real.'

So did I, until reality slapped me around the ears. She'd been an idiot to think there was a way around the problem on the other side of her front door. 'I'm sorry.' She didn't want his sympathy—or worse, was afraid of seeing a look of horror in his eyes when he saw how far gone her mother would be.

The sound of her front door being unlocked sent a wave of panic through her. 'You have to go. Now.'

'Olivia, darling, there you are. I've been wondering where you'd got to and when you'd be back. They wouldn't tell me anything at the hospital.'

Olivia was a dab hand at interpreting the alcohol-laden slur. One glance at Zac and she knew he was also right up to speed on the situation. Anger—at her mother, at Zac for learning her truth—rolled up and spilled out. 'Mum, what are you doing here? You know I don't like you in my house when I'm away.'

A firm hand on her arm stopped her diatribe. 'Olivia, it's okay.'

'No, it's not. You don't get it. This is my mother, Cindy Coates-Clark. Mum, meet Zachary Wright, a friend—' No, damn it. 'Zac and I have been in Fiji together. We have had a wonderful time and now we'd like to wind down from our flight home. Alone.'

'Pleased to meet you, Zachary. Call me Cindy.' A wave of alcohol fumes wafted between them all.

Her mother stepped back and held the door wide, as though it was her place to do so. 'Do come in.'

'Thank you, Cindy.' Zac picked up the cases and nodded Olivia through in front of him. 'I'll leave mine just inside the door while we have that coffee.'

'You still want it?' When she locked her eyes with his, he nodded.

'Yes.' Like there was nothing out of the ordinary, being greeted by a scantily clad woman who was obviously plastered.

Heavy black smudges of mascara covered Cindy's cheeks, and bright red lipstick had run into the lines around her mouth. Her low-cut top revealed way too much cleavage, and her skirt…

Olivia gulped as anger and disappointment again boiled over. 'Mum, that was a new suit. I haven't even worn it.' And never would now that three-quarters of the skirt had been hacked off. She'd been thrilled when she'd found the emerald-coloured outfit at her favourite shop.

'It's far sexier now. You can be so old-fashioned with your clothes, darling.'

'I wonder why.' From the day she'd turned thirteen her mother had spent a fortune on buying her clothes that had made her feel uncomfortable even around the cat, let alone the kids she'd hung out with. Humiliating didn't begin to describe it.

Now Zac was seeing things she never wanted him to know about. 'Zac, about that coffee…'

'I'll make it, shall I?' He hid his disgust very well. 'Would you like a coffee, Cindy?'

'Coffee? I don't think so. Why don't you two join me with a gin? Zac, I know you'd like one. You're a real man. Not like—'

'Mum, stop it. Now. We are not having gin.' She stepped into the kitchen and crumpled. *Welcome home, Olivia. Welcome back to life as you really know it.* Empty bottles lay everywhere. Half-full takeout food containers covered the bench, dirty cutlery and glasses filled the spaces. 'How long have you been here?'

'I don't know. Days?' Mum sounded confused all of a sudden.

Strong arms wound around Olivia, held her from dropping in a heap. 'Hey, we'll get it sorted.' Zac's low voice was full of compassion and wove around her like the comfort blanket she'd taken everywhere with her as a toddler. 'You're not alone, okay?'

Yes, she was. Her mother was her problem. This had nothing to do with Zac, and never would. Despite the warmth that stole through her at his words. She stayed in the circle of his arms—just for one more minute. Her chin rested on his chest. One minute, then she'd toughen up and face the consequences of having gone away without telling her mother where she was.

Finally she stepped away, put space between her and Zac. 'You have to go.'

Frustration deepened his voice. 'No, Olivia, I don't. I'm with you, at your side, looking out for you.'

On her phone she found the taxi company number and stabbed the button. Forcing a toughness she didn't feel on her face, she snapped, 'I'm not asking, I'm tell-ing you to go.' Someone from the taxi company answered and she rattled off directions, ended the call. 'They'll be five minutes.'

He gave no further argument, just kissed her softly. 'Good night, sweetheart. Talk to you in the morning.'

'No, Zac. Don't. It's over. We're done. Permanently.' It was the only way forward for her.

But when the front door had closed behind him Olivia leaned against the hall wall and felt her heart crack into pieces. It had taken this for her to realise her hope for the future with Zac was actually love for Zac. She wanted to be with him, to give him so much, to share a life. To openly show him her love. To try to be the woman she hadn't thought she could be. But that mess in her kitchen told her otherwise. Dreams were fairytales.

Sliding down the wall, she wrapped her arms around her legs, dropped her head on her knees, and let the tears come. She hadn't cried over her mother for so long but there was no stopping the torrent. For a brief time she'd let hope into her heart, had wanted more with Zac. How dumb could she get? This had always been going to happen. Therefore, the sooner the better. Now she could move on, without Zac, and do what she'd always done—survive and look out for her mother.

Zac stared at Olivia's house until the taxi turned the corner at the end of the street. His throat was dry, his heartbeat slow and his gut knotted tight. What a difference twenty-four hours made. From sexy and fun in that red dress to heartbroken at home, it was like Olivia had flipped from one person to another.

Now he understood so much. The control she constantly maintained over herself and everything around her was a coping mechanism.

There'd be no controlling her mother.

Olivia didn't want to be like her mother.

The glimpse of worry when he'd said that dress was so different from what he was used to seeing her in now made sense.

'Well, hello, you're nothing like your mum.' Despite having spent only a few minutes with Cindy and not knowing anything about her, he knew Olivia was the polar opposite from her mother.

But you didn't have to kick me out like I mean nothing to you.

When Olivia had mentioned her mother was an alcoholic he'd had no idea what that meant in real terms. Drunk and disorderly didn't cover it. Cindy whined like a spoilt brat, created chaos. She'd helped herself to her daughter's clothes, ruining them in the process. Helped herself to the house, the contents of the kitchen, and trashed it as only belligerent teenagers did. What had that woman done to Olivia's life? Her sense of belonging, her future?

The resignation in CC's eyes had hit him hard. She was responsible for that woman, and he knew all about responsibility. He'd learned it the hard way. Hopefully Olivia hadn't, but deep down he knew this situation went a long way to explaining why she ran solo.

You don't have to be alone any more.

Olivia wasn't made for that. She was loving, caring, sharing, and a whole load more.

The taxi pulled up in Quay Street. His apartment building loomed above, dark and unwelcoming. He'd rather be back at Olivia's house, no matter the mess inside. He wasn't thinking about the state of the kitchen.

But you sent me away, Olivia. Again.

As Zac rode the elevator to his floor a slow burn began in his belly. He'd been shoved out of Olivia's life for a second time. She hadn't given him a chance to stay, to talk about it, to do any damned thing except get out of her life. What had their holiday been about if not learning more about each other and getting closer?

Learning that I love you, Olivia. Do you know that? Do you know I've broken all my rules for you? That for the first time ever I'm seeing a future that's got people in it—you and our children.

The doors slid apart but Zac didn't move. The itch had gone.

The doors began closing. Sticking his foot in the gap so they opened again, Zac hoisted his bag and dragged his feet towards his apartment. He'd pour a whisky and try to fathom where to go from here.

How damned typical that when he'd finally fallen in love he wasn't wanted.

CHAPTER THIRTEEN

'DON'T HANG UP, OLIVIA.' Zac didn't give her time to say hello. 'This is about Josaia.'

'I'm listening.' Olivia could listen to him all day, but of course she'd spent the last ten days doing her damnedest to push him away, out of her head, her heart. She missed him so much it was unbelievable. It was like her heart and mind were stuck in Fiji mode with Zac, talking and laughing, while her real life was grinding along without any joy.

'Theatre's booked at the private hospital for Saturday morning. I've managed to inveigle a free bed for four nights so we're set to go.' Zac sounded upbeat and pleased with himself. As he should be. He'd been hassling everyone he knew to get Josaia's surgery organised. All the staff assisting were doing it gratis. No surprise there. When Zac wanted to he could charm the grumpiest of old men into putting his hand in his pocket and handing over his life savings.

'You should start a charity organisation for kids like Josaia,' Olivia acknowledged.

'*I* should? You're the one who knows how to pull at people's heartstrings. Look at how successful Andy's gala night turned out to be.'

Had she pulled Zac's heartstrings? Ever? Even a

teeny-weeny bit? Why was she wondering when a yes only added to her grief? Staying away from him was hard enough already. She only talked to him about Josaia's upcoming surgery, cutting him off the moment he started on about anything personal. 'I'll see you at the motel at five.' They'd decided between themselves to pay for a motel unit for the family close to the hospital. Zac was picking up Josaia and his family from the airport later in the day. Tomorrow they had a free day, and then it would be D-day.

'You could come with me.'

'I've got a clinic starting at two.'

Zac sighed, his upbeat mood gone. 'Promise me you'll be at the motel. It's important for Josaia.'

She didn't make promises. Her word was usually enough. 'I promise.' *I do?*

'Are you sure you're not a secret needleworker?' Zac asked from the other side of the operating table on Saturday. 'You're so patient, creating delicate stitches even where the outcome won't be visible to anyone.'

Olivia glanced up at him, her heart stuttering when his dark eyes locked on hers. 'I could've taken up knitting.'

'That'd be messy.' He grinned. She mightn't be able to see his mouth behind that mask but his eyes were light and sparkling.

Olivia concentrated on her patient. She'd reopened the wound that ran down the side of Josaia's face and removed tissue causing lumps where the previous stitches had been pulled too tight. Now she was painstakingly suturing layer after layer, careful with each and every stitch. While it was what everyone saw on the outside that upset Josaia, she could make it so much better by preparing the underneath muscle properly.

'You want to close the shoulder wound once I've worked on Josaia's shoulder?' Zac asked. 'We might as well go for broke and have everything looking as close to new as possible.'

'Make those kids want their friend back.'

Kay looked up from her monitors. 'I hope Josaia tells them where to go.'

'I suspect he might after this,' Zac told the anaesthetist. 'He's been different ever since we said we could operate. Hopeful, expectant. Which puts the pressure on us.'

Olivia clipped the end of her last suture and straightened her back. 'There you go, young man. As good as new.'

Zac swapped places with Olivia. It was his turn to set things right for Josaia. 'Let's hope I can do the same. At least no one gets to see what I do.' He picked up a scalpel.

'They will on the outside. It will be great to see Josaia with his confidence back, swimming and diving with the best of them.'

'I hope he finds some new friends. He doesn't need the old ones.' Olivia swabbed as Zac made incisions. 'But I guess Josaia doesn't have a lot of choice on the island.'

'It must be hell for his family, seeing how he's treated. No parent would want their child to suffer like that.' Zac exposed the collarbone, where it had been broken. 'Re-breaking this is kind of awful. The kid's going to be in pain for a while.'

'Think about how those pins you're going to put in will help him. One day he'll appreciate it.' The sooner the better if the boy was to make a full recovery with friends and school.

'Right, let's get this done.' He reached for the first pin.

As soon as the surgeries were completed and Josaia was wheeled away to Recovery, Olivia and Zac went to put the family at ease.

Then they headed for the car park and Zac suggested lunch downtown. 'We could go to the Viaduct.'

'Sorry, Zac, but I'm not hungry.' She'd eaten very little over the last couple of days, food making her feel nauseous.

'What's going on, Olivia? Don't give me the "nothing" reply. I won't believe you.'

The steel in his tone overwhelmed her. She could feel her body being pulled towards him. It would be so easy to lean in and let go of her problem for a while. The thing with that was that her mother wasn't going to go away; would be there causing havoc when she finally took up the reins again. Tightening her spine, she told him, 'I have an appointment in an hour, and before that I need to hit the supermarket.' Though why when she wasn't eating she had no idea. That had just dropped into her head when she was trying to sound convincing to Zac.

'An appointment with who?' Of course he went for the important part of her statement.

'A lawyer, a psychologist, and a cop,' she blurted, close to unravelling. Had to be why she'd answered with the truth. She needed to get away from Zac fast, before she became a blithering idiot and spilled her guts all over his classy leather jacket.

Where was her car key? Scrabbling around in the bottom of her bag didn't produce it. Tipping the contents onto the bonnet of her car, she couldn't believe it wasn't there. Great. Just great.

'This what you're looking for?' Zac swung a key from his finger.

Snatching it from him, she began throwing everything back in her bag. 'Where did you find it?'

'Where are you meeting these people?'

'At home.' She bent to pick up her wallet from where it had slipped onto the tarmac.

'I'll drive you. Come on.' He took her elbow.

She tugged free. 'I can drive myself. Anyway, I can't leave my car here.'

Zac's hand was back on her arm. 'You can and you will. I'm taking you home, Olivia.'

That got her. Slap bang in her heart. She didn't pull away. She couldn't. She needed Zac, and, as frightening as that was, she went with the desperate longing to have someone at her side. 'Next you'll be telling me you're coming to the meeting.' Geez, had she just said that with hope in her voice?

'I'll make the coffee.'

He did more than that. Even when she nodded at the door for him to leave he stayed and listened as the horrible facts about her mother were aired and discussion began on what to do about Cindy. The truth was that there wasn't a lot that could be done unless her mother committed to a programme and went into care. Her latest hideous deed, arrested for driving while drunk on Thursday, made Olivia's stomach churn, and when she lifted her eyes to Zac's she fully expected to see total disgust all over his face. But no. His hand engulfed her shaking ones, his thumb rubbed back and forth over her fingers, and his eyes were full of understanding.

Olivia *needed* to leap up and drag Zac to her front

door, push him out, and lock it behind him. She *wanted* him here with her, holding her hand as he was. Split right down the middle, her emotions were raw and out of control. She aimed to do what she always did when this happened and focus on her mother's current situation. But it wasn't working. The words were going in but they weren't registering as clearly as they should.

By the time the meeting was over she was as aware as ever that her mother was a ticking time bomb and unwilling to take charge of herself. It had been suggested Olivia walk away, make her mother face up to her situation, but she didn't think she could do that. It would go against everything she believed in. Even now, when she was fighting Zac's pull, fighting this deep, paralysing need to let him into her life, she had to hold on to the only way she knew how to cope with her mother—by standing strong, alone.

Shutting the front door behind the lawyer, she leaned back against it, closing her eyes. Did she even have the energy to make it to the kitchen where Zac was waiting? She had to tell him to leave. It was getting to be a habit.

'Hey,' Zac said from somewhere in front of her. 'You need to go to bed and get some shut-eye.'

'I have to check Josaia's doing okay.'

'I'm going to head in there shortly so I can let you know if there's anything you need to deal with. I spoke to the ward sister while you were showing that lot out and she says he's doing fine. The family are with him.' Zac draped an arm over her shoulders and led her down the hallway in the direction of her bedroom. 'When did you last sleep properly?'

'I have no idea.'

'Get into bed and I'll make you a hot chocolate.'

Olivia sank onto the edge of her bed. 'Hot chocolate? I haven't had one of those in years.' *Since I had measles and Dad looked after me.* Huh? Dad had done that? Yeah, he had, just as he'd once spent lots of time with her. Before he'd got jaded and bitter about Mum, and had made another life.

Zac pulled her to her feet again. 'No, you don't. Let's get you into your PJs first.' He began unbuttoning her shirt and it was nothing like last time when he'd made her body hot with need. This loving gesture filled her heart with gladness and relief.

'I'll manage.' Her fingers worked the zip on her trousers. When Zac reached her door she called, 'Hey, you. Thank you for…everything.'

He came back and kissed her on each cheek. 'Told you I was here for you.'

Scary. 'Zac, I don't do being looked after.' Deep, deep breath. 'You have to go. You have to stay gone this time. Please.' Her voice cracked over the lump of tears clogging her throat.

Zac shrugged. 'Here's the thing. I don't do walking away from someone I care about either.'

Had Zac just said he cared about her? No, he couldn't have. She must be asleep already, having a dream. At least it wasn't a nightmare.

Zac let himself out of Olivia's house and made sure the door locked behind him. With a bit of luck Olivia would sleep right through until tomorrow. One thing for certain was that she needed to.

It was about the only thing he was sure of, he thought as he climbed into his vehicle and slammed the door against the light rain. That, and the fact she wouldn't be letting him back into her house tomorrow morning.

Looking up the path to her house, he recalled some of the comments made by the lawyer, and wondered just what sort of childhood Olivia must've had with a mother so far off the rails. What woman wanted to dress up as her daughter's lookalike? Wanted to hang out with a bunch of giggly teens? One eyebrow rose. Olivia a giggly teen? Hard to imagine.

Slowly pulling away, he kept going over everything he'd heard about Cindy Coates-Clark. How cruel of Olivia's father to leave her to deal with her alcoholic mother, especially when she'd been so young.

Toot, toot. A quick glance in the rear-view mirror showed a truck up his boot. He waved. 'Sorry, mate.' And planted his foot, roaring away from the corner.

He'd go see Josaia, then head home for the night. Tomorrow morning he'd take breakfast to Olivia's house.

Think that's going to win you entrance to her lair, do you?

No, not a sod's chance, but he had to try, if only to show her he wasn't repelled by anything he'd heard today. If anything, he was more determined to be a part of her life. At the moment he'd take the crumbs, but he fully intended to win her over completely so they'd have a future together.

His hand clenched, banged the steering wheel. Damn—families could be such screw-ups. He and Olivia had got the pick of them. What was Mark like as a father? Did he show his boys he loved them? Would he blame them for everything or walk out of their lives when the going got tough? And if he did, who would be there for them?

I would. But he didn't know the boys. Not really. Only one way to rectify that. But he and Mark didn't get along. *So go fix that. Start at the beginning and get to know your brother again, learn to put the angst behind you and love him as you always did, always have.*

Olivia rolled over onto her back and stared up at the ceiling. The sunlit ceiling.

'What time is it?'

Eight thirty-five, according to the screen on her phone.

She'd missed a load of texts while in the land of nod, starting last night.

Josaia says hi to Dr Olivia. He's doing fine and can't wait to be up and running around, despite the pain. Hope you're sleeping and don't get this till the morning. Hugs, Zac.

Thinking of you, and wishing we were back on Tokoriki enjoying dinner under the palm trees. More hugs, Zac.

Hitting the sack now. See you in the morning.

No, you won't. I've got a mother to sort out, and wounds to lick.

Outside your door with breakfast.

Had Zac knocking on the door been what had woken her? Olivia leapt out of bed and headed down the hall.

Wait up. You're going to let Zac in? Think about this. Is it wise when you're going to walk away from him again? It's not fair on him to be running hot and cold all the time. Either let him into your life or cut all ties—now.

Her feet dragged as she turned for the kitchen and

the kettle. Strong coffee was needed. Her heart was so slow it was in danger of stopping. She didn't want Zac gone but what else could she do? She had nothing to offer him.

She loved Zac. She knew it bone deep. He was the one for her. *Sniff.* But she wasn't right for him. Never would be.

With two coffees on board and a hot shower having washed away the sleep sludge on her skin, Olivia headed out her front door to see Josaia, and tripped over a paper bag with a takeout logo on it. Breakfast. Gluggy cold pancakes, bacon, and maple syrup filled the container she opened. 'Oh, Zac, you're making this so hard for me.'

She dropped the bag into her rubbish bin and headed for her garage, only remembering when the door rolled open that her car was still in the hospital's car park. Back inside the house she changed her shoes. Walking to the hospital would help clear her head.

Maybe.

Josaia was arguing with Donny about getting out of bed when Olivia arrived at his room. 'I don't like staying in bed.'

'You have to wait until Dr Olivia's checked you over,' his grandfather growled.

'If Josaia's that keen to get up then there's no reason why he shouldn't,' Olivia told them.

Josaia grinned. 'See?' But when he moved pain filled his face and he stopped.

'Take it slowly.' Olivia spoke firmly. 'I need to look at your face first. Then you'd better be careful what you do until Dr Zac sees you.' She needed to get out of there before he turned up and started asking why she hadn't returned any of his messages.

'He came when I was asleep.' Josaia slowly sat up, his damaged cheek turned up to her. 'My face is better, isn't it?'

If he could think that with a line of stitches running down his cheek then he was well on the way to recovery. 'Lots better.'

'My friends are going to like me again.'

Thud. Olivia's heart sank. 'Josaia, you are still going to have a scar, just not as obvious and no more lumps and bumps.'

'My arm's going to work properly.'

'Soon, yes. You have to do a lot of work first, exercises that Dr Zac will show you.' But those friends? 'Let's take everything slowly, eh?' She sat down beside him and turned his head so that the overhead light shone on the wound. No redness or puffiness, just a neat line that would heal into a thin, flat scar that over time would fade to a pale mark on his skin. 'That's looking good.' Pride filled her. Hopefully she'd made this boy's life a little easier.

If only her mother was as easily pleased when she visited later.

'I am not going into one of those rehab places. They're full of pious do-gooders who think having a drink is a crime.'

Clocked driving at eighty-five Ks per hour in a residential area while drunk was a crime. 'You're lucky Judge Walters has given you another chance to fix your life. He's ordered you to go into a clinic. If you don't you'll appear before him again and this time he'll throw the book at you. You already have one drunk-driving conviction.' She drew in a breath. 'I've made you an appointment for tomorrow at the clinic in Remuera. I'll come with you.'

'Bet that man you went away with wouldn't do anything naughty, like having a drink too many.'

Olivia sighed at her mother's classic tactic of changing the subject. 'Leave Zac out of this.'

'Why? You got the hots for him?'

I don't want him sullied by you. 'We're friends, nothing more.' *Nothing less either. If only...*

'He's cocky, thinks he's every woman's gift.' Her mother looked smug as she raised her coffee to her lips, then put it down without a sip.

'No, Mum, he does not.' Confident, comfortable in his own skin, but not cocky.

'You watch. He'll get what he wants from you and walk away. He's not the settling-down type.'

Mum always aimed for the bull's-eye. Never missed either. 'You know an awful lot about Zac for having spent very little time with him.'

'He's going to hurt you, darling. Trust me, I know men and how they operate. You are fair game with this one.'

She snapped, 'Zac is not like you think. You're insulting him with your accusations.'

'Watch this space,' her mother drawled, before changing tactics again. 'Darling, I'm only thinking of you. I don't want to see you get hurt. I know what that's like, believe me.'

'Why are you doing this? You want to destroy everything I hold dear.'

'Ha, you care about him. Knew it. I worry about what happens to you. I'm your mother, I want you to be happy.' Her hands shook so badly coffee slopped onto the table.

Mum's frightened. Of what? She's been going on about Zac. Aha. Got it. She's afraid she'll have to share me. She's always done this. She drove Dad away, pushed friends out of my life, and I've gone along with it, believing I can't love two people at once, can't be there for anyone but her.

'Goddamn,' she said under her breath. *Have I been wrong?* 'Mum, I've got to go. I'll pick you up at ten tomorrow.'

'Come back, Olivia. I need to talk to you.'

'No, Mum, I'm done talking.'

She ran out to her car, leapt in, jerked the gearstick into drive, and sped away.

Cornwall Park was busy with families and their dogs, with joggers, walkers, and tourists heading up to the top of One Tree Hill. Olivia strode out under the massive trees, her hands stuffed in her jacket pockets, her chin down. And let it all in. Everything that had shaped her. Dad abandoning her. Her mother. Zac. *Her life.*

The answers for the future were elusive. *But I want to try. I love Zac. No denying it.* So now what? Race around to his apartment and tell him the good news? Leap into his arms and hang on for dear life?

Even as she spun around to return to her car and do just that, common sense prevailed.

Am I absolutely sure?

Hurting Zac was not on the agenda. There were a lot of things to think through, and she'd take her time, spend the next few days getting her head around the fact that she could be about to change her life for ever by giving her heart to Zac. By letting go of some of the control that had kept her on track most of her life.

Scary. Downright terrifying.

* * *

The days dragged. Sleep was elusive and work tedious. Her head was full of arguments for and against getting involved with Zac. *More involved.*

I love you, Zachary Wright. But I can't have a life with you, her old self told her. *I'll hurt you.*

Every day she got texts.

Hey, isn't Josaia doing well? He's like a new kid. Hugs, Zac.

Yep, their young patient had turned into a bright and bubbly boy desperate to get out and play.

CC, you want to have dinner at that new Italian place? Zac.

Absolutely, yes. But she didn't.

You okay? I'm here for you. Hugs, Zac.

No, I'm not okay. I'm missing you. So much it's like there's a hole where my heart used to be. She thought of those shoulders she liked to lean against, that strong body that made her feel safe and warm. And missed him even more.

Did your mother go into the clinic this week? More hugs, Zac.

Yes, surprisingly, Mum had.

Olivia didn't answer any of the texts. When she found a huge bunch of irises in gold and purple paper on her doorstep on Thursday night with a note saying,

'Love, Zac,' she wanted to cry. Oh, all right, she did cry. But she didn't ring to thank him. Or to acknowledge what his message might mean.

Friday night he sent photos of his nephews. 'Check these guys out. I'm mending bridges.' The cutest little boys hung off Uncle Zac's arms, beaming directly at the camera. Zac looked happy but wary. It wasn't hard to see him with his own kids hanging off him like that. Her heart rolled. She wanted that—with Zac. Children. She had no idea how to raise kids but with Zac at her side she'd learn.

Saturday morning her phone rang. She sighed when she saw the number. 'Hello, Mum.'

'Darling, come and get me. I hate it here. They treat me like a child. I can't have anything I want.'

'Where are you ringing from?' Patients weren't allowed any contact with family for the first few weeks.

'I'm at a coffee shop around the corner from the clinic. The coffee's terrible but the owner let me use the phone. Hurry, Olivia. I can't stand the place.'

'Mum, listen to me.' It hurt to breathe. 'I am not coming to get you. You have to go back and start getting better.'

'It's him, isn't it? He's told you to do this.'

'Don't blame Zac.' *I am finally opening my eyes and seeing that to be kind to you I have to be strong and hard.* '*I* want you to stop drinking.'

'Come and get me so we can talk about it,' her mother wheedled.

'Sorry, but I've got someone to see.' Why had she left it so long? Zac was her man.

'What about me?'

'Mum, I love you, but I am about to put me first.' *Me and Zac.* 'Don't bother coming around to my house. I won't be here. Please go back to the clinic. Do this for yourself.' She cut their conversation, then turned the phone off and put it in a drawer. She was on a mission and didn't want any interruptions.

In her bedroom she gazed into the wardrobe, trying to decide what to wear. That red dress stood out amongst the dark winter clothes. Reaching for it, she hesitated. Zac had lost his mind when she'd worn it in Fiji but this was early afternoon and it was very cold outside. The many trousers and blouses were too work-like. The green skirt she pulled out didn't excite her either. In the end she slipped into the designer skin-tight jeans and silk blouse she'd worn on the day of the gala when they'd caught up again at the hotel. Zipping up the knee-high boots, she did a twirl in front of her mirror. 'Not bad.' For the first time in days she could feel some control coming back, could feel her body tightening up. The thigh-length coat from that day completed the look, and made her smile briefly.

A quick check of her make-up and a swipe of her hair with the brush and she was on her way, not giving herself time to think about what she was doing. Laying her life on the line was what this was about.

Stop thinking, just concentrate on driving through the downtown traffic.

What if—?

No what-ifs, she told herself as she pressed the buzzer for Zac's apartment. *This is do or don't. And don't is no longer an option.*

'Hello?'

It's not too late to run. 'Zac, it's me.'

A soft buzzing and she was stepping into the elevator. She didn't hesitate but pressed the button for the penthouse floor and held herself ramrod straight, ready for anything, refusing to acknowledge the flapping sensations in her stomach.

Zac was standing outside the elevator door as it opened. His smile was friendly but cautious. 'Olivia.'

'Zac.' Suddenly the full import of what she'd come to say slammed into her like an avalanche. Her hand went out to the wall to steady herself.

He took her elbow. 'Come into the apartment.'

Through the thick layers of coat and silk blouse she felt heat spreading out from where his fingers touched her, filling her with courage. Reaching behind her, he said, 'Let me take your coat.'

As she shrugged out of the sleeves she breathed deeply, boosted her courage. Then she turned to face him. 'I'm sorry I haven't been returning your texts or thanking you for the flowers.'

'That's okay.'

'But it isn't. I was rude, and there is no excuse for that. Zac, I came to tell you I love you.' There. She'd done it.

That smile didn't change; didn't fade, neither did it widen or soften. 'I was hoping you might.'

'I think I always have, but I've been so busy trying to deny it that I've made a lot of mistakes.' This was hard, yet relief was catching at her. 'Is there a future for us?'

'What do you want, Olivia? Marriage? Children and a dog?

Too much too soon. She took a step back. 'Could we try living together first? See how that goes? I didn't have good role models growing up and I'd hate to make the mistakes my parents did.'

Zac closed the gap, standing directly in front of her. He ran a finger down her cheek and over her chin. 'No, sweetheart. It's all or nothing. I love you and I want the whole picture.'

He loved her. To hear those words did funny things to her heart. Wow. To hear Zac tell her he loved her was the most wonderful thing. She smiled at him, sure her face was all goofy-looking.

Then the rest of what he'd said hit her, and she shook her head. 'I know nothing about happy families. I don't even know if I can love you and kids and my mother. I've kept myself shut off from all that, only ever loved one person.'

His mouth softened and the kiss he placed on the corner of her mouth felt lighter than a butterfly landing. 'I'll help you. But I don't want a practice run. Let's get married, jump in boots and all, a full commitment to each other and our lives. I believe in you, Olivia. If you falter *we'll* work it out. Just as I expect you to do for me. My family history isn't any more encouraging than yours and yet I want to make it work with you.'

Hope began to unfurl at the bottom of her stomach. 'Really? You want all that with *me*?'

Now he gave her the full-blown grin she enjoyed so much. 'That's only the beginning, girl. There're the hot nights in bed, the lazy days lying in front of your fire and eating takeout food, the days when we're both working so hard the only contact we have is by text, but we'll always know we're there for each other.'

'What about the days my mother does her thing?' He'd seen what she could do.

'We support her and try to turn her back on track. We do not split up over her. We will be together, in love, war, and everything in between.' Those arms she'd been hankering for wound around her waist and drew her close so his eyes looked directly into hers. 'I love you,

Olivia, more than life itself. Please, say you'll marry me.' His mouth hovered close to hers, waiting.

'Okay. Yes, please. I will. Let's get married. Sooner rather than later.' Talk about jumping in at the deep end. But somehow she didn't think she was going to drown, not with Zac holding her. 'Did I mention I love you?'

'Not often enough for me to be absolutely sure,' he said just before claiming her mouth with his.

Minutes later Zac lifted his head. 'Now I know why I had the impulse to buy a bottle of your favourite bubbles. Come on, let's celebrate.'

'Just one glass.'

'CC, relax. You are not an alcoholic.'

'No, but I want to take you to bed and have my wicked way with your body, and too many glasses of champagne might spoil the fun.'

'Can't argue with that.' Zac grinned and hooked his arm through hers. 'Come on, we've got a cork to pop. And you can tell me why it took you so long to drop by.'

'Not tonight. Tonight's for us. But I'll fill you in soon enough. Promise.'

EPILOGUE

Fourteen months later

'HAPPY WEDDING ANNIVERSARY.' Zac sank onto the edge of their bed and placed a tray with breakfast on her knees. In the corner beside the small bowl of maple syrup for the pancakes and bacon was a tiny box.

Picking it up, she locked her eyes on the man she adored and who had been everything he'd promised and more since that night she'd told him she loved him. 'What's this?'

'Only one way to find out.'

When she flipped the lid a set of exquisite emerald earrings and a matching bracelet sparkled out at her. 'They're beautiful,' she squeaked.

'For a beautiful woman. Here.' He slid the bracelet over her hand. 'Perfect.'

She put the earrings in and then reached for the top drawer of her bedside table. 'Happy anniversary to you.' She placed a small, thin box in his outstretched hand and sat back to watch his reaction.

'What's this?' He gaped at the plastic stick he held up. 'Are we—?'

'Yes, we're pregnant. And I can hardly wait.' This past year had been wonderful, and not once had she faltered. Not even when Mum had run away from the clinic twice. With Zac there she could face anything. 'We're going to be parents, great parents.'

'Yeah, sweetheart, we are.' His kiss was made in heaven and had consequences that kept them busy for most of the morning and left the pancakes to go cold and gluggy on the plate.

Her hero for sure.

* * * * *

A CHILD TO OPEN
THEIR HEARTS

MARION LENNOX

My books in this series are dedicated to Andy,
whose help and friendship during my writing
career has been beyond measure.
I've been so proud to call you my friend.

CHAPTER ONE

THIS COULD BE a disaster instead of a homecoming. He could be marooned at sea until after his daughter's wedding.

Max wasn't worrying yet, though. Things would be chaotic on Wildfire Island after the cyclone, but the weather had eased and Sunset Beach was a favourite place for the locals to walk. If the rip wasn't so fierce he could swim ashore. He couldn't, but eventually someone would stroll to the beach, see his battered boat and send out a dinghy.

Max Lockhart, specialist surgeon, not-so-specialist sailor, headed below deck and fetched himself a beer. There were worse places to be stuck, he conceded. The *Lillyanna* was a sturdy thirty-foot yacht, and she wasn't badly enough damaged to be uncomfortable. She was now moored in the tropical waters off Wildfire Island. Schools of tiny fish glinted silver as they broke the surface of the sparkling water. The sun was warm. He had provisions for another week, and in the lee of the island the sea was relatively calm.

But he *was* stuck. The waters around the island were still a maelstrom. The cliffs that formed the headland above where he sheltered were being battered. To try and round them to get to Wildfire Island's harbour would be suicidal, and at some time during the worst of the cyclone his radio had been damaged and his phone lost overboard.

So now he was forced to rest, but rest, he conceded, had been the whole idea of sailing here. He needed to take some time to get his head in order and ready himself to face the islanders.

He also needed space to come to terms with anger and with grief. How to face his daughter's wedding with joy when he was so loaded with guilt and sadness he couldn't get past it?

But rest wouldn't cut it, he decided as he finished his beer. What he needed was distraction.

And suddenly he had it. Suddenly he could see two people on the island.

A woman had emerged from the undergrowth and was walking a dog on the beach. And up on the headland...another woman was walking towards the cliff edge.

Towards the cliff edge? What the...?

As a kid, Max and his mates had dived off this headland but they'd only dived when the water had been calm. They'd dared each other to dive the thirty-foot drop. Then they'd let the rip tug them out to this reef, where they'd catch their breath for the hard swim back. It had kept them happy for hours. It had given their parents nightmares.

For the woman on the headland, though, the nightmare seemed real. She was walking steadily towards the edge.

Suicide? The word slammed into his head and stayed.

He grabbed his field glasses, one of the few things not smashed in the storm, and fought to get them focussed. The woman was young. A crimson shawl was wrapped around a bundle at her breast. A child?

She was walking purposefully forward, closer to the edge. After the cyclone, the water below was a mass of churning foam. Even as a kid he'd known he had to get a run up to clear the rocks below.

'No!' His yell would be drowned in the wind up there, but he yelled anyway. 'Don't…'

His yell was useless. She reached the cliff edge and walked straight over.

Hettie de Lacey, charge nurse of Wildfire Island's small hospital, rather enjoyed a good storm. It broke the humidity. It cleared the water in the island's lagoons and it made the world seem fresh and new.

This, however, had been more than a good storm. The cyclone had smashed across the island three days ago, causing multiple casualties. Even though most wounds had been minor, the hospital was full to bursting, and Hettie had been run off her feet.

This was the first time she'd managed a walk and some blessed time to herself. Sunset Beach was relatively sheltered, but she was close to the northern tip, where waves flung hard against the headland. The seas out there were huge.

In another life she might have grabbed a surfboard and headed out, she thought, allowing herself a whiff of memory, of an eighteen-year-old Hettie in love with everything to do with the sea.

Including Darryn…

Yeah, well, that was one memory to put aside. How one man could take such a naïve kid and smash her ideals… Smash her life…

'Get over it,' she told herself, and she even smiled at the idea that she should still angst over memories from all those years ago. She'd made herself a great life. She was… mostly happy.

And then her attention was caught.

There was a yacht just beyond the reef. It was a gracious old lady of a yacht, a wooden classic, anchored to the south of The Bird's Nest. The Nest was a narrow rim of rock and coral, a tiny atoll at the end of an underwater reef running out from shore.

The yacht was using the atoll for shelter.

It'd be Max Lockhart, she thought, and the nub of fear she'd been feeling for Caroline dissipated in an instant. Oh, thank heaven. She knew the owner of Wildfire Island was trying to sail here for his daughter's wedding. Max had left Cairns before the cyclone had blown up, and for the last few days Caroline Lockhart, one of Hettie's best nurses, had been frantic. Her father was somewhere out to sea. He'd lost contact three days ago and they had no way of knowing if he'd survived.

She could see him fairly clearly from where she was, but she'd never met him—his few visits to the island during her employment had always seemed to coincide with times when she'd taken leave. But this must be him. The entrance to the harbour was wild so this was probably the safest place he could be.

She went to wave, and then she hesitated. The guy on the yacht—it must be Max—was already waving. And yelling. But not at her. At someone up on the headland?

Intrigued, she headed to the water's edge and looked up. Another islander out for a walk? Max must be stuck, she thought. He'd be wanting to attract attention so someone could send a dinghy out to bring him in. He'd seen someone up on the cliffs?

And then her breath caught in horror. Where the shallows gave way to deep water and the cliffs rose steeply to the headland, the wind still swept in from the cyclone-ravaged sea.

And up on the headland… Sefina Dason.

The woman was thirty feet above her but Hettie would know her anywhere. For the last few days Sefina had been in hospital, battered, not by the cyclone but by her oaf of a husband. She'd had to bring her toddler in with her because no one would care for him, something almost unheard of in this close-knit community.

There'd been whispers…

But this wasn't the time for whispers. Sefina was high on the headland and she was walking with purpose.

She was headed for the edge of the cliff!

And then she turned, just a little, and Hettie saw a bundle, cradled to her breast in a crimson shawl. Her horror doubled, trebled, went off the scale.

Joni!

No! She was screaming, running, stumbling over the rocks as beach gave way to the edges of the reef. *No!*

She could hear the echoes of the guy on the yacht, yelling, too.

But yelling was useless.

Sefina took two steps forward and she was gone.

Max knew the water under the headland like the back of his hand. In good weather this was a calm, still pool, deep and mysterious, bottoming out to coral. It was a fabulous place for kids to hurl themselves off the cliff in a show of bravado. The rip swept in from the north, hit the pool and tugged the divers out to the rocky outcrop he was anchored behind. As kids they'd learned to ride the rip to their advantage, letting it pull them across the shallow reef to the atoll. They'd lie on the rocks and catch their breath, readying themselves for the swim across the rip back to the beach.

But that rip would be fierce today, too strong to swim against. And the water in the pool…would be a whirlpool, he thought, sucking everything down.

All this he thought almost instantly, and as he thought it he was already tearing up the anchor, operating the winch with one hand, gunning the engine with the other.

His mind seemed to be frozen, but instinct was kicking in to take over.

Where would she be hurled out?

He hit the tiller and pushed the throttle to full speed, heading out of the shelter of the atoll, steering the boat as close as he dared to the beach. He couldn't get too close. Sheltered or not, there were still breakers pounding the sand.

There was a woman running along the beach, screaming. The woman with the dog? She'd seen?

But he didn't have time to look at her. He was staring across the maelstrom of white water, waiting for something to emerge. Anything.

He was as close as he could get without wrecking the yacht. As far as he could tell, this was where the rip emerged.

He dropped anchor, knowing he'd be anchoring in sand, knowing there was a chance the boat would be dragged away, but he didn't have time to care.

There... A wisp of crimson cloth... Nothing more, but it had to be enough.

If he was right, she was being tugged to twenty feet forward of the boat.

He'd miss her...

He was ripping his clothes off, tearing. Clothes would drag him down. If he used a lifejacket he could never swim fast enough.

He had so little chance the thing was almost futile.

He saw the wisp of crimson again, and he dived.

Sefina.

Joni.

Hettie was screaming but she was screaming inside. She had no room for anything else. Where...?

She'd swum here. There was a rip, running south. Hettie could swim well. Surfing had once been her life, but to swim against the rip in these conditions...

The guy on the boat had seen. If she could grab Sefina and tow her with the rip, maybe he could help.

A mother and a toddler?

She couldn't think like that.

As a teenager she'd trained as a lifeguard, hoping for a holiday job back when she'd lived at Bondi. Her instructor's voice slammed back now. *'Look to your own safety before you look to help someone in the surf.'*

This was crazy. Past dangerous.

Oh, but Joni... He was fifteen months old and she'd cradled him to sleep for the past few nights. And Sefina... Battered Sefina, with no one to turn to.

Forget the instructors. Her clothes were tossed onto the sand. 'Stay,' she yelled at Bugsy, and she was running into the waves regardless.

The rip was so strong Max was swept south the moment he hit the water. Anything in that pool would be tugged straight out, past the reef and out to sea.

He surfaced, already being pulled.

But Max had swum like a fish as a kid, and for the past few years gym work and swimming had sometimes seemed the only thing that had kept him sane.

He couldn't swim against the rip but if he headed diagonally across he might collide with...with what he hoped to find. That slip of crimson.

He cast one long look at the pool, trying to judge where he'd last seen that flash of crimson.

He put his head down and swam.

Was she nuts? Trying to swim in this surf? But if she got past the breakers she only had the rip to contend with. She could deal with the rip, she thought. She knew enough not to panic. The guy on the boat would have seen her. If she could reach Sefina and hold on to her, she could tread water until help came.

Even if the guy hadn't seen her, she was due to go on duty at midday. The staff knew she'd gone for a walk on the beach. If she didn't return they'd come down and find Bugsy, find her clothes... Once the rip dragged her out, she could tread water and hope...

Yeah, very safe, she thought grimly as she dived through another wave. *Not.*

What would she do if she reached them? The lifeguard part of her was already playing out scenarios.

The quickest way to kill yourself is to put yourself within reach of someone who's drowning. They'll pull you down as they try to save themselves.

There was her instructor again.

Sefina wouldn't try to save herself, though. Sefina wanted to die.

Sefina...

She'd known how unhappy the girl was, but in the post-cyclone chaos all Hettie had been able to give the young woman had been swift hugs between periods of imperative medical need. She'd promised her she was safe in the hospital. She'd promised they'd sort things out when things had settled.

She hadn't realised time had been so achingly short.

Hettie surfaced from the last breaker and looked around wildly. The rip was stronger than she'd thought. Maybe she'd missed them.

And then she saw someone else in the water, swimming strongly across the rip. The guy from the boat?

There went her source of help if she got into trouble, she thought grimly. All of them in the water? This was breaking every lifesaving rule, but it was too late to back out now. She was watching the rim of the foam where the deep pool ended and the relative calm began.

There! A sliver of crimson.

She must have shouted because the swimming guy raised his head. She waved and pointed.

He raised a hand in silent acknowledgement and they both put their heads down and swam.

He could see her now, or he could see the swirl of crimson shawl she'd wrapped around her body. If he could just get closer…

The pull of the rip was hauling him backwards. By rights it should've propelled the woman's body towards him.

Was she stuck on the edge of the reef? Had the shawl snagged?

The rocks were too close to the surface for safety. He should stay well clear…

He didn't.

This was crazy. Suicidal. She couldn't swim into the foam. She daren't. As it was, the rip was pulling so hard she was starting to doubt her ability to get herself to safety.

A breaker crashed on the rocks and threw a spray of water, blocking her vision. She could see nothing.

With a sob of fear and frustration she stopped trying and let herself be carried outward.

Free from the foam she could tread water. She could look again.

She could see nothing but white. Nothing…

There! Max's hands had been groping blindly in front of him, but the touch of fabric had him grabbing.

He had her, but she was wedged in rocks. He was being washed by breaker after breaker. He couldn't see. He pulled upwards to take a tighter hold—and a child fell free into his arms.

The child must have been clinging, or tied within the shawl. The rip caught them again and they were tugged outwards.

He had a child in his arms. He had no choice but to let himself go. To ride the rip…

He was pushing the child up, rolling onto his back, trying to get the little one into the air. The water was sweeping…

'Here!'

It was a yell and suddenly someone was beside him. A woman, dark-haired, fierce.

'Give him to me. Help Sefina. Please!'

'You can't hold him.' He didn't even know if the child was alive.

Her face was suddenly inches from his, soaking curls plastered across her eyes, green eyes flashing determination. 'I can. I know what to do. Trust me.'

And what was there in that that made him believe her?

What was there in that that made him thrust the limp little body into her arms and turn once again towards the rocks?

He had to trust her. He had to hope.

Joni was breathing. He'd been limp when he'd been thrust at her, but as she rolled and prepared to breathe for him—yes, she could do it in the water; lifesaver training had been useful—the little one gasped and choked and gasped again.

His eyes were shut, as if he'd simply closed down, ready for death. How many children drowned like this? Thirteen years as a nurse had taught Hettie that when children slipped untended into water they didn't struggle. They drowned silently.

Somehow, though, despite not fighting, Joni must have

breathed enough air to survive. As she touched his mouth with her lips he gasped and opened his eyes.

'Joni.' She managed to get his name out, even though she was fighting for breath herself. 'It's okay. Let's get you to the beach.'

His huge brown eyes stared upwards wildly. Joni was fifteen months old, a chubby toddler with beautiful coffee-coloured skin and a tangle of dark curls. He was part islander, part...

Well, that was the problem, Hettie thought, her heart clenching in fear for his mother.

She couldn't do anything for Sefina, though. The sailor—Max?—had handed her Joni and she had to care for him.

Where was he now? she wondered as she trod water. Her first impressions had been of strength, determination, resolution. His face had been almost impassive.

He'd need strength and more if he was swimming back against the reef. The risks...

She couldn't think of him now. Her attention had to be on keeping Joni safe.

Keeping them both safe?

She cupped her hand around Joni's chin and started sidestroking, as hard and fast as she could, willing him to stay limp. The rip was still a problem. Getting back to the beach was impossible. The boat was too close to the breakers, but the atoll at the end of the reef might just be possible. If she could just reach the rocks...

Blessedly Joni stayed limp. *It must be shock*, she thought as she fought the current, but she was thankful for it. He lay still while she towed.

But the rip was strong. She was fighting for breath herself, kicking, using every last scrap of strength she had, but she couldn't do it. She couldn't reach the atoll. It was so near and yet so far.

If she could just keep floating, someone would help, she thought. If she rode the rip out, if she could hold on to Joni...

But if he struggled...

She had no choice. The rip was too strong to fight.

She held him as far out of the water as she could and let herself be carried out to sea.

He had her. For what it was worth, he had her, but she was dead. He could see the head injury. He could see the way her head floated limply.

She must have crashed onto the rocks, he thought. She'd stepped straight down instead of diving outwards. Death would have been instantaneous. It had been a miracle that the child had stayed with her.

He had her free of the reef, but what to do now? He couldn't get her to the beach. There was no way he could fight the rip. It was carrying them out fast, towards the atoll. Did he have enough strength to get them both there?

By himself there'd be no problem, but holding this woman...

He couldn't.

She was dead. Let her go.

He couldn't do that, either. A part of him was still standing at his son's gravesite.

A part of him was remembering burying his wife, all those years ago.

Somewhere, someone loved this woman. To not have a chance to say goodbye... It would have killed him.

Holding on to her might kill him. He couldn't keep fighting for both of them.

Despite the strength of the rip, the water he was in was relatively calm. He was fighting to get across the current but he paused for a moment in his fight to get a bearing. To see...

And what he saw made him rethink everything. The woman he'd given the child to still held him, but they were drifting fast, so fast they'd miss the atoll. They were being pulled to the open sea.

The woman didn't seem to be panicking. She had the child in the classic lifesaver hold. She seemed to know her stuff, but she wasn't strong enough. In minutes she'd be past the atoll and she'd be gone.

A woman and a child, struggling for life.

A woman in his arms, for whom life was over.

Triage. Blessedly it slammed back. For just a moment he was a junior doctor again in an emergency room, faced with the decision of which patient to treat first.

No choice.

He gave himself a fraction of a second, a moment where he tugged the woman's body around and faced her. He memorised everything about her so he could describe her, and then, in an aching, tearing gesture that seemed to rip something deep inside, he touched her face. It was a gesture of blessing, a gesture of farewell.

It was all he could do.

He let her go.

She'd never reach it. Her legs simply weren't strong enough to kick against the current.

She was so near and yet so far. She was being pulled within thirty yards of the atoll and yet she didn't have the strength to fight.

If she was swept out… If Max didn't make it… How long before they could expect help?

The child in her arms twisted unexpectedly and she almost lost him. She fought for a stronger hold but suddenly he was fighting her.

'Joni, hush. Joni, stay still…'

But he wasn't listening, wasn't hearing. Who knew what he was thinking?

She was being swept…

And then, blessedly, she was being grabbed herself by the shoulders from behind. She was being held with the swift, sure strength of someone who'd been trained, who knew how to gain control.

Max?

'Let me take him.' It was an order, a curt command that brooked no opposition. 'Get yourself to the atoll.'

'You can't.'

'You're done,' he said, and she knew she was.

'S-Sefina?'

'She's dead. We can't do anything for her. Go. I'm right behind you.'

And Joni was taken from her arms.

Relieving her of her load should have made her lighter. Free. Instead, stupidly, she wanted to sink. She hadn't known how exhausted she was until the load had been lifted.

'Swim,' Max yelled. 'We haven't done this for nothing. Swim, damn you, now.'

She swam.

He could do this. He would do this.

Too many deaths…

It was three short weeks since he'd buried his son. The waste was all around him, and the anger.

Maybe it was Christopher who gave him strength. Who knew?

'Keep still,' he growled, as the little boy struggled. There was no time for reassurance. No time for comfort. But it seemed to work.

The little boy subsided. His body seemed to go limp but

he reached up and tucked a fist against Max's throat. As if checking his pulse?

'Yeah, I'm alive,' Max muttered grimly, as he started kicking again against the rip. 'And so are you. Let's keep it that way.'

Rocks. The atoll was tiny but she'd made it. The last few yards across the rip had taken every ounce of her strength, but she'd done it.

She'd had to do it. If Max and Joni were swept out, someone had to raise the alarm.

She wasn't in any position to raise any alarm right now. It was as much as she could do to climb onto the rocks.

She knew this place. She'd swum out here in good weather. She knew the footholds but her legs didn't want to work. They'd turned to jelly, but somehow she made them push her up the few short steps to the relatively flat rock that formed the atoll's tiny plateau.

Then she sank to her knees.

She wanted—quite badly—to be sick, but she fought it down with a fierceness born of desperation. How many times in an emergency room had she felt this same appalling gut-wrench, at waste, at loss of life, at life-changing injuries? But her training had taught her not to faint, not to throw up, until after a crisis was past. Until she wasn't needed.

There was a crisis now, but what could she do? She wasn't in an emergency room. She wasn't being a professional.

She was sitting on a tiny rocky outcrop, while out there a sailor fought for a toddler's life.

Was he Max Lockhart?

More importantly, desperately more importantly, where was he? She hadn't been able to look back while she'd fought to get here, but now…

Max…Joni…

She was a strong swimmer but she hadn't been able to fight the rip.

Please… She was saying it over and over, pleading with whomever was prepared to listen. For Joni. For the unknown guy who was risking his life…

Was he Max? Father of Caroline? Owner of this entire island?

Max Lockhart, come home to claim his rightful heritage?

Max Lockhart, risking his life to save one of the islanders who scorned him?

So much pain…

If he died now, how could she explain it to Caroline? For the last three days, when the cyclone had veered savagely and unexpectedly across the path of any boat making its way here from Cairns, Hettie's fellow nurse had lost contact with her father. She'd been going crazy.

How could she tell her he'd been so near, and was now lost? With the child?

Or not. She'd been staring east, thinking that, if anything, he'd be riding the rip, but suddenly she saw him. He was south of the atoll. He must have been swept past but somehow managed to get himself out of the rip's pull. Now he was stroking the last few yards to the rocks.

He still had Joni.

She'd been out of the water now for five minutes. She had her breath back. Blessedly, she could help. She clambered down over the rocks, heading out into the shallows, reaching for Joni.

She had him. They had him.

Safe?

CHAPTER TWO

FOR A WHILE they were too exhausted to speak. They were too exhausted to do anything but lie on the rocks, Joni somehow safe between them.

The little boy was silent, passive...past shock? Maybe she was, too, and as she looked at Max collapsed beside them she thought, *That makes three.*

'S-Sefina,' she whispered.

'Neck,' he managed, and it was enough to tell her what she needed to know.

Oh, God, she should have...

Should have what? Cradled Sefina yesterday as she was cradling Joni now?

Yes, if that's what it would have taken.

If this had happened at a normal time... But it hadn't. Sefina had been admitted into hospital, bashed almost to the point of death, while the cyclone had been building. With the cyclone bearing down on them Hettie hadn't had time to do more than tend to the girl's physical needs.

Afterwards, when there'd been time to take stock and question her, Keanu, the island doctor on duty, had contacted the police. 'I want her husband brought in. With the extent of these injuries it's lucky he didn't kill her.'

It's lucky he didn't kill her...

She remembered Keanu's words and her breath caught on a sob.

Hettie de Lacey was a professional. She didn't cry. She held herself to herself. She coped with any type of trauma her job threw at her.

But she sobbed now, just once, a great heaving gulp that shook her entire body. And then somehow she pulled herself back together. Almost.

Max's arm came over her, over Joni, enfolding them both, and she needed it. She needed his touch.

'You're safe,' he told her. 'And the little one's safe.' And then he added, 'Keep it together. For now, we're all he has.'

It was a reminder. It wasn't a rebuke, though. It was just a fact. She'd been terrified, she was shocked and exhausted, and she still had to come to terms with what had happened, but the child between them had to come first.

And Max himself… He'd swum over those rocks. Over that coral…

She took a couple of deep breaths and managed to sit up. The sun was full out. The storm of the past days was almost gone. Apart from the spray blasting the headland and the massive breakers heading for shore, this could be just a normal day in paradise.

Wildfire Island. The M'Langi isles. This was surely one of the most beautiful places in the world.

The world would somehow settle.

She gathered Joni into her arms and held him tight, crooning softly into his wet curls. He was still wearing a sodden hospital-issue nappy and a T-shirt one of the nurses had found for him in the emergency supplies. It read, incongruously, 'My grandma went to London and all she brought me back was this T-shirt'.

It was totally inappropriate. Joni didn't have a grandma, or not one who'd acknowledge him.

Max had allowed himself a couple of moments of lying

full length in the sun, as if he needed its warmth. Of course he did. They all did. But now he, too, pushed himself to sitting, and for the first time she saw his legs.

They'd been slashed on the coral. He had grazes running from groin to toe, as if the sea had dragged him straight across the rocks.

What cost, to try and save Sefina?

He'd saved Joni.

'I never could have got him here,' she whispered, still holding him tight. The toddler was curled into her, as if her body was his only protection from the outside world. 'I never could have saved him without you.'

'Do you know…? Do you know who he is?' Max asked.

'His name is Joni Dason. His mother's name is…was Sefina.'

'A friend?' He was watching her face. 'She was your friend?'

'I… A patient.' And then she hesitated. 'But I was present at Joni's birth. Maybe I was…Sefina's friend. Maybe I'm the only…'

And then she stopped. She couldn't go on.

'I'm Max Lockhart,' Max said, and she managed to nod, grateful to be deflected back to his business rather than having to dwell on her shock and grief.

'I guessed as much when I saw your yacht. Caroline will be so relieved. She's been out of her mind with worry.'

'My boat rolled. I lost my radio and phone three days ago. Everything that could be damaged by water was damaged.'

'So you've been sitting out here, waiting for someone to notice you?'

'I reached the island last night. It was too risky to try for the harbour, and frankly I wasn't going to push my luck heading to one of the outer islands. So, yes, I've been here overnight but no one's noticed.'

'I noticed.'

'Thank you. You are?'

'Hettie de Lacey. Charge nurse at Wildfire.'

'I'm pleased to meet you, Hettie.' He hesitated and then went on. 'I'm very pleased to meet you. Without both of us… Well, we did the best we could.'

'You're injured. Those cuts need attention.'

'They do,' he agreed. 'I need disinfectant to avoid infection, but the alternative…'

'You never would have saved Joni without swimming over the coral,' she whispered, and once again she buried her face in the little boy's hair. 'Thank you.'

'I would have…I so wanted…'

'Yes,' she said gently. 'But she jumped too close to the rocks for either of us to do anything.'

'Depression?'

'Abuse. A bully for a husband. Despair.'

The bleakness in her voice must have been obvious. He reached out to her then, the merest hint of a touch, a trace of a strong hand brushing her cheek, and why it had the power to ground her, to feed her strength, she didn't know.

Max Lockhart was a big man, in his forties, she guessed, his deep black hair tinged with silver, his strongly boned face etched with life lines. His grey eyes were deep-set and creased at the edges, from weather, from sun, from…life? Even in his boxers, covered with abrasions, he looked… distinguished.

She knew about this man. He'd lost his wife over twenty years ago and he'd just lost his son. Caroline's twin.

'I'm sorry about Christopher,' she said gently, still holding Joni tight, as if holding him could protect him from the horrors around him.

'Caroline told you?'

'That her twin—your son—died three weeks ago? Yes. Caroline and I are fairly…close. She flew to Sydney for the funeral. We thought…we thought you might have come back with her.'

'There was too much to do. There was financial stuff to do with the island. To do with my brother. Business affairs have been on the backburner as Christopher neared the end, but once he was gone they had to be attended to. And then…'

'You thought it might be a good idea to sail out here?'

'I needed a break,' he said simply. 'Time to get myself together. No one warned me of cyclones.'

'It's the tropics,' she said simply. 'Here be dragons.'

'Don't I know it!'

'But we're glad you're back.'

That got her a hard look.

Max Lockhart had inherited the whole of Wildfire Island on the death of his father. The stories of the Lockharts were legion in this place. Max himself had hardly visited the island over the past twenty years, but his brother's presence had made up for it.

Ian Lockhart had bled the island for all it was worth. He'd finally fled three months ago, leaving debt, destruction and despair…

Ian Lockhart. The hatred he'd caused…

She hugged the child in her arms tighter, as if she could somehow keep protecting him.

How could she?

The sun was getting hotter. She was starting to get sunburnt. Sunburn on top of everything else?

She was wearing knickers and bra. But they were her best knickers and bra, though, she thought with sudden dumb gratitude that today of all days she'd decided to wear her matching lace bra and panties.

They were a lot more elegant than the boxers Max was wearing. His boxers were old, faded, and they now sported a rip that made them borderline useless.

'You needn't look,' Max said, and she flashed a look up at him and found he was smiling. And in return she managed a smile back.

Humour… It was a tool used the world over by medical staff, often in the most appalling circumstances. Where laypeople might collapse under strain, staff in emergency departments used humour to deflect despair.

Sometimes you laughed or you broke down, as simple as that, and right now she needed, quite desperately, not to break down. Max was a surgeon, she thought gratefully. Medical. Her tribe. He knew the drill.

'My knickers are more respectable than your knickers,' she said primly, and he choked.

'What? Your knickers are two inches of pink lace.'

'And they don't have a hole in them right where they shouldn't have a hole,' she threw back at him, and he glanced down at himself and swore. And did some fast adjusting.

'Dr Lockhart's rude,' she told Joni, snuggling him some more, but the little boy was drifting towards sleep. Good, she thought. Children had their own defences.

'My yacht seems to be escaping,' Max said, and she glanced back towards the reef.

It was, indeed, escaping. The anchor hadn't gripped the sand. The yacht was now caught in the rip and heading out to sea.

'One of the fishermen will follow it,' she told him. 'The rip's easy to read. They'll figure where it goes.'

'It'd be good to get to it now.'

'What could a yacht have that a good rock doesn't provide?' she demanded, feigning astonishment. And then she looked at his legs. 'Except maybe disinfectant and dressings. And sunburn cream.'

'And maybe a good strong rum,' he added.

'Trapped on an island with a sailor and a bottle of rum?

I don't think so.' She was waffling but strangely it helped. It was okay to be silly.

Silliness helped block the thought of what had to be faced. Of Sefina's body drifting out to sea…

'Tell me about yourself,' Max said, and she realised he was trying to block things out, too.

'What's to tell?' She shrugged. 'I'm Hettie. I'm charge nurse here. I'm thirty-five years old. I came to Wildfire eight years ago and I've been here ever since. I gather you've been here once or twice while I've been based here, but it must have coincided with my breaks off the island.'

'Where did you learn to swim?'

'Sydney. Bondi.'

'The way you swim… You trained as a lifesaver?'

'I joined as a Nipper, a trainee lifesaver, when I was six.' The surf scene at Bondi had been her tribe then. 'How did you know?'

'I saw how you took Joni from me,' he reminded her. 'All the right moves.'

'You were a Nipper, too?'

'We didn't have Nippers on Wildfire. I did have an aunt, though. Aunt Dotty. She knew the kids on the island spent their spare time doing crazier and crazier dives. I've dived off this headland more times than you've had hot dinners. We reckoned we knew the risks but Dotty said if I was going to take risks I'd be trained to take risks. So, like you, aged six I was out in the bay, learning the right way to save myself and to save others.' He shrugged. 'But until today I've never had to save anyone.'

'You are a surgeon, though,' she said gently, looking to deflect the bleakness. 'I imagine you save lots and lots.'

He smiled at that and she thought, *He has such a gentle smile*. For a big man…his smile lit his face. It made him seem younger.

'Lots and lots,' he agreed. 'If I count every appendix…'

'You should.'

'Then it's lots and lots and lots. How about you?'

'Can I count every time I put antiseptic cream on a coral graze?'

'Be my guest.'

'Then it's lots and lots and lots and lots and lots.'

And he grinned. 'You win.'

'Thank you,' she managed. 'It takes a big surgeon to admit we nurses have a place.'

'I've never differentiated. Doctors, nurses, even the ladies who do the flowers in the hospital wards and take a moment to talk... Just a moment can make a difference.'

And she closed her eyes.

'Yes, it can,' she whispered. 'I wish...oh, I wish...'

He'd stuffed it. Somehow they'd lightened the mood but suddenly it was right back with them. The greyness. The moment he'd said the words he'd seen the pain.

'What?'

Her eyes stayed closed. The little boy in her arms was deeply asleep now, cradled against her, secure for the moment against the horrors that had happened around him.

'What?' he said again, and she took a deep breath and opened her eyes again.

'I didn't have a moment,' she said simply. 'That'll stay with me for the rest of my life.'

'Meaning?'

'Meaning Sefina was brought into hospital just before the cyclone. Ruptured spleen. Concussion. Multiple abrasions and lacerations. Her husband had beaten her to unconsciousness. Sefina's not from M'Langi—she came here eighteen months ago from Fiji. Pregnant. Rumour is that... Joni's father...brought her here and paid Louis to marry her. Louis's an oaf. He'd do anything for money and he's treated her terribly. She's always been isolated and ashamed, and Louis keeps her that way.'

There was a moment's silence while he took that on board, and somehow during that moment he felt the beginnings of sick dismay. Surely it couldn't be justified, but once he'd thought of it he had to ask.

'So Joni's father…' he ventured, and she tilted her chin and met his gaze square on.

'He's not an islander.'

'Who?'

'Do I need to tell you?'

And he got it. He looked down at the little boy cradled in Hettie's arms. His skin wasn't as dark as the islanders'. His features…

His heart seemed to sag in his chest as certainty hit. 'My brother? Ian? He's his?' How had he made his voice work?

'Yes,' she said, because there was no answer to give other than the truth. 'Sefina is… Sefina *was* a Fijian islander. As far as I can gather, Ian stayed there for a while. He got her pregnant and she was kicked out of home. In what was a surprising bout of conscience for Ian, he brought her here. He paid Louis to marry her and he gave her a monthly allowance, which Louis promptly drank. But a few weeks ago the money stopped and Louis took his anger out on Sefina. The day before the cyclone things reached a crisis point. They were living out on Atangi. We flew her across to Wildfire, to hospital, but then the storm hit…and I didn't have that moment…'

'I'm sure you did your best.' It was a trite thing to say and he saw a flash of anger in response.

'She needed more.'

'She had no one else?'

'You need to understand. She was an outsider. She was pregnant by… And I'm sorry about this—but she was pregnant by a man the islanders have cause to hate. She married an oaf. Her mother-in-law wouldn't have anything to do with her, and vilified anyone who did. And the only person responsible—your brother—is now missing.'

'He's dead,' he said, and her gaze jerked to his.

'Dead?'

'That's another reason I couldn't get back here until now. Ian's been gambling—heavily. Unknown to me he racked up debts that'd make your eyes water. That's why he's bled the island dry. And that's why…well, his body was found two weeks ago, in Monaco. Who knows the whys or where-fores? The police are interested. I'm…not.'

There was a long, long silence.

She was restful, this woman, Max thought. Where others might have exclaimed, demanded details, expressed shock, disgust or horror, Hettie simply hugged the child in her arms a little tighter.

She was…beautiful, he thought suddenly.

Until now, despite the lacy knickers and bra, despite the attempt at humour, she'd seemed a colleague. A part of the trauma and the tragedy. Now, suddenly, she seemed more.

She was slight, five feet four or five. Her body was tanned and trim, and the lacy lingerie showed it off to perfection.

Her dark hair was still sodden. Her curls were forming wet spirals to frame her face.

Thirty-five, she'd said, and he might have guessed younger, apart from the life lines around her shadowed green eyes.

Life lines? Care lines? She'd cared about Sefina, he thought. She was caring about Joni.

Her body was curved around him now, protective, a lioness protective of her cub. Everything about her said, *You mess with this little one, you mess with me.*

His…nephew?

'You realise he's yours now,' she whispered at last into the stillness, and the words were like a knife, stabbing across the silence.

'What…?'

'This little boy is a Lockhart,' she said, deeply and evenly. 'The M'Langi islanders look after their own. Joni's not their own. He never has been. He was the child of two outsiders, and the fact that an oaf of an islander was paid to marry his mother doesn't make him belong. The islanders have one rule, which is inviolate. Family lines cross and intercross through the islands, but, no matter how distant, family is everything. Children can never be orphaned. The word "orphan" can't be translated into the M'Langi language.'

'What are you saying?' There was an abyss suddenly yawning before him, an abyss so huge he could hardly take it in.

She shrugged. 'It's simple,' she said softly. 'According to the M'Langi tradition, this little one isn't an orphan, Dr Lockhart. This little boy is yours.'

He had complications crowding in from all sides but suddenly they were nothing compared to this one.

Ian had had a son.

The boy didn't look like Ian, he thought. He had the beautiful skin colour of the Fijians but lighter. His dark hair wasn't as tightly curled.

He was still sleeping, his face nestled against Hettie's breast. Max could only see his profile, but suddenly…

It was a hint, a shade, a fleeting impression, but suddenly Max saw his mother in Joni.

And a hint of his own children. Caroline, twenty-six years old, due to be married next week to the man she loved.

Christopher, buried three weeks ago.

Christopher, his son.

This little boy is yours...

How could he begin to get his head around it? He couldn't. Every sense was recoiling.

He'd loathed Ian. Born of gentle parents, raised on this island with love and tenderness... There'd never been a reason why Ian should have turned out as he had, but he'd been the sort of kid who'd pulled wings off flies. He'd been expelled from three schools. He'd bummed around the world until his parents' money had dried up.

Max thought back to the time, a few years back, when Ian had come to see him in Sydney.

'I'm broke,' he'd said, honestly and humbly. 'I've spent the money Mum and Dad left me and I can't take the lifestyle I've been living anymore. I need to go back to Wildfire. Let me manage the place for you, bro. I swear I'll do a good job. We both know it's getting run-down and you don't have time to be there yourself.'

It was hope rather than trust that had made him agree, Max thought grimly. That and desperation. It had been true; the island had needed a manager. But Max had needed to be in Sydney. Christopher had been born with cerebral palsy and he'd lurched from one health crisis to another. Max had been trying to hold down a job as head of surgery at Sydney Central, feeding as much money as he could back into the island's medical services. Caroline, too... Well, his daughter had always received less attention than she'd needed or deserved.

If Ian could indeed take some of the responsibility...

Okay, he'd been naive, gullible, stupid to trust. That trust was coming home to roost now, and then some. He was having to face Ian's appalling dishonesty.

But facing this...

This little boy is yours...

His son was dead. How could he face this?

'You don't need to think about it now,' Hettie was saying gently, as if she guessed the body blow she'd dealt him. 'We'll work something out.'

'We?'

'I love Joni,' she said simply. 'I'm not going to hand him over until I'm sure you want him.'

'How can you love him?'

Her eyes suddenly turned troubled, even a little confused, as if she wasn't quite sure of what she was feeling herself. 'He has no one,' she said, tentatively now. 'His mother trusted me and depended on me. I was there at his birth.' She took a deep breath. 'Maybe...until you're ready to accept your responsibilities, I can take care of him for you.'

'My responsibility...'

'Whatever,' she said hastily. 'Until there's another alternative, I seem to be all he has. He needs someone. He has me.'

'You're not saying you'll take him on?'

'I'm not saying anything,' she whispered, and once again her lips touched the little one's hair. 'All I'm saying is that for now I'm holding him and I'm not letting go. Oh, and, Max...'

'Yes?'

'There are people on the beach,' she said. 'Waving. I think rescue is at hand. Time to get back to the real world.'

He glanced around sharply. There were, indeed, people on the beach.

'Caroline will be overjoyed,' Hettie told him. 'Your daughter. Your family.'

And there was something in the way she said it...

He knew nothing about her, he realised. Nothing at all. He was a Lockhart. The islanders, including Hettie, must know almost everything there was to know about him. But Hettie? He knew nothing about her other than she was holding…

His son?

CHAPTER THREE

THE CORAL CUTS on Max's legs were treated by his about-to-be son-in-law. Keanu, the island doctor Max's daughter was about to marry, greeted him with overwhelming relief, but was now insisting Max submit to his care.

It seemed Sam, the island's chief medical officer, had had to fly out that morning, transporting an urgent case to the mainland. 'We're always short on medical staff,' Keanu told him, 'so you're stuck with me. But I think we can get away with no stitches. Now, anaesthetic?'

'The last thing I need is a general anaesthetic,' Max growled. 'And no blocks. I've wasted enough of my time here. I don't intend to lie round, waiting for anaesthetic to wear off. Keanu, leave it. I can clean them myself.'

'So who'll explain to Caroline that you can't give her away because your legs are infected?' Keanu demanded. 'Not me. You'll let me clean them properly.'

So he had no choice. He lay back and thought about biting bullets as Keanu cleaned, disinfected and dressed his cuts.

Thankfully the cuts were on his legs and not his face, he thought. He might still manage to look okay at Caroline's wedding.

'You have no idea how relieved she'll be when she finds you're here,' Keanu told him as he worked. 'She's been out at a clinic at Atangi but she's due back any time now. Our wedding plans are all in order and now she has her dad. We were starting to think we'd have to send Bugsy down the aisle in your place.'

'Bugsy…'

'The dog,' Keanu said briefly, inspecting a graze that almost qualified as a cut. 'This one's nasty. Hold your breath for a bit, there's a bit of muck stuck in here.'

Max held his breath. Maybe an anaesthetic wouldn't have been such a bad idea.

'Dog,' he said at last when he could concentrate on anything other than pain.

'Bugsy, the golden retriever. He's responsible for us finding you so fast. Hettie left him on the beach. Normally Bugsy would loll around, waiting for her to come out of the water, or go for a swim himself, but he must have figured something was wrong. He came haring up to the hospital, soaking wet. We were already worried about Sefina and Joni. Sefina had discharged herself but we knew she couldn't go home, so when Bugsy appeared looking desperate, running back and forth to the beginning of the path to Sunset Beach, and we couldn't find Hettie, we put two and two together and figured we needed to investigate.'

'You let Sefina discharge herself?'

'Junior nurse,' Keanu said grimly. 'But it wasn't her fault. Short of holding Sefina by force, which was impossible, there wasn't a lot she could do when Sefina decided to leave. She let us know as soon as she could, and then Bugsy arrived.' He hesitated. 'Bugsy's a shared dog, devoted to all of us. He officially belongs to one of our fly in, fly out doctors, but Maddie's on maternity leave right now so Bugsy's main caregiver is Hettie.'

'Hettie has…no one else?'

Keanu cast him a sharp look. 'Hettie has everyone on the island.'

'Is that a warning?'

There was a moment's silence, and then Keanu gave a reluctant shrug. 'I know you're not Ian,' he conceded. 'I need to keep reminding the islanders.'

'Meaning they think if I was Ian I couldn't be trusted with anything in a skirt.'

'Ian couldn't be trusted with anything at all,' Keanu said bluntly. 'But he was your brother and Hettie tells me he's dead. I'm sorry.'

'Are you? Will anyone on this island be sorry?'

'No,' Keanu admitted bluntly. 'Maybe Sefina might have mourned him, but now...' He shrugged again, and then went back to focussing on Max's knee. 'Maybe a stitch here...'

'Steri-Strips,' Max growled. 'A scar or two won't hurt.'

'You can always cover it with pantyhose,' Keanu said, and grinned. 'It's good to have you home, Max. You've done so much for the island.' And then he glanced up as the door opened a crack. 'Hettie. Come in. That is, if Dr Lockhart doesn't mind you seeing his bare legs.'

'I saw a lot more than his legs out in the water,' Hettie retorted. 'And there's nothing our Dr Lockhart has that I haven't seen a thousand times before.'

'Shall we let the lady in?' Keanu asked.

And Max thought, *What the heck?* It was true, Hettie was a professional. Right now, he was a patient, she was a nurse. There was no reason he should feel odd at the idea of her seeing him dressed in a hospital gown with bare legs.

'Sure,' he growled, and Hettie popped in, smiling. It was a professional smile, he thought, just right, nurse greeting patient. She was in nurse's uniform, blue pants and baggy blue top. Her curls were caught back in a simple ponytail.

She looked younger than she'd looked on the atoll, he thought, and then he thought... She looked lovely?

She wasn't beautiful in the classical sense, he conceded.

Her nose was too snub, her cheeks were strong-boned, and her mouth was maybe too generous to be termed lovely.

She was wearing no make-up.

He still thought she looked beautiful.

'How's Joni?' Keanu asked, before Max could form the same question, and Hettie smiled, albeit sadly.

'Clean and dry and fast asleep in the kids' ward. He's the only occupant, now that any kids with minor injuries after the storm have gone home. I left Bugsy asleep beside his cot.'

'The dog?' Max stared. What sort of a hospital let dogs stay in the children's ward?

'We have monitors,' Hettie told him. 'The moment Joni stirs I'll be in there, but the first thing he'll see when he wakes will be Bugsy. Bugsy's a friend, and Joni...well, Joni needs all the friends he can get.'

'What will you do with him?' Keanu asked. Keanu was still cleaning. Hettie had moved automatically to assist, handing swabs, organising disinfectant. They were both focussed on Max's legs, which was disconcerting, to say the least.

The question hung and suddenly Max realised Keanu was talking to *him*.

What will you do with him?

'He's not mine to do anything with,' Max growled, and Keanu raised his brows.

'That's not what the islanders think.'

'They'll think he's yours,' Hettie said. 'I told you. He's your brother's child, your brother's dead, therefore he's your family. You don't want him?'

'Why would I want him?'

'Goodness knows,' Keanu said, and kept on working. It was disconcerting, to say the least, to be talking to two heads bent over his legs—plus talking about a child he'd only just learned existed. 'Family dynasty or something?' Keanu suggested. 'He is a Lockhart.'

'I have no proof he's a Lockhart.'

'You don't, do you?' Hettie was concentrating—fiercely, he thought—on his legs, and yet he could tell that her thoughts were elsewhere. On a little boy in the kids' ward. 'He could be anyone's.'

Yeah, but he looked like a Lockhart.

'Is there any sort of Child Welfare in the M'Langi group?' he asked.

'We don't need Child Welfare,' Hettie snapped, and Keanu cast her a surprised look. But then he shrugged and addressed Max.

'We don't normally need Child Welfare,' Keanu agreed. 'The islanders usually look after their own, but Joni's an exception. He's an outsider.'

'He's not an outsider. He belongs here, and if Max won't look after him, I will.' Hettie murmured the words almost to herself, but for a murmur it had power. The words were almost like a vow.

They made Keanu pause. The doctor stood back from the table and stared at Hettie, who was still looking at Max's legs fiercely.

'What the…? Het, are you suggesting you adopt him?'

'If no one else claims him, yes.'

'You can't decide that now.'

'I have decided. If his family doesn't want him, I do. I mean it. Keanu, do you want to keep cleaning or will I take over?'

Keanu stared at her for a moment longer and then silently went back to cleaning. There was a tense stillness, broken only by the sound of tiny chinks of coral hitting the kidney basin.

His legs really were a mess but, then, everything was a

mess, Max thought grimly. So what was new? When hadn't life been a mess?

For just a moment, this morning, watching the sun rise, watching the fish darting in and out of the water, watching a pod of dolphins give chase, he'd given himself time out. He'd thought, What if…?

What if he finally let himself be free?

Twenty-six years ago his wife had died on this island, giving birth to twins. He and Ellie had been babies themselves, barely twenty.

He'd met Ellie at university. They'd both been arts students, surrounded by friends, high on life. They'd fallen in love and when they'd discovered a baby was on the way they'd accepted the pregnancy with all the insouciance of youth.

'Maybe it's not a mistake,' Ellie had told him. 'Maybe we're meant to be a family.' The knowledge that she'd been carrying twins had only added to their feeling of excitement.

'How do you feel about marrying on Wildfire?' he'd asked, and she'd been ecstatic.

'The Lockhart family home? Your real-life island? Max, can we?'

They could, but not until summer vacation. They'd travelled to the island as soon as exams had ended. Ellie had been thirty-two weeks pregnant, excited about her pregnancy, excited about her sheer bulk.

He remembered their welcome. His mother had been wild with joy at their homecoming. His father had been gravely pleased that his son had found someone so beautiful to wed. No one had worried that Ellie had been pregnant at the ceremony. After all, what trouble could come to this truly blessed couple?

No one had worried that twin pregnancies sometimes spelled trouble.

He remembered his brother the night before the wedding. Ian had been blind drunk, toasting him for the hundredth time. They'd lit a campfire on the beach. Ian had waved his glass towards the island and then out at the stars hanging bright and low over the ocean.

'Here's to us, bro. We've got it all.'

He'd even been stupid enough to agree. The next day, he'd married. They'd danced into the small hours.

Ellie had gone into labour that night.

There had been no medical centre on the island then. They'd faced an agonising wait for medical evacuation, while Ellie had bled and bled.

She'd died before help arrived. The twins, Caroline and Christopher, had survived, but prematurity and birth trauma meant Christopher would be burdened with cerebral palsy for the rest of his life.

Christopher. His son.

'Family dynasty or something? He is a Lockhart.'

No. Christopher was his son, he thought grimly. Not some child called Joni. How could he ever want another child?

He closed his eyes and Keanu paused again.

'If this is hurting too much, let me knock you out.'

'Just go for it.'

There was silence as Keanu started work again. Undercurrents were everywhere, Max thought, gritting his teeth against the pain.

'Het, you won't be able to just…adopt him,' Keanu said at last into the stillness. 'You'll have to go through channels. If it's really what you want then we'll support you, but you're not deciding this today. This suggestion seems right out of the blue. It's a huge decision and there are legal channels to be dealt with. You know we come under Australian legal jurisdiction. If Joni doesn't have relatives on the island…' Here he cast a quick glance at Max. 'As the island's acting medical director, I'll need to report Sefina's death and Joni's status to the mainland authorities. A kid like Joni…there'd be mainland couples lined up to adopt a toddler like him. You'll need to plead some special case to be allowed to keep him.'

'Sefina was my friend,' Hettie told him.

'Sefina was your patient.'

'I let her down.'

'We all let her down but her death is not our fault. I'm not about to let a guilty conscience force you into adoption.'

'I'm not being forced.'

'Why would you want to adopt?' Max asked, and they both paused in their work, as if they'd forgotten he was there.

Maybe they should have had this discussion without him, Max thought. After all, it had nothing to do with him. Just because it was Ian's child…

This little boy is yours.

No. He wanted nothing to do with Ian's child.

His own son was dead. His daughter was about to be married to the man of her dreams and he might even be free of another responsibility.

All his life he'd accepted the responsibility the Lockharts had carved for themselves through generations of ownership. Every spare cent he'd earned had been ploughed back into this hospital. He'd worked so hard…

But now… In the next couple of days Max would meet the man who'd funded a world's best tropical diseases research facility and tropical resort on Wildfire. Ian had conned a Middle Eastern oil billionaire—a sheikh, no less—into purchasing island land for the resort, but the sale had been built on forged signatures and falsehoods. Island land was held in a Lockhart family trust for perpetuity and Ian had had no power to sell. Amazingly, though, once he'd known the facts, the sheikh had still been prepared to invest, leasing instead of buying. He had seemingly limitless money and resources. He was giving work to the islanders, giving hope, and for the first time since that night before his wedding, twenty-six years ago, Max was feeling a taste of freedom.

Maybe he could walk away from here and never come back.

This little boy is yours. Hettie's words, Keanu's words meant nothing. They couldn't. He did not want any more responsibility.

But finally Hettie was answering his question. 'I want to adopt because I can,' she said. It was as if she'd needed time to work out her answer, but now she had it clear. 'I've spent my life looking out for no one but myself. Sitting out on the atoll this morning, holding Joni, knowing Sefina was dead, it crowded in on me. I give nothing. I love…nothing. If I can have Joni…I will love him, Keanu. I promise.'

'But it won't be up to me,' Keanu told her, giving her a searching look. 'We'll report Sefina's death to the authorities and see what happens.'

'I won't let him leave the island.'

'Het, the islanders won't accept him,' Keanu said gently. 'He's Ian's child and Ian robbed them blind.'

'He'll be my child.'

'Let's see what the authorities say.' Keanu fastened a last dressing on Max's legs. 'There you go, Dr Lockhart. All better. You're free to go.'

Free to go…

It sounded okay to him, Max thought, swinging his legs gingerly from the examination table. Hettie held his arm while he stood, and he had the sense to let her. Lying supine during medical procedures could make anyone dizzy.

And dizziness did come, just a little, but it was enough for him to be grateful for Hettie's support.

She was small and slight. She'd been through an appalling experience, too, and yet he could feel her strength. She was some woman. How many women would have backed up such a morning with heading into work; with continuing to keep going?

With offering to adopt a child?

'Are you okay?' Hettie asked, sounding worried.

She was worried about him?

'I'm fine. Just a bit wobbly.'

'Take your time,' Keanu told him. 'We'll find you a bed in the ward.'

'If you can find me some clothes I'll head up to the house.' His clothes were either in the water or on board the boat. And where was his boat?

'You need someone to keep an eye on you,' Hettie said. 'With those legs, you need care. I'm not sure where Caroline is…'

And, as if on cue, the doors to the theatre swung open. Caroline burst through the doors, looking frantic.

'Dad,' she said as she saw him. 'Oh, Dad…' And she flung herself into his arms and burst into tears.

Hettie stepped back.

'You'll be okay now,' she said softly. 'You're with your family.'

And she walked out and left him with his daughter.

Keanu was waiting as Hettie finished her interview with the local constabulary. He'd protested as she'd donned her nurse's uniform instead of civvies the moment she'd reached the hospital. Now, though, with Max settled with his daughter and Joni asleep, there seemed no reason for her to stay. The hospital on Wildfire had settled to a new norm. Without Sefina.

Hettie could hardly think of Sefina without wanting to be sick. Of all the senseless deaths…

'There's nothing more you can do, Het,' Keanu told her as the policeman left. The young doctor was starting to sound stern. 'You've had an appalling shock. For you and Max to save Joni was little short of miraculous. You need to give your body time to recover. Take Bugsy home with you and sleep.'

'How can I sleep? Keanu, we failed her.'

'The island failed her,' he said. 'The islanders hated Ian Lockhart, and Sefina was someone they could vent that anger on.'

'It wasn't her fault.'

'We all know that. Even the islanders know that. It was only her husband who was overtly cruel and he'll be prosecuted. Now you need to take care of you.'

'I'll stay with Joni.'

'Not on my watch, Het,' he said, even more firmly. 'Joni's a problem we need to solve but not now, not when you're emotionally distraught. If I let you stay with him all the time it'll tear your heart out when he leaves. I don't know where your offer of adoption came from, but it's crazy. You know it is. You haven't had time yet even to absorb the enormity of Sefina's death. So let's be professional. We're taking care of him. Go home.'

'I don't want to.'

'I'll give you something to help you sleep,' he said, as if he hadn't heard her objection, and he took her shoulders and propelled her to the nurses' station. 'But you're signing off now and that's an order.'

It was all very well, following orders, but Hettie needed to work. She was exhausted but work seemed the only way to get the events of the morning out of her head.

She couldn't—but neither could she get rid of this certainty of what she had to do.

She'd tried hard not to get emotionally involved with her patients. Why did she suddenly, fiercely, want to adopt Joni?

Why did she *need* to adopt Joni?

She walked slowly around the lagoon, in no hurry to get to her neat little villa overlooking the water. The island was lush, beautiful, washed with rain. Most of the storm damage had been cleared. A few palms had fallen but tropical rain forest regenerated fast. Soon there'd be nary a scar.

Except Sefina was dead.

Maybe it'd be easier, she thought, if there was a body to bury. To keen over?

It'd be a tiny funeral if the body was ever found. Nobody here had loved Sefina.

No one would love Joni. He was Ian Lockhart's son.

He'd be adopted off the island, she thought bleakly. Here he'd never get over the stigma of being Ian's son. He'd never be accepted.

'I could make him be accepted.' She said it out loud but even as she said it she faced its impossibility. On this island Joni was an illegitimate outsider. He always would be.

'But I want him.'

Why? She sank onto a fallen log and stared sightlessly over the lagoon. Why did she want, so fiercely, to hug Joni to her? To hold?

Her maternal instinct was long dead. Killed by Darryn...

'Oh, get over it.' She rose and stared out at a heron standing one legged at the edge of the water. She often saw this guy here. He was a lone bird.

'And that's what I am, too,' she told herself. 'Today was an aberration. Joni will find himself some lovely parents on the mainland who'll love him to bits. And I...' She took a deep breath. 'I'll take the pills Keanu gave me and go to sleep. And I'll wake up in the morning feeling not maternal at all. I'll feel back to normal.'

But she couldn't stop thinking of Joni.

And, strangely, she couldn't stop thinking of Max. Max, swimming strongly towards her in the water as she felt herself pulled out to sea. Max, risking his life to save a woman he didn't know, almost killing himself in the process. Max, tugging a small child from a dead woman's arms.

A decent Lockhart?

She'd watched his face when he'd told her Sefina was dead. She knew it had almost killed him to release her body, to make the choice to save her son instead.

He'd be feeling sick, too. She knew it.

Would Max stay in hospital for the night? Would Keanu insist he stay, or would he let Caroline take him home to the big house, the homestead owned by the Lockharts for generations?

'So what's that got to do with you?' she demanded of herself. 'You've never had anything to do with the Lockharts.'

Which wasn't quite true. As nurse administrator she'd had conflict after conflict with Ian Lockhart. The funds for the medical administration came from the Australian government, augmented by donations from a trust Max Lockhart had set up when his wife had died. Ian, however, had swaggered onto the island a few years back and had tried to take control. For a while, because of his name, they'd let him sit on the hospital board but pretty soon they'd realised the hospital hadn't been a priority. Equipment had been purchased from the trust but had mysteriously never appeared. If she hadn't been on the ball…

She had been. There'd been an almighty row, she'd threatened to bring in lawyers and she and Ian had hardly spoken after that.

Max looked like his brother.

They were so different…Ian was a con man, out for what he could get, morally empty.

This morning Max Lockhart had risked his life trying to save a woman and her child.

Max had poured money into this island's medical services for years.

Max had mourned his dead wife and had cared for his son until the end.

'Yeah, he's a hero, and he looks great in boxers.' She ran her hand through her hair and her tight ponytail came free, letting her curls cascade to her shoulders. She hauled them back up with something akin to anger.

She was so confused.

No, she thought. What she was feeling was shock. It'd be shock making her thoughts so tumultuous.

'So go home and sleep,' she said out loud. 'You know that's the most sensible thing to do. Go home and stop thinking of Joni. And stop thinking of Max.'

She tried. The pills Keanu had given her put her to sleep but her sleep was full of dreams.

Sefina's body, drifting on the tide.

A little boy, unloved, lying alone in the hospital ward.

Max Lockhart.

Why was he superimposing himself over all the rest?

Despite Keanu's objections, Max discharged himself. 'I have my own home and my daughter's a qualified nurse. She can report in if my condition gets interesting,' he'd told Keanu. So Caroline drove him the short distance to the Lockhart homestead, but once in the jeep a silence fell between Max and his daughter.

Where to start? There'd been silence between them for twenty-six years, he thought grimly. He hadn't treated her fairly and he knew it. He'd had two children. Ninety five per cent of his attention had been taken by Christopher. Caroline had had to fit into the edges.

'Caro,' he started, dubiously, and she flashed him a look that might even have been amusement.

'You're going to say sorry again?'

'There's not a lot else to say. I shouldn't have tried sailing here. Hettie says you were terrified.'

'I was.'

'And...I shouldn't have left you alone for so long.' He had to say it. He'd had no choice, but now that Christopher was dead the ghosts had to be hauled into the open. 'I'm so pleased you and Keanu are together.' Keanu was an island kid, grown up to be a fine doctor. He was loyal, intelligent and courageous. There was no one he'd rather have for a son-in-law, but that Caroline had met him and was marrying him was in no way down to her father. He'd done so little for her.

'Dad, I understand.' They pulled up in front of the homestead. She switched off the ignition but made no move to get out. 'Yes, there were times during my childhood when I resented the time you spent with Christopher, but the older I get the more I understand. You could never have looked after two babies on your own, not with Christopher's needs. And Grandma and Aunt Dotty were wonderful. I had Keanu as a playmate and his mum as our housekeeper. I had this whole island and I had freedom. If you'd taken me to Sydney I'd have had childcare and no one apart from the snatches of time you could spare.'

'I should have spared more.'

'And taken that time from Christopher? How could you?' She put her hand on his and held. 'Dad, you know I loved him. You know how much I wanted him to live—how much I've been hoping a miracle would save him. That last rally, I so hoped... It wasn't to be, but my comfort was that you were there, loving him for me, for us, right to the end. I guess I've accepted now that he was always on borrowed time, but it must have broken your heart, watching him fade. Yet all the while you've supported the medical needs of this island every way you know how. And I know you're blaming yourself for Ian's dishonesty but maybe you had to trust him. Ian was *your* brother, and this was his island, too.'

Redemption? Forgiveness? His daughter was handing it to him, but could he take it? His legs ached. His head hurt. The morning's tragedy hung heavily in his thoughts.

So much tragedy…

'Hey!' Caroline released her seat belt and gave him a hug and then kissed him. 'Don't look like that. Dad, it's over. The new guy investing in the resort is pouring money into the island—did you know he wants to help with the medical facilities, as well? I know there are legal things you have to sort, but they're minor. And, Dad…Christopher's dead. You did everything you could do for him, but now it's over. And I'm marrying the man of my dreams. For the first time in your life you're responsible for nobody, for nothing. You're free, Dad. It's time you shook off the guilt and enjoyed yourself.'

'And Joni?' He said it heavily, as if he couldn't help himself, and maybe he couldn't. 'Joni's a Lockhart. I can't escape that.'

Caroline took a deep breath. 'So he is,' she said gently. 'So I guess he's my cousin. If no one else will take him, maybe Keanu and I could.'

'You can't go into a marriage with someone else's child.'

'Honestly, it's not something I ever planned for,' she said diffidently. 'But if Joni is indeed my cousin… Dad, we may have no choice.'

'That's crazy. The social welfare system works well for orphaned children. Lots of families will want him.'

'Dad, you don't understand.' Caroline put her hand on

his. 'You were born here. You should get it. According to the islanders, Joni's now yours.'

'How can he be mine?' He felt as if a vast leaden weight was descending onto his shoulders. 'Hettie wants him,' he said abruptly, and Caroline's eyes widened.

'Hettie?'

'She wants to adopt him.'

'That's crazy.' She shook her head in disbelief. 'She's shocked. It's been an appalling morning. She'll be devastated by Sefina's death. We're all upset but as for taking him on...'

'Yet you're saying you could take him.'

'It wouldn't work with Hettie,' Caroline said, thinking it through. 'He'd be the illegitimate son of an outsider, with the stigma of Ian as a father to add to it. He'd have no father to watch his back. If Keanu and I adopted him, the islanders would know he's our family. They love Keanu. They'd come to accept him soon enough.'

'But he's my responsibility.' There. He'd said it. The words were heavy and hard, but they were true. Whether he liked it or not, he was the closest kin. To have a situation where his daughter took on that responsibility because he wouldn't...

It made him feel ill, but what was the alternative?

Adoption off the island? It *was* an option, but no one else was seeing it.

'You're tired,' Caroline said at last into the stillness. 'Come into the house. You can have some sandwiches and those nice painkillers Keanu's given you. Then you can sleep until morning. Problems always seem smaller in the morning.'

'I need to visit the mine. I need to talk to—'

'You need to do nothing except sleep,' she said soundly. 'Bed, this instant.'

'Yes, Mum,' he said meekly, and she chuckled and

hugged him, and he thought that at least he was here with his daughter.

But...why was he still thinking of Hettie?

CHAPTER FOUR

SLEEP WAS NOWHERE. At 3:00 a.m. Hettie lay staring into the dark, and ghosts she'd thought were long buried resurfaced and started swirling.

Dawn, long ago, a morning like this one. Breakers hurling in from the east, pounding the beach. The lingering remnants of a vast southerly storm.

Darryn, waking her, exuberant with excitement. He'd organised the press for a photo shoot.

'Come on, babe. The surf's perfect.'

She'd protested, still sleepy, still tired. 'Darryn, the waves are huge. You know the doctor said—'

'Honey, the doctor's just covering himself. Our kid's born to surf. Honest, he'll come out hanging ten. Let's go.'

'I don't want to.' There, she'd said it. 'I'm seven months pregnant. I'm off balance on my board. It's dangerous.'

'You're not turning into a wuss on me. Babe, I married you because you're a surfing legend. The pictures will be awesome. Come on!'

And now, sixteen years on, her hands moved instinctively to her belly.

For sixteen years she'd buried this hunger. Today one little boy had unleashed it to the extent it was threatening to overwhelm her.

She couldn't go back to sleep. She was trying to be logical but logic was nowhere. All she could see when she closed her eyes was Max, in the water, holding his arms out for Joni. Demanding she release him to keep him safe.

She could still feel the wrench as she'd let him go. A little boy who needed her.

How could she let him go again?

This was nonsense. It was emotional fluff. She had no business to be thinking of it.

But she was more than thinking of it. She was tossing back the bedclothes, tugging on jeans and heading for the children's ward.

He was in the bedroom he'd moved into when he'd married.

When he'd been a kid Max had had a small room at the back of the house. From his window he'd been able to see all the way to the sea.

But Caroline had that bedroom now. She'd assumed he'd want to sleep in this big room. This place of ghosts.

He and Ellie had hardly had any time at all here, he thought bleakly. A break from university while they'd planned the wedding, the wedding itself, and then tragedy.

Ellie had given birth in this bed. How could a man sleep in it?

It was history. Twenty-six years of history.

He'd decided to come back now, see Caroline married, sort out the financial affairs with the sheikh who was prepared to pour money into the place and then walk away.

For the first time since the birth of the twins he'd be responsible for nobody.

Except one little boy. Fifteen months old.

A Lockhart.

Caroline had suggested she could take him on. She would, too, he thought. His daughter had a heart big enough to take on all comers. But, like him, she had her whole future ahead of her. She was marrying Keanu.

He couldn't—he wouldn't—ask them to take on Joni.

Hettie, then?

A single woman. A woman who'd instinctively said she'd care.

It'd be different in the morning, he thought. Hettie would be back to being sensible.

So... Adoption off the island...

Why did that feel so wrong?

This little boy is yours.

'I'm too much of an islander,' he said into the dark. 'But I don't believe it. The child needs parents who want him. Adoption's the only way.'

This little boy is yours.

And suddenly he was thinking of a toddler, waking in the small hours, calling from his cot. As Christopher had called for him.

Where was sleep when he needed it? Nowhere?

He lay and stared into the dark until the dark seemed to take shapes and mock him.

This little boy is yours.

Useless. He swore and threw back the sheets. He hauled on pants and a shirt and headed for the children's ward.

The children's ward was empty, apart from Joni. 'He's asleep,' the night nurse told Hettie. 'I checked on him twenty minutes ago.'

But he wasn't asleep anymore. He was lying on his back, wide-eyed, staring upward. The ward had luminescent stars all over the ceiling but Hettie wouldn't mind betting Joni wasn't looking at the stars. He seemed almost to be looking past them. He had a corner of the sheet in his mouth and was sucking fiercely, but he wasn't making a sound.

'Louis hits us both if Joni cries,' Sefina had told her. 'Joni's good, but he can't be good forever.'

'Joni?' she said softly, and the baby's gaze flicked to her and then away again. He went on sucking fiercely.

'Hey.' It was too much. Hettie scooped him up and cradled him against her. He was stiff and unresponsive. She tugged the sheet with her so he could keep on sucking. Anything that gave him comfort was okay by her. Anything...

'How is he?'

It was a low growl. Max. He was standing in the doorway. She wasn't startled. For some reason it seemed almost inevitable that he was here.

'He should be crying,' Hettie whispered. 'But even so young he's been trained not to cry. With his stepfather... there were consequences.'

'You're kidding.' Max spoke softly, his words seeming little more than another shadow in the night. 'What kind of creep...?'

'He's nothing to do with Joni anymore.' Hettie kissed Joni on the top of his head. 'Louis didn't let Sefina name him as father on the birth certificate. She named Ian. He never adopted Joni so he has no hold. No one will hurt you, little one. You're safe with me.'

She stood and rocked while Max watched. He could retreat. There was no need for him to stay.

He stayed.

'He's not sleepy?'

'Are any of us?' Hettie asked hollowly, and Max shrugged.

'Not me.' Then he looked up at the ceiling. 'How about bringing him outside so we can see some real stars?'

She nodded without a word, and carried the little boy out through the glass doors to the courtyard and down to the lagoon beyond. The courtyard and walkway down to the lagoon were set up so healing patients could lie under the palms, still under the watchful eye of the staff on duty. Hettie sank down onto one of the loungers, still cradling Joni.

Most children would be wailing, Max thought. It was the middle of the night. Joni was with strangers. Why wasn't he sobbing for his mother?

How did you train a child not to cry? The question made him feel cold.

'See the stars?' Hettie whispered to Joni. 'See how many there are? They're up there, guarding us. Every one of them is your friend. Aren't they, Max?'

'They surely are.'

'And the moon's the biggest friend of all. He watches over the whole sky and keeps us safe.'

She almost had him believing it.

He sat on the lounger beside them while Hettie crooned her words of comfort to the little boy. In truth, he wasn't quite sure what he was doing here. Keeping guard? That's what it felt like, but who needed guards when there was Old Man Moon and his minion stars?

But it felt okay. More, it almost felt as if something inside him was settling. The last few weeks had been fraught and this day had been steeped in tragedy and grief. Sitting here under the stars with this gentle woman brought a measure of peace.

Around them was strewn the detritus from the cyclone. Trees had been uprooted, stripped foliage was everywhere and clearing up had barely started, yet here the darkness hid the damage. Here was an oasis of calm. Here was peace.

Hettie rocked and rocked, and then she started a gentle singing, a silly little tune that children must know the world over.

'My nanny sang that to me,' Max said softly, as he watched Joni's body finally lose its rigidity. The little boy was slumped, exhausted, against Hettie's breast, as if he'd finally lost the fight. He had no one else to turn to. Hettie was his last resort and he may as well submit.

'My grandma sang it to me, too,' Hettie whispered back between tunes. 'Hush, little one. Sleep.'

And amazingly Joni did. His eyes fluttered as he fought against the inevitable but finally he slept.

There was a long silence, broken only by the faint lapping of the water at the edges of the lagoon. It felt okay, Max thought. It felt good.

'Did you sing it to your twins?' Hettie asked at last.

'To Christopher,' he said shortly. 'I had to leave Caroline behind.'

'On the island?'

'Yes.'

He didn't tell people his personal business, but suddenly it was out there. A long-ago tragedy.

'My wife went into labour here on the island,' he said. 'We had no medical facilities. The twins were premature and came fast. Caroline was four pounds, big enough to survive. Christopher was only three. He survived but with cerebral palsy. Ellie haemorrhaged and died the day before she could be evacuated.'

'I guess... I knew that much,' she said. 'That's why you set up the hospital.'

'I was twenty.' He said it with muted fury, remembering the waste, the realisation of a loss he could never make good. 'We were arts students, studying in Sydney, young enough to think we knew everything. We came home to the island in our summer vacation to shock everyone with our pregnancy and to marry. We never thought...'

'Kids don't.' She hugged Joni a little tighter.

'So I grew up fast,' he said. 'Christopher needed excellent medical care. I decided there and then that Wildfire was going to get the best medical facilities I could manage, but I couldn't care for twins, not with Christopher's needs. So Caroline stayed here with my mother—her grandma. She came to Sydney later when she was ready for boarding school. I went back straight away, though. I moved from studying arts to medicine. I studied and I cared for Chris. Then I worked and cared for Chris. So, yes, I sang to Chris but I never sang to Caro.'

'She doesn't resent it,' Hettie said softly, as if she guessed his bone-deep grief. 'I'm sure she understands.'

'It doesn't stop me feeling like I've failed her,' he said heavily. 'At least she has Keanu now. At least she has someone who she knows will love her.'

'I'm sure she knows you love her.'

He paused and stared at Joni and tried to get his thoughts in order. 'We should never have got pregnant,' he said at last. 'We were two kids without a sense of responsibility between us. It was an accident but we weren't being careful. Planning a baby is huge.'

'It is.'

'And yet you say you want Joni.'

'Yes.'

'Within a day of his mother dying. It's an impulse decision.'

'That doesn't make it bad. Having Christopher and Caroline…no, it wasn't planned but they were loved. Joni will be loved.'

More silence. Sitting under the stars with this woman seemed to lead to silence. There was something about her, he thought, some restful quality that seemed to make his world settle. The huge bundle of regret and grief that had been his world since Christopher's death all at once seemed to take a step back.

'Tell me about you,' he said into the night, and was it his imagination or did she stiffen?

'What about me?'

'You know about me,' he told her. 'Max Lockhart, owner of Wildfire Island, brother of criminal Ian, father of Caroline…'

'Uncle of Joni,' she added, and he winced.

'Don't. Just tell me about you. You're the head nurse here. You've been here for years. Did you come here to escape?'

'Why would I do that?'

'People do. My great-great-grandfather bought this place as an escape after a scandal with a married woman. He brought her here, waited for years for her divorce to come through and then married her with all honour. But the initial decision to buy the island was as an escape.'

'I didn't know that.'

'You have no idea how many skeletons there are in the Lockhart family closet. So show me one of yours. Why did you run here?'

'I didn't!'

And for a while he thought she wouldn't say more. It didn't actually matter if she didn't, he decided. The night was warm and still, Joni was deeply asleep and the sky was aglow with stars. There was a sense of peace that couldn't be messed with, no matter what skeletons were exposed.

'I'll tell you,' she said at last, though. 'If you'll support me caring for Joni.'

'I can't decide if you can have Joni.'

'No. Sorry. I guess… All I'm thinking is that you're Joni's uncle. You deserve to know a little about the woman who's fighting for custody, and I will need your support.'

'So you will fight for custody?'

'Yes.' She said it harshly, and Joni stirred uneasily in her arms. She hushed and crooned and Joni slipped back to sleep, and Max sat on while she decided what she wanted to tell him.

'I was a bit like you,' she said at last. 'I married young. My parents were surfers, hippies, based at Bondi Beach in Sydney but following the waves. I learned to surf when I was three but they often left me behind. My grandma was my rock. She died when I was fifteen and after that I sort of drifted. But by then, wow, I could surf. I was competitive. I won a couple of world championships and then I met Darryn.'

'Your husband.'

'We thought we were so cool,' she told him. 'Both champion surfers. Both invincible. We had this crazy, amazing wedding on the beach in Hawaii. We had the world at our feet—nothing could touch us.' She shrugged. 'Only then I fell pregnant and I was fat and clumsy and I backed off in the surf. Darryn wasn't doing too well, either, and he couldn't stand it. He hated not being in the limelight. Finally he organised a photo shoot with one of the big American surfing magazines. He said it'd be stunning publicity, me hanging ten when I was so pregnant. It'd tell the world why we weren't out front in the surf scene anymore. But on the day, the swell was huge. I should never have agreed to do it.'

'And…' He hated to ask but he had to.

She sighed. 'And something went horribly wrong. To this day I have no idea how, but I bombed and the board hit my belly. I lost my baby and I also lost the chance to have any more children.'

'Oh, Hettie…'

'So Darryn couldn't cope with my grief,' she said, as if she hadn't heard him interrupt. 'He left me as soon as he decently could. I went back to Sydney, knowing I had to make a living. I scraped through a nursing course but I hated being anywhere I could meet any old friends. I got the best qualifications I could, and then this job came up. I've been here ever since.'

'So you're hiding?'

'I'm not hiding,' she snapped, and then bit her lip as Joni stirred again. 'This is my family. I love the island, the islanders, the hospital, my colleagues. I'd never had a place to call home until I reached here. This is where I want to be.'

'And now you want a baby?'

'I didn't know I did,' she murmured, cradling Joni to her. 'I thought I'd blocked it out. Until today. Until I held him. Suddenly I realised that this was someone I could help. He's injured, Max. Not just today, though heaven knows how he'll remember the terror of today. But he's already had his tiny lifetime marred by abuse at the hands of the man who was supposed to be his father. He's been hit. Sefina told me on that last appalling day when she was admitted. He's seen his mother being hit. How old do you have to be to remember such things? All I know is that he's quiet when he should cry. I know his background. I knew Sefina, and I can bring him up to love her. I've been thinking and thinking. It may seem selfish to you, but it's not. I can give him…all the love he needs and more. If he's adopted on the mainland this part of his life will be a blank. It shouldn't be. He needs to be here.'

'And you need him.' It wasn't a question.

'Maybe I do,' she said softly. 'Maybe until today I didn't realise how much. But I will look after him. We will be a family.'

'He might not be accepted on the island.'

'Because he's Ian's? He's not Ian's. He's mine.'

Was there anything else to be said? There were questions everywhere, Max thought, but he couldn't voice them.

He should go back to bed. His legs ached and he had a power of issues to face in the morning. Ian had left a legacy of debt and deceit. He needed to start sorting the mess. The sooner he got it sorted, the sooner he could leave.

But somehow, tonight, the thought of leaving was slipping into soft focus. Ever since Ellie had died, twenty-six years ago, he'd thought he hated this island. The horror of Sefina's suicide should have made it worse.

Somehow it didn't, though. Somehow, sitting here in the

peace of the night, with this woman, with this child, the grief of the past seemed to lessen.

'Has Caroline told you all her wedding plans?' Hettie asked.

And he thought, *Great, we're moving on, away from the grey of the past.* But there was another shadow.

'I guess she doesn't have to. She'll have it all arranged.'

'She hasn't run things by you?'

'She's been independent forever. She's known she can't count on her dad.'

'She's known why,' Hettie said gently. 'You can't beat yourself up over something that's not your fault.'

'You'd be amazed at what I can beat myself up over.'

'Well, that makes two of us.' She grinned. 'Glum and Glummer, that's us. It doesn't help, though. Tell you what, how about a swim tomorrow?'

'The sea...' he said, startled, and she shook her head.

'Not in the surf. I'm no longer a surfer. You needn't worry, a wave doesn't have to be very big to have me a screaming wuss and backing away.'

'You weren't a wuss today.'

'Neither were you. No choice gives us no choice. But below the resort...'

'The resort?'

'The research station. You know it? Have you seen it yet? I don't suppose you have. But you must know that Sheikh al Taraq—or Harry, as he's known, the guy who's rebuilt the research centre—has converted it into a world-class conference venue. It'll take your breath away. I know you're leasing the land to him. I know the scandal. Everyone here knows now that Ian conned him into thinking the land was his, but he seems to have accepted the facts and moved on. So as owner I reckon you need to do a tenancy inspection, and if you do, how about in your swimming gear? There's a lagoon between the resort and the sea. It's fed by rainwater from the mountains so it won't hurt your legs—but you'll know that.'

Then she glanced at Max's legs and grimaced. 'Okay, maybe not tomorrow,' she conceded. 'Maybe tomorrow's for sitting on the verandah and trying not to wince. But by Tuesday you should be up for a swim. It might even do you good. I swim most mornings so if you're up for it...Tuesday morning? Seven o'clock?'

'Hettie...'

'I know, you have a power of stuff to face,' she said, gently again. 'And so do I. Neither of us may be able to do it. But if we can... Look, it's just a thought. I'll be at the track at the back of the house at seven. If you're there, you're there. If you're not, you're not, and no hard feelings.' And then she stood, still cradling Joni. 'That's it,' she said briskly. 'Time to move on. Goodnight, Dr Lockhart.'

'Goodnight, Hettie.'

She smiled and gave a brisk little nod and turned away.

He stood and watched her as she walked back into the hospital. A woman holding his nephew. A woman claiming him as her own?

The child was a Lockhart, if not in name, certainly in everything else.

Hettie wanted Joni.

And Max... Who knew what he wanted?

Hettie disappeared and he dug his hands into his pockets and gazed back out over the lagoon.

He could settle things here and disappear, to a life, finally with no responsibilities.

That's what he'd thought he wanted. So why did watching a woman disappear into the darkened hospital suddenly make him feel...hungry?

Hettie returned Joni to his cot, then settled in a chair beside him. There was no need to stay—the night staff would be here in moments if there was a peep out of him—but somehow it seemed impossible to leave him. Whatever ties had been created in the morning's drama seemed to be strengthening by the moment. She couldn't leave him.

She might have to. She had no right to him. He was an orphan. Keanu had already told her that the mainland social services had been contacted. She'd have to fight.

'And I will,' she whispered into the night, and part of that fight seemed to start right now. She fetched a rug from the linen bank, tugged it over herself and tried to settle.

But not to sleep. Sleep was nowhere. The events of the day were too horrific.

Joni's needs were too overwhelming.

Max's presence was too...invasive.

What was that about?

She didn't know. All she did know was that every time she closed her eyes, instead of the horrors of the day, somehow superimposed was Max.

Max, sitting beside the lagoon, gazing reflectively into the night. Max, describing his past, the pain of choices he'd had no part in making.

Max, taking Joni from her just as she'd felt herself sweeping out to sea, out of control. Saving her baby.

Not her baby. Joni.

Max, trying with everything he had to save Sefina.

She shouldn't be thinking of Max. The day had been a swirl of trauma. There was so much else to be thinking of besides Max, so why did he seem beside her now? Why had sitting beside him on the edge of the lagoon seemed to settle not just the terrors of today but past terrors?

She'd asked him to go swimming with her. How stupid was that?

He wouldn't come. Even if his legs didn't hurt, why would he come?

But if he did...

Stop thinking about it, she told herself fiercely. Her life was suddenly complicated. It'd get more complicated if she was to have a hope of adopting Joni, and stupid teenage thoughts about a guy with a good body could mess things completely.

But he has more than a good body. She almost said it aloud but she was in the hospital so the monitors were on and anything she said could be heard at the nurses' station. She still had some remnants of sense.

Did she want…more than a good body?

The question was suddenly out there. Why?

Relationships terrified her. She'd stepped into marriage that one horrendous time and the scars were still with her. She'd made a vow to stay single, to stay in control, for the rest of her life.

So why was Max Lockhart messing with that control? Why did the image of him, the sound of his voice, make something inside her feel as if it was stretching to breaking point?

'It was the day,' she said, and it seemed her subconscious was taking over her sense as well as her thoughts because she did say it out loud. 'It's just the way he held Joni and the way he saved him—it's the way he saved me… We both could have drowned without him. It's made me feel vulnerable.'

But…vulnerable? Was that the word she was looking for?

She was gazing down at the sleeping Joni, aching to lift him and hold him again. But there was suddenly a deeper ache, and it was an ache she couldn't acknowledge. She couldn't begin to define it. Max…

But she had spoken out loud, and Beth, the nurse on duty, was bustling down the corridor to see what was happening.

'Hettie? Is anything wrong?'

'No.' It was as much as Hettie could do not to snap but

somehow she managed it. She was off balance and if she was to have a chance to adopt Joni then she needed to be more on balance than she'd ever been in her life. She certainly didn't need to be letting her subconscious have weird thoughts about his uncle. 'I'm just muttering to myself before I go to sleep.'

'You know, if you want to go home to bed, I can look after him,' Beth said, and Hettie nodded.

'Of course you can. And me sleeping here is ridiculous. But that's pretty much how I'm feeling right now. Ridiculous. Indulge me.'

'He's pretty good-looking, isn't he?' Beth said softly, and to her horror Hettie felt herself blush. Blush! She hadn't done such a thing since she was a kid.

'You're talking about Dr Lockhart?'

'Who else would I be talking about? Only the guy you were stranded on the reef with. Who risked his life with you. Also, the guy you've been sitting outside with for an hour.'

'An hour?'

'And five minutes. I timed you. And all the time I thought, he's gorgeous.'

'He's too old to be gorgeous.'

'Are you kidding?'

'He's Caroline's father!'

'And Caroline's twenty-six and her parents were twenty when she was born. That only makes him forty-six.'

'For heaven's sake, after all that's happened today…'

'Especially after what's happened today,' Beth said, becoming serious. 'Honest, Hettie, you do so much for everyone, and now you're talking about adopting Joni…'

'That's not being generous. It's entirely selfish.'

'Maybe, but it's left out a whole chapter of your life. It's called your Love Life. You run this hospital brilliantly, you watch all your staff have affairs, fall in love, have fun. But you—'

'Am I or am I not your boss?' Hettie demanded, and Beth chuckled.

'Yes, you are, ma'am.' And she gave a mock salute. 'But I've never heard that giving your boss a bit of well-meaning advice is insubordination. Max Lockhart's gorgeous. I say go for it.'

'Beth…'

'That's all,' Beth said, and stooped and kissed her. So much for respect, Hettie thought. Beth was an island girl, born and bred, and she knew everything about this island. She probably knew far too much about Max Lockhart. 'But, honest, Hettie, it's been an appalling day and we all know there's appalling stuff behind that mask you wear. You're going to fight for Joni? Good for you, but while you're about it, what about fighting for his uncle, as well? He might be Ian's brother but to my mind he's *bee-yoo-ti-ful*.'

CHAPTER FIVE

To HIS ANNOYANCE Max slept half the next day. He emerged from his bedroom at noon, feeling disoriented. Weird.

Caroline was in the kitchen, cooking and humming an old island folk tune. For an instant she could have been his mother. The tune was an ingrained part of his childhood, as was the smell of the meal she was cooking.

She turned as he entered, and smiled, and she was his daughter again and time had moved on, but the surge of emotion didn't move with it.

He'd been raised on this island. He loved it. He loved its people. He loved this house.

He'd been away for more than half his life, yet it still felt like home.

'Hey,' Caroline said, and smiled some more.

And he thought, *That was Ellie's smile*. But he could hardly conjure her now. Ellie. His wife.

'Welcome to the world of up,' Caroline said. 'Would you like breakfast or would you like curry? Keanu will be here in ten minutes. I've made his mum's recipe—fish curry with a magnificent red emperor caught this morning. Coconut milk and limes picked an hour ago. There's nothing like it. Oh, and Hettie rang to find out how you were. I asked her for lunch, too, but she's staying with Joni.'

'She still wants to keep him?'

Caroline looked troubled.

'Yes, but I don't see how she can. Keanu's contacted social services. A couple of welfare officers will be on the flight the day after tomorrow. They'll make an interim decision.'

'So soon?'

'If he's to be adopted, the sooner the better. His stepfather doesn't want him.' She eyed her father for a couple of moments and then ventured, 'Unless… Dad, do you want to keep him yourself?'

And there it was, front and centre, and with her words the past slammed back. Standing in the intensive care nursery in a Sydney hospital, with the two tiny scraps of humanity that were his children. He'd been twenty years old, a kid himself. Ellie was dead. The doctor had just spelled out Christopher's probable future.

'How will you care for them?' the doctor had asked, and Max hadn't been able to answer. But he'd muddled through. His parents had suggested taking Caroline home to Wildfire. Christopher had needed specialist care, though, so unless he abandoned him to foster care, Max was stuck on the mainland. His father had agreed to fund him through a medical degree, and somehow he'd cared for Christopher. After Ellie's death, though, he was determined to get a decent medical service for Wildfire, so somehow he'd found time to put pressure on politicians. He'd made noise in the right places and even sent money home to help get the Wildfire hospital up and running.

It had all just been reaction, though. He'd done what had come next. That's what he'd been doing for twenty-six years. Was this another such moment?

'Hey, Dad, don't look like that,' Caroline said softly. 'If Hettie really wants him, we'll support her. Maybe we can organise things so she can. If worst comes to worst, we've discussed it and Keanu and I will adopt him. No one's forcing Joni on you.'

'No one's forcing anyone.' He shook his head. 'And you can't adopt a child as worst-case scenario. Sorry, love. Let's think this through later. Your curry smells great.'

'It does, doesn't it?' Caroline agreed, and then Keanu arrived, filthy after clearing fallen palms from behind the hospital. There was cyclone damage to talk over, then the wedding to discuss and island affairs and arrangements to be made. The rest of the day passed in a blur and Max had to put the thought of one small boy aside.

And the thought of the woman who loved him?

Hettie had a busy day at the hospital, followed by another sleepless night, and then she was faced with something she would have rather forgotten.

Had she been nuts, suggesting this? It had been an off-the-cuff suggestion and she was hoping Max had forgotten. What had she been thinking, suggesting an early morning assignation? A swim below the research station? Why would he want to do such a thing—and with her?

She should leave a message at the Lockhart place for him to forget it. Or tell Caroline.

Ha!

'Tell your father I don't want to meet him tomorrow morning,' she'd say. She could imagine Caroline's reaction.

He would have forgotten, she decided, but if he hadn't…

Okay, if he hadn't then he had a choice. He'd be there or he wouldn't. It wouldn't worry her either way. She loved swimming—she swam most mornings. If you blocked out the fallen trees and mass of leaf litter, the island was at its gorgeous best and she wasn't on duty today.

But did she want to go swimming with Max?

Who wouldn't? He was…

Gorgeous?

Yes, he was, she told herself, and if she was interested she'd think he was very gorgeous indeed, but she wasn't interested, at least not like that. She was well over such nonsense. She had to be.

But if he happened to be there...

Then they'd have a brisk, businesslike swim, she told herself. Joni was still in the children's ward—Keanu wasn't letting her take him home until after the welfare visit. Caroline was on duty. Bugsy was asleep under his cot. The child welfare visit the next day was looming large and she needed exercise to drive her thoughts from it.

And she reached the fork in the track and Max was sitting on a fallen palm, looking for all the world like he was waiting for her.

But he didn't look like he was heading for a swim. He was dressed almost formally, in chinos and a short-sleeved, open-neck shirt, almost a business shirt. He was wearing brogues, for heaven's sake. He was clean-shaven, smart— no, more than smart.

He was almost breathtakingly good-looking.

She was wearing a sarong and sandals. She'd let her hair cascade to her shoulders.

All of a sudden she felt practically naked. Like she should turn and run?

'I thought you might have forgotten.' He rose and smiled at her, for all the world like he'd been looking forward to this strange assignation.

'I don't...I don't forget appointments.'

'I can see that about you,' he said approvingly. 'Nice sarong.'

'I... Thank you. Neat...shirt.'

'Thank you, too.'

'And brogues?' She couldn't help the note of teasing.

'You know they found my boat?'

She did know. They'd towed it into harbour yesterday.

They'd also found Sefina's body, but Hettie wasn't going there.

'I... Yes.'

'So I have my clothes—and I have an assignation other than the one with you. I hoped we might combine them.'

'Sorry?'

'With the sheikh,' he told her. 'The businessman who's funded the reopening of the research station and the resort. He's invited me for breakfast. I've never met a sheikh. I've only spoken to him on the phone. See me nervous.'

'Hence the brogues.'

'It seems disrespectful to wear sandals.'

'So you're inviting me? With sarong and sandals?'

'Women get latitude. I dare say every woman in his harem wears sarong and sandals.'

'He's not like that,' she said sharply, and he raised his brows.

'You've met him?'

'Sheikh Rahman-al-Taraq? Otherwise known as Harry? Yes, I have. You know he's an oil billionaire? He's also a brilliant paediatric surgeon but a near-fatal brush with encephalitis has left him with hand tremors that prevent him from operating. He's now intent on wiping encephalitis from the face of the planet, which is why he invested here. But you must know that already, and we all know now that your brother conned him into thinking he could buy the land here. We're just so grateful he's bigger than...'

'My shady brother?' Max sighed and fell silent.

They started walking towards the resort, easily, almost with the familiarity of longtime friends. There was still fallen timber on the track. They needed to concentrate on where they walked. A couple of times they faced logs fallen over the path. The first time it happened Max offered his hand to Hettie to help her over.

'You're the one with the cut legs,' she said, and he smiled.

'I'm the one with brogues. Indulge me.'

'I'm fine on my own.'

'Aren't we both,' he said softly, but still he held out his hand. 'Indulge me,' he said again, and there was nothing for it but to put her hand in his and let him support her as she stepped over or through the litter.

It was nothing more than a gentlemanly gesture, she told herself when it happened the second time. It was good old-fashioned courtesy, and why it had the power to make her feel…?

She didn't know how she was feeling.

As if she was almost looking forward to the next fallen log?

Weird.

Focus on practicalities, she told herself, trying hard to block out the feel of Max's hand holding hers. Trying to block out the strength of him, the way he made every nerve ending seem to tingle.

Think of Max, the man. Max, the owner of Wildfire Island, finally about to meet the sheikh who was helping to save it.

For the last couple of years things on the island had been a mess. While Max's son had been gravely ill in Sydney, Max's brother had illegally 'sold' the land and buildings to Sheikh al Taraq. By the time Max had discovered that documents had been signed in his name, the research station had been rebuilt as a state-of-the-art conference centre.

The Sheikh would have been within his rights to walk away and sue for millions. Thanks to Max's frantic phone negotiations, somehow the situation had been saved.

It seemed almost ludicrous now, though, that Max had never met him.

'I've only seen the sheikh in my work gear, though, and

only as a nurse,' Hettie told him. 'Breakfast in my sarong…
You do realise I'm wearing my bikini underneath.'

'Excellent.' Max's magnetic smile flashed out again.
'I'm wearing boxers.'

'Better than the last ones I saw?'

His grin broadened. 'Yes, indeed. I'm almost respectable.'

'As opposed to me.' She tried to glower, which was
hard when his grin made her want to smile back. His grin
seemed to be made for sharing. His grin seemed…almost
dangerous. 'One slip of the tie at my breast and I'm… Well,'
she managed. 'I'll sit still, that's all I'm saying.'

'So you will join us?'

'You'll be wanting to talk business. I can't imagine it's
anything to do with me.'

'I can't imagine there's anything on this island you don't
know about,' Max said gently. 'Support me, Hettie. I need
your strength.'

'You know, I'm very sure you don't.'

'Then you don't know anything about me,' he said, and
suddenly his voice was grim. 'Not many people do.'

The breakfast with the sheikh went brilliantly. They sat
outside the resort's wonderful new restaurant, under the
bougainvillea and frangipani, with brilliantly coloured island parrots squawking in the trees above them and occasionally daring a brave foray to try and filch a sugar
lump. The sheikh—'Call me Harry'—was polite, gentle
and non-accusatory.

'Every family has troubles,' he told Max, when Max
tried to apologise as he'd apologised over and over, via
telephone, via his lawyers. 'And now your brother is dead.
I'm so sorry, but we need to move forward. You know I
invested in this facility to make a difference to the world-
wide scourge of mosquito-borne encephalitis. This is my

passion. I have other facilities around the world but this one is important to me, and Wildfire itself seems to have found its way into my heart.' He smiled. 'You know I've married a woman who loves Wildfire as much as I do? How can I argue with my heart? So now how can we make the best of the situation, for us, for the islanders and for the researchers who I hope will use this island?'

He then launched into plans that Max found impossible not to engage in. Clinical trials for the encephalitis vaccine were well under way, but meanwhile Harry was offering Max assistance in an insect eradication programme, and in other island medical needs, as well. The two men were soon deep in conversation, and Hettie sat back and listened.

She listened with intelligence, though, Max thought. Through the hour they sat there she asked four questions, each simple but each intensely focussed. She spoke little, but when she did, it was to maximum effect.

It took him little time to realise she already had Harry's respect. She spoke and Harry deferred to her local knowledge—and to her intellect.

As she sat, demure and quiet, he found himself more and more drawn to her. She was wearing no make-up. Her curls were free to tumble to her shoulders. The tie of her sarong sat low in the curve of her breasts.

The work he and Harry were talking of was vital. All his attention should be on business, but it was as if there was some magnetic pull, tugging his gaze to that tie.

Hettie looked…almost like a girl.

Except she wasn't. There were life lines around her eyes. Her hands were worn from a career in nursing where she washed them a hundred times a day. And the way she held herself, with quiet dignity…

She was no girl. She was every bit a woman.

'But I'm holding you up.' With their business finished,

the sheikh rose. 'I can see by Hettie's outfit that you're heading for the beach. For the rock pool below the resort?'

'You've taken away the barriers,' Hettie said. 'I assume it's okay?'

'The barriers were only there during construction,' the sheikh told them. And then his voice softened. 'The rock pool where Joni's mother died is a favourite place to swim, as well. I know you swim there, Hettie. I hope you can return to swim there again, but for now please use our pool. I'm so sorry. It's an appalling tragedy and I know this is none of my business, but, Max... The little boy...your nephew... How will you care for him?'

And there it was again.

This little boy is yours.

'The welfare people will be on the island tomorrow,' Max said brusquely. 'They need to assess what's best for him.'

Harry glanced at Hettie. 'My sources say you would take him.'

'I could,' Hettie said, and unconsciously tilted her chin. 'I would. If I'm permitted.'

'You know that isn't an ideal solution.'

'Why not?' Max asked, and Harry cast him a curious glance.

'This is your island. You don't know the mood of the community?'

'Max hasn't spent any time here for years,' Hettie told the sheikh, obtusely defensive on Max's behalf. 'He's been supporting his son in Sydney. He's also been doing everything he can to support the islanders.'

'This I already know.' Harry held up a hand as if in apology for what he had to say. 'But, Max, I also know how your brother has besmirched your name. Your brother was hated. The mine collapse, the death of a beloved island elder... These are only two of the many crimes put to his account.' His voice gentled. 'I've only been on this island a short while, but already I know the stigma the child will carry. And Hettie, as a single mother, you won't be able to protect him from that stigma.'

'I can.' Hettie rose abruptly. 'This isn't the time to discuss it, though. Meanwhile, if you two need to talk more, I'll leave you to it. Max, if you still want a swim, I'll see you in the pool. Otherwise I'll see you back at the hospital.'

She walked out, leaving the two men gazing after her.

But she couldn't disguise her distress. Harry's words had battered her.

'She might be able to care for him,' Max said softly into the stillness that followed, but Harry shook his head.

'The child will be seen as a Lockhart.'

'I'm a Lockhart.'

'Yes. And I understand the situation. Even though your brother was hated, this community still looks to you for leadership. If you stayed…you might afford this child some protection.'

'I'm not staying. I'm here for my daughter's wedding and then I'll leave.'

'To be free?'

'I… Yes.' What was the purpose of denying it? Besides, this man deserved honesty. 'This island killed my wife. I've been away for twenty-six years. The island has little to do with me.'

'And yet you love it.'

'I don't.' It was an angry snap but as he stared out over the sea to the cluster of islands beyond he felt that age-old tug that made a liar of him. And Harry knew.

'How can you not?' Harry shook his head. 'I know. You don't want the mantle of responsibility and yet it's yours regardless. I, too, have responsibilities I can't walk away from. This is your community, and, like it or not, the child, Joni, is your responsibility.'

'Hettie can have him.'

'That's just the problem,' Harry said gently. 'You know and I know that Hettie can't.'

When all else fails, swim. It was a mantra that had held her in good stead all her life. Maybe that was one of the reasons she loved Wildfire. The sea was tropically warm, turquoise waters washed over brilliant coral, and freshwater pools dotted the island. Apart from the occasional storm, she could swim year round.

She needed to swim now. The pool behind the resort was a naturally formed rock pool, fed by waterfalls from the mountains above, with an outlet at the end where the water tumbled to the sea. The water was crystal clear, the rocky bottom dotted with clumps of water grasses. Brilliantly coloured fish darted from clump to clump, but here in this protected place there were no large predators. If she floated she could almost touch the fish with her fingers.

But today Hettie wasn't floating. She put her head down and swam the full length of the rock pool, up and back, up and back. She blocked out everything except the need to expend energy, to get rid of this grey hopelessness that had been with her since she'd seen Sefina walk off the cliff edge.

Or maybe before that. Maybe a long time before. Maybe Joni's helplessness was bringing out emotions she'd suppressed for years.

And with that thought came another. Did she want to adopt Joni for Joni's sake—or for hers?

And then there was the way she was feeling about Max. The way he made her feel...

Like she was a vulnerable kid again. Out of control.

Scared.

Her mind was a kaleidoscope of emotions that swimming couldn't settle. She swam and she swam...

And suddenly Max was swimming with her. Suddenly he was right beside her, pacing her stroke for stroke.

He swam with ease. She was pushing herself but she was aware that his power was constrained. He could lap her if he wished.

He didn't wish. He simply chose to swim beside her.

For a moment she considered stopping, pulling back, telling him to find his own space to swim. But that'd be impolite. Besides, he owned this island. Okay, Harry was leasing this part but she wasn't too sure of landlord rights and she didn't feel up to treading water and telling Max Lockhart to take himself off.

So she kept on swimming and Max kept on pacing her. Stroke for stroke. On and on.

And finally she found herself relaxing, just a little. The tension that had been with her since Sefina's death eased. Her mind was focussing on Max instead, and strangely, thankfully, her irrational fear was fading, as well.

But it was a strange sensation, swimming in tandem with this man. He'd eased his power back so he exactly matched hers. It meant there was no sound apart from the precise, matched strokes. The morning sun was glinting on the water. The fish were darting every which way underneath them and the grasses were swaying lazily as they passed.

It was almost mesmerising. It was…beautiful.

So was the man beside her.

That was dumb. She was trying to make her thoughts practical. Prosaic. She needed to be matter-of-fact about this. She'd invited Max to swim with her this morning and that's what he was doing. Nothing more, nothing less.

So do it.

They swam length after length, diving as they reached the rocks at the ends, tumble-turning and swimming back. Over and over. Not connecting. Simply pacing each other.

Except they were connecting in a way she didn't understand. It was disturbing. It wasn't bad. It wasn't threatening. But it was…disturbing.

She shouldn't have asked him to join her, she decided. She was a loner. Since divorcing Darryn all those years ago, she'd retired into herself. She had friends, she was sociable enough, but she held herself to herself.

Over the past few months there'd been a flurry of romances between the medics on the island, so much so that she was thinking of buying wedding gifts in job lots. But each time she'd watched one of her staff fall in love, a part of her had been flinching. *Be careful*, she'd wanted to warn them. *Fall with your head, not your heart.*

They wouldn't have listened. Hormones had held sway.

And right now hormones were having a fine time with her and she couldn't prevent it. The sensation of Max's body beside her, not touching and yet moving so his strokes matched hers, the rush of water that followed his strokes… It was almost a caress. His body was so large. So male…

And this water wasn't cold enough. She needed to go and find a cold shower—but that'd mean breaking the moment and she couldn't. Whether she willed it or not, she was held in thrall by the sensation of a man she hardly knew swimming beside her.

The sun warmed her body, glinted on the water, glistened on the large male body beside her. This was like a trance, a dream. Soon she'd wake up, but not yet, not yet.

For some reason an illusion crept into her mind and stayed. The illusion that she wasn't alone. Not just here. Not just now. But somehow her customary solitude had been invaded in a way she…wanted?

This was crazy. Her mind was all over the place.

All she could do was keep on swimming.

He hadn't meant to lap with her. At first Max had settled onto a rock at the water's edge. He'd watched Hettie for a while—she really was a wonderful swimmer—and finally he'd stroked out to meet her.

But she hadn't seen him come, and as he'd reached her it had seemed right not to interrupt her solitude. But somehow it had also seemed right to keep swimming, to stroke beside her, and then to match his pace to hers.

Maybe it was an intrusion. If it was, though, surely she'd have raised her head and glared? She knew he was with her. At the last turn she'd fallen a stroke behind. Instead of staying behind, though, she'd raised her stroke rate until once again they'd been in rhythm.

They were swimming as one.

It was almost a kind of lovemaking.

Where had that thought come from? And how crazy was it? This wasn't a woman to make love to. This was Henrietta de Lacey, charge nurse of Wildfire Island hospital. She was practically his employee.

She was not his sort of woman.

Who was…his sort?

No one, he thought as he swam. His one foray into marriage had catapulted him into a catastrophe so great it had overtaken his life. Since then he'd had the occasional relationship but they'd mostly been with colleagues, and all had been on a strict no-future basis. There were many women in medicine who welcomed such friendships. They were career oriented, focussed on getting ahead, knowing a family would interfere with what they wanted in life.

What did he want in life?

Why was he wondering that now, as he stroked back and forth?

Because he hadn't had time to think about it until now? Because there'd never been a choice? Christopher's needs, the island's needs, his daughter…

Now suddenly the future lay ahead like a blank slate. What did he want?

Freedom? Yes!

He swam some more and Hettie swam with him, and he found himself thinking of what Hettie wanted. To take on a child who wasn't her own.

To knowingly step into responsibility.

The thought made him shudder. Freedom had hung before him for twenty-six years, unattainable, a dream he could barely imagine. To give it up…

What was Hettie thinking of?

He shouldn't want to know, he told himself. It was none of his business—as the child she wanted was none of his business.

He should stop swimming alongside her. He should…

No. There was no *should.* He was free. Harry was willing to pour money into the island's medical facilities, making his own small contribution almost unnecessary. Christopher was dead. Caroline was marrying the man of her dreams.

And one little boy? If Hettie wanted that responsibility it was up to her. He could walk away.

Except for now all he wanted was to swim.

They swam for almost an hour and in the end it was Max who called a halt. He reached the flat rock at the end of the pool, and as Hettie turned to do another lap he hauled himself out of the water.

She did another two laps alone. It felt like she'd lost something.

That was fanciful. She'd lost nothing. She'd swum in this pool often since she'd arrived on the island. Sometimes colleagues swam with her but mostly she swam alone.

She didn't mind being alone.

She wouldn't be able to do it with Joni.

Yes, she would. She could teach him to swim. The thought gave her a surge of pleasure, of hope, but it wasn't enough to dispel the weird, desolate sense of losing Max's presence beside her.

Wow, she was being dumb. She had no right to be thinking like this.

Right? That was the wrong word, she decided. She had no *desire* to be thinking like that.

Desire. There was a loaded word.

She shook it off, almost with anger. She finished another lap.

If she kept swimming, would Max go away? How ungracious was that? She slowed, reached the rocks and pulled herself out.

The rocks were slippery. Max's hand came out and caught her wrist. She was tugged up, faster than she expected, a little closer than she expected.

He was so…male. He must spend serious time in the gym, she thought tangentially. A twenty-year-old would kill for Max's body.

A twenty-year-old could never have this body. Wet, clad only in board shorts, his silver-shot black hair dripping, rivulets of water running down his bare chest, he looked…

Distinguished?

It was the wrong word but she was too close to him to think of another.

Mature. Strong.

Very, very sexy.

Whoa…

'That was some swim,' he said, and smiled at her, and that smile was almost her undoing. How could a guy's smile light up his face? More. How could it light up…something inside her she didn't know had been dark?

He'd tugged her up on the rocks to sit beside him. Mosses covered the surface. The sun was warm on her face. The moss was as soft as bedding, and this man beside her was so…

Near.

She should edge away. She couldn't. Her body wouldn't move.

'You're some swimmer,' he said, and she tried smiling herself. She wasn't sure it came off.

'You're not so bad yourself. Not many men can keep up with me.'

'I can see that about you.' One of her curls had flopped over her eye. He leaned forward and tucked it behind her ear.

'Th-thank you.'

'My pleasure.' His voice was deep and resonant, almost a caress on its own. 'So…no men in your life?'

'Is this a come-on?'

'It's not.' His smile lit his face again. 'Not that I'm not interested…'

'Don't do that,' she snapped, and his smile died.

'What?'

'You sound like your brother.'

That produced a sharp intake of breath—and instant anger. 'You'd judge me like Ian?'

She hesitated. 'No,' she said at last. 'That's not fair. But you look like him.'

'And he…came on?'

'He tried,' she said darkly. 'He regretted it. He also tried messing with a couple of my nurses. He regretted that, too.'

'That sounds scary.'

'I invoked you,' she told him, and lightened up a little, remembering a late-night conversation when she'd found Ian propositioning one of her very young ward assistants. 'Rumours were that you didn't know half the stuff Ian did, so I told him that if he messed with my staff I'd personally fly to Sydney and lay every folly I knew about him in front of you. I said it once in desperation, and to my astonishment he backed off. After that I only had to glare at him.'

'He was scared of me?' Max said incredulously.

'I believe he was afraid of you finding out what a toerag he was.'

'I wish you *had* told me.'

'You had enough to worry about,' she said gently. 'That was the island consensus. We knew how ill Christopher was. I'm glad we didn't worry you.'

'But if you had...'

'No.' And this time it was her turn to touch him. His face had grown grim. She could see the pain of remembrance, of regret, and she couldn't help herself. She reached out and traced the strong contours of his face, a feather touch, a touch of comfort and nothing more. 'Max, you've done all you can for this island. To stop Ian you would have had to leave Christopher, and that would have been unthinkable. Your first care had to be for your son.'

'As your first care will be?'

'If I'm allowed to keep Joni, yes.'

'You'll make a formidable mother.'

'Don't you believe it,' she said, suddenly feeling shaky. 'I'm tough on the outside but I'm squishy in the middle.'

'Which is the best combination for a mum.'

'You think so?'

'I know so.' His hand came up and caught hers. 'Hettie, you know it'll be hard.'

'It'll be hard but it'll be fun.' She should pull away from his touch, she thought. His hand was holding hers and it was totally inappropriate, but to pull away seemed...ungracious?

Impolite?

Unthinkable.

'It might not happen,' Max warned.

'I know that. But I will fight for it.'

'You have no one to help you.'

'I won't need help. Like you, I've learned to be independent.'

'I don't see Child Welfare seeing independence as an attribute.'

'Strength must be.' She looked down at their linked hands. Once more she thought about pulling away, but once more came the realisation that pulling away was impossible.

'I hope you're right.' He, too, was looking at their linked hands and his face twisted into a wry, self-mocking smile. 'Strength has to be fed, though.'

'So how did you stay strong? All those years?'

'I'm not sure I did,' he confessed. 'Maybe on the outside…'

'I guess that's the important part. The part we show to the world.'

'That's the part you'll show to Child Welfare when they assess you?'

'What else should I show them?'

'Maybe the softer bits,' he suggested.

'Softer?'

'The distress you feel at Sefina's death. The regret. And the way Joni makes you feel…'

'How do you know how he makes me feel?'

'I had twins, remember?' he said gently. 'I was twenty years old, I was grief-stricken, I was terrified, and I held them and knew I'd do anything in my power to protect them. It was enough to make me study medicine, to make me vow to learn everything I could for Christopher. It was even enough for me to send Caroline back to the island to live with my parents and my aunt. I loved her enough to let her go.'

There was a long silence at that.

Their hands were still linked. It *was* inappropriate, Hettie thought inconsequentially, and everything seemed inconsequential just now.

Everything except that link.

But somewhere in that conversation was something she had to pursue. A warning?

'Are you saying…maybe I should let Joni go?' she asked into the stillness, and he didn't answer for a while. His fingers started massaging hers. It was a comfort touch, maybe something he'd learned to do for Christopher, she thought, but it didn't feel like something he'd do for Christopher.

Or maybe it was just that she was a woman and he was every bit a man…

A man who was too close.

A man to whom she wouldn't mind being closer.

'I don't know,' Max said at last, heavily now, still massaging her fingers, using his thumb and middle finger to knead their length, strong, firm, sure. 'I only know you're offering something I can't. To commit… Hettie, it's for a lifetime.'

'That's what I want.'

'I've done a lifetime.' His words were suddenly angry. She flinched. He closed his eyes and shook his head. 'I'm sorry.' He released her hand, then absently lifted the other and started massaging again. She had a sudden image of Max, a surgeon, always on call, finding time every day to be at his son's bedside, gently working his magic.

For a lifetime…

'You can't regret,' she whispered, and he shook his head.

'No. Except the time I couldn't spend with Caroline.'

'Caroline understands.'

'Will Joni understand that you need to work?'

'Other women work when they're on their own.'

'So do men, as I did, but believe me it's usually not by choice. Sole parenthood is just plain hard.'

'So if they ask—Child Welfare—will you support me?'

'Why would you need my support?'

'You're his uncle. His legal guardian. Your wishes should make a difference.'

There was a long pause.

'Why do you want him?'

And what did she say to that? She hardly knew herself.

She thought of all the things she should say, the logical arguments she'd already lined up for the welfare people. How she had a secure job, a supportive community. How she already knew Joni and he seemed to trust her. How she'd been a friend of Sefina's, and how, with her, Joni would grow up knowing his background, his heritage. How she'd raise him with love and with all the skill her nursing background could give her.

But that didn't answer Max's question.

Why do you want him?

And there was no answer to that other than the truth.

'I don't know,' she confessed. 'I know I can't have children. Yes, I lost my baby and I mourned, but then I got on with life. My work satisfies me. I love caring for people. I've loved caring for Joni. And yet I've cared for many children without wanting them.'

'But you want Joni.'

'All I know is that when you handed him to me in the water, something changed,' she whispered. 'I held him to me and I wouldn't have let go, even if the rip had carried us both out. Something just…stuck. It was suddenly like he was part of me. Keanu's sent me away now. He says I shouldn't take on all the caring because it'll hurt more when…*if* I have to give him up. But it can't hurt more than it'll hurt right now. Because in that moment…' She shook her head. 'I'm sorry. It doesn't make sense.'

'But it does,' he said gently. 'At twenty years old I held my twins and that was how I felt.'

'They were yours. Their mother was your wife. It did make sense.'

'I don't think sense comes into loving.'

'No,' she said bleakly, 'it doesn't. But Keanu's right. My chances of keeping him…'

'Hettie, I will support you. I will ask that you be allowed to keep him. I can't do more than that, but I'll do my best.'

She closed her eyes. Swallows were swooping across the pool. It was so quiet she could hear their wingbeats as they fluttered back and forth, snatching insects above the water.

Joni wasn't hers yet—but this man would help her.

'Thank you,' she whispered, and he put a hand under her chin and lifted her face and waited until her eyes were open.

'You'll make a good mother,' he told her. 'You're a good person, Hettie. You deserve…'

'I don't deserve…'

'Okay, maybe "deserve" is the wrong word. But you long for a family. I'm over family. I'm free, so holding on to Joni would hold me down. But you… You'll give him all the love he needs. I know you will.'

'How can you know that?' She shouldn't ask, she thought. He'd given her the assurance she wanted. Why ask for more? But the question was out there.

'Because you're you,' he said, and she looked into his eyes and the combination was too much. The stress of the last two days, the tragedy, the shared danger. The shared worry for a small boy. The swim this morning, the sun, the gentle lapping of the water, the sound of the birds…

Whether she raised her face still more, or whether he bent to her, she could never afterwards remember. All she knew was that he was cupping her face. She was moving those last few inches.

And he was kissing her.

CHAPTER SIX

HE HADN'T MEANT to kiss her. Why should he? There was nothing between them. There could be nothing.

His life had just stopped being complicated, and he needed another complication like a hole in the head. He did not need to have an affair with the woman who wanted to adopt his nephew.

But she wasn't just the woman who wanted to adopt his nephew. She was Hettie, a woman who'd risked her life trying to help him, a woman of strength and character, a woman of past tragedy and determination born of that tragedy.

Or…she was none of those things. She was a nymph, a water creature who'd swum beside him, a desirable, beautiful woman.

She was wearing a sliver of a crimson bikini. She was wet but sun-warmed. Her curls were tumbling, still dripping, in tendrils, to her shoulders.

Her eyes were a deep green, slightly shadowed as though she hadn't slept. She had crinkly life lines at the corners of her eyes… Smile lines?

Which brought him to her mouth…

Yeah, it was her mouth where the trouble was. Her lips were full, her mouth was slightly open and his whole consciousness centred on it.

When her face tilted to his, when he drew her to him and he touched her…

When he tasted…

It was an explosion of senses that almost blew him away.

He'd had women—of course he had—lovers as well as friends. A widower was sexy, he'd discovered early. It evoked a nice mix of availability, sympathy and, for some reason, intrigue. It was much sexier than a divorcée. More reliable, too.

Or maybe it was Christopher who evoked the reliability response. Christopher had been his out, but, then, he'd never really needed an out. He'd never let himself get close enough.

I have a disabled son…

He'd used it in his head more than he'd used it out loud. It stopped him getting close. He didn't want to get close.

He was close now. He was so close his brain was in danger of shorting out. Hettie's body was against his, wet and sun-warmed and soft and curvaceous. Her slip of a bikini was barely there. Her mouth was lush under his, and she was taking as well as giving.

This kiss was blowing his mind.

When had a kiss ever tasted like this? When had a woman ever felt like this?

She was ordinary! She was a thirty-something charge nurse, a career medic, someone employed in the hospital he helped fund. She was sensible, determined, capable.

She had no right to be making him feel…

Like this kiss had to be deepened. Like he needed to hold her tighter and tighter still, until her breasts were crushed against his chest and until it felt as if their bodies were melting into each other. Becoming one. He heard a whisper of a moan. Her hands were clutching the small of his back, tugging him as close as he wanted to tug her.

The sea grasses were soft. This place seemed deserted. They could…

'No.'

And suddenly she was pulling away.

The world somehow steadied. Or sort of steadied.

Thank heaven she had some sense, he told himself, because he seemed to have lost his.

He had still lost it. She'd pushed back from him, but her gaze was still locked to his. She was breathing too fast. She put a hand to her heart as if to try and control its beating.

Control. That was what they both needed. This was madness.

'This is crazy.' It was a whisper, words he could barely hear, but behind the whisper he suddenly heard…fear.

What was she afraid of?

And then the image of his brother flashed into his mind. *Anything in a skirt…*

'I'm not like Ian.' If she could think that…

'I know.' Her voice wobbled. 'It's just…'

She couldn't explain further but the moment was shattered. How could she be fearful? Her fear made him feel ill.

'You don't trust me and why should you?' He snagged her sarong from the rocks and tossed it to her, then watched as she tugged it round herself like a shield. She was shaking. Because he'd kissed her?

What sort of damage had his oaf of a brother done on this island?

He was a Lockhart. He couldn't escape that. His neglect had caused grief and heartache for the islanders. Was it now causing this woman to back away?

'I'm sorry.' She had herself under control now, and she even managed a weak smile. 'Whew. That was some kiss.'

'But I'm not Ian.' It was all he could think of to say.

'I know you're not.' But still her voice trembled.

'That kiss,' he said slowly into the silence, 'was not a

kiss of seduction. Neither was it a kiss that said I'll kiss anything in a skirt. Or in your case—' he managed a smile himself '—anything in a bikini.'

'I know you're not like Ian. Of course I do. But it didn't mean anything,' she whispered. And then she took a deep breath, hauling herself together. 'Sorry. I'm not usually a wimp. It's just... I'm usually in control. That feeling...okay, it scared me. Max, I'm not in the market for a relationship, and I don't think you are, either.'

'I'm not.' He had to be blunt. 'I'll be leaving the island after Caroline's wedding. Harry has the research station under control. The mine's being made safe and will be running as a co-operative from now on, and Caroline and Keanu are happy to oversee things. If I need to, I'll come back, but only for fleeting visits.'

'Can I ask why?'

'My wife died here.'

'That seems a bit...excessive.'

'It does, doesn't it?' He shrugged. 'I can't help that. My father brought me up to be the lord of the island, Lord Lockhart, if you like. Dad never had a title but he acted like he did, as did my grandfather before him. I rebelled. I insisted on heading to Australia to university. Then I met Ellie and brought her here and she died.'

'Which was the end of your freedom,' she ventured, and he shrugged.

'What do you think? Dad wanted me to put Christopher in a home. He insisted the island needed me. In my conceit I thought medicine needed me more. Christopher needed me more. And I was right. My grandfather set up a trust for the islanders' medical care but it wasn't enough for a hospital. With me on the ground in Australia, and with my medical knowledge, I was able to badger the authorities into proper funding, and for years now my income has augmented the terrific service you provide. But the choice

I made had costs, so much so that even stepping on the island fills me with regret. So now? I'll see Caroline married, and then I'll go back to work. I still command an exorbitant salary so I can still feed funds here. But Harry is promising to help so the load is lessening. Now, in my spare time…'

'You'll be free?'

'Yes.' He said it with vehemence. 'What's wrong with that?'

'Nothing, if it makes you happy.'

'It will.'

'Be careful what you wish for,' she said softly, and looked out over the sunlit water and smiled. Her smile wasn't for him, though. It was a smile filled with sadness, filled with the same regret he was feeling. A smile that looked back over the years and saw…nothing.

Enough. What was he doing here with this woman? She stirred things up in him he had no wish to be stirred. He needed to get back to the house.

Back to…what?

'You had Christopher,' she said gently. 'You loved him. And you have Caroline.'

'I've let her down…'

'It doesn't matter what you have or haven't done in the past,' she snapped, suddenly angry. 'It's what you do today and tomorrow that counts. I can't see running away as an option.'

'I'm not running. No one needs me.'

'Joni…'

'Has you.'

'What if I'm not allowed to adopt him?'

'Then he'll go to adoptive parents in Australia who'll love him. He'll get over this awfulness and so will you.'

'And I'll be free again,' she said in a strange voice, and he couldn't bear it. He wanted to kiss her again. He needed to kiss her.

But she was backing away even more, slipping her feet into her sandals, fastening her sarong tighter.

'I need to get back to the hospital. Joni might be awake. I don't want to leave him for too long.'

'You might have to leave him forever.'

'So why would you care?' she snapped. 'You think freedom's so great? You might even think it's a good thing for me to be alone again.'

'Hettie...'

'No. I didn't say that.' She bit her lip. 'I have a great life. I'm perfectly happy. I don't need Joni. And I don't need you, either, Max Lockhart, which is just as well, seeing you're flying in and flying out. So you can just keep your hands and your mouth to yourself while you're here.'

'You liked kissing me.'

'What if I did?' she snapped. 'I have very poor choice in men.'

And with that she turned and stalked away, leaving him to follow if he wished.

He decided...maybe he shouldn't follow.

Joni was awake when Hettie reached the hospital. She hadn't stopped for a shower or to change. For some reason she felt deeply unsettled.

She needed to ground herself.

But if she needed Joni to ground herself, then she was in trouble. She knew it but she couldn't help herself. She headed for the children's ward and Caroline was sitting beside Joni's cot. She had him out of the cot and was cuddling him, but the little boy was asleep.

'Hey,' she said as Hettie walked in. 'What's up?' Her eyes widened as she saw what Hettie was wearing. Hettie was nothing if not proper in the way she dressed for work.

'I just thought I'd drop by and see how he's doing,' Hettie said defensively.

'I'm not talking about the sarong,' Caroline said gently. 'I'm talking about your face. What's wrong?'

'Nothing.'

'Liar, liar, pants on fire. Hettie, I've only worked with you for three months so I still don't know you very well, but I do know enough to recognise trouble.'

'Your dad...' Hettie said, before she could stop herself, and Caroline's face stilled.

'What about my dad?'

'I...' Hettie shook her head. 'Sorry. Nothing. I was just talking to him...'

'In bathers and a sarong?'

'He was telling me...' She fought for a minute for composure. What if she really said what had happened? That Max had kissed her until her toes had curled, that he'd made her feel as young and vulnerable as a teenager, and she'd felt so out of control she was terrified? Um...not.

'He'll support me if I want to keep Joni,' she managed.

'But he doesn't think it will happen?'

'I think he thinks it's a whim.'

'It's not?'

'No.'

'But you're not family.' Caroline looked down at the little boy in her arms. 'He's my family. My uncle's child. My cousin.'

'Do you want him?'

'N-no,' Caroline told her. 'Is that selfish? But if no one else will...'

'He'll be adopted in Australia. It's sensible.'

'Yeah,' Caroline muttered. 'Sensible. Like Dad sending his daughter back to Wildfire while he stayed in Australia. Sensible.'

'Did he have a choice?'

'No,' Caroline conceded. 'But it did hurt, no matter how

much I reassure Dad. And it'll hurt Joni. He should stay here. I'll talk to Dad. See if he can apply more pressure...'

'He's said he'll support me,' Hettie said again, and Caroline's eyes frowned.

'Is there something between...?'

'No!'

'There is! Hettie... You and Dad?'

'There's nothing!'

But Caroline's eyes had lit with excitement. 'Hettie, that'd be awesome. You and Dad and Joni...'

'Caro, cut it out. It was one kiss.'

'He kissed you? My dad kissed you?'

'That makes me feel about eighty. Stop it.'

'It shouldn't make you feel eighty. Dad's gorgeous. Oh, Hettie... You could make him stay here. He could take on work at the hospital—heaven knows, the islands could use a full-time surgeon. You could be a family. Hettie, this is amazing. We just have to get it sorted before the welfare people arrive...'

'Will you stop it?' Hettie was half angry, half laughing. 'Of all the ridiculous... One kiss doesn't make a romance.'

'No, but the way you're looking...I know a romance when I see one. Oh, it'd be so wonderful for both of you.'

'Caro, don't.' The laughter faded. She looked down at the little boy in Caroline's arms and she felt...ill.

And Caro's teasing faded. She looked up at Hettie for a long moment and then she rose and gently lowered Joni back into his cot.

'I won't,' she said softly. 'It's just...it would be so perfect. Why did he kiss you?'

'Heaven knows. He's a Lockhart?'

'That's unfair,' Caroline told her. 'As far as I know, Dad hasn't had a single serious affair since Mum died. I asked him once when I was a kid when he was getting married again. You know what he said? He said he had his family.

He'd married my mother, he had Christopher and me, and we were all the family he ever needed. Only you know what? From here, with Chris gone and Mum gone and me marrying Keanu, his family's looking a bit lean. But I'd imagine he's still not even thinking about anything serious. Twenty-six years…maybe he's out of the habit.'

'That's none of my business.'

'It's not, is it?' Caroline said seriously. 'But, oh, Hettie, wouldn't it be great if it was?'

Sam, the island's medical director, arrived back later that morning, and he strode from the plane looking immensely pleased with himself. Apparently the patient he'd escorted to the mainland was on the way to full recovery. There was also a woman, Caroline told Max, a paramedic called Lia whom Sam had hoped to see in Brisbane. His grin said that he had seen her, and his love life was just fine.

His grin got even broader when he learned that Max was back. 'Great to have you here, sir,' he told him, and they celebrated by going through the hospital finances. Maybe both men wanted to be thinking of other things but it had to be done. Ian had managed to bleed funds from the hospital, but not enough to cause significant problems. Max's job was to figure out where the gaps were and plug them.

There was also the damage done by the cyclone. There'd been a power surge, and the CT scanner was damaged. A leak had also caused problems behind the kitchen stoves and one of the wards was unusable.

He needed to get back to the mainland and start working again, he thought. He couldn't ask Harry to donate for general maintenance.

Some things he was still responsible for.

'I'm sure Harry would help with this if we asked him,' Sam said as they reached the end of the bookwork. 'If he was allowed. You know he's a doctor himself, a surgeon and a good one. Encephalitis damaged the nerves in his hands so he can no longer operate but he appreciates what we're doing and supports us to the hilt.' He hesitated. 'Speaking of surgeons…I have an islander with suspected appendicitis in room three. Our only surgeon, Sarah, is currently completing her fly in, fly out roster—did you know she and Harry have just married? But at the moment she's on the mainland. Tomas seems to be settling, but if he flares in the night can I call on you?'

'Of course. You'd normally fly him out?'

'Keanu and I can cope with a simple appendix, which is what this looks like, but Tomas is in his sixties. With the CT scanner out of action I'd like to send him to the mainland. I'm all for avoiding surprises when we open things up, but the islanders hate leaving.' He hesitated. 'Max, there are many things we could use a specialist surgeon for. At the moment we have Sarah for one week a month but it's not enough and now she's married Harry. Harry loves this place but he has his own country. He has research facilities elsewhere and Sarah will travel with him.'

'You're telling me the position's vacant.'

'Interested?'

'For tonight, yes.'

'But not forever?'

'A week and then I'm gone.'

'You hate it here so much?'

Max hesitated. Did he hate the island?

No. He loved it. The island was like a siren song, calling him home.

The problem was, though, he'd never been able to see it as home. He saw it as responsibility.

When he'd been born his grandfather had still been alive. He had vague memories of walking with the old man, hand in hand, as old Henry Lockhart had started the process of handing over.

'You'll own this,' he'd said. 'You'll own every square inch, but don't you dare waste it. And don't think of it as pleasure. It's a burden, boy, a sacred trust. My grandfather bought this island and what he didn't realise was that buying it meant responsibility for every islander who makes their living from it. These are your people, Max, boy. You'll work for them for the rest of your life.'

Even then—aged, what, about six?—Max had felt the burden of responsibility. As a kid, roaming the island with the island kids who were his friends, he'd already felt it. If anything happened to his mates, his family and their families, had looked to Max. He remembered his best mate, Rami, falling from the cliffs while they'd been checking birds' nests. Rami had broken his leg. Max's father had belted Max and then sent him to Rami's family to apologise.

'You're a Lockhart,' he'd growled. 'Your responsibility is to keep people safe, not put them in danger.'

Keep people safe...

That's what he'd been juggling all his life. Keeping his children safe. Keeping the islanders safe.

If he allowed Harry to fully fund the hospital... To finally walk away...

'This is your home, isn't it?' Sam asked curiously, and Max dug his hands into his pockets and thought about it.

'I don't do...home,' he said at last. 'When I was in Sydney with Christopher I always thought I should be here. When I was here, Christopher needed me. Home has always meant...guilt.'

'Hell, Max.'

'I'd been thinking I might take a break. I thought I might take *Lillyanna* and sail round the world.' He was attempting lightness he wasn't feeling. 'Until she rolled. The night of the cyclone put me off like you wouldn't believe.'

'I can imagine it would.' Sam hesitated. 'But if you did decide to settle... We might not need your money anymore but your presence would be a godsend. The islanders need a figurehead. Persuading them to get their kids vaccinated. Mosquito eradication. Disease control. So many things... They still look up to you.'

'Even after Ian?'

'Especially after Ian. They knew he was the wrong Lockhart. And, Max...'

'Yes?' He was starting to feel...goaded.

'Hettie and Joni.'

'What about Hettie and Joni?'

'Joni's Ian's son and the islanders treat him as that. If you stayed...he'd be your son. The difference would be unimaginable.'

'I can't take on another family.'

'No one's asking you to take on another family,' Sam said gently.

'But you are pressuring me.'

'I'm just telling you the truth.'

Hettie was on duty that afternoon and she was busy. All she wanted was to be in the children's ward with Joni, but Joni was happy, playing with Leah, the ward clerk, and the hospital seemed suddenly to be full of acute patients who needed her skills.

Tomas Cody was one of them. Sam had examined him and given him pain relief but Tomas wasn't settling and was obviously afraid.

By late afternoon Hettie was thinking of calling Sam back, just to reassure him, but before she could, Max appeared.

He was dressed semi-formally again, and he carried a stethoscope. He paused at Tomas's door and smiled at her.

'Good afternoon, Nurse. Good afternoon, Mr Cody. Dr Taylor's asked me to see you, Mr Cody, in my capacity as a surgeon. Do you know who I am? Max Lockhart...'

'I know who you are,' Tomas muttered. 'Damned Lock-hart who ran away…' And then he paused and seemed to regroup. 'Nope, that's wrong. You've been the one send-ing money, I know that. Keeping this place going. It's your brother who was the bad egg. Blasted pain's got me con-fused.'

'That's why I'm here,' Max said gently. 'Dr Taylor—Sam—suspects appendicitis. He could send you to the mainland tomorrow but if it is appendicitis I could whip it out here. That is, if you trust me.'

'Of course I trust you. Your mother used to say you'd made a brilliant surgeon. If you can stop this gut ache I'd be grateful.'

'It's okay to examine you?'

'Be my guest.'

So Hettie watched as Max gently questioned, gently ex-amined, gently probed. His questions said he'd confronted this situation hundreds of times before. His very assurance as he performed the examination had Tomas relaxing. Pain could often be augmented by fear, Hettie knew, and some-how Max's very assurance was taking the fear out of it.

And at the end of the examination Max sat by Tomas's bed as if he was prepared to chat.

How many surgeons did that? Hettie thought in aston-ishment. In her experience surgeons arrived, did a fast ex-amination and then left to discuss the outcome with the lower orders. Not with the patients themselves, at least not first off.

'I think it is appendicitis,' Max told him. 'You have a tender abdomen and a slight temperature, but I can't be sure without a CT scan. Sadly our CT scanner is out of order. It was damaged by a power surge during the cyclone.'

'I don't want to go to the mainland,' Tomas said, star-tled. 'Not for just an appendix.'

'Well, here's the thing.' Max glanced up at Hettie, a single glance that somehow encompassed her, that told Tomas that Max was part of a medical team, working for the best for him. How did he do that? Hettie wondered. She didn't know. All she knew was that this man engendered trust. It seemed to ooze from him like radio waves, encompassing all in range. 'You're older than most people who present with appendicitis. There's a slight chance you could have some kind of bowel blockage, something that might have caused your appendix to get inflamed. You don't seem very sick so I doubt if that's the case, but it might be. Without a CT scan I can't guarantee it.'

There was a long silence while Tomas took that on board. 'I guess...' He hesitated but then forged on. 'You're saying... Guys of my age... You're saying things can go wrong, huh? If it was a kid with a bad appendix, you'd just think it was their appendix, but with me...well, there's all the C-word stuff. You're saying there's a chance it's cancer?'

He'd repeated what Max had told him in terms of acceptance. How had Max done that? Hettie thought. More and more, she thought, this man had skills that were needed here.

If he could stay...

He wasn't staying, and it was just as well, she reminded herself. After that kiss...

'The chance is small,' Max said. 'But we can't exclude it.'

'So if you operated...' Once more Tomas hesitated and then he forged on. 'If there is something in there, you could fix it?'

'I could try.'

'No promises, right?'

'There never are in medicine,' Max told him, and once more Hettie was stunned by Max's skill in telling it like it was.

'So if I went to the mainland and they did one of those CT scan things and it told them there was cancer...'

How hard had that been to say? Hettie thought, but Max didn't react. It was like cancer was just like a normal word. A non-scary word. A workaday word.

'If I was in Cairns,' Tomas forged on. 'If it was cancer... Someone like you would do the operation, right?'

'That's right.'

'And you'd cope with what's in there when you found it.'

'We'd have a better idea of what we were dealing with,' Max told him. 'We might be better prepared but, yes, it'd be someone like me doing the operating.'

'So you can operate here?'

'I can,' Max said steadily. 'If you trust me. But, Tomas, remember, there's still a very good chance it's just appendicitis.'

But Tomas had relaxed, Hettie thought. The big man had straightened in the bed and was looking directly at Max, man to man. It was like saying the word 'cancer' out loud had brought the bogeyman out in the open where it could be fought, not just by Tomas but by all of them as a team.

'I trust you, Doc,' Tomas said, and Max grinned and reached for his hand to shake it.

'I'm glad to hear it. After so long off the island...'

'You're a real Lockhart,' Tomas muttered. 'Not like the other one. Now, about this gut ache...'

'I'll do something about that right now,' Max said. 'Nurse de Lacey...'

'Hettie,' Tomas growled. 'She's one of us. Our Hettie.'

And what was there in that that made Max flinch? Hettie saw the brief flash of bleakness, but then it was gone.

'Hettie,' Max corrected himself, and he smiled at her, and there it was again, that smile, and why it had the power to disconcert her so much she didn't have a clue. 'I'll write Mr Cody up for—'

'Tomas,' Tomas growled, and Max grinned.

'Only if I'm Max.'

'You're Mr Lockhart,' Tomas growled. 'Some things don't change. Some things shouldn't change. We've needed a Lockhart to be in charge here forever.'

Max's smile faded. He stood looking down at Tomas for a long, long moment and finally he nodded.

'I'll see what I can do,' he said. 'But, meanwhile, we'll give you painkillers and let you sleep. Sam's started you on antibiotics and there's still a good chance things will settle down. But if nothing's changed in the morning then we'll go in and fix things.'

'That's exactly what this island needs,' Tomas muttered. 'Finally, a Lockhart who can fix things.'

Max had dinner at the resort that night. He spent time with Harry, discussing out how to keep the islands, Wildfire and the rest of the M'Langi group, safe into the future.

Yes, Harry was prepared to put funds into the hospital. Yes, there were good men prepared to oversee the mine. Yes, the mosquito eradication and the vaccination programmes could go ahead.

Things were under control. There was no need for Max to stay after Caroline's wedding.

He walked home—no, he walked back to the homestead—late. He walked around the lagoon and then he paused. Hettie was where she'd been that first night he'd sat with her. Looking out over the lagoon.

He paused, and decided not to intrude. He could sense her need for space even from where he was.

There'd been a burial service for Sefina late that afternoon. He'd stood in the background then, too, hating to intrude.

It had been a simple island service with less than a dozen people in attendance. Hettie had stood at the graveside with a couple of the nurses from the hospital. She'd held Joni, and she'd placed a spray of frangipani on the grave. Sefina's son and Sefina's friend saying goodbye.

A part of him had ached to go and stand by them, but he had no right. It wasn't his place. His brother had done such harm...

Some of the island women watched from the background as well, as if, like him, they were ashamed.

In time these women could support Hettie, he thought, if she was allowed to keep Joni. The anger and resentment of Sefina's husband had driven them away, but maybe the fact that Joni was Ian's son could eventually be forgotten.

That had been a moment of hope amid the bleakness, but there seemed only bleakness now.

Hettie was still in her nurse's uniform. She must have just come off duty. She didn't have Joni with her. She was simply staring out over the moonlit water.

He could feel her desolation.

He'd only known her for three days. How did he feel he knew her so well?

Shared experience? They'd been through grief, but hers had been the bleaker harvest. He'd been left with two children. Despite his appalling medical problems, Christopher had brought him joy. Caroline would continue to bring him joy. Hettie had none of that.

In time Caroline and Keanu could even give him grandkids. That was a sudden blindside. Surely he was too young to be a grandfather, but the thought was...amazing. He'd have to come home for that.

Home?

This wasn't home.

Nowhere was home.

He stood on, in the shadows of the palms, and watched Hettie for a few moments more, careful not to make a move, not wanting to intrude. Was he being a stalker, just watching? The thought crossed his mind, but he pushed it away. He needed this time to watch her.

She seemed so bereft. So alone.

Sam seemed to think the authorities would come down hard on her wish to keep Joni. Maybe she was mourning that already, as she was mourning the death of her friend. But Hettie must've known more than most that she could survive grief and move on.

But did she need to?

An image flashed into his mind, a tiny nebulous thought. A thought so ridiculous...

He and Hettie and Joni. A family. They'd let Joni stay then.

A family. Was he out of his mind? This was tiredness speaking, he decided, and grief, and a bit of shock and pain thrown in for good measure.

Enough. He could justify watching her no longer. He turned and slipped away, aware as he did so of a sharp stab of loss.

Like leaving part of him behind?

No!

He was still raw from Christopher's death, he told himself. He was in no state to be thinking of anything other than the needs of himself, his daughter and the island.

So why were the needs of one nurse suddenly so important?

Why, when he went to bed, did he lie awake and think of Hettie?

Why did the faint idea of family suddenly seem possible?

How did she know he was there?

She had no idea. It was like a sixth sense, telling her there was someone among the shadows.

Maybe she should be nervous. Maybe she should be creeped out.

She wasn't. It was Max. She knew it, and she also knew he was fighting shadows that were as long as her own.

She didn't move. She didn't by as much as a blink let on that she knew he was there. There was no need, for it seemed he was doing the same as she was.

He'd be looking into the future and seeing only echoes of the past.

This was dumb. She was tired and she had to be at her best tomorrow. She had to make a good impression on the welfare people. More, she had to convince them she could be mother and father to Joni and that she could care for him better than some adoptive parents in Australia.

Could she?

It was too huge a question for her to answer.

Max would support her. The thought was comforting but strangely it wasn't enough.

She wanted more. From Max?

Why was she thinking that? She had no right.

'Enough.' She said it out loud, knowing, once again without understanding how, that Max had gone, and the night felt emptier for his going.

CHAPTER SEVEN

TOMAS WAS NO better the next morning. The drugs Max had prescribed had had to be topped up in the small hours and when Max saw him at eight, he was starting to slip into an abyss of pain.

'Enough,' Max told him. 'If it's okay with you, Tomas, we're going in. I'll operate. Sam will do the anaesthetic.'

'And Hettie will be there, too?' Tomas demanded. Hettie had come into the ward with Max and was standing at his side, waiting for orders.

'I'm not much use,' Hettie told him. 'I just get to stand around and watch the doctors do their thing.'

'Yeah,' Tomas growled. 'Like we know that's true. There's no one on this island we'd rather have than Hettie in an emergency,' he told Max. 'We're limited in doctors. The number of times she's had to step in, stitch people up, help mums with bubs, cope until a doc can get here... She ought to be a doctor, our Het. Some of us reckon she already is.'

'Hush,' Hettie told him. 'Don't give him any ideas. If you think it's fun to chop people open...'

'I reckon you could do it if you had to,' Tomas said stubbornly, and Max glanced at Hettie and saw her blush, and thought he wouldn't be the least bit surprised if Tomas was right.

'So you want Hettie there in case Sam or I fall over?' he asked, and Tomas managed a weak grin.

'That's the one. With Hettie I know nothing will go wrong.'

She's that sort of woman, Max thought. Though the weird fantasies of last night had slipped back where they belonged, into the realms of tired night dreams that could be safely ignored, it still gave him curious comfort to think that when he left the island Hettie would stay on. It was as if the island was safe in her hands.

His daughter intended to stay here. Maybe in time Hettie could even deliver her babies. She could be here for her.

As he couldn't? Because he could no longer do family?

Enough. He turned to the drug chart and started writing up pre-meds.

He had a patient to operate on. Medicine.

He needed to concentrate on practicalities, not emotion.

How many appendectomies had he performed in his working life? Max had lost count. He should be able to do this in his sleep, and yet enough had presented challenges over the years for his adrenaline levels to rise as he stepped into the theatre.

This place didn't have back-up, either. It had no highly equipped intensive care unit and no specially trained theatre staff.

It shouldn't matter. He'd already figured that Sam Taylor was extremely competent. A fly in, fly out surgeon and anaesthetist came once a month, but in the interim Sam and Keanu did most of the low-key surgery, even though they weren't specifically surgically or anaesthetically trained. Sam surely knew what he was doing now. He discussed the levels of anaesthesia with a calmness that spoke of years of practice.

And Hettie was good, too. She worked silently in the

background, not ready to pick up doctors as they collapsed, as Tomas had suggested, but surely ensuring nothing would collapse on her watch.

As Tomas slipped into drugged oblivion Max checked and rechecked the monitors, and got the go-ahead from Sam—'All systems go!'

And from Hettie came a curt, 'Yeah, why are you asking me?'

He made a neat incision—and almost immediately suspected something was wrong.

The appendix was gangrenous.

'No wonder he was hurting,' he muttered, and then concentrated a bit more and the mood in Theatre became tense around him.

Hettie and Sam had assisted in enough surgical procedures to know when things weren't great. There'd been the odd comment, a joke from Sam as Max had made the incision, and now there was silence.

'Blast,' Max muttered, and the silence intensified.

He closed his eyes for a nanosecond and then stepped back from the table. Hettie moved in with swabs.

'I need to change the incision to midline,' he told Sam. 'I'm thinking caecal carcinoma. That's what it looks like.'

'Can you cope with that here?' Hettie asked. It was a dismayed whisper.

Max was looking at Sam. 'It's extensive—I'm thinking a right hemicolectomy. Couple of hours, mate. You up for it?'

'We can't close him up and send him to Cairns?' Sam asked, and Max shook his head.

'Worst case—if we have to—but the mess of the gangrenous appendix is going to knock him around anyway. There's no way I can close and leave it. To close and send him for further surgery... The outcome's shaky anyway.'

'Okay,' Sam said grimly. 'What are we waiting for?'

And as if on cue the door to Theatre swung open. Caroline stood there, in her nurse's uniform, looking...scared.

'Dad?'

'Problem?' Max was checking the equipment tray with Hettie, figuring what else they needed on hand before he did the midline. 'We'll be a while, Caro.'

'That's just it,' Caro said, and he thought, *Uh-oh, she's scared.* 'We need a doctor out here. Billy Tarla's just come off his boat. He was dropping lobster pots on the reef and the rope wound round his leg. He fell and the pot pulled him under. His mate got him out but he was five minutes underwater. They've got him breathing but he's still unconscious. The boat landed five minutes ago. They should be arriving now.' She paused and listened and they could hear a car being revved up the hill, engine screaming. 'That'll be him. Dad, Sam...'

'Where's Keanu?' Max snapped.

'On one of the outer islands. Clinic.'

'Damn.' Two doctors. Two patients. Two situations ideally calling for two doctors each.

'Close and wait?' Sam asked, and Max looked down at the incision he'd already made and swore. The appendix was a mess. The longer he took, the more likely it would be that infection would spread through Tomas's body.

'If it's important... If I have to,' Hettie ventured. 'If you give me instructions every step of the way...I've given anaesthetics before.'

And Sam's face cleared. 'She has. She's good, Max.'

'Good enough to give an anaesthetic?' he demanded.

'I know it's unusual but we've used her before. She follows instructions to the letter. I trust her.'

And he knew Hettie well enough by now not to argue. Moving on... If Sam left... If Hettie took over the anaesthetic...

'I'll still need an assistant.' He wasn't being precious.

To do the complex surgery he was proposing and have to turn constantly to locate the equipment he needed was impossible.

'How about I stay?' Caroline suggested.

'Sam'll need the best help possible,' Hettie said. 'Send in Beth. She's not theatre trained but—'

'What's her training?' Max demanded, and Hettie gave a strained smile.

'Registered nurse, basic qualifications. She's only just returned from the mainland after qualifying. So no theatre experience yet but she's calm and she doesn't faint. You talk me through the anaesthesia, I'll talk Beth through what she needs to be doing.'

Outside the truck had screeched to a halt. 'Okay, Max?' Hettie said. 'Caro, Sam, go. Billy's Tomas's mate's son. If we give up on his life to save Tomas, Tomas will never forgive us. Let's give it our best shot and save them both.'

Hettie was, quite simply, incredible.

The surgery he was performing was complex, technically difficult and messy. Normally there'd be a team of at least four highly qualified medics. Beth was a scared newly qualified with just basic training. She was totally reliant on Hettie's directions. The thing was, though, that Hettie gave directions softly and succinctly, and so subtly that Max found himself snapping a request for something and it was in his hand almost before he needed it. Hettie was watching Tomas's breathing, watching the monitors, watching Max's hands, as if she had six hands and six eyes. And she wasn't even a doctor!

Occasionally she'd slip the odd query his way—or a warning as blood pressure dropped—and once she hit the intercom with her elbow. A scared kitchen lad came to the door and she requested plasma. He returned before Max needed it.

She was amazing.

He couldn't pay her any attention. If Tomas was to end up with a working bowel, Max needed to use all the skill at his disposal, and he could only be grateful that Hettie's skills seemed to match his.

Grateful? 'Astounded' was the word he wanted, he thought as he finally stepped back from the sutured and dressed wound and moved to help Hettie reverse the anaesthetic. He saw the sag of her shoulders as he took control; he knew how much stress she'd been under.

This woman must have spent her entire working life learning 'more', he thought. She must have watched and watched, and learned and learned, and he thought that for Tomas's sake, the day she'd decided to move to Wildfire had been a blessing.

'Thank you both,' he said simply, as Hettie started to help Beth clear up. 'You're two amazing women.'

'You're not so bad yourself,' Hettie murmured, but her voice shook and he thought she could hardly talk. Her concentration had been so fierce…

'We all did good,' Beth said in satisfaction, and then looked down at Tomas's drawn face. 'Will he…? Is he…?'

'He'll need chemotherapy,' he told her. 'But it's looking good. I'm pretty sure I've removed everything. He'll need to go to the mainland for scans and to see an oncologist. It's unfortunate but it's a small sacrifice when he's looking at years of life ahead of him. The appendix was a bit of a blessing. If it hadn't flared, the tumour could have grumbled and spread for a long time without us knowing. As it is, we've caught it early. Also, Sam ran blood tests yesterday and there's no sign of anaemia. Lack of anaemia in caecal carcinoma is related to a better outcome. If I was a betting man I'd say he has a few good years left.'

'Oh, thank goodness,' Beth said, and burst into tears.

* * *

No man is an island… Nowhere was that so true as on Wild-fire. Tomas was Beth's uncle. Hettie had known that when she'd asked her to assist. It hadn't been fair but there hadn't seemed a choice and Beth had handled herself brilliantly. Now it was over, it was fine to burst into tears—and Max had said exactly the right thing.

He hadn't treated Beth as a junior helping out, Hettie thought. His response to her had been as one medic to another. He hadn't patronised or sympathised and Beth had taken his words and held them. They'd be repeated to Tomas's wife, his mother, his children, and the reassurance would be all the better coming from Beth.

And by adding the comment about going to the mainland for chemotherapy… By the time Tomas was fit enough to put up a fight the family would have plans in place.

It's a small sacrifice when he's looking at years of life ahead of him.

That line would be repeated across the island, and Tomas wouldn't have a leg to stand on.

Max had saved Tomas's life today, Hettie thought, and he'd save it into the future.

So why did her knees suddenly feel like jelly?

'Sit,' Max said, and her gaze jerked up to his in surprise. *What…?*

'Sit,' he said again, more gently, and suddenly his hands were on her shoulders and he was propelling her into a chair at the side of the room. It was a chair put there for just such a purpose, only she'd never used such a chair in her life. But she was sitting and Max was easing her head down between her knees with gentle, inexorable pressure.

'Watch Tomas,' he growled to Beth. 'Tell me the minute his breathing changes. The second.'

'Go back to him,' Hettie muttered. 'I can manage.'

'I know you can,' he said softly. 'You can and you can

and you can. You're amazing, Henrietta de Lacey. I wonder if this whole island knows how wonderful you are.'

'She needs to be even more wonderful now,' Beth interjected. The nurse was bent two inches from Tomas's nose, watching his breathing with total attention, following Max's instructions to the letter.

'What—' Max started.

'The Child Welfare people.' Beth pointed to the clock. 'They'll be here in thirty minutes.'

'I need to check on Billy,' Hettie murmured. 'Sam and Caroline might need help.'

'I'll check on Billy,' Max said firmly. 'You go and get yourself ready to be a mother.'

Billy looked like he'd make it. He had water on his lungs. He'd need intravenous antibiotics and careful watching for a couple of days but for a potentially lethal accident the outcome looked promising.

'He was under for almost five minutes,' Sam told Max. 'He's probably knocked off a neural pathway or two, and, to be honest, he didn't have all that many pathways to begin with. Not the sharpest knife in the block is our Billy, which explains why he was tossing out lobster pots without checking where the ropes were. But he's conscious, he knows what day it is and with luck he'll walk away with no consequences. And Tomas?'

'Hopefully the same.'

'Excellent,' Sam said. 'You sure you don't want to join us permanently, Dr Lockhart?'

'No,' he snapped, possibly with more force than necessary, and Sam looked at him quizzically.

'I've hit a nerve?'

'I've had responsibility since I was twenty. I wouldn't mind some freedom.'

'Right,' Sam said slowly. He glanced at his watch. 'You going to this meeting with Child Welfare?'

'I'll go for Hettie but he's not my responsibility.' Why did he feel the need to say that so forcefully? Sam was looking at him in mild astonishment.

'He is your brother's child,' Sam reminded him. 'Ian's name is on the birth certificate. It seemed even though Ian paid for Sefina's marriage, Sefina was still adamant that Joni was a Lockhart.'

'He was Ian's son, not mine.'

'Yes,' Sam said gently. 'But with Ian's name on his birth certificate, and you being next of kin to Ian, you're his closest relative. You get to choose.'

'I choose Hettie.'

'I meant choosing whether to keep him yourself,' Sam said. 'I've been on the phone to the mainland for a couple of hours, being grilled on the situation, and I can tell you that Hettie will need your support and more if she's to be allowed to adopt him. So why are you still here? Or does your lack of responsibility mean you're not even interested enough to attend?'

'There's no need—'

'To be blunt? Maybe there is,' Sam said. 'If you care about Hettie, you need to be there now.'

He'd always intended to be there. Joni was his last responsibility. This was the last of Ian's messes to be cleared up.

But because of the medical emergencies of the morning he was late. He walked into the meeting, he looked at Hettie's face and he knew things weren't going well.

Sam had volunteered his office for the meeting and two officials were seated behind Sam's desk. They had a chair apiece and had pulled in a folding chair for Hettie. She was sitting facing them. It had the effect of making Hettie seem younger, vulnerable, like a schoolkid in front of two headmasters.

The man and woman were both suited, formal. Hettie had changed in a rush. She was wearing a simple blue skirt and white blouse. Her hair was still tugged back as it had been in Theatre. She was wearing no make-up.

She looked scared.

'Good afternoon,' Max said, and formally introduced himself. 'I apologise for being late—we've had medical emergencies, which have also prevented Dr Taylor from being here. I believe those incidents have also meant Ms de Lacey is less prepared than she'd wish to be. However, we have saved two lives so I'm sure it was worth the inconvenience. Now, before we go any further, this seating arrangement seems inappropriate. Let's pull this desk back and get ourselves a couple more decent chairs. Ms de Lacey has had a stressful morning; we don't want to put her under more stress.'

There were harrumphs and sighs but he went ahead and reorganised the room. He'd learned early with patients that behind-the-desk consultations could push stress levels through the roof. Informality put everyone on an equal footing and Hettie needed that.

Hettie cast him a grateful glance as they all re-settled, but he saw her fingers clench as soon as the woman in the suit started talking again. It seemed they were well into the discussion.

'Dr Lockhart, please understand that we've done some intense research on Joni's situation in the last two days.' The woman addressed Max as if she'd already finished her discussion with Hettie. 'His mother is dead. His stepfather doesn't wish to have anything to do with him—indeed, he's making threats if the child stays on the island. We understand criminal charges are pending but we can't take that into consideration—our principal job is to keep Joni safe.

We've made some tentative enquires to his grandparents in Fiji but it seems they'd lost contact with their daughter and want nothing to do with her child. Dr Lockhart, you're Joni's uncle but Dr Taylor says you don't wish to take on the responsibility, either.'

Then her voice softened a little. She became the compassionate counsellor, still talking only to him. Ignoring Hettie.

'Dr Taylor told us your son died three weeks ago,' she murmured. 'If that's the case, we don't blame you for stepping back now. You have no wish to replace your son. No one would.'

You have no wish to replace your son.

The words felt like a kick to his gut, and Max felt himself freeze. He'd never thought of such a concept.

He felt ill.

But to his astonishment Hettie's hand came out and touched his. She flashed him a look that said she understood; that the woman's words were ridiculous.

'No one can replace Christopher,' Hettie said, to the room in general. 'We all know that. Joni and Christopher are two different people. "Replacement" is the wrong word, and to put Joni's care into the context of Max's grief is inappropriate.'

'I didn't mean…' The woman paused, disconcerted, looking towards her colleague for help.

'What Maria means,' the man said evenly, 'is that you don't want the child, Dr Lockhart, and that's understandable. Your grief aside, you are his next of kin. We've made tentative enquiries. You've raised two children already. You seem admirably responsible so of course you could have custody if you want him. But you don't, so we need to make other arrangements. Ms de Lacey here has kindly offered—'

'There's no *kindly* about it. I *want* Joni,' Hettie said, and maybe only Max heard the faint tremble in her voice. Her hand was still touching his. Was she taking reassurance now instead of giving it?

'Very well,' the man said. 'Ms de Lacy has expressed a desire to keep him, but we fail to see it as an appropriate option.'

'Well, I do,' Max said firmly, and he found himself holding Hettie's hand. Staring down this officious pair together. 'Hettie's competent, caring and loving, and she has the backing of the entire hospital staff. She also has my backing. As Joni's uncle, do I have a right to ask that Joni stay in her care?'

'Frankly, no,' the woman said, collecting herself and moving on. 'As next of kin, if you want him yourself it's a different matter, but you have no right to delegate. Ms de Lacy, we've talked to the island doctors and to some of the island elders. It seems there's reluctance to accept the child among the islanders. As well as that, Ms de Lacey, you've never expressed a wish to adopt a child before. You knew Joni's mother only in a professional capacity. You certainly didn't know her well enough to prevent her suiciding—'

'That's unfair,' Max snapped, beginning to seriously dislike this woman. But the woman shook her head and continued.

'Ms de Lacey was occupied with her professional duties while Mrs Dason was distressed. We understand that, but we also understand that she'd still be occupied with professional duties if we allow her to try and raise Joni. She has no means of financial support apart from her career. Also, Ms de Lacey, if we allowed you to adopt Joni, he'll be staying on an island where the local community consider him an outsider. That disadvantage might be mitigated if he were to have the support of two loving parents, but our feeling is that you alone have little chance of providing sufficient support. We therefore think it's best for the child if he leaves the island and starts life in a new community with two parents. We're sorry, Ms de Lacey, but Joni will be returning to the mainland with us. Tonight.'

Silence.

Other women might have sobbed, Max thought. Other women might have reacted with anger. Hettie simply sat staring at the woman who'd made the pronouncement.

The silence lengthened. Max tried to think of something to say, and couldn't. Her hand still lay in his. He found himself gripping tighter. Was he feeding her reassurance—or taking it himself?

Or was it something other than reassurance? Guilt?

Or more. She was hurting and he couldn't bear it. And the vision of Joni was all around him, too, a little boy who was partly a Lockhart, his parents' grandchild, a toddler in his cot, keeping quiet because he'd been hit...

Hettie had had the courage to do something about it. Why didn't he?

And the thought he'd had the previous night suddenly was there, front and centre. Family...

Could he?

'Is there any way I can appeal?' Hettie asked at last in a small voice, and the woman gave her a sympathetic smile.

'My dear, you're not family. From all reports you're hardly even a friend. You have no support for the child among the islanders, and you have no family support yourself. What do you possibly have to offer Joni?'

'Love?' Hettie said in a bleak voice, in a voice that said it was already hopeless. And then she seemed to pull herself together. She tugged her hand from Max's and she made one last try.

'What if I leave the island?' she said. 'I can get a job in Cairns. That takes away one of your objections.'

What? Max thought. For the island to lose Hettie...

But it seemed that also wasn't an option. 'The islanders' antagonism is only one of many objections,' the woman said, more firmly now. 'This seems a spur-of-the-moment offer and we can't decide a child's future on such a whim. The issue is settled.'

More silence. Hettie stared down at the floor, her face blank. She looked…stoic, Max thought. She'd accept it and she'd move on.

But why should she?

What had the woman called this? A spur-of-the-moment offer? It was no such thing, Max thought. What Hettie was offering—had, in fact, given—was something as old as time itself. It was love. He'd watched Hettie when she'd realised Sefina was dead and he'd seen the grief—and the love. He'd seen her at the simple burial service for Sefina. Hettie had looked stoic then. She'd loved and she'd lost.

Hettie had offered to move to Cairns. The woman had called it a spur-of-the-moment offer. It hadn't worked.

Love…

The situation was a muddle, a chaotic tangle in his head. He was trying to get it clear, but, no matter how tangled, one thing stood out.

For whatever reason, however unlikely, Hettie loved Joni. And wasn't love the most important thing?

And as he looked at Hettie he felt something deep within his gut, something that hadn't stirred for years.

Love?

No. He didn't understand it. It was too soon, too fast, too crazy. He had to get himself together. He had to get this on a solid, unemotional footing.

He had to say the only sensible thing there was to say.

'I have a proposition,' he said into the silence.

Behind him the door swung open. Sam had promised to try and attend to back Hettie up, and here he was. He opened the door but then he paused, as if he knew how momentous were the words Max was about to say.

'I've told you,' the woman snapped, her professional smile slipping. 'You can't delegate responsibility.'

'No, but I can share,' Max said, and he thought, *What am I doing? I want no responsibility.*

But surely this wasn't taking it. This was simply handing it over in another way.

'How?' the woman snapped, and Max turned to Hettie and took her hand and smiled at her.

'Easy,' he said. 'Hettie de Lacey, will you marry me?'

Up until now this discussion had been loaded with silences. None had been as long as this one. It stretched seemingly all the way to the horizon and back, and then zoomed off into the distance again.

The woman was the first to recover. 'Is this some kind of joke?' she snapped, but Max didn't take his eyes from Hettie.

'I'd get down on one knee if I didn't have coral grazes all over both of them,' he said. 'But, Hettie, I'm serious.'

She didn't look like she thought he was serious. She looked like she thought he'd lost his mind.

'What...? Max, for heaven's sake...'

'Think about it,' he said, urgently now because he could feel the rising anger of the two officials behind him. 'Hettie, can we go outside for a moment?'

'Say what you need to say here,' the woman snapped angrily. 'We'll not condone any arrangement made purely—'

'For the good of Joni?' Max finished for her. 'Isn't this what the entire meeting is about?' Still he watched Hettie. 'Hettie, think about it. I believe I'm Joni's lawful guardian. I'm his closest kin. As Louis has refused any responsibility, any court in Australia will give me first right of custody, especially as I know what parenthood entails. I know what I'm taking on.'

'You don't intend to take it on,' the woman snapped, and finally Max turned back to her.

'In times of stress families need time to adjust,' he said. 'You know that. I've changed my mind, and that's understandable in the circumstances. The responsibility's mine, and I'll take it on as long as I have a wife to support me. If Hettie agrees to marry me, we'll take Joni for our own.'

'But...you don't even want to stay on the island,' Hettie whispered, and Max turned to her again, his gaze meeting and holding hers. His gaze was an urgent message— *Hush*, he was saying without speaking. *Don't argue. Go along with this.*

'I will need to come and go,' he agreed. 'But half the workers on these islands seem to work on a fly in, fly out basis. I will support you, Hettie, and I'll support Joni. I swear.'

'You can't...' Hettie whispered.

'Why can't I?'

'This is ridiculous,' the woman snapped, and Max shook his head, determined not to look at her again.

'It's not ridiculous. Hettie and I share a very deep friendship. She's been in my employ for many years now.' There was no need to mention it wasn't totally his employ—the hospital was part funded by the Australian Government and he hadn't actually met Hettie until this week. That was irrelevant.

'Hettie's one of the best nurses I've ever met,' he continued. 'She's competent, she's caring, she's wonderful. She also swims like a champion and when she kisses me she knocks my socks off. Hettie and I have both been married before. Up until now we've been looking at life through sensible, pragmatic glasses, but suddenly I'm thinking, Why not? Why not, Hettie, love?'

To say Hettie looked astounded was an understatement. She looked like she'd just been slapped on the face with a wet fish. It couldn't matter. There was nothing he could do to make this proposal more romantic. Or sensible.

He wanted to whisk her outside and talk through practicalities, but there was no way he'd leave these officials time to reorganise their opposition. This was a rearguard attack. They'd been left floundering—it was just a shame that Hettie had, too.

'Well, about time.' It was Sam, coming to Hettie's rescue. Coming to both their rescues. He stooped to kiss Hettie, as if the thing was already decided and she'd said yes. 'You two have been smelling of April and May forever.' He grinned across at the officials. 'The whole island's been wondering…I had a text from one of my more impudent twelve-year-old patients when I flew in yesterday morning,' he told them. 'Bobby "borrowed" his dad's phone to take a picture of the big fish he was planning to catch. Instead, he spotted our Hettie and Max at one of the most beautiful of the island's waterholes. He sent me the photo in twelve-year-old indignation, and asked should Nurse Hettie be allowed to do "yucky stuff"?'

His grin broadened as he flicked open his cellphone and held it up. And there were Max and Hettie after their morning swim yesterday. Or rather there was Max—you could scarcely see Hettie but there was no denying she was under there.

It had been quite some kiss. All the emotion in the world was in that kiss.

Hettie opened her mouth to say something but nothing came out. Actually, Max was fighting for anything to say, as well. Hettie's normal tan had turned to bright crimson. She looked like she was blushing from the toes up.

This was one kiss recorded for the world to see. It was one kiss that meant these officials just might see their relationship as real.

It was one kiss that didn't mean anything?

'So we have Joni's uncle and Joni's mother's friend,' Sam said, smiling from Hettie to Max and back again. 'Two people who risked their lives trying to save Sefina and who saved Joni. Two people who love Joni and who wish to marry.'

'But Dr Lockhart doesn't want the child,' the woman managed.

'I didn't see how I could love him,' Max told her, deciding he should stop looking at Hettie. He'd sprung this on her with no warning. It wasn't fair, but then, he hadn't planned this. He just had to go with it. 'But if Hettie's willing to share,' he continued, 'then I think we can provide Joni with a safe and loving home. Hettie? This is much earlier than I'd like. I know it's rushed but suddenly it seems the only sensible option.'

He turned fully to her then and took her hands in his. He held them, firmly, and waited until she looked up at him. His gaze held hers. *Trust me,* he was saying in his head, but the words he said out loud were different.

'Hettie, we can be a family,' he said. 'We can make a home for Joni.'

'And no one will ever give Joni grief about his background when he's our Hettie and our Doc Lockhart's son,' Sam said triumphantly.

'Sam?' Max was still focussed on Hettie.

'Yes?' Sam was practically bouncing.

'Shut up,' Max growled. 'It's time for Hettie to speak. Hettie, do you think…? Is it too soon to ask you to marry me?'

His eyes were doing all the talking. He'd thought previously that this woman seemed to be a kindred spirit. Could she guess what he was thinking now?

She looked at him for a long time. The lady from welfare made to say something but the guy beside her put his hand on her arm as if to restrain her. All attention was on Hettie.

'We can do this,' Max said softly. 'We can work this out. Together.'

And she got it. He saw the moment when she decided to trust him. He saw the moment she decided to put Joni's fate—and hers—in his hands.

'You really want to marry me?'

'I do.' How hard was that to say? To be honest, though, it didn't seem to be adding to his responsibility. In some way it seemed to lessen it.

'Yes,' he said. 'We can give Joni a home. We can make it work.'

'Okay, then,' she said, and he blinked.

'Okay?'

'Until I get a ring, okay is all you get,' she managed. 'Okay is fine until I see the diamond to match.'

And amazingly he saw the hint of laughter, the slight twitch of her lips. She was amazing, he thought. Stunning.

'When?' the woman snapped in a last-ditch attempt to gain control, and Sam looked from Hettie to Max and back again and obviously decided a little help was needed.

'The islanders don't have mandatory waiting periods like the mainland does,' he said, grinning broadly. 'I know,' he added as the woman made an involuntary protest. 'They'll need to satisfy the Australian legal requirements, but for now…I'm sure you won't object to an island marriage. This island is, after all, part of Joni's heritage, or it will be with these two as his parents. Now, is there anything else, or is Joni's future settled?'

The officials left soon after, without Joni, making angry noises about Max's indecision costing them time and money but with no arguments left. Sam needed to head back to the wards.

'But this is the best possible outcome,' he told them, shaking Max's hand and kissing Hettie. 'Brilliant. Max, we'll make an islander of you yet.' He left, still grinning, and they were left alone in Sam's office.

What had just happened? Max was feeling like he'd been hit by a truck, but Hettie looked like she'd been hit by a bigger truck. The wet-fish analogy was no longer big enough.

'You know this won't be a real marriage.' He said it too fast, wanting to wipe the look he didn't understand from her face. Was she feeling trapped? He hadn't meant that.

'I didn't...' She took a deep breath and tried again. 'I didn't think so. You're offering...'

'A marriage in name only.' Once again he'd said it too fast. 'I don't intend to stay on the island, but neither do I... did I...intend to marry again. I've had enough of responsibility to last a lifetime.'

'You will be responsible...for Joni. If you marry me...'

'I'm already responsible for Joni.' He said it more forcibly than he'd intended, but he seemed to have little control over his emotions right now. 'What I'm doing by marrying you is assuring his future.'

'By delegating the responsibility.' Her voice sounded as if it came from a long way away.

'I'll pay,' he said. 'Of course I'll cover the cost of his upbringing. And, Hettie, I will treat Joni as my son.'

'Even though you won't be here.'

'I'll visit. He'll be a Lockhart of Wildfire.'

There was a pause. 'How will Caroline feel about that?' she asked at last.

'I think she'll be pleased. She said if worst came to worst she and Keanu would take him.'

'But worst hasn't come to the worst,' Hettie whispered. 'Because you're marrying me to stop that. Max, I don't think I want to be married.'

'But we've both been married,' he said, cautiously now because there was no need to bulldoze her. If indeed she didn't want Joni enough to take this step, things had to be reassessed. 'We married with our hearts before. This is marriage made for practical reasons, sensible reasons. It's a marriage made with our heads.'

'But you kissed me.'

And there it was, the elephant in the room. The kiss...

'In retrospect,' he said cautiously, 'maybe that was a mistake.'

And, amazingly, a glint of laughter crossed her face again. It was an echo, a trace, and it was gone as fast as it had appeared, but it left him disconcerted.

'Meaning kissing could get in the way of a marriage of convenience?' she asked.

'It could,' he said, just as cautiously, and she nodded and fell silent again, and then she turned and looked out the window.

'Why?' she asked, without looking back at him.

'Why?'

'Why are you making this offer?'

He had to get this straight. 'Because I know how much you want Joni. Because I believe you'll make Joni a wonderful mother. Because it'll give you and Joni the respect you deserve on this island.' He took a deep breath. 'And because there's no one else I want to marry.'

She didn't turn back. 'What if...what if there's someone else I'd like to marry?'

'Is there?'

'Call me stupid,' she whispered. 'But I've always thought...one day I'd like to end up with someone who loves me. Darryn never did. My parents never did.' She shrugged. 'Sorry. Pipe dream. It's not going to happen. This is a fine offer, a wonderful offer. It's more than kind.'

'I don't believe I made the offer to be kind.'

'You did,' she said gently. 'And of course I knew as soon as you said it that the sensible thing was to accept.'

'You can still back out.'

'And lose Joni? No.'

'If you meet someone else… Hettie, there's always divorce.'

'You think I don't know that?' Still she was staring out the window, as if there was something out there that took her entire concentration. 'Max, you took my breath away—back there. I was prepared to lose him.'

'I wasn't prepared to let you lose him.'

She turned then to face him. Her face had lost its colour. She looked strained to breaking point. 'It'll have to seem… real,' she whispered. 'At least while you're on the island. I mean, if we marry in name only and never go near each other it'll get back to them soon enough. The authorities. For the first year at least…'

'The Lockhart house is huge,' he told her. 'Caroline doesn't want to live there after her marriage. You could move right in. It's big enough for us…'

'To be separate?'

'Yes.' And then he added, and afterwards he wasn't sure why, 'If that's what you want.'

'Why would I want anything different? But, Max…the big house? I'm staff.'

'You won't be staff. Of course you could still nurse if you want—but you'd be my wife.' And then he paused. The word seemed to echo.

My wife.

He'd had a wife once. It had been a disaster. He'd sworn…

'Things don't need to change,' she said—fast, as if she'd read his mind. 'Max, my villa is fine. I'm happy to stay there.'

'Your villa isn't my home. You said yourself the marriage needs to be seen to be real, and if Joni's to be a Lockhart he has the right to be raised in the big house.'

'But you don't want a wife there.'

'I'll get used to it.'

'You won't have to. You'll be coming and going.'

'Yes.'

'You really won't expect…'

'You to be a wife?' He tried to smile. 'I'm pretty good at cooking for myself these days. I iron a mean shirt. I've even been known to scrub a bathroom.'

'Wow, now we really are getting into the nitty-gritty of marriage proposals.'

'I do have a housekeeper, though,' he added. 'So we don't need to take turn about.'

'This is getting more and more romantic.'

'It is, isn't it?' he agreed, and then he grinned, suddenly relaxing. This'd be okay. He'd marry Hettie. Hettie would live in the big house and care for Joni. He'd stay here for a little longer than he'd intended, but he'd go back to work in Sydney. He'd fly in, fly out, maybe once a month to check things were okay.

They could live in separate wings of the house. He could still be independent. He could still be free.

But there were a few words that niggled, that Hettie had said, that couldn't be unsaid.

But I've always thought…one day I'd like to end up with someone who loves me.

She deserved that, he thought, and suddenly he was back at the pool, with Hettie in her crimson bikini, with Hettie melting into his arms.

He wouldn't mind—

'Don't even think about it,' she snapped, and he stepped back as if she'd slapped him.

'What?'

'If you're thinking about a little nookie on the side.'

'Nookie?'

'You know what I mean.' She glowered. 'This is complicated enough. No nookie.'

'Sheesh, Het, no sex? What sort of marriage is that?'

'A marriage of convenience. It'll be like the olden days. You're a Lord Wotsit with debts up to your ears and I'm a plain little heiress with warts and a crooked nose and millions you can use to restore your castle.'

'I can't see a crooked nose. But do you have warts?' he demanded, fascinated.

'Not that I'm admitting to.'

'You can show me. I'm a doctor.'

She choked then, laughter bubbling up again unbidden. But then it faded and her lovely green eyes grew serious. 'Max, if you indeed do this…it will be the kindest—'

'It won't be the kindest. It's self-interest,' he growled.

'Marriage with no nookie is not self-interest.'

'Providing my nephew with a woman like you for his mother is self-interest. You're brave, kind, funny… Not to mention skilled.'

'My head will explode. Cut it out.' Still her gaze was serious. 'Max, can we really do this?'

'I think we can.' He reached out and took her hands. He looked down at them for a long time. They were good hands, slim, tanned from years in the island sun, worn from years of nursing. Years of caring.

'I know we can,' he said, more surely now. 'This is sensible, Hettie. We can make this work. So when? Next week? We'll get Caroline married off and then do the deed ourselves.'

'No fuss,' she said anxiously, and he could only agree. He was having trouble getting his head around…everything.

'I need to find Caroline,' he managed. 'I need to tell my daughter I have a brand-new family.'

'A family of convenience.'

'I suspect you and I both know that's the only type to have.'

CHAPTER EIGHT

FOR THE NEXT few days Max hardly saw Hettie. Lawyers arrived from the mainland to help him sort out the mess Ian had left. He and Harry spent hours planning directions the island management could take. A new fly in, fly out nurse arrived and Hettie took leave from nursing. She took Joni back to her villa.

They weren't avoiding each other on purpose—were they?

Max couldn't think about it. After so many years of neglect, all his focus had to be on seeing his daughter wed. Arrangements between him and Hettie had to take second place.

Which suited him. He needed time to get his head around what was about to happen.

Caroline and Keanu had organised a wedding rehearsal and then a dinner for their closest friends the night before their wedding. Max dropped by Hettie's villa that morning and asked her to be there, but she refused.

'It's Caroline's time,' Hettie said firmly. 'She needs her dad to herself. She's had to share him often enough.'

Max had to agree. He went to the dinner alone but Caroline cornered him afterwards.

'What's going on, Dad? Are you marrying Hettie or not?'

'Not until after your wedding. Hettie and I both agree that comes first.'

'But Hettie's my friend and your fiancée. She should be here.'

That's what he'd thought but Hettie had been adamant. 'I don't need a social life,' she'd told him. 'Especially not now. Joni needs me. We need to bond.'

Hettie had been dressed in shorts and a T-shirt. She'd let her hair loose. She'd been hugging Joni. She'd stood in the doorway of her villa and she hadn't invited him inside, and he'd thought that was just as well.

After they were married they'd move to the big house and things would change. Or would they? He'd be leaving, heading back to Sydney, doing what came next.

'Dad, talk to me,' Caroline was saying. 'You are marrying Hettie?'

'You know I am.'

'Then she has to be included in tomorrow's ceremony. I thought the hope was that the islanders start looking on Joni as yours and Hettie's. You need to be a family for that to happen.'

'You're my family.'

'Yes, but now I have Keanu, and you have Hettie and Joni. You offered this marriage, Dad. You need to go through with it.'

How to tell his daughter that one part of him would love to 'go through with it'? One part of him thought Hettie was the most beautiful woman he'd ever met.

But the other part of him wanted—needed—to head back to the mainland and soak up the freedom he'd wanted for so long.

'You'll walk me down the aisle tomorrow,' Caroline said, and he forced his attention back to the here and now.

'Of course.' He smiled at his beautiful daughter. Caroline was showing no signs of nerves. She was glowing in anticipation of spending the rest of her life with the man she loved.

Was he jealous?

'I love it that you're here,' she said softly, and suddenly she reached out and hugged him. 'I know responsibility has always kept you in Sydney but I've always known you love me. I'm so glad the *Lillyana* didn't sink. I'm so glad you're free to start again.'

To start again... What did that mean?

'But you have to start,' Caroline continued. Since when had his little girl got bossy? She was certainly bossy now. 'Dad, tomorrow you'll walk me down the aisle, you'll give my hand to Keanu and then you'll sit in the front pew. And you'll sit with Hettie and Joni. I've chosen my new family. You've chosen yours.'

'Caro—'

'It's the way it is,' she said gently. 'We're both moving on, and isn't it wonderful?'

Max went round to Hettie's as soon as the dinner finished. It was late but there was still a light on in her front room. He knocked and she opened the door a notch and peered out.

The door was on a chain. That took him aback a bit. Most islanders didn't even bother to lock their doors.

'Hettie?'

'It's you.' She sounded relieved. She closed the door and fumbled with the chain and a moment later the door swung wide.

She was wearing pyjamas. Pale blue pyjamas adorned with pink flamingos. Her hair was tousled. Her feet were bare and she looked so desirable it was all he could do not to gather her up and claim her as his wife there and then.

Boundaries would have to be worked out, he thought. Boundaries were like fine gossamer threads—he had to look close to see them and they could be broken with one misstep. But they were important.

So he forced himself to stop looking at the woman before him and looked instead at the chain.

'Do you get nervous?' And then he looked more closely. The chain was shiny new, and there was a trace of sawdust on the doorknob. Like it had only just been put on.

'Is this about you and me?' he managed lightly. 'Are you scared I'll come to claim my own?'

'What, club me and drag me by the hair back to your lair?' She said it lightly but he could hear the trace of strain behind her words. 'Nope. It seems to me that I've agreed to go willingly to the big house—if that is indeed your lair.'

'It's the closest thing to a lair I can think of. You reckon I should put down a few bearskin rugs and hook mirrors to the ceiling?'

'And pop in a dungeon complete with shackles and whips. Um…maybe not.' She was smiling but still there was that strain.

'Hettie, what are you afraid of?'

'N-nothing.'

'You don't put chains on your doors for nothing. What's going on?'

'I…Louis was here,' she said.

'Sefina's husband?'

'Yes.' She bit her lip. 'Look, I'm overreacting. He was drunk. You know he bashed Sefina before she died? There's a warrant out for his arrest but Ky's the only policeman on Wildfire and he hasn't been able to find him.'

'But he was here?'

She tilted her chin, looking all at once brave, defiant and vulnerable. 'He was drunk,' she said. 'Well, that's nothing new. But it seems things have changed for him. He's a bully. He accepted Ian's money to marry Sefina but he bad-mouthed her and he threatened everyone who even tentatively tried to befriend her. He threatened me.'

'When?' She was so small, he thought, but then he thought she wasn't small. She was defiant even now. She was five feet four of courage.

'When I reported her injuries to the police,' she said. 'When I told Louis he'd pay for what he was doing to her. He said he'd hurt me and anyone else who tried to interfere with...well, I won't tell you what he called Sefina.'

'That didn't worry you?'

'I told Ky.' She flinched and he saw her regroup. 'And now Louis's in hiding but he's running out of places to hide. He came to find me today, and he yelled at me. He says the islanders are starting to blame him for Sefina's death. They are, too. There are a lot of guilty consciences; a lot of people who looked the other way. Her death has made people see the appalling place she was in. So Louis is getting a hard time and no one's willing to support him. He says... He said, "The kid should never have survived. If you keep him the locals'll be rubbing my nose in it for the rest of my life. Don't you dare try and keep him. You and the doc... Bloody do-gooders. Get rid of the kid or I'll do it for you."'

There was silence at that, silence while Max assimilated her fear; while he looked down at the chain she'd obviously had installed in a hurry; while he looked at the defiance of that tilted chin and saw the fear behind it.

'You told Ky this, too?'

'Yes. He's trying to find him. But word is that he's all talk and he's gone back to Atangi. It was only the booze talking. I should be okay. But Ky sent a guy to put on the chain.'

'Wise but not wise enough,' Max growled. 'You'll stay in the big house tonight. Both of you. We'll pack what you need and you can come now. There's room.'

'Max, it's ten o'clock. I'm in my pyjamas.'

'And very cute they are, too. You can put on some slippers, or I'll carry you.'

She choked on that, laughter bubbling despite the seriousness of what she'd been saying. 'You couldn't.'

'Want to see me try?'

'Yeah, you might manage it if you sling me over your shoulder like a bag of potatoes, and I cling to Joni while you carry me. Not. Max, I've just got Joni to sleep. I can't move now.'

'But you would feel safer in the big house?'

'I… Yes,' she admitted. 'Bessie and Harold are there. With a housekeeper and gardener on site, Louis wouldn't dare come near.'

'And me.'

'And you,' she admitted with another attempt at a smile. 'Macho Max.'

'There's no need to be sarcastic.'

'Believe it or not, I'm not being sarcastic,' she told him. 'You are macho. I've watched you swim into danger to try and save Sefina. You did save Joni. I've also watched you perform as fine a piece of surgery it's ever been my privilege to watch, and now you're threatening to throw me over your shoulder in a fireman's hold. So, yes, macho.'

'So you will come.'

'No,' she said. She took a deep breath. 'Not because I'm being stubborn. Not because I have any sense of bravado. I know I'll have to live there when we're married. But not tonight, Max, when it's Caroline's last night in her home before she marries. Tell me the house isn't full of guests? It is, isn't it?'

'You could sleep in my room. I could sleep in the living room.'

'And have all your guests trip over you in the morning? Max, I'm not moving in until Caroline is well and truly married, until we can divide the place into sensible sleeping quarters, until we can start as we mean to go on.'

And she was right. The place was full.

He thought of Sefina. He'd seen the pictures Hettie had taken when she'd been admitted before the cyclone. She'd been thoroughly, brutally bashed.

Somewhere out there was the guy who'd done it. Somewhere out there was the guy who was threatening Hettie. Rumour said he'd gone back to Atangi. Rumour wasn't enough.

'I'll sleep here tonight, then.'

'You're kidding.' She shook her head. 'Max, you can't. Firstly, I only have one bed. Secondly, it's the night before Caro's wedding. She needs you.'

'Caroline is surrounded by bridesmaids,' he said. 'We've arranged to have breakfast together, alone. I can go home by then, after I've checked with Ky that he has someone to keep an eye on this place. I can kip on your sofa. Okay?'

'I… Okay,' she managed, and he realised that underneath it all she really was scared.

'And, Hettie, you are coming with me to the wedding tomorrow.'

'Caroline's already invited me. I thought I'd slip in…'

'You're slipping nowhere.'

'But—'

'You'll sit with Joni, in the front pew, as my future wife, as my family. You and Joni are under my protection and the sooner Louis understands that, the sooner the threat to you will fade. We're a united front, Hettie. That's what this marriage is all about.'

'Until you leave.'

'I'll keep returning. I'll keep you safe. You're my—'

'Responsibility,' she said flatly. 'I know.'

'I meant to say you're my family.'

'It's the same thing, isn't it?' she said, attempting lightness. 'I'm sorry, Max. I'll try to make your load as light as possible.'

'I didn't mean—'

'I don't want you to explain,' she said, and he heard the faint note of bitterness in her voice. 'I'm enormously grateful and I'm sure Joni will be, too. Okay, then. Let's go find you a blanket and a pillow. My sofa's not bad. Let's both of us see if we can get some sleep.'

As a surgeon on call, and as a father of a disabled son who had spent his life in and out of hospital, Max should have been used to sleeping wherever he found himself. He usually could.

Tonight he couldn't. He found himself staring up at the ceiling, listening to the bush turkeys scrabbling in the undergrowth outside the villa. It wasn't that he was nervous. In truth, he wouldn't mind if Louis appeared. He had Sergeant Ky's number on his phone. He'd spent time training in karate. He wouldn't mind a chance to face off with the guy who'd caused so much grief.

So it wasn't that that was keeping him awake. It was the fact that Hettie was sleeping right through that door.

She had Joni in with her. Soon after she'd left him to his sofa, he'd heard him stir. She'd heard Hettie rise and comfort him, crooning him back to sleep.

For years Max had cuddled Christopher to sleep. The sound of someone else doing it…

Someone else taking his responsibility?

Someone else doing the loving?

It was a strange sensation and it left him feeling unsettled. Especially as the one doing the loving was Hettie.

His wife-to-be.

Wife. The word kept echoing in his head. She wasn't his wife yet, but she would be.

She was so different from Ellie. Ellie had been young,

vibrant, carefree. She'd been full of the promise of life to come.

Hettie was sensible, practical, bruised by life.

Which was why this would be a sensible, practical marriage.

She'd be taking on Joni. He wouldn't have to feel responsible.

Why did he suddenly want to feel responsible?

There was a crazy thought. It wouldn't go away, though, and at four in the morning, when Hettie padded through the lounge in her bare feet to heat a bottle, he was still wide awake.

He watched her from the shadows as she quietly heated Joni's milk, and when the bottle was ready he spoke.

'Bring him out here,' he said softly.

She jumped almost a foot. She yelped.

'Yikes,' she managed when she came down to earth. 'Don't do that. I forgot you were there.'

So much for the vague thought—hope?—that she might be lying in the dark, thinking about him.

'Sorry,' he told her. 'I just thought…maybe Joni should start seeing me as part of the furniture.'

'Because?'

'Because I will be,' he growled. 'Hettie, I will keep coming back. He should see me as…'

'His father? He's never had one.'

'I don't—'

'How about he calls you Papa?' Hettie suggested. 'That's a nice encompassing word that could be Dad or could be Papa.'

'And you'll be Nana?'

'That's the Fijian word for mother,' Hettie said softly. 'I can't replace Sefina. I have no wish to try.'

'But you could be Mama.'

'I guess…'

'At least Mama doesn't sound like Grandpa,' he growled, and she chuckled.

'That's settled, then…Papa. He's waiting.'

'Bring him out. Unless you think it'd distress him.'

'No,' she said softly, slowly, as if thinking it through. 'He's got so much to get used to but he needs to get to know his papa.'

Which explained why two minutes later Hettie was perched on the sofa, watching him feed Joni.

She'd simply walked out and handed him over. 'Papa is going to give you your bottle,' she told Joni, and she sat right down beside Max, easing the little boy onto Max's knee. They were right beside each other. Feeding their… son?

Together.

And for some unknown reason it evoked sensations so strong it almost blew him away.

He'd never done this.

Oh, he'd fed children, all right, mostly Christopher. He remembered hours, days, weeks in the nursery for premature babies, and then in a succession of hospitals. Feeding his son. Watching nurses feeding his son.

In the times when his mother had brought Caroline to the mainland, she'd leave her to him to feed so they could 'bond'—but Caroline had hardly known him. Feeding her had been fraught, tense, with Caroline making it very clear she preferred her beloved grandma.

But now… Joni didn't know him. Joni hardly knew Hettie. Yet somehow he was lying cradled in Max's arms, sucking fiercely at his bottle, casting an occasional glance at Hettie as if to make sure she was going nowhere but then looking up at Max again.

It was like he was learning Max's face.

'He's learning to know you, Papa,' Hettie whispered, and Max managed a grin.

'Don't you start using it. I can see it now. One marriage ceremony with a difference. Will you, Mama de Lacey, take you, Papa Lockhart…?'

She chuckled, a lovely low chuckle that lit the night. That even had Joni looking up in wonderment and his eyes lighting with something that might even be a smile—if he wasn't concentrating so fiercely on his bottle.

'You want me to call you Max?' Hettie asked.

'Of course.'

'You mean you want it to be personal?'

There was a question. It hung between them while Joni kept feeding, his sucking slowing as he grew sleepier. He shouldn't need a night bottle anymore, Max thought obliquely, but it was a comfort. A personal need.

Do you want it to be personal?

Was that what Hettie wanted? Support in more ways than one?

A proper marriage?

'Max, I didn't mean… With personal…I'm not asking for romance. I'm not one for hearts and flowers,' she said hurriedly.

'I didn't think you were.'

'But I'll not have a husband who calls me Mama.'

'And if anyone else on this island's seen you in your bikini and heard me call you Mama they'd think I was nuts.'

She chuckled again. 'So I'm not past it?'

'You're not past it at all,' he murmured. 'You're beautiful.'

'There's no need to get carried away.'

'I'm not carried away,' he said, and suddenly the laughter was gone from the room. 'Hettie, you are beautiful.'

'I'm thirty-five years old. I might have been beautiful a long time ago.'

'How long since you looked in the mirror? How long since you listened to your chuckle? How long since you saw your smile?'

'Max...don't.'

'I'm only speaking the truth.'

She sighed then and lifted the now sleeping Joni from Max's knee. She carried him into the bedroom. She had a nightlight on. He watched through the open door as she settled the little boy into the hospital cot she'd borrowed. She took her time settling him, crooning a little, making sure he was deeply asleep.

Then she straightened and he thought she'd close the door on him and return to bed. Instead, she came back to the doorway and stood and looked at him. It was a direct look that seemed to bore straight through him.

'Max, don't,' she said.

'Don't what?'

'Start something you have no intention of continuing.'

'Hey, I only said—'

'That I'm beautiful. I know. At least, I don't know that I'm beautiful, and you know what? I can't afford to think it. I put beautiful away a long time ago and it's staying away. We need to keep this impersonal. If we need to refer to ourselves as Papa and Mama...'

'In your dreams...'

'Max, that's all we can be to each other.'

'We can be friends.'

'Friends don't call each other beautiful.'

'Of course they do.'

'Friends don't kiss each other...as you kissed me,' she whispered and he had no answer.

'You want to be free,' she said, still whispering. She made no move to come forward out of the doorway. It was as if she was making sure she had an escape route. 'You'll leave after the marriage ceremony.'

'I'll come back.'

'As often as you need to. I know. You take your responsibilities seriously and I honour you for that. I'm not exactly
happy that Joni and I need to be your responsibility, but I'll
wear that. It's…anything else that I can't wear.'

'Like?'

'Like falling in love,' she said, and her whisper was so
low he could hardly hear it. 'Max, I can't do that. I can't
afford to. Not with a man who doesn't want to be here.'

'I don't want you to…'

'Fall in love? Of course you don't, and I won't, at least I
think I won't, unless you keep calling me beautiful. Unless
you keep cradling Joni and looking up at me as if you want
me to share how you're feeling. Unless you kiss me again.'
And then she hesitated but finally the rider…

'Unless you care.'

'I don't think…' he said, carefully, because in truth he
had no idea how to respond to this. 'I don't think I can
stop caring.'

'Care as my boss, then. Care as my acquaintance. You
can't care as my husband.'

'How can I not?'

'Stay separate,' she said. 'We've both been separate for
many years now. We're probably good at it.'

'I'm not.'

'But you don't want to love me. You don't want me to
love you.'

There was a long silence at that. A loaded silence.

Love.

He thought of the way he'd loved Ellie, fiercely, pas-
sionately, throwing all cares to the wind. What a disaster.

He thought of the pain of loving Caroline, knowing he
couldn't give her what she wanted, knowing he'd had to let
her go to keep her safe.

He thought of the agony of loving Christopher, of losing him little by little by little.

Did he want to love again? Could he?

It was too hard an ask, and Hettie saw it. She smiled, a tiny, rueful smile that was almost self-mocking.

'Don't, Max. Don't even think about going there. You've done an amazing thing for Joni and for me. All I'm saying is that we can't complicate things by going further. Yes, I'll call you Max. I won't call you Dr Lockhart because you'll be my husband but you'll be my husband in public only.'

'So you'll call me Dr Lockhart in private?'

'Are you kidding?' she said with sudden asperity, with the return of the Hettie with courage and humour. 'That would be just plain kinky. You know exactly what I mean, Max Lockhart. I have no need to explain further. Just cut it out with the beautiful. Now, if you don't mind, I'm going to bed.'

'But you will sit beside me at the wedding tomorrow.'

'Yes, because that's public.'

'Of course.' He didn't have a clue where to take this from here, and apparently neither did she, because she backed a few steps into her bedroom.

'Goodnight,' she managed, and closed the door behind her.

'Goodnight,' he repeated, but it was all he could do not to add a rider.

Goodnight, beautiful.

'Fall in love? Of course you don't, and I won't.'

That was what she'd said but she was wrong. She'd just uttered an out-and-out lie.

Hettie settled Joni into his cot and tried to settle herself but settling was impossible. She'd just watched a man who would be her husband feed a child who would be her son, and while she'd watched, she'd felt her world shift.

He was big and tender and kind. He'd held Joni as she knew he'd held his own son for years. She'd watched the expert way he'd held the bottle, his big hands cradling Joni, manoeuvring the bottle so Joni wasn't sucking air. She'd watched the way he'd constantly checked that all was right with the baby's world.

With her baby's world.

He was staying here to protect her.

He'd put his life on the line to try and save Sefina.

He held her heart in his hands.

And there it was, as simple and as complicated as that. It was crazy to say she'd fallen in love. It was far too soon, far too crazy, far too unthinkable.

But still…

He was lovely. He was in her living room.

He was to be her husband and if he wanted her…

It was totally, absolutely unthinkable but the sentence kept ringing in her head.

He held her heart in his hands.

CHAPTER NINE

HAPPY IS THE bride the sun shines on?

It wouldn't have made one speck of difference if it had been pouring, Max thought as he walked his daughter down the aisle. Caroline clung to his arm as if she needed his support, but he knew it wasn't true. She'd woken smiling and she hadn't stopped smiling since.

His beautiful daughter was marrying a man whose smile matched hers. Her Keanu was an islander, a doctor, a man of fierce intelligence and integrity, and Max couldn't have chosen a man he'd be more proud to call his son-in-law. Caroline didn't need his support.

No one did.

'Who giveth this woman…?'

'I do,' he said in a voice that was choked with emotion. He released his daughter's arm and stepped back to the pew reserved for him. The pew where Hettie sat, cradling Joni. At his insistence.

Hettie reached out and took his hand and he was grateful for it. The way his daughter looked… A man could dissolve into tears.

'Hold Joni,' Hettie said, and suddenly the sleeping Joni was on his knee. He had something…someone…to hold. To care for.

He didn't need him, he thought, but as the ceremony pro-

ceeded he was more than grateful for the baby's presence.
And for Hettie's. She sat by him, pressed lightly against
him as if there wasn't quite room in the pew, but of course
there was, for this pew was reserved for the bride's family
and there was only him.

The ceremony was over. Handel's Trumpet Voluntary
sounded out through the little chapel, joyfully triumphant,
across the headland and over the island beyond. Caroline
was laughing and crying all at once. She was hugging her
father and because he was holding Joni she was hugging
the bemused little boy, as well. And then she took her husband's hand and somehow enveloped them all in a wedding hug—Caroline and Keanu, Max and Hettie and Joni.

'I have so much family,' she whispered through tears.
'I'm so happy. Dad, you need to go for it, as well. Love
Hettie as much as I love Keanu.'

And then she was gone, in a mist of white lace, to en-
velop Keanu's aunts and uncles, his grandma, the staff of
the hospital and anyone else who was brave enough to come
into her orbit.

'You must be very proud.' The voice behind him made
Max turn. It was Harry, holding the hand of a woman Max
now knew as Sarah, the woman who'd acted as a fly in, fly
out surgeon one week a month. Sarah enveloped Hettie in
a hug. They turned to talk, and Max was left with Harry.

'Are you ready to leave?' Harry asked, smiling across at
Caroline and Keanu. For all his distraction, though, Max
knew this man to be an astute businessman. A billionaire
with power. It behoved him to stop thinking about Caroline for a moment—and also stop thinking about the way
Hettie had felt beside him in the chapel.

'You're wanting to take over responsibility?'

'In a word, yes. These islands… In a sense they've cured
me,' Harry said. 'They've made me see there's life beyond
my injury and it would be my privilege to give back. But

you, Max, you've been injured, too, and you've been giving back for years. Forgive me but I've made some enquiries about your background. It seems you're a skilled surgeon working in the public sector but you've also honed your skills in cosmetic surgery. You're the go-to surgeon for Sydney's society darlings. Do you enjoy that?'

Did he enjoy it? After a day working in the public sector, operating as he had here, to turn to men and women who were paying to keep the years at bay... No, he hadn't enjoyed it.

'It's lucrative,' Harry said softly, watching his face. 'I, too, am a surgeon. I know the choices we make. I know the doctors who choose to work for money and those who don't. I know you, Max Lockhart, and I believe you're the latter. But my spies also tell me that every cent of your lucrative cosmetic practice has been channelled back to the Wildfire hospital. Max, we've already discussed this, but the money you contribute would be a drop in the ocean compared to my fortune. I've already said I would like to assist. It would be my very great privilege to endow the hospital in perpetuity. You no longer need to do cosmetic surgery. You can step back and let someone else take over. Will you accept?'

And with that Max felt the last great burden of responsibility lift from his shoulders. He thought of the CT scanner, blown in the power surge at the hospital, and of the usual mass of paperwork to try and get government help to repair it, or the scores of cosmetic surgical procedures he would have had to perform if government help wasn't forthcoming.

Would he accept? Here was freedom in a form he had never dreamed.

'Thank you,' he said simply. 'The whole island would be honoured to accept your help.'

And then he paused as a burst of delighted laughter

sprang from the crowd. The islanders were tossing armfuls of frangipani over the bride and groom. Some had landed in Joni's hair. The toddler had lifted a handful, stared in wonder and then tossed the petals towards Caroline.

And he crowed in delight.

It was the first time Max had seen the little boy laugh, and, by the look of it, Hettie hadn't seen him laugh, either. Max watched Hettie blink away tears. He watched her hug Joni and then stoop with him, gathering more flowers to toss again. She was wearing a soft blue dress—incredibly simple, elegant, right. She had a frangipani tucked behind her ear. She looked…happy.

A happy ending.

And for a brief moment he forgot about freedom and let himself think, *What if?*

What if he stayed?

What was he thinking? Abandoning his dream? Harry was right beside him, telling him his dream was real.

For years, from the time he'd been twenty years old and he'd stood in the premature nursery as the father of twins, he'd thought of freedom. And now it was being handed to him. His financial obligations had been lifted. Caroline was safely married. Joni? He had to take responsibility there, but Hettie had shouldered that, as well. He could easily support them, from a distance.

Louis had been a threat to Hettie but the news there was reassuring, as well. Sergeant Ky had arrested him late last night, drunk, outside Wildfire's only bar. With island sympathy for Louis completely gone, the bartender had rung Ky to tell him where he was. Louis had broken the bartender's jaw, he'd smashed furniture, he'd even lunged at Ky with a knife. He was currently on his way to the mainland, facing a lengthy jail term, and the consensus was that the islanders, both on Wildfire and Atangi, were pleased to see him go.

So that left Max free. Hettie was safe. Joni was cared

for. He could do whatever he wanted. He could work wherever he wanted.

He could lie on a beach in Hawaii and do nothing at all.

Suddenly Hettie was back beside him, linking her arm in his. But this was a plan they'd talked about before the ceremony. This whole family thing was a pretence, a plan to have Joni accepted by the islanders. It wasn't real.

'What are you two plotting?' she asked. Joni was still on the ground, happily sorting frangipani flowers. She smiled down at him and then smiled up at Max, a smile that took his breath away.

She was beautiful. This place was beautiful.

Freedom... He did want it—didn't he?

'Harry's making plans for the island,' he managed, and Hettie turned her smile on Harry.

'Good ones?'

'Excellent ones,' Harry told her. 'We'll make your hospital first class. I'm thinking we won't stop at repairing the cyclone damage. I'm thinking we need a new wing with the extra services we could offer. More full-time staff.' He eyed Max speculatively. 'You know, if you decide to stay, Wildfire needs a good surgeon.'

'Of course it does,' Hettie said stoutly, and her arm tightened in Max's. 'But don't you look to Dr Lockhart. Apart from a few fly in, fly out visits to check on his new family, our Max is free.'

And that should've made him feel amazing.

It did—didn't it?

Their own marriage took place three days later. It was a quiet ceremony. 'Max's son died so recently. There's no way we want a fuss,' Hettie told everyone, and their friends were disappointed but understanding. But they had enough people in attendance to make a public point.

Caroline and Keanu were there, smiling and smiling.

They were leaving the next day on an extended honeymoon but they'd stayed to see Max wed.

'Because even if this is only a marriage of convenience, I think it's lovely,' Caroline told Max before the ceremony, hugging him soundly. 'And if you can make it more…'

'Neither Hettie nor I want more.'

'Really?' Caroline looked across to where Keanu was talking to Hettie and her eyes reflected her love and her happiness. 'I can't think why not. Dad, why don't you go for it?'

'You know why not.'

'I do,' she said, softening and hugging him again. 'But, honestly, Dad, freedom's not all it's cut out to be. I understand what's driving you,' she said, as he tried to frame words to explain. 'I've figured it out but I don't have to like it. Off you go and see the big wide world but know always there are people who love you. Including, I suspect, your Hettie.'

'She's not my—'

'She would be,' Caroline said softly. 'Given half a chance. She has all the love in the world to give, your Hettie. Just say the word.'

'Caro…'

'I know. Not my business. But let's get you wed and see where things go from there.'

So here they were. *Getting wed…*

They didn't use the chapel. It didn't seem right to make time-honoured vows in the chapel when their vows were being made for convenience, not for love.

Instead they stood by the lagoon, in the place where he'd sat that first night with Hettie and Joni. Hettie was wearing the same blue dress she'd worn at Caroline's wedding. Caroline had made her a wreath of frangipanis and pinned it to her hair. Her curls were tumbling softly to her shoulders. She was bare-legged, wearing simple golden sandals.

She was devoid of all jewellery and as Max slipped the ring of gold on her finger he thought he'd never seen her look as lovely.

With this ring, I thee wed.

He'd made that vow before, as a carefree student, a boy who'd never imagined what responsibility that vow entailed.

Now he was making that same vow—without the responsibility?

It felt wrong.

'I will look after you,' he murmured, as she placed a matching ring on his finger and made the same vow, and she flashed him a look that might almost be anger.

'I don't need looking after,' she whispered. 'This island is my home and my family. Max, I love that you're doing this. I love your reasons, but I don't need your care. I'm not your responsibility, so if that's what you're thinking I'll take off this ring right now.'

'Really?'

'Really.'

'That would be the shortest marriage in the history of the universe.'

'I'm up for record breaking.' She was smiling, for the sake of their audience, he thought, but her voice was deadly serious. 'We're doing this for Joni. Don't you dare take me on, as well.'

'I want to take you on.'

'As my friend.' Her chin tilted. 'As your wife in name only. As someone you can leave and leave again. I'll not hold you down.'

He couldn't reply. Their tiny audience was watching, a little bemused. They were speaking in undertones, only to each other. What did brides and grooms generally say to each other in such circumstances?

'Go ahead or not?' Hettie whispered. Still her eyes were challenging.

And how could he not go ahead? Why would he not?

But he would take care of her, he thought. He just wished…

What? There was no time to decide.

The vows were made. They were man and wife. The island's celebrant beamed a blessing.

'You may now kiss the bride.'

Their friends were smiling and waiting. Caroline and Keanu, with Keanu cradling Joni. Harry and his Sarah. Sam and his Lia, just flown in from Brisbane, via Cairns. Bessie and Harold.

Couples who'd listened to the wedding vows and were remembering or looking forward to their own. He could see it in their eyes as they smiled and clapped and waited for him to kiss his bride.

As they waited for him to kiss Hettie.

And it felt…wrong? It felt dishonest, like some sort of travesty, that he'd make these vows to this woman, that he'd kiss her now and claim her as his wife and not mean it.

It was sensible. It was what they both wanted.

He needed to kiss his bride and move on.

He set his hands lightly on her shoulders and drew her to him.

He kissed his bride.

She should take this lightly. She'd deliberately pulled back during the ceremony and she'd deliberately added a prosaic reminder that this wedding was in name only.

So this kiss should be a brief, formal kiss, as this ceremony was supposed to be. And indeed for an instant that was all it was. Max's hands took her shoulders, she tilted her face to meet his and their lips brushed.

She should have pulled back fast. He should have released her. They should have turned to their audience, job done, formalities complete.

Except they didn't. They couldn't.

Because they were still kissing?

How did that happen? One moment there was a light brushing of lips against lips. The next moment the hold on her shoulders tightened. The brush of lips was repeated and then she found herself standing on tiptoe so the brush could be something more.

For it was something more. It was a whole lot more. Max was kissing her as if he meant it, as if this was no mock wedding. He was kissing her as if he wanted her.

Want…

It was such an alien sensation that she had no way of dealing with it. She was shocked into submission—but no. Submission? This was no such thing.

She was shocked into desire.

He was kissing her and she was giving as good as she got. Why not? she thought in the tiny amount of brain she had left for processing such thoughts. It's not every day a woman gets married.

It's not every day a woman marries a man like Max.

And with that thought came another, insidious, sweet, a siren song. What if this marriage was real?

What if Max wanted her?

It was a fleeting thought in the few sensuous moments as his mouth claimed hers, as warmth flooded her body, as his hands held her to him.

As she felt herself mould against him.

As she kissed him as she'd never dreamed she could ever kiss.

And as the kiss ended, as she surfaced to laughter and applause and Max smiling down at her, his hands on her shoulders, she thought, *My world has changed.*

She was married.

It was a marriage of convenience.

Yes, it was, she told herself. Her head knew that it was true. It was only her body telling her it was a lie.

Or maybe it was more. For somehow she knew, deep down, admit it or not, it was her heart that was telling her that for richer or poorer, in sickness and in health, for as long as they both should live, this man was her husband.

Her heart was saying, Marriage of convenience or not, from his moment, with this kiss, she was truly married.

Only, of course, it *was* just a marriage of convenience. They signed the register. They received laughing congratulations from their friends. They got through a sumptuous wedding feast that Caroline had organised and then their friends dispersed and they were left alone.

With Joni.

'Let Keanu and I take him for the night,' Caroline had begged, but Hettie wouldn't hear of it.

'He's only just starting to relax with me. And with Max. He needs to stay with us.'

Plus she needed the little boy, she thought as she walked up the steps into the palatial Lockhart mansion. She looked at all the photographs of Lockhart ancestors and felt the presence of her new husband behind her and thought, *What have I done?*

Joni was practically a shield. She hugged him tight, thinking this was for him. Joni's rightful place was here. Max had wanted her to move in here three days ago but when Ky had assured her there was no further threat from Louis she'd opted to stay in her villa.

'Only until our wedding,' Max had growled, and she'd agreed, but now there was no reason not to live here.

Except she wasn't a Lockhart. This wasn't her home. It'd be more suitable if she was here as Joni's nanny, she thought, and a bubble of laughter that was half fear rose within her.

She should be the hired help. She had no place here.

And the way she felt about Max... It scared her.

'This is your room,' Max told her. He'd led her across the grand entrance hall and along a short passage. He threw open double doors and she caught her breath in awe.

This room was amazing. This room was bliss.

For a start it was vast. It was also old. The worn, wooden floor was honey gold and faded by sun. The bed was an enormous four-poster, with soft white netting draped around it. There was a faded chintz sofa and armchairs, a small, elegant antique table, faded rugs, and wide French windows opening to the verandah and the lagoon beyond.

The room invited her in, welcomed her in a way nothing else could. A woman could sink into this room.

'Check the bathroom,' Max said, smiling, watching her face. He threw open a door and revealed an enormous tub on crocodile feet, a shower the width of the room and massive towel rails with lush, white towels. All still looking over the lagoon.

'And this is where Joni can sleep,' he told her. He opened another door and there was a perfect child's room, already decorated with pink wallpaper. With ponies and roses and tiny forget-me-nots.

'This was Caroline's. Maybe we should get rid of the pink.'

'I don't think Joni's noticing,' Hettie said. 'But we... Maybe I can do something later? Max, it's beautiful. But where do you sleep?'

'At the other end of the house. But I'm leaving next week so you'll have the whole house to yourself.'

'That's...fine,' she managed, and hugged Joni a bit tighter.

'Bessie and Harold will be here. Ky says Louis is no longer a threat.'

'You don't need to worry.' But she must have sounded strained because Max looked at her in concern.

'Hettie, I didn't resign from my job,' he told her. 'I took leave. I'm not sure what I'll be doing in the future but for now, my job at Sydney Central is waiting.'

'Of course it is.' She struggled to make her tone light. 'But you will come back?' Heck, she sounded needy. She could have slapped herself but the words were out and she couldn't get them back.

'Once a month,' he told her. 'I have it planned. If I stay at Sydney Central I'll do what most fly in, fly outers do. I'll work through a couple of weekends and then spend five or six days here once a month. That way I can catch up with Caroline and with you and Joni.'

That was the deal, she thought. This was the agreement going into their marriage. This arrangement had given the little boy to her, and more. It had given her the backing of the Lockhart name, this sumptuous place to live, and a live-in housekeeper and groundsman to help with Joni's care.

How could she possibly want more?

It was just that kiss.

Those kisses.

They were somehow imprinted on her heart. How Max could stand there and calmly talk about catching up with her once a month when he'd kissed her like that…

'What you're planning… That doesn't sound like freedom to me,' she ventured. 'Max, this has been all about me. I wanted Joni and I have him. What do you want?'

'I have everything I need.'

'I didn't say need. I said want.'

'Want doesn't come into it.'

'So all that talk of freedom…'

'Leave it.'

It was a snap and she flinched. He saw it and swore. 'Hettie, I didn't mean—'

'It doesn't matter.' She cut him off. 'I'm tired. Max, I need to settle Joni and go to bed myself.'

'Of course.' But there was a strain between them that was almost tangible. He was standing back, apart. That's what he wanted, she thought. His body language was almost spelling it out.

Why did she want to weep?

Some wedding night, she thought bleakly, with the groom backing out of her room as fast as he could go, with her holding Joni like a shield.

They were alike. Two people with ghosts, with shadows so deep they'd never move past them.

But she was overthinking things. This, after all, was a business arrangement, a great outcome for all concerned. If she could just get the kisses out of her head... If she could just look at Max and see the patriarch of the island, the hospital's benefactor, a fine surgeon, her friend...

Not the man. Not the toe-curlingly sexy male her heart told her he was. Not a man who knew how to love and who could be loved in return.

Not a man with needs he couldn't admit to.

No. That was wishful thinking and she needed sensible thinking. And action.

'I don't need anything else,' she told him, striving to sound brisk and efficient. 'I know where the kitchen is if Joni needs a bottle and everything else can wait until morning. Thank you, Max. Thank you for everything and goodnight.'

'It's me who should be thanking you,' he said heavily. 'You're the one taking on the responsibility for Joni.'

'I'm not taking on responsibility for anything,' she snapped, suddenly angry. 'I'm choosing. They're very different things and I'm sorry you can't see it. Meanwhile, I don't need gratitude.'

'Hettie—'

'Goodnight, Max,' she said, as firmly as she could manage, and she turned away fast, and if it was to hide the sudden moisture welling behind her eyes, well, how stupid was that?

A woman had to be sensible. A sensible woman said goodnight to her brand-new husband and closed the door behind him.

And where was sleep after that?

Max didn't even try to go to bed. Instead, he wandered down to the lagoon where a few short hours ago he'd made the vows to love and to honour Hettie de Lacey for the rest of his life.

They'd been mock vows.

They hadn't felt like mock vows.

It didn't matter, though, he thought as he stared out over the still water. He'd always look out for her. He'd keep her safe and he'd keep his nephew safe.

He was responsible for them—and he didn't want to be responsible.

But neither did he want to walk away.

He could stay. He could pretend those vows were real. To love and to honour… Well, the honour was real at least.

Love? He'd known her a week.

She was a convenient answer to the problem of Joni.

Could he love Joni?

As he'd loved Christopher?

A few short weeks ago he'd stood by his son's grave and he'd felt his heart break. Simple as that.

He'd done the same when Ellie had died. He'd had no idea that grief was a physical thing, a crumbling from within, a physical reaction that had left him gutted, helpless, without an anchor. Drifting as the *Lillyanna* had drifted, buffeted by whatever wind, whatever tide took her.

That's what grief did to you. That's what love did to you.

He'd longed for freedom and now he had it. If anything happened to Caroline, yes, he'd be gutted again, but she had her Keanu to look out for her. He was free.

A man without responsibilities.

Why did it feel so empty?

He was still feeling grief; of course he was. With his son so recently gone...how could he think of making new connections?

Of filling the void.

Of replacing Christopher?

Hell.

It was hell. His head was filled with a special kind of torment, a tangle of pain and confusion and emptiness.

What he wanted—what he ached for—was to walk back into the house, take Hettie into his arms and hold her. To take comfort in her body. To forget himself in the love he suspected she could give.

She'd given her heart to Joni but he was starting to know this woman. He'd kissed her and she'd kissed him back, and there was a matching need in that kiss. The difference was that her need wasn't a product of aching loss.

What was it, then?

The beginnings of love?

If it was...

If it was then he had to move away fast. It wasn't fair on Hettie to take this one step further. He'd married her because it had been the sensible thing to do. To even think about making that marriage something other than a signed contract would be to invite disaster.

To let her hold him when he couldn't give back... To ask her to love him when all he felt was fear... It was unthinkable.

He swore and a night heron startled and flew straight upward into the starlit sky.

The night stretched on but still he didn't go inside. He

needed to go back to Sydney, he thought, and quickly. He needed to bury himself in his work. There was always enough medicine to fill the void. In Theatre, with lives under his hands, there was no room for the questions hammering in his head.

He could go back to swimming laps, lifting weights, running, filling the empty crevices of his life. He could finally figure where he could go from here without pain.

Except...why was the pain still with him?

It was Christopher, he told himself. Of course it was Christopher. He ached for his son.

He stood and looked out over the lagoon until the first rays of dawn tinged the sky.

He thought about Christopher. And Ellie.

It was sheer discipline that stopped him thinking about Hettie.

CHAPTER TEN

THE NEXT FEW DAYS were busy—deliberately so. He and Harry spent hours delving into the island's finances, deciding what needed to be invested and where. The knowledge that he wasn't on his own was incredible. Since his father's death he'd felt the full responsibility for the island's welfare. Now...the sensation of sharing made him feel almost light-headed.

'Harry's hiring choppers from the mainland within the next week,' he told Hettie on the night before he left. 'We've planned a full spray of all the M'Langi islands. Until now I've only been able to do Wildfire but if we can get rid of the mosquito breeding grounds... With the new vaccine available for clinical trials, with the money injected to get stocks, with the spray covering the swamp areas, encephalitis might become a thing of the past. And the ulcers... Without them, this island will be so much safer.'

He'd come back to the house—briefly. He'd done a couple of minor operations during the week and he'd told Sam he'd do a ward round that night.

'There's no need,' Sam had growled. 'Spend your last night with Hettie.'

But that was dangerous territory. He did need to be seen to spend time with her. That was part of the plan—to have the islanders see them as a family, to see Joni as a Lockhart—but that could easily be done with Hettie living in the house and Max dropping in and out at need. And sleeping—or not sleeping—there. Lying in the dark, thinking…

Trying not to think.

'You and Harry seem to have done a wonderful job,' Hettie was saying. She was sitting at the kitchen table. Joni was in his highchair. She was giving him his dinner, making the spoon into an aeroplane, making him giggle.

What was there in this scenario that made him want to run?

He didn't need to run. He was leaving tomorrow.

'Harry's amazing. I'm leaving the island in great hands.'

'But you still own the island,' Hettie said.

Was that a rebuke?

Maybe not. The aeroplane swooped, Joni chortled and the moment was past.

'You will be okay,' he told her.

'I'm not worrying about me,' she said, and then she stopped zooming the aeroplane and turned and looked directly at him. 'I'm worrying about you.'

What was there in that that took the air from his lungs?

'Why would you worry about me?'

'Going back to the mainland alone. Max, tell me you have good friends who'll meet you at the airport, who'll take you out to dinner, who'll watch your face and know you need to be taken for a drink or a walk or just have silent company. Christopher's so recently gone. Tell me you have friends who care.'

'My colleagues care.' They did, too, he thought. The hospital team had been incredibly supportive throughout Chris's illness. Some of his colleagues had attended the funeral. There'd been a vast arrangement of exotic flowers delivered to his apartment. His anaesthetist and a couple of his fellow surgeons had clapped him on the shoulder and said things like, 'We're with you, mate. Anything we can do, just ask.'

But he'd been so busy… For twenty-six years he'd been busy, working two jobs and caring for Christopher. He'd had an apartment at the hospital and a full-time carer for Chris, so that any gap in his working day could be spent with him.

Gaps hadn't included making friends.

Maybe he could now. Maybe that was what this new-found freedom would give him.

Friends.

He looked down at Hettie serenely feeding Joni, and he thought…

No. Run. Get out of here before the whole nightmare starts again. The nightmare of caring.

'I'm heading back to the hospital now,' he told her. 'I'll do a ward round tomorrow, too, before I go. I expect I'll see you at breakfast.'

She didn't move. 'I expect you will.'

'What will you do while I'm away?'

She concentrated on another aeroplane. 'Pretty much what I'm doing now, I expect. My role as charge nurse will be filled while I have some family leave.' She smiled up at him then. 'Actually, you know what? I intend to do…nothing. Or not quite nothing. I intend to play with Joni, to hug him, to take him to the beach and teach him to paddle, to lie under the palm trees and read silly kids' books to him. I intend to feed him his dinner via aeroplanes. I expect to leave my hair untied, wear my sarong, wake when Joni wakes, sleep when Joni sleeps. I intend to love my son.'

There was nothing to say to that. He glanced at Joni, who was picking up a rusk and inspecting it for possible poison. It was obviously a Very Suspicious Rusk, covered with Vegemite, the lovely black goop beloved by every true Australian kid but obviously not by Joni. He eyed it from every which way, then smeared it carefully onto his nose before carefully dropping it overboard.

Bugsy had been lying unnoticed in his basket by the corner. With the speed of light the rusk was hoovered up and Bugsy was back in his basket, smirking.

Joni chortled with delight and then looked expectantly at Hettie and held out his hand.

'Rusk?' he said, and Hettie giggled and Max grinned. But inside…his heart twisted.

'I have to go,' he said, and Hettie rose and searched his face.

'Do you?'

'You know I do.'

'I guess I do,' she said evenly, and then she took a deep breath. 'Max…I have to tell you, though…'

And then she fell silent.

Don't ask, he thought. *Just go.* But she was standing in front of him, shorts, T-shirt, snub nose, her curls a bit tangled. One curl had dared to drift across her eyes and she didn't seem to notice.

He really wanted to lift it and tuck it behind her ear.

He couldn't.

He should turn and walk out the door but his feet seemed glued to the floor.

'What?' he asked, heavily, and here it came.

'You should know that there's a choice,' she whispered. 'These last few days… I know you don't want it and I don't want you to take it any further. But what I feel for you… It's not gratitude. It's not respect and it's not friendship. You know how I held Joni after his mother died and I knew I could love him? Well, like it or not, that's how I feel with you.' She gave a wry grin then, as she heard what she'd said.

'Okay, sort of different,' she conceded. 'It's something to do with you being six feet tall and so gorgeous it's not fair to expect my hormones not to react.' She caught herself,

trying to make what she was saying make sense. 'Um...
Max...hormones or not, I understand you need to leave.
I respect that. I know your reasons. But when you come
back...I'll stay at my end of the house for as long as you
wish, for Joni's sake, but if you ever want me... If you ever
want to take it further...'

And then she broke away. She took a step back, looking appalled.

'Whoa, I'm sorry,' she managed. 'I can't imagine why
I'm laying this on you. I know it's not fair. But, Max, you
know I'm fine on my own. You know I'm happy. It's just
that I thought maybe if we're husband and wife I should
just say it. Just so you know...the hormone thing is sort
of...there.'

'I can't,' he said, because it was all he could think of to
say, and she nodded as if this was a normal conversation
between a married couple, maybe Mum asking Dad to take
the kid to school, Dad saying he couldn't.

Dad saying he couldn't commit.

Dad saying he couldn't be a dad. Or a husband.

Or a lover.

And there was the crux of everything. He wouldn't mind
being a lover. No, that was wrong. He *wanted* to be a lover.
The more time he spent with Hettie the more he wanted
to pick her up and carry her to his bed. To love, to protect,
to honour...

To hold her as his own.

But with that came the rest. Husband. Father. Island
patriarch. All the things that had weighed on him for
twenty-six years.

'Hettie, love...'

'I know I'm not your love.' She managed to say it
evenly, emotion gone from her voice. She sat down again
and started wiping Joni's face. 'I'm not your anything,' she
added mildly. 'I shouldn't have said it but it seemed only

honest and I think honesty has to be front and foremost in this…arrangement. Go back to work, Max. Go back to what you do and forget all about my dumb little confession. It means nothing. Your plane gets in at ten in the morning. I'll feed Joni between seven and eight but then we'll go and play by the lagoon. So if you can arrange not to be in the kitchen between seven and eight…'

'Why?'

'Because goodbye should be now,' she said, and she looked up at him and he saw the emotionless facade slip. He saw distress. 'Because I've just made a fool of myself and I need time to recover. You'll be back in a month and by then I'll have myself nicely under control. Joni and I will have our lives sorted. So you head off and sort your life as you want it to be—as you deserve it to be—and leave us to get on with ours.'

'Hettie—'

'Leave it, Max,' she said, and she tugged Joni from the highchair and held him close. 'I'm taking Joni for a bath so we'll say goodbye now.' And then she slipped forward and reached up and kissed him, lightly, a faint brush on the cheek. And then she stepped away fast.

'Goodbye, Max,' she whispered. 'And thank you.'

How was she to calmly bath Joni after that?

Luckily Joni pretty much bathed himself. He splashed in the big tub, crowing with delight as he ran water from a plastic mug down his tummy. He was entranced with his cleverness.

So was Hettie, but not completely. She sat on the floor next to the tub and she kept a hand on Joni's shoulders, keeping contact, keeping the reassurance that she was always there, and stupidly, foolishly, she let herself weep.

She'd just let down all her defences.

She was married and, for better or worse, she wanted

her husband. She wanted to keep contact. She wanted the reassurance that he was always there.

More, she wanted him.

At midnight, twelve-year-old Indi Hika and his two mates sneaked out of their parents' houses, took Indi's dad's dinghy and tried to catch flounder in the lagoon. Two hours later, hauling the dinghy out through the marshes, Indi felt a sting on his ankle. It hurt, but twelve-year-olds didn't make a fuss in front of their mates. By the time he limped home it was hurting a lot, but he was understandably reluctant to let his parents know he'd been out on the water after midnight. He sneaked back into bed and pulled up the covers.

He didn't even look at his ankle. If he had he would have seen two distinctive fang marks. Instead, he lay silent for two hours while his foot grew more and more painful and the venom spread through his body. Finally he cried out loud. His parents investigated, to find him twisting in agony and having trouble breathing.

The family had no phone. Max was standing on the house verandah, staring into the darkness, when he saw the truck race up the hill.

His thoughts were so tangled that a medical emergency was almost a relief. He reached the hospital almost as the Hikas did, and by the time Sam arrived he had the lad intubated.

It took the two doctors' combined efforts, considerable skill and the rest of the night to keep the boy breathing. Finally, though, Indi decided to live and Max walked out of the hospital to a new day. The day he was to leave.

He glanced at his watch. He had an hour until the plane left.

Hettie and Joni would have already breakfasted. She'd have taken him to the little beach at the end of the lagoon.

His time on the island was over.

He walked back to the house to shower and collect his gear. His thoughts were still drifting, the drama of the night fresh and real. Just do what comes next, he told himself as he walked up to the airstrip with his kitbag. Any number of people would have driven him but he wanted no one. He felt curiously disengaged, as if he was moving in a vacuum.

The *Lillyana* was in harbour, waiting for repairs. Most of his gear was still on her and could stay there.

His kitbag was light. He was…free.

It was the end of an era. He'd come back, he knew, but only as a visitor. The responsibilities had all been taken care of.

He'd be welcomed as a friend.

He wasn't part of this island.

The incoming plane hadn't arrived yet and the airstrip was deserted. He sat on a cyclone-smashed palm beside the hangar and looked out over the island. From here he could see the sea and the lagoons dotting the island. He could see across to the research station with the beautiful pool where he and Hettie had swum.

She'd keep swimming there.

And suddenly her words from the night before were replaying in his head. Not the ones concerning him. Not the ones that had him closing down, the words he didn't know what to do with. What he was remembering was her talking of taking family leave to get to know her new son.

'You know what?' she'd said. 'I intend to do…nothing. Or not quite nothing. I intend to play with Joni, to hug him, to take him to the beach and teach him to paddle, to lie under the palm trees and read silly kids' books to him. I intend to feed him his dinner via aeroplanes. I expect to leave my hair untied, wear my sarong, wake when Joni wakes, sleep when Joni sleeps. I intend to love my son.'

He found himself smiling at the thought of Hettie free

from her responsibilities as nurse manager, free to do what she wanted.

Free to love her son.

And all at once he was hit by a sensation so powerful he couldn't deal with it. It was like a blow to the side of the head, a blow that sent him reeling.

He wanted…what Hettie had chosen.

Of course he did, he told himself, rising and striding across to the edge of the clearing, staring across at the island and then out to the farther islands dotting the sea beyond. He wanted freedom. He'd ached for freedom. That's what Hettie now thought she had.

So…had he got it wrong?

Was freedom sitting under a palm tree, reading a kids' book to a child who wasn't his?

Was freedom dipping his toe again into the pool of loving?

Was freedom jumping right in?

The memories of the night just gone were still swirling in his head. Indi, twelve years old, agonisingly close to death. Indi's parents, clutching each other in terror, every fibre of their being centred on the life of their son. If he'd died, everything would have fallen apart.

As his life had fallen apart when Ellie had died. And then when Christopher had died.

He never wanted that pain again. If he walked away now, he'd never have it, and that was what he wanted—wasn't it?

'I intend to love my son.'

There was the rub. What if Joni were to be bitten by a snake or stand on a stonefish? Hettie would bear the trauma alone.

No, she wouldn't, he told himself savagely. She'd have every islander beside her. His own daughter and her husband would be here. Caroline and Keanu would support her. Everyone here would love her and stand by her.

It should be him.

He wanted it to be him.

He thought tangentially of Christopher. His grief for his son was still a raw and jagged wound. Surely he couldn't open his heart to that sort of loving again?

Surely he couldn't.

But as he stood in the morning sun, as he watched the silver glint of the incoming plane slowly grow bigger, he thought somehow, some way, he already had.

It wasn't a betrayal of Christopher. Or of Ellie.

He remembered Chris in one of the last few lucid moments before he'd slipped into unconsciousness. His lovely son had reached out and taken his hand.

'Dad, get a life...'

Chris had said it to him often, sometimes teasing, sometimes exasperated, a kid not able to see how seriously a man had to take the world.

Get a life.

A life could be...right here on the island.

Hettie was right here.

The choking fog that seemed to have enveloped him since Christopher's death was lifting, and with its lifting came a knowledge so deep, so fundamental that he must have been blind not to see it all along.

He was free to choose.

He could choose to love.

If she'd have him.

'Please,' he said out loud, and he left his kitbag where it lay and turned and started walking down towards the house. Towards his home.

And then he started to run.

Hettie and Joni and Bugsy had sat on the beach at the lagoon for a couple of hours. Joni was ready for a sleep but she hadn't wanted to risk running into Max by heading back to the house too soon. The plane's schedule was tight, though. It'd come in, drop off, pick up and be gone, so as soon as she saw it coming in the distance she knew it was safe to go home.

Home? To the Lockhart homestead.

She was a Lockhart. It'd take some getting used to. She was Max Lockhart's wife.

She was a wife without a husband.

She pushed the all-terrain stroller along the path to the house. The going was rough through the bushland, over leaf litter strewn from the cyclone. Joni was growing sleepier and she was in no hurry. What was the use of hurrying?

As she walked somehow she kept noticing the glint of gold on her ring finger.

She was married—and yet not.

She was married to a man who was even now boarding a plane to head back to Australia.

'Well, what did you expect?' she muttered to Bugsy, who was trailing at her side. 'He's given you Joni. What else did you want from him?'

'Nothing,' she told Bugsy.

She lied.

'Yeah, and didn't I do that well,' she demanded. 'Telling him I was available if he wanted me. Throwing myself at him. What sort of a goose must he take me for?'

Bugsy looked supremely disinterested. Joni, however, looked up sleepily from the stroller and looked a bit worried.

'It's okay, sweetheart,' she said, giving the stroller a final shove up the path into the clearing by the house. 'I'll forget to blush in a while. Life will settle down. We're fine on our own.'

But then Bugsy gave a joyful woof, as if he'd seen someone in the bushes. He lurched ahead. Hettie shoved the stroller up the last bit of rough path—and Max was in front of her. Max, looking dishevelled. Max, out of breath.

Max, looking as if he'd been running.

For a moment neither of them spoke. She couldn't, and it seemed neither could he. Possibly because he had no breath.

'Hey,' she whispered at last. 'You'll miss...you'll miss your plane. It's landed.'

He told her where the plane could go and she blinked. 'Pardon?'

'You heard. But I hope Joni didn't.' He smiled then, a tired, rueful smile. They were standing eight feet apart, as if he wasn't ready to venture closer. 'I guess...I need to start watching my language all over again. Toddlers are parrots.'

She hesitated, still confused. 'Joni's nearly asleep. I think you're safe. But...Max, I saw the plane coming in to land. That's why we're going home. Because you won't be there.'

There was a silence at that. It stretched on, while a couple of crazy parrots turned somersaults in the palms above her head, while a blue-winged butterfly idled past her nose, while she became aware of the look of strain behind Max's eyes.

'I guess,' Max said at last, as if he'd finally regained his breath and was ready to go on. 'What I'm about to ask... Hettie, do you think, in the future—or even now—do you think you can go home because I *am* there?'

She thought about it. Thinking was hard when there was a butterfly doing circles around her head, but it seemed it needed to be done. She needed to concentrate really hard.

She waved away the butterfly. The butterfly was beautiful but Max's words were better.

But this was a time to be practical, she told herself. She needed to say it like it was.

'Max, I'm truly grateful,' she managed. Why was it so hard to get her voice to work? 'I'm incredibly grateful for all you've done, but you've done enough. I won't have you staying because you feel responsible for me. For us. You need your freedom, and you deserve it. You need to leave.'

The silence stretched on. There were sunbeams filtering through the wind-battered canopy of palms. They were making odd shadows on the path. She concentrated on the patterns, on the shifting shadows.

Joni was drifting off to sleep in his stroller. He gave a tiny, sleepy murmur and Hettie checked him, grateful for the distraction. When she glanced up again Max's face had changed a little. The tension on his face lifted.

'Hettie, I know you don't need me,' he said, and it was as if he was talking from a long way away. This was a voice she hadn't heard before. 'But what if I realised…' he said slowly. 'What if I said I needed you? You take the world on your shoulders, Hettie, love. Could you take me on, too?'

What was he saying? She stared at him and then looked down at the shadows again. This felt terrifying. She felt as if she was on the edge of something so huge…

So fragile…

'Hettie, this might not make any sense to you,' he said slowly, as if he was still putting the words together in his head before he spoke. 'But I sat up on the runway, waiting for the plane to land, and I thought of you building sand-castles with our son—*our son*—and I had a wash of need so great it knocked sense into me.'

'Sense?' She was having so much trouble getting her voice to work.

'Perspective? Heaven knows what. I only know that at twenty I was landed with twins and financial obligations and responsibility and I coped. But you know what? Sometimes I even had fun. I loved Chris. I adored my daughter, even though I seldom saw her. But I loved it that Caroline grew to love this island, so much so that she's now married an islander. And I loved my work. Heaven help me, sometimes I even loved the weird and wonderful people who lined up to have themselves look younger. But all the while, all these years, a voice has been hammering in my head, saying, *What if you were free? What if you had none of these responsibilities?* And then suddenly…I was.'

'You deserve—'

'Who knows what I deserve?' he said frankly. 'But is what I deserve what I want?'

'I don't know what you mean.' It was barely a whisper.

'I mean I sat up there, waiting for the plane to take me to this new freedom, and I thought, Harry's taken financial responsibility from me. You've taken the care of Joni from me. Caroline and Keanu are here to take care of the island. I'm not needed. I can go and lie on a beach in Hawaii. I can do anything I want. And the plane was coming closer and I thought, I can get on that plane and go anywhere in the world. I'm needed nowhere. But then I thought, *Where do I want to be?* And suddenly the answer was so obvious it was like a punch to the side of the head. Because I knew. Hettie, I knew that you were at the lagoon, playing with our baby—*our* baby, Hettie—and I realised that this is where I want to be. More, this is where I need to be. Hettie, love, I'm not here because you need me. I'm here because I need you.'

The butterfly had landed on the leaf litter just beyond her feet. Its wings were still fluttering, seemingly in time with the beats of her heart.

She was trying to get Max's words into some sort of order. Some sort of sense.

For some reason, it was easier to watch the butterfly.

'This is probably way too soon,' Max said ruefully. 'I know you said you could love me but maybe you need time. Maybe we both need time.'

'Do you need time?' Her voice was still strangely calm.

'No,' he said, and he said it almost fiercely. 'I need no time at all. For I know what I want and I want you. Hettie, love, suddenly I have freedom and it's the greatest gift of all. Up on the airstrip as the plane was coming in to land… It was like a clearing of the fog. I could see it and why I couldn't see it before… But I am seeing it now. Hettie, it means I have the freedom to love. If you'll have me, my love. If you'll take me on, then I have the freedom to love you.' He paused, still apart from her, still holding himself back. 'But if it's too soon…if indeed we are rushing things… Hettie, tell me to go away and I will.'

'N-no.' It was so hard to make her voice work. 'Can you really want to stay?' she managed.

'For as long as you need me.' And then he shook his head. 'No. Let's make that as long as I need you.'

'And how long could that be?' Her voice was scarcely a whisper.

'Forever?'

Maybe she hadn't heard right, she thought. Maybe this was nothing but a dream.

But he was stepping forward. He was moving the stroller with the sleeping Joni aside and he was taking her hands. He was smiling at her, tenderly, lovingly but, oh, so uncertainly.

He thought she didn't need him.

Ha!

But let him think it, she decided, a hint of the inner Hettie returning. A man who thought he wasn't needed… A man who wanted to be needed… This could be excellent. She could graciously allow him to unblock her plumbing. She could kindly permit him to push the stroller up the rough part of the track—or maybe she could even suggest if he could rebuild the track.

'Hettie?' He sounded nervous.

'Yes?'

'What are you thinking?'

'Nothing,' she said with insouciance, and suddenly Max

was grinning. He could read her, her Max, and suddenly he was with her, the Max she knew and loved, the Max in charge of his world, who'd returned to take his rightful place as Lockhart of Wildfire.

Her husband.

The father to her son.

'You get to push the stroller,' she said firmly, and he looked astonished.

'What, now?'

'Certainly now. You can push faster than me and we need to go home.'

'I… Yes.' And then he added, still not completely sure, 'Back to the homestead?'

'Certainly. We have work to do.'

'Work?'

'We need to shift those bedrooms,' she said astringently. 'Get all your stuff up to my end of the house, or my stuff up to your end of the house. Depending on whose bed's biggest.'

'Het—'

'And we need to do it before Joni wakes up,' she told him. 'We could make a bed right here but I'm scared of small boys and cameras.'

He choked on joyful laughter, and then, even though speed was imperative, even though his beautiful, bossy Hettie was giving orders he fully intended to comply with, he firmly gathered her into his arms.

'Hettie de Lacey?' he managed and then he kissed her so her answer couldn't come for quite a while.

'Y-yes?' she managed when she came up for air.

'Will you marry me?'

'I thought…I thought I already did.'

'Not properly,' he told her. 'Not the way it ought to be done. I'm a Lockhart of Wildfire and I know what's due to my bride.'

'What?'

'The whole island,' he said in satisfaction, holding her against him, folding her to him so she moulded against his breast, so she felt truly as if she'd found her home. 'We need to repeat our vows in front of every islander, from Wildfire, from the whole of M'Langi if they'll come. Every single islander present, a feast that lasts for days, a celebration to say this is a new beginning. You and me, my love, with Joni and Bugsy and Harry and all our hospital friends and all the islanders… It's a joyous beginning for all of us. I want to work here, Hettie, and I hope I can be needed. I hope together we can make a difference to this place. But we'll do it side by side, my love. As husband and wife. I know you don't need me, but this new system, do you think we could share?'

'It sounds good to me,' she told him, and smiled and smiled. And then she pulled back so she could see him. So she could see all of him, this man she loved with all her heart.

'It sounds wonderful,' she told him. 'Let's start now.'

EPILOGUE

EIGHTEEN MONTHS ON marked the twenty-fifth anniversary of the opening of the Wildfire hospital. When Ellie had died Max had vowed to get a hospital on the island. It had taken a herculean effort to see it built but now every islander, plus every medic who'd ever worked in the hospital, seemed to be here to celebrate. They were also here to celebrate the new Christopher Lockhart Surgical Wing, built by Harry.

Harry had also funded tonight's *hangi*. It was held on Sunset Beach, below the hospital, and it was a feast to outdo any feast the island had seen before. All day there'd been hospital tours, tours of the new research centre, tours of the amazing new resort, even an underground tour of the now fully operating gold mine. Two years before, Wildfire had been in such financial straits that half the islanders had been unemployed and the hospital threatened with closure. Things couldn't be more different today.

'We've done well.' Harry and Max were standing apart, looking out over the crowd of islanders and medics gathered around the vast fire pit on the beach. Harry gripped Max's shoulder in a gesture of companionship, a gesture that spoke of shared troubles and a similar happy ending. 'This is better than we could ever have hoped,' Harry said in quiet satisfaction, and Max could only agree.

And he wasn't only thinking of the hospital.

Harry's Sarah was helping Hettie build a sandcastle for Joni. At three, Joni was a bossy toddler, happy and self-assured and certain that his way was the right way to get those turrets up, even when they kept falling over. Sarah and Hettie were giggling over the latest disaster, while Joni stomped down to the water's edge with his bucket to get more water.

Both men watched and both men had goofy smiles on their faces.

'We have done well,' Max said softly. 'Thanks to you.'

'Thanks to us,' Harry said firmly. 'Mine was the money. Yours was the persistence and power. Not to mention the encouragement of the two women in our lives.'

'We wouldn't have done it without them,' Max agreed. He tried to change his smile from goofy and failed. Hettie was laughing. Hettie was gorgeous. She was his wife. How could he do anything but smile?

And there was so much more to smile about than the laughter of his lovely wife, he conceded. He had a grand-child now, tiny Christie, born six weeks ago to Caroline and Keanu. Ana and Luke were here, with their daughter, Hana, and their baby, Julien. Sam and Lia were helping Joni scoop up water but Lia was having trouble bending. Eight months into pregnancy, Lia had an excuse not to bend.

And she wouldn't have to go to the mainland to have her baby. That was an amazing source of satisfaction. With the new wing on the hospital and with Harry's funding, they now had a full-time obstetrician on the island, plus an an-aesthetist. Max's grandchild had been born on Wildfire with every precaution taken care of.

'And we've not had a single case of encephalitis for the season.' Harry's beam was almost as wide as Max's. 'The trials of the new vaccine seem to have been a resounding success. We can almost rest on our laurels, Dr Lockhart.'

Max grinned back. 'Do you think my Hettie will let me rest? That woman has so many projects…'

'She did tell me you like to be needed,' Harry conceded, smiling across at the doctors in charge of the new clinic out on Atangi. Josh and Maddie and their beautiful baby daughter had come to Wildfire for the celebrations. 'Has she told you her idea for a preschool?'

'No,' Max said, startled, and Harry chuckled.

'I might have known. The elementary school's good but she thinks early schooling's important, especially now we have so many more babies. She's thinking of setting one up on each of the islands and she's already hit me for funding.'

'You've done enough,' Max told him, but Harry shook his head.

'How can I ever have done enough? If I've done enough then I'm not needed. What about you, Max? Have you done enough?'

And Max thought of what he had.

He had enough surgery here to keep him busy full time. He had a wife who loved him. He had a son who came running every time he came into the house, greeting him with joy. He had his daughter and son-in-law and he had a granddaughter who was already promising to be Joni's best friend.

He had friends, he had family, he even had a dog because Hettie decreed that since Maddie had taken Bugsy out to Atangi, there had to be another hospital mascot. Not that Roper was much of a mascot, but the great shaggy cross-bred was certainly a favourite. Max needed to put in a bit of dog training. He had projects to make the M'Langi islands better and better, and Hettie kept thinking up more.

He smiled at her now and she looked up from what she was doing and smiled back, almost as if she could sense he was thinking of her. Her smile was warm, intimate, loving, and it still had the capacity to make his heart turn over.

'What are you plotting?' she called. 'You and Harry?'

'Just what comes next,' he called back, and he couldn't help it. His smile turned goofy again, just like that. 'Just how to be needed for the rest of my life.'

* * * * *

A ROYAL
AMNESIA SCANDAL

JULES BENNETT

I have to dedicate this book to the fabulous Andrea Laurence and Sarah M. Anderson who always come through for me when I need a plot fixed five minutes ago. Wouldn't go through this crazy journey without you guys!

One

Escaping to the mountains would have been much better for his sanity than coming to his newly purchased private seaside villa off the coast of Portugal.

Kate Barton fully clothed was enough to have any man panting, but Kate running around in a bikini with some flimsy, strapless wrap that knotted right at her cleavage was damn near crippling. The woman had curves, she wasn't stick-thin like a model and damn if she didn't know how to work those dips and valleys on that killer body. Not that she ever purposely showcased herself, at least not in the professional setting, but she couldn't hide what she'd been blessed with, either. Even in a business suit, she rocked any designer's label.

Luc Silva cursed beneath his breath as he pulled his Jet Ski back to the dock and secured it. His intent in coming here was to escape from the media, escape from the woman who'd betrayed him. So why was he paying a penance with yet another woman?

To ensure privacy for both of them, he'd given Kate the guesthouse. Unfortunately, it and the main house shared the same private beach, damn it. He'd thought purchasing this fixer-upper on a private island, barely up to civilization's standards, was a brilliant idea at the time. With no internet access and little cell service, it was a perfect hideaway for a member of Ilha Beleza's royal family. He didn't want to be near people who knew of or cared about his status. Luc had only one requirement when searching for a hideout: a place to escape. Yet here he was with his sexy, mouthy, curvy assistant.

Not only that, the renovations to the property were only half-done, because he'd needed to get away from reality much sooner than he'd thought he would.

A lying fiancée would do that to a man.

"Your face is burning."

Luc fisted his hands at his sides as he approached Kate. Was she draped all over that lounge chair on purpose or did she just naturally excel at tormenting men? She'd untied that wrap and now it lay open, as if framing her luscious body covered only by triangles of bright red material and strings.

"I'm not burned," he retorted, not slowing down as he marched up the white sand.

"Did you apply sunscreen?" she asked, holding an arm over her forehead to shield her eyes from the sun.

The movement shifted her breasts, and the last thing he needed was to be staring at his assistant's chest, no matter how impressive it was. When she'd started working for him about a year ago, he'd wanted her... He still wanted her, if he was being honest with himself.

She was the absolute best assistant he'd ever had. Her parents still worked for his parents, so hiring Kate had been an easy decision.

A decision he questioned every single time his hormones shot into overdrive when she neared.

He never mingled with staff. He and his parents always kept their personal and professional relationships separate, so as not to create bad press or scandal. It was a rule they felt very strongly about after a scandal generations ago. Rumor had it the family was quite the center of gossip for a while after an assistant let out family secrets best left behind closed doors.

So once Luc had become engaged to Alana, he'd put his attraction to Kate out of his mind.

For the past three months, he'd been ready to say "I do" for two very valid reasons: his ex had claimed to be expecting his child, and he needed to marry to secure his crown to reign over Ilha Beleza.

Now Alana was gone and he was trying like hell to hang on to the title, even though he had just a few months to find a wife. And the second he was in charge, he'd be changing that archaic law. Just because a man was nearing thirty-five didn't mean he had to be tied down, and Luc wanted nothing to do with holy matrimony... especially now that he'd been played.

"You're frowning," Kate called as he passed right by her. "Being angry isn't helping your red face."

There were times he admired the fact she didn't treat him as if he was royalty, but just a regular man. This wasn't one of those times.

Before climbing the steps to the outdoor living area, Luc turned. "Did you cancel the interview with that journalist from the States?"

Kate settled back into her relaxed position, dropping her arm to her side and closing her eyes as the sun continued to kiss all that exposed skin.

"I took care of canceling all media interviews you

had scheduled regarding the upcoming wedding, or anything to do with Alana," she told him. "I rescheduled your one-on-one interviews for later in the year, after you gain the title. By then I'm positive you'll have everything sorted out and will be at the top of your game."

Luc swallowed. Not only was Kate his right-hand woman, she was his biggest supporter and advocate. She made him look good to the media, occasionally embellishing the truth to further boost his family's name.

"I simply told each of the media outlets that this was a difficult time for you, playing up the faux miscarriage, and your family's request for privacy."

Kate lifted a knee, causing a little roll of skin to ease over her bikini bottoms. Luc's eyes instantly went to that region of her body and he found himself wanting to drop to his knees and explore her with more than his eyes.

"If you're done staring at me, you need to either go inside or put on sunscreen," she added, without opening her eyes.

"If you'd cover up, I wouldn't stare."

Her soft laugh, drifting on an ocean breeze, hit him square in the gut. "If I covered up, I wouldn't get a tan. Be glad I'm at least wearing this. I do hate those tan lines."

Gritting his teeth, Luc tried but failed at keeping that mental image from his mind. Kate sunbathing in the nude would surely have any man down on his knees begging. Forcing back a groan, Luc headed up the steps and into the main house. She was purposely baiting him, and he was letting her, because he was at a weak spot in his life right now. He also couldn't hide the fact that his assistant turned him inside out in ways she shouldn't.

He'd been engaged, for pity's sake, yet before and after the engagement, he'd wanted to bed Kate.

Sleeping with an employee was beyond tacky, and he wasn't going to be so predictable as to fall into that cliché. Besides, the house rule of no fraternizing with employees was something he stood behind wholeheartedly.

He and Kate were of like minds, and they needed to remain in a professional relationship. Period. Kate stood up for him, stood by him, no matter what, and he refused to risk that by jumping into bed with her.

She had been just as shocked as he was when Alana's deception had been revealed. For once, Kate hadn't made a snarky comment, hadn't tried to be cute or funny. She'd instantly intervened, taking all calls, offering up reasons why the engagement had been called off.

In fact, it was Kate's brilliant plan that had saved his pride. She'd informed the media that Alana had miscarried, and the couple had opted to part ways as friends. At first he'd wanted to just come out with the truth, but he'd been so hurt by the personal nature of the lie, he'd gone along with the farce to save face.

So, for all the times Kate got under his skin with their verbal sparring and her torturous body, he couldn't manage this situation without her.

There were times, even before the fiancée debacle, that he'd just wished he had a place to run to and escape all the chaos of being royalty. Purchasing this home— even though it needed some updating—was like a gift to himself. The view had sold him immediately. With the infinity pool overlooking the Mediterranean Sea and the lush gardens, the previous owners obviously had to have been outdoor enthusiasts. At least Luc had a dock for his Jet Ski and his boat.

Too bad he'd had to come here before all the remodeling was complete. Kate had informed the workers they would have the next two weeks off because the house would be in use. The contractors had managed to get a few of the rooms fully renovated, and thankfully, Luc's master suite was one of them.

He stripped off his wet trunks and stepped into his glass-enclosed shower, which gave the illusion of being outside, but in fact was surrounded by lush tropical plants. The shower was an addition to the master suite and one of his favorite features in the house. He loved having the feeling of being outdoors while being ensured of the privacy he craved. That had been his top priority when he'd bought the house.

An image of sharing this spacious shower with Kate slammed into his mind, and Luc had to focus on something else. Such as the fact she was ten years younger than him, and when he'd been learning to drive, she'd been going to kindergarten and losing her first tooth. There. That should make him feel ridiculous about having such carnal thoughts toward his assistant…shouldn't it?

Water sluiced over his body as he braced his hands against the glass wall and leaned forward. Dropping his head, he contemplated all the reasons why bedding his assistant was wrong. Not only would things be awkward between them, but any bad press could threaten his ascension to the throne. Not to mention the no-fraternization rule, which had been implemented for a reason. He didn't want to be the cause for a black mark on his family's name. One major issue was all he could handle right now. Unfortunately, the one and only reason for wanting to claim her kept trumping all the mounting negatives. He had to find a way to keep her at arm's length, because if he kept seeing her parading around in that skimpy gear, he'd never make it through these next two weeks alone with her.

Scrolling through the upcoming schedule, Kate jotted down the important things she needed to follow up on once she was back at the Land of the Internet, aka the palace. Even though Luc was taking a break from life, she had no such luxury, with or without cyberspace. He might be reeling from the embarrassment of the breakup, and dodging the media's speculations, but she still had to stay one step ahead of the game in order to keep him pristine in the eyes of the people once the dust cloud of humiliation settled. Damage control had moved to the top of her priorities in her role as assistant.

Being the assistant to a member of the royal family hadn't been her childhood aspiration. Granted, he wasn't just any member of the royal family, but the next king of Ilha Beleza, but still.

At one time Kate had had notions of being a dress designer. She'd watched her mother, the royal seamstress, often enough, and admired how she could be so creative and still enjoy her work. But Kate's aspirations hit the wall of reality when she'd discovered she excelled at organizing, being in the thick of business and playing the peacemaker. The job appealed to the do-gooder in her, too, as she felt she could make a real difference in the lives of others.

Once she'd received her degree, Kate knew she wanted to work with the royal family she'd known her entire life. She loved them, loved what they stood for, and she wanted to continue to be in that inner circle.

Kate had first met Luc when she was six and he was sixteen. After that, she'd seen him at random times when she'd go to work with her parents. As Kate grew older and well into her teens, Luc had become more and more appealing to her on every level a woman starts to recognize. Of course, with the age gap, he'd paid her no mind, and she would watch as he'd parade women in and out of the palace.

She'd never thought he would settle down, but as his coronation fast approached, with his thirty-fifth birthday closing in, the timing of Alana's "pregnancy" couldn't have been better.

Too bad the spoiled debutante had had her hopes of being a queen shattered, tarnishing the tiara she would never wear. Alana had tricked Luc into believing she was expecting their child, which was absurd, because there's only so long that lie could go on. Alana hadn't planned on Luc being a hands-on type of father, so when he'd accompanied her to a doctor's appointment, he'd been stunned to realize there was no baby.

At least now Kate wouldn't have to field calls for "Lukey" when he was in meetings and unable to talk. Kate was glad Miss D Cup was out of the picture…not that there was room in the picture for Kate herself, but having that woman around had seriously kept her in a bad mood for the past several months.

As she glanced over Luc's schedule after this two-week hiatus, all she saw was meetings with dignitaries, meetings with his staff, the wedding ceremony and the ball to celebrate the nuptials of his best friend, Mikos Alexander, and a few outings that were just "spontaneous" enough for the media to snap pictures but not get close enough to question Luc. A quick wave as he entered a building, a flash of that dimpled grin to the camera, and the paparazzi would be foaming at the mouth to post the shots with whatever captions they chose.

For the past year Kate had tried to get him to take

on charity projects, not for the media hype, but because he had the power to make things happen. Good things, things that would make a difference in people's lives. What good was power and money if they weren't used to help those less fortunate?

But Luc's focus had always been on the crown, on the bigger prize, on his country and what it would take to rule. He wasn't a jerk, but his focus was not on the little guys, which occasionally made Kate's job of making him look like a knight in shining armor a little harder.

Still, working for a royal family had its perks, and she would have to be dead to ignore how sexy her boss was. Luc would make any woman smile with a fantasy-style sigh. But no matter how attractive the man was, Kate prided herself on remaining professional.

She may have daydreamed about kissing him once. Okay, fine. Once a day, but still. Acting on her attraction would be a colossal mistake. Everyone knew the royal family's rules about not fraternizing with staff. The consequences could mean not only her job, but also her parents'. A risk Kate couldn't take, no matter what she ached for.

With a sigh, Kate rose to her feet and set her day planner aside. Luc had warned her that she'd be "roughing it" at this guesthouse, but she sort of liked the basic charm of the place. The rooms were pretty much bare, the scarred hardwood floors desperately in need of refinishing and the kitchen was at least thirty years out of date, if not more. But she was in her own space and had water, electric power and a beach. She wasn't working nearly as much as she had been at the palace in the midst of wedding-planning chaos. All of those media interviews had been canceled or rescheduled, and she was on a secluded island with her hunky boss. So roughing it wasn't so "rough" in her opinion.

Kate headed out her back door, breathing in the fresh scent of the salty ocean breeze. Following the stone path lined with overgrown bushes and lush plants, which led to the main house, she was glad she'd come along even if the circumstances made Luc only edgier, grouchier and, well, difficult. He had every right to be furious and hurt, though he'd never admit to the pain. Luc always put up a strong front, hiding behind that tough-guy persona.

Kate knew better, but she still chose to refrain from discussing the incident too much. Keeping things more professional than personal was the only way she could continue to work for him and not get swept away by lustful feelings.

When Kate had first started working for Luc, they'd had a heated discussion that led to a near kiss before he'd pulled back. He'd informed her right then that under no circumstances did he bed, date or get involved with employees.

Still, long nights spent working together, trips abroad and even the close quarters of his office had led to heated glances and accidental brushes against each other. The attraction most definitely wasn't one-sided.

Then he'd started dating Miss D Cup, and the obvious physical attraction between boss and employee had faded...at least on Luc's side. Typical playboy behavior. Kate had chided herself for even thinking they would eventually give in to that underlying passion.

Yet here they were again, both single and utterly alone. So now more than ever she needed to exercise this ability to remain professional. In reality, she'd love nothing more than to rip those designer clothes off him and see if he had any hidden tan lines or tattoos, because that one on his back that scrolled across his taut muscles and up onto his left shoulder was enough to have her lady parts standing at attention each time he took his shirt off.

As tempted as she was to give in to her desires, too much was at stake: her job, her parents' jobs, the reputation she'd carry of seducing her boss. That wouldn't look good on a résumé.

Kate had left her phone behind and contemplated changing. But since she was comfortable and would be only a minute with Luc—five at the most—she wanted to see if he'd take her up on this venture she'd been requesting his help with for the past year. Now that his life was turned inside out, perhaps he'd be a little more giving of his time.

With her sandals slapping against the stone pathway, Kate rehearsed in her head everything she wanted to say as she made her way to the house, passing by the picturesque infinity pool.

The rear entrance faced the Mediterranean. Of course, there wasn't a bad view from any window or balcony that she'd seen, and her guest cottage was definitely on her list of places she never wanted to leave. Regardless of the updates that needed to be done, this house was gorgeous and would be even more so once Luc's plans were fully executed.

When she reached the glass double doors, she tapped her knuckles against the frame. The ocean breeze lifted her hair, sending it dancing around her shoulders, tickling her skin. The wind had kicked up in the past several minutes and dark clouds were rolling in.

Storms…she loved them. Kate smiled up at the ominous sky and welcomed the change. There was something so sexy and powerful about the recklessness of a thunderstorm.

When she knocked again and Luc still didn't answer, she held her hand to the glass and peered inside. No Luc in sight. The knob turned easily and she stepped inside the spacious living area. It led straight into the kitchen, which was only slightly more modern than hers. Basically, the main house looked the same as the cottage, only supersized, with the entire back wall made up of windows and French doors.

"Luc?" she called, hoping he'd hear her and she wouldn't startle him.

What if he'd decided to rest? Or what if he was in the shower?

A smile spread across her face. Oh, yeah. What if he *was* in the shower? Water sliding over all those glorious tanned muscles…

Down, girl.

She wasn't here to seduce her boss. She was here to plant a seed about a charity project close to her heart. If Luc thought he'd formulated the plan, then he'd be all for it, and she desperately wanted him to donate his time and efforts to an orphanage in the United States she'd been corresponding with on his behalf. For reasons he didn't need to know about, the place held a special spot in her heart. She didn't want him to go there out of pity. She wanted him to do so on his own, because he felt it was the right thing to do.

But Kate couldn't get the twins who lived there, Carly and Thomas, out of her mind, and she was driving herself crazy with worry. For now, though, things were out of her control, so she had to focus on getting Luc on board with funding and volunteering. What would that little bit hurt him, anyway? In all reality, the visit and the monetary gift wouldn't leave a dent in his time or finances, but both would mean the world to those children.

"Luc?" She headed toward the wide, curved staircase with its scrolled, wrought-iron railing. She rested her hand on the banister, only to have it wobble beneath her palm. Definitely another item for the list of renovations.

She didn't even know what room he'd opted to use as the master suite, as there was one downstairs and one upstairs. "Are you up there?" she called, more loudly this time.

Within seconds, Luc stood at the top of the stairs, wearing only a tan and a towel. Kate had seen him in swimming trunks, knew full well just how impressive his body was. Yet standing here looking up at him, knowing there was only a piece of terry cloth and a few stairs between them, sent her hormones into over-drive. And she had to keep reminding herself she was only his assistant.

Still, that wouldn't stop her from appreciating the fact her boss was one fine man. Her "office view" was hands down the best she could ever ask for.

"I'm sorry," she said, forcing her gaze to stay on his face. If she looked away she'd appear weak, as if she couldn't handle seeing a half-naked man. If her eyes lowered to the flawless chest on display, he'd know all her fantasies for sure. "I'll just wait until you're dressed."

Before she made a fool of herself by staring, babbling or drooling, Kate turned and scurried back to the liv-ing area, where she sank onto the old sofa that had been draped with a pale yellow cover until the renovations were completed and new furniture arrived. Dropping her head against the saggy cushion, she let out a groan.

Lucas Silva was one *atraente* prince. Sexy prince. After living in Ilha Beleza for a full year now, she was growing more accustomed to thinking in Portuguese as opposed to English. Even thinking of Luc in another language only proved how pathetic she was.

Get a grip.

She should've waited in the living room, or just come back later after her walk. Then she wouldn't have been tortured by seeing him wearing nothing but that towel and the water droplets that clung to those taut muscles. Had he been standing closer, the temptation to lick away all the moisture from his recent shower might have been too much to handle.

She'd held on to her self-control for a year and didn't intend to let it snap now. A man like Luc would enjoy that too much, and Kate refused to be like all the other women who fawned over the playboy prince.

Smoothing her floral, halter-style sundress, she crossed her legs, hoping for a casual look instead of the assistant-hot-for-her-boss one. The second she heard his feet crossing the floor, she sat up straighter and silently scolded herself for allowing her thoughts and hormones to control her.

"Sorry I interrupted your shower," she told him the second he stepped down into the sunken living area. "I was heading out for a walk, but I wanted to run something by you first."

He'd thrown on black board shorts and a red T-shirt. Still, the image of him wearing next to nothing was burned into her mind, and that's all she could focus on. Luc fully or even partially clothed was sexy, but Luc practically in his birthday suit was a much more dangerous thought.

"I'm not working, if that's what you want to discuss." He strode across the room and opened the patio doors, pushing them wide to allow the ocean breeze to stream in. Kate came to her feet, ready to be firm, but careful not to anger him, because this project was too important to her.

"It's just something you need to think about," she retorted as she went to stand near the open doors. "I know we've discussed charity work in the past—"

He turned, held up a hand to cut her off. "I'm not scheduling anything like that until I have the crown. I don't want to even think beyond right now. I've got a big enough mess on my hands."

Crossing her arms, Kate met his gaze...until that gaze dropped to her chest. Well, well, well. Looked as if maybe he wasn't immune to the physical attraction between them, after all.

"I was working on your schedule for the next several months and you have a gap that I could squeeze something into, but you have to be in agreement."

The muscles in his jaw clenched as Kate waited for a response. Whenever he stared at her with such intensity, she never knew what was going through his mind. If his thoughts had anything to do with the way he'd been staring at her moments ago, she was totally on board. Sign her up.

Before she realized what he was doing, Luc reached out and slid a fingertip across her bare shoulder. It took every bit of her willpower not to shiver beneath such a simple, yet intimate touch.

"Wh-what are you doing?" she asked, cursing the stammer.

When his finger trailed across her collarbone, then back to her shoulder, Kate continued to stare, unsure what he was doing. If he was trying to seduce her, he needn't try any harder. With the way he kept looking at her, she was about to throw out the window all the reasons they shouldn't be together. One jerk of the knot of fabric at her neck and that halter dress would slide to the floor.

She waited, more than ready for Luc to make her fantasy come true.

Two

Luc fisted his hands at his sides. What the hell had he been thinking, reaching out and touching Kate like that? He was nothing but a *tolo*, a fool, even to allow himself the brief pleasure.

With all Kate's creamy skin exposed, silently inviting his touch, his last thread of willpower had snapped. And as much as he hated to admit it, even to himself, he was too emotionally drained to think straight. Part of him just wanted someone as a sexual outlet, an escape, but he wouldn't use his assistant…no matter how tempted he was.

Luc hadn't tried hard enough to keep himself in check, which was the main problem. He was still reeling from the fact that Kate had stood at the base of the steps looking as if she might leap to the second floor and devour him if he even hinted he was ready. And *misericórdia*, mercy, he was ready for some no-strings affection. Still, not with his employee. How did this number-one rule keep slipping from his mind?

"You're burned," he replied, surprised when his tone came out stronger than he'd intended. "Looks like you should've taken your own advice about that sunscreen."

With a defiant tilt of her chin, a familiar gesture he'd come to find amusing, she propped her hands on her hips, which did amazing things to the pull of the fabric across her chest. The woman was slowly killing him.

The no-dating-staff rule also covered no sleeping with staff. Damn it, he was a mess after Alana. More so than he feared if he was thinking even for a second of risking his family's reputation, and his own reputation as a worthy king, by sleeping with Kate. Nothing good would come from his moment of weakness, and then he'd be out an amazing assistant, because he couldn't allow her to work for him further. And she'd have a wealth of fodder for the press if she chose to turn against him.

That was precisely the reason he needed to keep his damn hands off his assistant.

"Maybe tomorrow we can rub it on each other, then," she suggested with a mocking grin. "Anyway, back to the charity."

Charity, the lesser of two evils when compared to rubbing sunscreen over her luscious curves... But he wasn't getting into this discussion again. He sponsored several organizations financially, but his time wasn't something he'd considered giving. The main reason being he didn't like it when people in power used that type of opportunity as just another publicity stunt. Luc didn't want to be that type of king...that is, if he actually got the crown.

"We need to figure out a plan to secure my title first," he told Kate. "Everything else can wait."

Pursing her lips, she nodded. Apparently, she was backing down, which was a first. She never shied away from an argument.

"You're plotting something," he said, narrowing his gaze. "You may as well tell me now."

"I'm not plotting anything," she replied, that sweet grin still in place, confirming his suspicion. "I've been thinking about your title, but I haven't come up with a solid solution, other than a quick wedding, of course."

She turned and started through the patio doors, but Luc reached out, grabbing her arm to halt her exit. Her eyes darted down to his hand, then back up to his face, but he didn't release her.

"Why is this particular charity so important to you?" he asked. "You mention it so often. If you give me the name, I'll send as much money as you want me to."

Her eyes softened, filled with a sadness he hadn't seen there before. "Money isn't what I wanted."

Slipping from his grasp, she headed down the stairs toward the beach. Money wasn't what she wanted? Had he ever heard a woman say that before? Surely any organization could benefit from a sizable donation.

Kate was always surprising him with what came out of her mouth. She seemed to enjoy a good verbal sparring as much as he did. But something about the cause she kept bringing up was bothering him. Obviously, this was something near and dear to her, and she didn't feel like opening up about it. She'd worked for him for a year, but he'd known her longer than that, though they didn't exactly hang in the same circles. Didn't she trust him enough to disclose her wishes?

Luc shook his head as he watched her walk along the

shoreline. The woman was mesmerizing from so many different angles, and it was a damn shame she was his assistant, because having her in his bed would certainly help take the edge off this title-throne nightmare.

Glancing up at the sky, he noticed the clouds growing darker. A storm was on the horizon and he knew how much Kate loved Mother Nature's wrath. She'd always been fascinated by the sheer power, she'd told him once. And that summed Kate up in a nutshell. She was fierce, moved with efficiency and had everyone taking notice.

Part of him wanted to worry, but he knew she'd be back soon, most likely to watch the storm from her own balcony. Luc still took a seat on his patio to wait for her, because they weren't done discussing this charity business. She was hiding something and he wanted to know what it was. Why was this mysterious organization such a secret? And why did discussing it make her so sad and closed off?

He sank down onto the cushioned bench beside the infinity pool. Everything about this outdoor living space was perfect and exactly what he would've chosen for himself. From the stone kitchen for entertaining to the wide, cushioned benches and chaise lounges by the pool, Luc loved all the richness this space offered.

Glancing down the beach where Kate had set out, he found he couldn't see her any longer and wondered when she'd start heading back. Ominous clouds blanketed the sky, rumbles of thunder filling the previous silence.

When the first fat drop of rain hit his cheek, Luc continued to stare in the direction she'd gone. Since when did he give anyone such power over his mind? He didn't like this. Not one bit.

He was next in line for the throne, for pity's sake.

How could his hormones be led around so easily by one petite, curvy woman, and how the hell could he still want her after months and months of ignoring the fact?

This pull was strong, no doubt, but Luc just had to be stronger. There was no room for lust here. He wouldn't risk his family's stellar reputation, or his ascension to the throne, just because he was hot for his assistant.

The wild, furious storm had been magnificent, one of the best she'd seen in a long time. Kate had meant to get back to the house before the weather got too bad, but she'd ended up finding a cove to wait it out in and couldn't resist staying outside. She'd been shielded from the elements, but she'd gotten drenched before she could get hunkered down.

With her dress plastered to her skin, she headed back toward the guesthouse. Even being soaking wet and a bit chilly from the breeze caressing her damp skin didn't dim her mood. She had to walk up the steps to Luc's patio in order to reach the path to her place. Noticing a light on the dock and lights on either side of the patio doors, she realized she'd been gone longer than she'd intended. It was clearly very dark and not because of the storm.

"Where the hell were you?"

Startled, Kate jumped back at the sound of Luc's angry, harsh tone. He stood in the doorway to his living area, wearing the same clothes as he had before, but now his hair stood on end, as if he'd run his fingers through it multiple times.

"Excuse me?" She stepped closer to him, taking in his flared nostrils, clenched jaw and the firm line of his mouth. "I told you I was going for a walk. I wasn't sure I had to check in, Dad."

Luc's lips thinned even more. "That storm was nasty. I assumed you'd have enough sense to come back. What the hell were you thinking?"

The fact he'd waited for her warmed something in her, but the way he looked as if he was ready to throttle her had her defensive side trumping all other feelings. This had nothing to do with lust or sexual chemistry.

"I purposely left the palace, the guards and everyone to get away from my troubles," he went on, his voice laced with irritation. "You're here to help me figure this whole mess out. But if you can't be responsible, you can either go back to the palace or I'll call in one of my guards to stay here and make sure you're safe."

Kate laughed. "You're being ridiculous. I'm a big girl, you know. I was perfectly fine and I sure as hell don't need a keeper. Next thing you know you'll be calling my parents."

With her father being head of security and her mother the clothing designer and seamstress for the family, Kate had been surrounded by royalty her entire life… just without a title of her own. Oh, wait, she was an assistant. Equally as glamorous as queen, princess or duchess.

Actually, she liked being behind the scenes. She had an important role that allowed her to travel, make great money and do some good without being in the limelight. And she would continue to try to persuade Luc to visit the orphanage so close to her heart. They'd taken care of her there, had loved her and sheltered her until she was adopted. Now she was in a position to return some of their generosity.

"Your father would agree with me." Luc stepped forward, closing the gap between them as he gripped her arm. "Don't go anywhere without your phone again. Anything could've happened to you."

"You can admit you were worried without going all Neanderthal on me, Your Highness." She jerked from his grasp, but he only stepped closer when she moved back. "What is your problem? I was out, I'm back. Don't be so grouchy because you can't admit you were scared."

"Scared?" he repeated, leaning in so close she could feel his warm breath on her face, see the gold flecks in those dark eyes. "I wasn't scared. I was angry that you were being negligent."

Kate really wasn't in the mood to be yelled at by her boss. She didn't deserve to be on the receiving end of his wrath when the issue he had was clearly with himself.

Her soggy dress needed to go, and she would give anything to soak in a hot bubble bath in that sunken garden tub in her master bathroom. She only hoped it worked. She hadn't tested it yet, and the sink in her kitchen was a bit leaky...

"I'm heading home." Kate waved a hand in the air to dismiss him and this absurd conversation. "We can talk tomorrow when you've cooled off."

The instant she turned away, she found herself being jerked back around. "I'm getting real sick of you manhandling—"

His lips were on hers, his hands gripping the sides of her face, holding her firmly in place as he coaxed her lips apart. There was nothing she could do but revel in the fact that Prince Lucas Silva was one potent man and quite possibly the best kisser she'd ever experienced.

And he was most definitely an experience. Those strong hands framed her face as his tongue danced with hers. Kate brought her hands up, wrapping them around his wrists. She had no clue if she should stop this before it got out of hand or hang on for the ride, since he'd fueled her every fantasy for so long.

Arching against him, she felt his firm body do so many glorious things to hers. The chill she'd had from the rain was no longer an issue.

But just as quickly as he'd claimed her mouth, he released her and stepped back, forcing her hands to drop. Muttering a Portuguese curse, Luc rubbed the back of his neck and kept his gaze on the ground. Kate honestly had no clue what to do. Say something? Walk away without a word?

What was the logical next step after being yelled at by her boss, then kissed as if he needed her like air in his lungs for his survival? And then pushed away with a filthy term her mother would blush at…

Clearing her throat, Kate wrapped her arms around her waist. "I'm not quite sure why you did that, but let's chalk it up to the heat of the moment. We'll both laugh about it tomorrow."

And dream about it tonight.

"You just push me too far." His intense gaze swept over her, but he kept his distance. "For a year I've argued with you, but you've always had my back. I know there've been times you've intervened and stood up for me without my even knowing. As far as employees go, you're the best."

Confused, Kate ran her hands up and down her arms as the ocean breeze chilled her damp skin. "Okay. Where are you going with this?"

"Nowhere," he all but yelled, flinging his arms out. "What just happened can't happen again because you're an employee and I don't sleep with staff. Ever."

Kate couldn't help the laugh that erupted from her. "You kissed me. Nobody mentioned sex."

His gaze heated her in ways that a hot bubble bath never could have. "I don't have to mention it. When I look at you I think it, and after tasting you, I feel it."

If he thought those words would deter her, he didn't know her at all. Kate reached forward, but Luc stepped back.

"Don't," he growled. "Just go on back to your cottage and we'll forget this happened."

Smoothing wet tendrils off her forehead, Kate shook her head. "Oh, no. You can't drop that bomb, give me a proverbial pat on the head and send me off to bed. You went from arguing to kissing me to throwing sex into the conversation in the span of two minutes. You'll understand if I can't keep up with your hormonal swings tonight."

The muscle tic in his jaw, the clenched fists at his sides, were all indicators he was irritated, frustrated and angry. He had no one to blame but himself, and she wasn't going to be caught up in his inner turmoil.

"This is ridiculous," she said with a sigh. "We're both obviously not in a position to talk without saying something we don't mean."

"I always mean what I say," he retorted. "Otherwise I wouldn't say it."

Rolling her eyes, Kate again waved a hand through the air. "Fine. You meant what you said about wanting to have sex with me."

"Don't twist my words," he growled.

Kate met his leveled gaze, knowing full well she was poking the bear. "Did you or did you not say you thought of having sex with me? That you actually feel it."

He moved around her, heading for the steps leading to the beach. "This conversation is over. Go home, Kate."

She stared at his retreating back for all of five seconds before she took off after him. Just because he was royalty and she was his assistant didn't mean he could dismiss her anytime he wanted. Rude was rude no matter one's social status.

She didn't say a word as she followed him. Luc's long strides ate up the ground as he headed toward the dock. Surely the man wasn't going out on his Jet Ski now. Granted, the water was calm since the storm had passed, but it was dark and he was angry.

Just as she was about to call his name, he went down. The heavy thud had her moving faster, her thighs burning from running across the sand. She prayed the sound of him falling was much worse than any injury.

"Luc," she called as she approached. "Are you all right?"

He didn't move, didn't respond, but lay perfectly still on the wet dock. Dread consumed her. The second she stepped onto the dock, her feet slid a bit, too, and she tripped over a loose board that had warped slightly higher than the others.

The dock obviously hadn't been repaired like the rest of the outdoor spaces on this property.

Kate crouched next to him, instantly noticing the swollen knot at his temple. He'd hit his head on a post, from what she could tell.

"Luc." She brushed his hair off his forehead, afraid to move him, and hoping he'd only passed out. "Can you hear me?"

She stroked his cheek as she ran her gaze down his body to see if there were any other injuries. How could he be up one second and out cold the next? Fear threatened to overtake her the instant she realized she didn't have her phone.

Maybe she was irresponsible, but she'd have to worry about that later. Right now she had no clue how serious Luc's injury was, but the fact he still hadn't moved had terror pumping through her.

Shifting so her knees weren't digging into the wood, Kate sat on her hip and kept patting Luc's face. "Come on, Luc. Wake up. Argue with me some more."

Torn between rushing back to the house for her phone to call for help and waiting to see if he woke on his own, Kate started patting down his shorts, hoping he carried his cell in his pocket.

One pocket was empty, and before she could reach to the other side, Luc groaned and tried to shift his body.

"Wait," she told him, pressing a hand to his shoulder as he started to rise. "Don't move. Are you hurt anywhere?"

He blinked as he stared up at her. Thankfully, the bright light from the lamppost was helping her assess his injuries, since the sun had set.

Luc's brows drew together in confusion. "Why were you feeling me up?"

Relief swept through her. "I wasn't feeling you up," she retorted, wrapping her arm around his shoulders and slowly helping him to sit up. "I was checking your pockets for a cell phone. You fell and hit your head on the post. I was worried because you were out for a few minutes."

Luc reached up, wincing as his fingers encountered the bump on his head, which was already turning blue. "Damn, that hurts."

"Let's get you back up to the house." Kate helped

him to his feet, then slid her arm around his waist to steady him. "You okay? Feeling dizzy or anything?"

He stared down at her, blinked a few times and frowned. "This is crazy," he muttered.

"What?"

With his thumb and index finger, he wiped his eyes and held the bridge of his nose. He probably had the mother of all headaches right now. All the more reason to get this big guy moving toward the house, because if he went back down, she couldn't carry him.

"I know you," he murmured. "I just... Damn it, your name isn't coming to me."

Kate froze. "You don't know my name?" This was not good. That ball of fear in her stomach grew.

Shaking his head, he wrapped an arm around her shoulders and started leading them off the dock. "I must've hit my head harder than I thought. Why isn't it coming to me?"

Kate pressed a hand to his abdomen, halting his progress. She shifted just enough to look him in the eyes. Since she wasn't a medic and never had any kind of training other than a basic CPR course, she had no idea what signs to look for with a head trauma.

"Look at me," she ordered. "You know me, Luc. You know my name."

Blowing out a breath, he hung his head. "I... It's on the tip of my tongue. Damn, why can't I remember?"

He glanced back up at her, worry filling his dark eyes. This was not good, not good at all. She was going to have to get him back to the house and call the palace doctor. Obviously, Luc's memory wasn't cooperating. But she didn't want him panicking; she could do enough of that for both of them.

"My name is Kate." She watched his eyes, hoping

to see some recognition, but there was nothing. "I'm your—"

"Fiancée." A wide smile spread across his face. "Now I remember you."

Luc leaned in to capture her lips once more, with a passion she'd never known.

Three

Fiancée? What the hell?

Mustering all her willpower, Kate pushed Luc and his intoxicating mouth away as his words slammed into her.

"Let's get you inside," she told him, trying not to focus on how hard he must've hit his head, because he was clearly not in his right mind. "I'm not comfortable with that knot you have, and you may have a concussion. I need to call your doctor. Hopefully, with the storm gone, we'll have cell service."

Luc stared at her another minute, then nodded. Slipping his arm around her shoulders again, he let her lead him up to the house. Something was definitely wrong with him. The Luc from only twenty minutes ago would be arguing that he didn't need a doctor, and he certainly wouldn't be leaning on her for support.

She couldn't even think about the fact that he believed they were engaged. Because if he thought they were sleeping together, this situation would get extremely awkward really fast.

Though she'd be lying if she didn't admit to herself just how much she liked him thinking they were a couple. How long would his mind play this trick on him? How would he treat her now that he believed they were together?

Once she had him inside and settled on the sofa, she stood up and caught her breath. Luc was one massive, thick, muscular man. She'd known he was cut, but she'd had no clue how solid and heavy he would be.

His body had leaned against hers, twisting her dress on their walk. As Kate readjusted herself, trying to refill her lungs with air and not panic, she found him staring up at her, that darkened gaze holding her in place. Shivers rippled through her at the intensity of the moment—and the man.

"What?" she asked.

"Why are you all wet?"

Plucking at the damp material that clung to her thighs, Kate shook her head. "I got caught outside in the storm earlier."

Those eyes continued to rake over her body. "You're sexy like this," he murmured as his heated stare traveled back up. "With your dress clinging to your curves and your hair messy and wavy."

Kate swallowed, because any reply she had to those intimate words would lead to a lie, and she couldn't let him keep thinking they were anything more than employee-employer, servant-royal.

"Where's your cell?" If she didn't stay on task, she'd get caught up in all those sultry looks he was giving her...and she desperately wanted to get caught up in the promise behind those sexy stares. But he wasn't himself right now. "I need to call the doctor. I hope we have service."

Luc glanced around, raking a hand through his hair. "I have no idea. I don't even remember why I was outside."

He slapped his hand on the cushion beside him and let out a string of curses. "Why can't I remember anything?"

The worry lacing his voice concerned her even more than the fact he thought they were engaged. Luc Silva never let his guard down. Even when faced with losing the crown, the man was the epitome of control and power. Sexy and strong and she wanted him. Plain and simple…or maybe not so simple considering she could never have him.

"It's okay," she assured him as she leaned down to pat his shoulder. "I'll find it. Once the doctor comes, we'll know more. Maybe this will only last a few minutes. Try not to panic."

That last bit of advice was for herself as much as him, because she was seriously in panic mode right now. She didn't know much about memory loss, but the fact that something had set his mind so off balance concerned her. She couldn't even imagine how he felt.

Kate walked around the spacious but sparsely decorated living room, into the dated kitchen and then back to the living room. Crossing to the patio doors they'd just entered, she finally spotted his cell lying on the old, worn accent table most likely left by the last tenants.

Thankfully, she knew the passcode to get into the phone. "I'm just going to step out here," she told him, trying to assure him he wouldn't be alone. "I'll be right back."

She didn't want Luc to hear any worry in her tone when she described the incident to the doctor. And for now, she wasn't going to mention the whole "fiancée" bit. She would ride this out as long as possible. Yes, that was selfish, but, well...everyone had their moments of weakness and Luc Silva was definitely her weakness.

Kate was relieved to get the doctor on the phone and even more relieved when he promised to be there within the next hour. For the next sixty minutes, Luc would most likely believe they were engaged and she would play right along until she was told otherwise.

Luc's private beach villa just off the coast of Portugal wasn't far from his own country. He was pretty much hiding in plain sight. This way he could be home quickly in an emergency—or someone could come to him.

Kate was grateful the doctor could use the private boat to get to the island. There was no airstrip and the only way in or out was via boat. Only yesterday she and Luc had been dropped off by her father, so Luc could keep his hideout a secret.

When she walked back inside, Luc had his head tipped back against the sofa cushions. Eyes closed, he held a hand to his head, massaging his temples with his fingers.

"The doctor is on his way."

Without opening his eyes, he simply gave a brief nod.

"I know you're hurting, but I don't want to give you anything before the doctor can examine you."

What if his injuries were more serious than she thought? Amnesia, temporary or not, wasn't the worst thing that could happen. People died from simple falls all the time. Even when they felt fine, they could have some underlying issue that went unnoticed.

The possibilities flooded her mind as she continued to stand across the room and stare at Luc. Should he be resting or should she keep him awake? She prayed she didn't do the wrong thing. She would never forgive herself if something happened to him because they'd been fighting and he'd stormed off. If she didn't always feel the need to challenge him, this wouldn't have happened.

The kiss wouldn't have happened, either, because that was obviously spawned from sexual frustration and anger. Luc's full-on mouth attack had been forceful, not gentle or restrained. She'd loved every delicious second of it. But now she needed to focus, not think about how good it had felt to finally have him touch her the way she'd always wanted.

As she watched him, his lids kept fluttering, and finally remained closed for a minute.

"Luc," she said softly. "Try not to fall asleep, okay?"

"I'm not," he mumbled. "The lights are too bright, so I'm just keeping my eyes closed."

Crossing to the switches, she killed the lights in the living room, leaving just the one from the kitchen on so she could still see him.

"Does that help?" she asked, taking a seat beside him on the couch, relishing in the warmth from his body.

He opened one eye, then the other, before he shifted slightly to look at her. "Yeah. Thanks."

When he reached over to take her hand, Kate tensed. This wasn't real. The comfort he was seeking from her was only because he was uncertain—and he thought they were engaged.

Oh, if they were truly engaged, Kate could hold his hand and not feel guilty. She could wrap her arms around him and give him support and love and...

But no. She wasn't his fianceé so thinking along those lines would get her nowhere.

For now, she could pretend, she could keep her fingers laced with his and feel things for him in ways she never had before. This was no longer professional... they'd crossed that threshold when he'd captured her mouth beneath his.

"I'll be fine." Luc offered a wide smile, one rarely directed at her. "Just stay right here with me."

Swallowing the truth, Kate nodded. "I'm not going anywhere."

She tried not to relish the fact that Luc's thumb kept stroking the back of her hand. She tried to fight the thrill that he was looking at her as more than just an employee.

None of this was reality. He was trapped in his own mind for now. She didn't know if she should focus on the kiss earlier or the nasty knot on his head. Both issues made her a nervous wreck.

The hour seemed to crawl by, but when Dr. Couchot finally knocked on the back door, Kate breathed a sigh of relief. Beneath her hand, Luc tensed.

"It's okay." She rose to her feet, patting his leg. "We'll figure this out and you'll be just fine."

Dr. Couchot immediately came inside, set his bag down and took a seat on the couch next to Luc.

"Tell me what happened," he said, looking at Kate. Worry was etched on the doctor's face. This man had cared for Luc since the prince had been in diapers, and held all the royals' medical secrets.

Kate recounted the events, omitting the fiancée bit, and watched as the doctor examined his patient while she spoke. He looked at Luc's pupils with his minuscule light, then lightly worked his fingertip around the blue knot. With a frown, he sat back and sighed.

"Have you remembered anything since I was called?" he asked.

Luc shook his head. "I know Kate, but she had to tell me her name. I know I'm a member of the royal family because of my name, and I believe I'm the prince. I know this house is mine and I know I wanted to fix it up, but apparently I didn't get too far, so I had to have just bought it."

All this was right. A little burst of hope spread through Kate. Maybe his injuries weren't as bad as she'd first feared.

"From what I can tell, you've got temporary amnesia," the doctor stated. "I'm not seeing signs of a concussion and your pupils are responsive." Dr. Couchot looked up at Kate. "I would like him to have a scan to be on the safe side, but knowing Luc, he'll be stubborn and refuse."

"I'm sitting right here," Luc stated, his eyes darting between Kate and the doctor. "I don't want to get a scan. I'd have to go home and face too many questions. Unless I'm at risk for something more serious, I'm staying here."

Kate shared a look with the doctor. "What about if I promise to monitor him? You said there was no concussion, so that's a good sign."

"Fine," Dr. Couchot conceded. "I won't argue. But Kate will have her eyes on you 24/7 for the next few days and I'll be in contact with her. At the first sign of anything unusual, she will get you back to the palace, where we can treat you. No exceptions."

Luc nodded. "Agreed."

After receiving her instructions and a list of things

to look for in terms of Luc's behavior, Kate showed the doctor out.

Once they reached the edge of the patio, Dr. Couchot turned to face her. "Make sure you don't force any memories on him. It's important he remembers on his own, or his mind could become even more confused and his condition could actually worsen. It's a blessing he remembers as much as he does, so I believe he's only lost a few months of his memories."

A few months. Which would explain why he didn't recall the real fiancée or the fake pregnancy.

"I'll make sure not to feed him any information," Kate promised. Smoothing her hair back, she held it to the side in a makeshift ponytail. "Can he see photos or listen to his favorite music? Maybe just subtle things that will spark his thoughts?"

"I think that would be fine. Just don't push all of that on him at once. Give this some time. He may wake tomorrow and be perfectly fine, or he may be like this for another month. Every mind is unique, so we just don't know."

Kate nodded, thanking the doctor for coming so quickly. She watched as he made his way back down to the boat, where a palace guard was waiting. Thankfully, it wasn't her father, but his right-hand man.

Kate gave a wave to the men and took in a deep breath. When the doctor mentioned unusual behavior, did that include believing you were engaged to the wrong woman?

Weary and worried, she stepped back through the doors. All her stuff was at the guesthouse, but she would need to stay here.

Luc's eyes were instantly on hers when she returned to the living room. That warmth spread through her once again as she recognized that look of need. She couldn't let him keep this up. There would be no way she could resist him. And based on his reaction after that kiss, he wouldn't be happy that he'd indulged his desire for her, no matter how good together they might be.

The warning from the doctor played over in her mind. She couldn't force memories, so for now she'd have to let him think what he wanted, until his mind started to cooperate.

"Sit with me," he whispered, holding his hand out in invitation.

Kate cringed, wanting nothing more than to take his hand and settle in beside him. "I need to go get some of my things."

Lowering his hand, he frowned. "Where are your things?"

Coming up with a quick excuse, she tried to be vague, yet as honest as possible. "I have some things next door at the guesthouse. Let me get them and I'll be all yours."

Okay, she didn't necessarily need to add that last bit, but it just slipped out. She'd have to think through every single word until Luc fully regained his memory. For now, she'd have to play along…and still try to maintain some distance, or she could find herself in a world of hurt when he snapped out of his current state. Getting wrapped up in this make-believe world, even for a short time, wasn't the wisest decision. Still, he would need her during this time and they were on this island together. How could she resist him? How could she resist more touching, more kissing?

"Why do you have anything next door?" he asked.

"I was working there earlier." Still not a lie. "Give me five minutes. I'll be right back."

She escaped out the back door, unable to look at the confusion on his face any longer. If she got too far into the truth as to why she had things at the cottage, she'd have to come clean and produce the information his mind wasn't ready for.

As quickly as she could, she threw a change of clothes into her bag, adding a few essential toiletries. Everything else she'd have to smuggle over a little at a time, provided she stayed at the main house for longer than a few days.

Her biggest concern now was the fact she hadn't packed pajamas, assuming she'd be living alone. She stared at her pile of silky chemises in various colors. There was no getting around this. She didn't even have an old T-shirt to throw on for a sleep shirt.

With no other choice, she grabbed the pink one and shoved it in her bag before heading back to the main house. There was no way she could let Luc see her in this chemise, but how could she dodge a man who thought they were engaged? Most likely he assumed they slept together, too.

Kate froze on the path back to the main house. There was no way she could sleep with Luc. None. If they shared the same bed, she'd be tempted to give in to his advances.

As the moonlight lit her way back, Kate was resigned to the fact that things were about to skyrocket to a whole new level of awkward.

Four

Kate glanced over her shoulder, making sure she was alone as she slipped back out onto the patio to call her mother. There were times in a woman's life she just needed some motherly advice, and for Kate, that time was now.

"Darling!" Her mother answered on the second ring. "I was just thinking of you."

"Hey, Mama." Kate leaned against the rail on the edge of the patio, facing the doorway to make sure Luc didn't come up behind her and overhear things he shouldn't. "Are you busy?"

"Never for you. You sound funny. Everything all right?"

Not even close. Kate sighed, shoving her hair behind her ear. "I'm in a bit of a bind and I need your advice."

"What's wrong, Katelyn?"

Her mother's worried tone slid through the line. Kate swallowed back her emotions, because tears wouldn't fix this problem and they would only get her a snotty nose and red eyes. Not a good look when one was shacking up with one's sexy boss.

"Luc fell earlier."

"Oh, honey. Is he okay?"

"Well…he has a good-sized goose egg on his head. And he has temporary amnesia."

"Amnesia?" her mother repeated, her voice rising an octave. "Katelyn, are you guys coming back to the palace? Do his parents know?"

"I actually called them before I called you. Dr. Couchot was just here and he's assured us that Luc is okay, no concussion or anything. He isn't sure when Luc will regain his memory, but he's confident it's a short-term condition."

"I can't even imagine how scary this must be," her mother commented. "What can I do to help?"

"Right now Luc and I are staying here as planned," Kate stated, her eyes darting to the patio doors on the far side of the house. Luc stood there for a moment, looking out at the ocean, before he turned and disappeared. "The doctor said keeping him relaxed and calm is best for now. Luc had wanted to get away, so staying here is still our best option."

"I agree. So what else has you upset? If the doctor has assured you this is temporary, and you're staying there as planned, what's wrong?"

Pulling in a deep breath, Kate blurted out, "He thinks we're engaged."

Silence settled over the line. Kate pulled her cell away from her ear to make sure the connection hadn't been cut.

"Mom?"

"I'm here. I just need to process this," her mother stated. "Why does he think you're engaged?"

"He's only lost the past few months. He knew I was familiar, but at first he couldn't place me. When I told him my name, he assumed we were engaged. I was worried and didn't say anything, because I wanted the doctor to look him over. Dr. Couchot said not to feed Luc any information, because giving him pieces of his recent past could mess up his memory even further."

Kate rambled on. She knew she was talking fast, but she needed to get all this out, needed to get advice with Luc out of earshot.

"The doctor and Luc's parents have no clue that Luc believes we're engaged," Kate went on. "That's what I need your opinion on. What do I do, Mom? I don't want to go against the doctor's orders, but at the same time, I can't have him thinking we're a couple, but he doesn't even recall I work for him. You know how this family feels about dating or having such personal relationships with their staff."

"Oh, Katelyn." Her mother sighed. "I would wait and see how tonight goes. If this is temporary, maybe Luc will wake up tomorrow and everything will be fine. You can't go against the doctor's wishes, but I wouldn't let this lie go on too long. Luc may cross boundaries that you two shouldn't cross if he thinks you're his fiancée."

Cross boundaries? Too late. The kiss they'd shared moments before his fall flashed through her mind.

"Thanks, Mom. Please don't say anything. You're the only one who knows Luc thinks we're getting married. I don't want to humiliate him any further or have anyone else worry. I just needed your advice."

"I'm not sure I helped, but I'm definitely here for you. Please, keep me posted. I worry about you."

Kate smiled, pushing herself off the railing and heading back toward the doors. "I know. I'll call you tomorrow if the cell service is good. It's pretty sketchy here."

"Love you, sweetheart."

"I love you, Mama."

Kate disconnected the call as she grasped the doorknob. Closing her eyes, she pulled in a deep breath and blew it out slowly. She needed strength, wisdom and more self-control than ever.

And she needed to remember that Luc was healing. That he was confused. Whatever emotions she'd held on to after that kiss had no place here. Being this close to grasp onto her fantasy, yet not being allowed to take all she wanted was a level of agony she hadn't even known existed.

Luc stood in the spacious bedroom. Apparently, his master suite and luxurious attached bath, with a most impressive shower that gave the illusion of being outdoors, had been at the top of his list for renovations. Fine with him, because this room was fit for romance, and his Kate had looked all sorts of sexy the way she'd worried over him, assuring him he would be okay.

When she'd said it, her sweet, yet confident words had sliced through the fear he'd accumulated. He'd seen the worry in her eyes, but she'd put up a strong front for him. Was it any wonder she was the one for him? Dread over the unknown kept creeping up, threatening to consume him, but Luc wasn't giving up. Being unable to recall bits of his life was beyond weird and frustrating. He actually didn't have the words to describe the emotions flooding him. All he knew was that his beautiful fiancée was here, and she was staying by his side, offering support and comfort.

His eyes drifted from his reflection in the glass patio doors back to the king-size bed dominating the middle of the room. Sheers draping down from the ceiling enclosed the bed, giving an impression of romance and seduction. There was a reason this bed was the focal point of the room, and he had to assume it all centered around Kate. He could already picture her laid out on those satin navy sheets, her black hair fanned out as they made love.

Damn it. Why couldn't he remember making love to her? Why couldn't he recall how she felt against him? How she tasted when he kissed her? Maybe their intimacy would help awaken some of those memories.

Luc cringed inwardly. No, he wasn't using sex or Kate in that way. He wanted to remember their love on his own, but he definitely wanted her by his side tonight while he slept. He wanted to hold her next to him, to curl around her and lose himself to dreams. Maybe tomorrow he'd wake and all this would be a nightmare. His memory would be back and he and Kate could move forward.

There had to be something lying around, some clue that would spark his memory. Granted, he hadn't really brought anything personal to the place, judging by the hideously dated furniture in the majority of the rooms, but surely there was something. Even if he looked through the clothes he'd brought, or maybe there was something in his wallet that would kick his mind back into the proper gear. Perhaps he'd packed something personal, like a picture, or maybe he should go through the contacts on his cell. Seeing a list of names might be just the trigger he needed.

Luc searched through his drawers, finding nothing of interest. It wasn't as if his underwear drawer would reveal any hidden clues other than the fact that he liked black boxer briefs.

Slamming one drawer shut, he searched another. By the time he was done looking through the chest and hunting through his bathroom, he was alternating between being terrified and being furious. Nothing new popped up except a healthy dose of rage.

There had to be something in his cell phone. He started out the bedroom door, only to collide chest to chest with Kate. Her eyes widened as she gripped his biceps in an attempt to steady herself.

"Sorry," she said, stepping back. "I just got back with my things. I called your parents and gave them the rundown. They're worried, but I assured them you would be fine and you'd call them yourself tomorrow. I also called my mother. I didn't mean to be gone so long. Are you heading to bed?"

Was she shaking? Her eyes darted over his shoulder toward the bed, then back to meet his gaze. The fact she had been rambling and now kept chewing on her lip was proof she was nervous. About the amnesia?

"Are you all right?" he asked, reaching out to smooth her hair away from her forehead. He tipped her chin up, focusing on those luscious, unpainted lips. "You seem scared, more than you were just a few minutes ago."

Kate reached up to take his hand in hers. "I guess all the events finally caught up with me. I'm tired and worried. Nothing more."

"That's more than you need to handle," he told her, stroking his thumb over her bottom lip. "Let's go to bed."

That instant, holding Kate completely trumped finding his phone and seeking answers. There was a need inside him, an ache he had for this woman that was so primal he couldn't even wrap his mind around it. His phone would be there when he woke up, and right now all he wanted was to lose himself in Kate. She looked dead on her feet, and she still hadn't changed from her wet dress, which had now mostly dried. There was no way she was comfortable.

"Why don't you grab a shower and meet me in bed?" he asked.

Her eyes widened. "Um…I'm not sure we should…"

Luc waited for her to elaborate, but she closed her eyes and let out a soft sigh. When her head drooped a little, Luc dropped his hand from her chin and squeezed her shoulder.

"Are you afraid to be with me because of the memory loss?"

Her lids lifted, her dark eyes searching his. "I'm not afraid of you, Luc. I think it would be best if we didn't… you know…"

"Make love?"

A pink tinge crept across her tan cheeks. "Yes. You're injured. You need to rest and relax. Per the doctor's orders."

Luc snaked his arms around her waist as he pulled her flush against his body. "I plan on relaxing, but I want you lying beside me. It's obvious we came here to get away, and I don't want to ruin this trip for you."

Delicate hands slid up his chest, fingers curling up over his shoulders. Just her simple touch was enough to have his body quivering, aching. Everything about her was so familiar, yet so new at the same time.

"You're not ruining anything for me." She offered a tired, yet beautiful smile. "Let's just concentrate on getting you better, and everything else will fall into place."

"So no sex, but you'll lie down with me?"

Her eyes held his as she nodded. "I'll lie with you."

He hadn't recalled her name at first, but he'd instantly felt a pull toward her. No wonder they were engaged. Obviously, they shared a special, deeply rooted bond. Their chemistry pushed through the damage to his mind, and that alone would help him pull through this.

"I'll just go shower in the guest bath, real quick," she told him, easing away from his embrace. "Give me ten minutes."

Confused at her need to retreat, Luc crossed his arms over his chest. "Why not just use the shower in here? The other bathroom hasn't been renovated and this one is much more luxurious."

She looked as if she wanted to argue, but finally nodded. "You're right. A quick shower in here would be better. I just didn't know if I would disturb you trying to rest."

"You won't bother me. You can take advantage of the sunken garden tub, you know." He took her hands, leading her farther into their bedroom. "No need to rush through a shower. Just go soak in a tubful of warm water and relax."

"I'll be quick in the shower. Why don't you lie down?"

He leaned forward, gently touching his lips to hers. "Don't take too long or I'll come in after you."

She shivered beneath his touch, and it was all Luc could do to keep from hauling her off to the bed and taking what he wanted, throwing every reason he shouldn't straight out the window.

Retreating into the bathroom, she closed the door. Luc frowned. Was she always so private? Why did some things seem so familiar, while other, mundane things had disappeared from his mind?

As he stripped down to his boxer briefs, he heard the

shower running. An image of a wet, soapy Kate flooded his mind. He couldn't wait to get beyond this memory lapse, beyond the annoyance of the headache, and make full use of that spacious shower with her.

He would make this up to her, somehow. His Kate was exhausted, and still worried about him. She was sacrificing, when this was supposed to be a romantic trip away.

As of right now he only remembered they were engaged. He recalled some buzz about wedding invitations and upcoming showers. He'd let his assistant handle all of that…but he couldn't recall who his assistant was at the moment.

Raking a hand down his face, Luc sighed. Now wasn't the time to think of staff, not when he was about to crawl into bed with his fianceé. Right now he wanted to focus on Kate, on their trip and somehow making this up to her.

Kate showered quickly, constantly watching the door she'd closed. She should've known he'd want her in his room, that he wouldn't even question the fact.

But sleeping with him under false pretenses was an absolute no.

No matter how Luc made her body tingle and the nerves in her belly dance…she couldn't let her thoughts go there.

She was still Luc's assistant, which meant looking out for his best interest. And it was in the interest of both of them to keep their clothes on. Easier said than done.

Kate dried off, wrapped her hair up in a towel and slid into her chemise. She truly had no other option unless she asked Luc for a T-shirt, but she didn't know if he was one of those guys who would be even more turned on by seeing a woman in his clothes, so she opted for her own gown.

Rubbing the towel through her wet hair, she got all the moisture out and took her time brushing it. Perhaps if she stayed away a few extra minutes, Luc would get tired and fall asleep before she went back out there.

Their argument before his fall had taken on a life of its own, and she still couldn't get that kiss from her mind. Of course, if her lips weren't still tingling, maybe she could focus on something else. Such as the fact that the man was suffering from memory loss and was scared and angry over this sudden lack of control with his own mind.

Still, between the toe-curling kiss and the fact she was about to slide between the sheets with her boss, Kate didn't know how to act at this point. What was the proper protocol?

After applying some lotion on her legs and shoulders, Kate hung up her towel and faced the inevitable: she was going to have to go out into the bedroom and get in that bed. The sooner she moved beyond the awkward, uncomfortable stage, the sooner she could breathe easily. All she needed to do was go in there, lie beside Luc and wait for him to fall asleep. Then she could get up and go to the sofa or something. No way could she lie nestled next to him all night. The temptation to pick up where their kiss had left off would be too strong.

But the doctor had been adamant about not saying too much, to allow the memories to return on their own. Kate didn't want to do anything that would cause Luc more damage.

Somehow she had to abide by his no-fraternization

rule and still manage to play the doting fiancée. Was that combination even possible?

Taking a deep breath, she opened the bathroom door. The darkened room was a welcome sight. At least this way she wouldn't have to look him in the eye and lie. Now the only light spilled from the bathroom, slashing directly across the bed in the center of the room as if putting all the focus on Luc and his bare chest. The covers were up to his waist; his arms were crossed and resting on his forehead.

"Turn off the light and get in bed."

The memory loss didn't affect his commanding ways. The man demanded, he never asked, and he expected people to obey. Still, the low, powerful tone he used was enough to have her toes curling on the hardwood. This was her fantasy come to life, though when she'd envisioned Luc ordering her into bed, she never imagined quite this scenario.

What a way for fate to really stick it to her and mock her every dream with this false one.

"Is your head still hurting?" she asked, remaining in the bathroom doorway.

"It's a dull pain, but better than it was."

Kate tapped the switch, sending the room into darkness, save for the soft moonlight sweeping through the balcony doors. The pale tile floor combined with the moon was enough to light her path to the bed.

Pulling the covers back, she eased down as gently as possible and lay on her back. On the edge. As stiff as a board. And the ache for him only grew as his masculine scent surrounded her and his body heat warmed the minuscule space between them.

The bed dipped as Luc rolled toward her. "Are you okay?"

His body fitted perfectly against hers. Just the brush of the coarse hair on his legs against her smooth ones had her senses on alert…as if they needed to be heightened.

Was she okay? Not really. On one hand she was terrified. On the other she was completely intrigued…and spiraling headfirst into arousal. And arousal was taking the lead over so many emotions. With his breath tickling her skin, she was fully consumed by the one man she'd wanted for so long. It would be so easy, yet so wrong, to roll over and take what she wanted.

"I'm fine," she assured him.

With the darkness surrounding them, the intimacy level seemed to soar. She should've insisted on a small light or something. But then she would see his face. Honestly, she had no clue what was more torturous.

"You're tense."

Understatement of the year.

Luc's hand trailed up her arm, moving to rest on her stomach. If he thought she was tense before, he should just keep touching her. She was about to turn to stone.

She needed to regain control of her body, her hormones. Unfortunately, her mind and her girlie parts were not corresponding very well right now, because she was getting hot, restless, as if she needed to shift toward him for more of that delicate touching he was offering.

No. This was wrong. Her even thinking of wanting more was wrong. Just because he'd kissed her earlier didn't mean a thing. He'd done so to shut her up, to prove a point and to take charge as he always did.

Yet given the way he'd masterfully taken over and kissed her with such force and passion, there was no way he'd been unmoved. And she would've called him on it, but now she was dealing with a new set of issues surrounding her desires.

"If you're worried about me, I'm fine," he assured her. "I just want to lie here and hold you. Scoot over against me. I feel like you're about ready to fall out of the bed."

Just as she started to shift, her knee brushed against him. His unmistakable arousal had her stopping short.

"Ignore it," he said with a laugh. "I'm trying like hell."

Squeezing her eyes shut, Kate sighed. "I can't do this."

Five

Luc grabbed Kate around the waist just as she started to get up. Pulling her flush against him, her back against his chest, he held on tight. Her silky gown slid over his bare chest, adding fuel to the already out-of-control fire.

"Don't," he whispered in her ear, clutching the silk material around her stomach, keeping her body taut against his own. "Just relax."

"You need to be sleeping."

Her body was still so stiff, so rigid beneath him. Something had seriously freaked her out and she wasn't telling him what it was. Damn it, was it something he already knew but couldn't recall? Or was this not about her at all, but something to do with his fall?

A sliver of fear slid through him.

"Did the doctor say something you're not telling me?" he asked.

"What? No."

She shifted, relaxing just a touch as she laid her hand over his on her stomach. The first contact she'd initiated since climbing into bed.

"He didn't say much when I walked him out," she went on. "Just that he felt it necessary for you to remember on your own."

"The only thing I want to do right now is to get you to relax."

Luc slid his hand out from beneath hers, to the lacy edge of her silk gown. Her body stiffened briefly, then arched as if she was fighting her own arousal. When she sucked in a breath, Luc knew he had her.

"Luc, you need to rest."

Her shaky voice betrayed her, indicating she was just as achy and excited as he was. He pushed one of her legs back, easing his fingers beneath the silk until he found the delicate elastic edge on her panties.

"What I need to do is pleasure my woman," he whispered in her ear, pleased when she trembled.

Kate's back arched again and her head fell against his shoulder. "Luc, you don't have to—"

He nipped at the tender flesh of her earlobe as he eased his hand inside her panties to stroke her. "I want to."

Her soft moans, her cry when he found just the right spot, left his mouth dry. It didn't take long for her body to give in and shudder beneath his touch. She gasped, trembled all the while Luc trailed kisses along her shoulder, her neck when she'd turn just so and the soft spot below her ear.

Yet nothing triggered any memories.

All the same, he didn't regret giving her pleasure. Everything about this private moment only made him want her, yearn for her more.

"Are you always this responsive?" he whispered.

Slowly, she rolled toward him, rested a palm on his chest. With the pale glow from the moon, he didn't miss the shimmer in Kate's eyes.

"Baby, don't cry."

She blinked, causing more tears to slide down her flushed cheeks. "You didn't remember, though, did you?"

He smoothed her damp hair away from her face. "No."

When her hand started down his abdomen, toward the top of his boxer briefs, he gripped her wrist.

Kate had been through a rough time, and even though he was the one suffering the medical concern, he wasn't about to let her think he'd given her pleasure only to get his own. This moment was all about her, reassuring her that he—no, that they—would be okay.

"We both need to rest right now," he told her, dropping a kiss to her forehead. "You're exhausted, I'm recovering. We'll make love tomorrow and I'll make this up to you, Kate. Our trip won't be ruined. I promise."

So stupid. Foolish, careless and flat-out irresponsible.

First she'd let him touch her, then she'd cried. The tears came instantly after she'd crashed back into reality after the most amazing climax she'd ever had.

The moment had been so consuming, so mind-blowing. That's when she knew Luc hadn't remembered anything, or he would've been angry to be in that position with her.

So when the tears fell, she'd had no way to stop them.

What should've been a beautiful moment was tarnished by the situation. She hadn't expected Luc to be so powerful in bed. She truly had no idea how she'd hold him off from becoming intimate now that they'd shared such passion.

Kate had eased from the bed early this morning. Her vow to leave and sleep on the couch as soon as he fell asleep had gone out the window. After his mission to relax her had been a success, she'd been dead to the world.

How had this bizarre scenario spiraled so far out of control? She'd just spent the night in her boss's arms, a boss who was a prince, a boss who thought she was his fiancée. He was a man who prided himself on control and keeping his professional and personal lives separate. The rule was very clear at the palace.

Everything that had happened in the past eighteen hours was a colossal mess.

Kate had hurried back to her cottage early this morning while Luc slept. She'd managed to smuggle a couple sundresses and her swimsuit over. That should get her through the next few days, though she prayed she wouldn't be here that long.

Her cell phone vibrated in the pocket of her short dress. Pulling it out, she was thankful the service seemed to be holding up. The doctor's name lit up her screen.

"Good morning, Dr. Couchot," she said, as if she hadn't had the most life-altering night she'd ever experienced.

"Kate, how is Luc this morning?"

Glancing over her shoulder toward the open patio doors, she saw him still sprawled out on the bed, asleep. She kept checking on him, but he'd grumble and roll back over. She had to assume he was fine, since he was resting so well.

"He's sleeping in today," she told the doctor, turning back to watch the gentle waves ebb and flow against the shoreline. "He was exhausted last night."

"I imagine so. Still nothing new to report? No change in the memory or new symptoms?"

Kate leaned against the wrought-iron railing and wondered if the toe-curling intimacy was worth reporting. Probably best to leave that out of the conversation.

"No. He's the same."

The same sexy, determined, controlling man he always was, just with a sweeter side he was willing to share. And he was oh so giving between the sheets...

Dr. Couchot reiterated how Kate was to just let Luc think on his own, let the memories return as slowly or as fast as his mind needed them to. As if she needed reminding. Nearly all she could focus on was keeping this colossal secret.

Once she hung up, she turned, leaning her back against the rail. Watching him sleep was probably wrong, too, but why stop now? She hadn't done anything right since she'd gotten here. In the span of three days she'd fought with him, kissed him, come undone in his bed and played the part of the doting fiancée. How could she make things any worse?

Kate just prayed he'd get his memory back so they could move on. The lies were eating at her and she didn't know how she could keep up this charade.

Luc was a fighter in every way. He wouldn't let this memory loss keep him down. He'd claw his way back up from the abyss and then...

Yeah, that was the ultimate question. And then... what? Would he hate her? Would he fire her? Would he look at her with disdain?

A sick pit formed in the depths of her stomach. Would her parents lose their jobs? Surely her mom and dad would be disappointed in her for breaking the royal protocol.

This couldn't go on. Luc had to remember. So far she hadn't given Luc any extra information regarding his past, and she didn't intend to because she didn't want to make his issue worse. But there was only so long she could go on not telling him things. The man wanted to sleep with her.

How did she keep dodging that fact when she wanted it, too?

The way he'd looked at her, with affection, was so new and so tempting. And all built on lies.

Luc called out in his sleep. Kate straightened as she slowly moved closer. When he cried out again, she still couldn't make out what he was saying. She set her phone on the nightstand and eased down on the edge of the bed. His bronze chest stared back at her and Kate had a hard time not touching him, not running her fingertips over the tip of the tattoo that slid perfectly over one shoulder.

The sheet had dipped low, low enough to show one hip and just the edge of his black boxer briefs. She'd felt those briefs against her skin last night. More impressively, she'd felt what was beneath them.

"Tell me," he muttered, shifting once again. His eyes were squeezed tight, as if he was trying to fight whatever image had him twisting in the sheets.

Kate froze. Was he remembering something? Would his memory come back and play through his mind like a movie?

When his face scrunched even more and his chin started quivering, she knew he was fighting some demon, and she couldn't just sit here and watch him suffer. She might not be able to fully disclose the truth, but she didn't have to witness the man's complete downfall, either.

"Luc." She placed her hand on his shoulder and shook him gently. "Luc."

Jerking awake, he stared up at her, blinking a few times as if to get his bearings. Kate pulled her hand back, needing to keep her touching at a minimum.

Raking a hand down his face, his day-old stubble rustling beneath his palm, he let out a sigh. "That was insane. I was dreaming about a baby," he murmured, his gaze dipping to her midsection. "Are we having a baby, Kate?"

On this she could be absolutely honest. For once.

"No, we're not."

"Damn it." He fell back against the pillows and stared up at the sheers gathered together at the ceiling. "I thought for sure I was having a breakthrough."

Kate swallowed. He was remembering, but the memory was just a bit skewed. With the pregnancy lie from his ex still fresh, Kate figured it was only a matter of time before he had full recollection of the situation.

She didn't know whether to be terrified or relieved. They still hadn't slept together, so she prayed their relationship could be redeemed once the old Luc returned.

"It just seemed so real," he went on. "My hand was on your stomach, and I was so excited to be a father. I had no clue what to do, but the idea thrilled me."

Her heart swelled to near bursting at his reaction. The thought of having a baby with him made her giddy all over. But they were treading in dangerous territory. This was going to go downhill fast if she didn't do something. She might not be able to feed him his memories, but that didn't mean she couldn't find other ways to trigger him.

"How about we take the Jet Skis out for a bit?" she suggested.

His eyes drifted from the ceiling to her. "I don't want to go out right now."

Wow. She'd never known him to turn down anything on the water. Especially his Jet Ski or his boat. She needed to get him out of the house, away from the temptation of the bed, the shower...anyplace that might set the scene for seduction.

"Do you want to just go relax on the beach and do absolutely nothing?"

Though the thought of them lying next to each other wearing only swimsuits didn't seem like a great idea, now that she'd said it aloud. Granted, they'd seen each other that way before, but not with him thinking they were in love and planning holy matrimony...not to mention his promise to make love to her today.

A wide smile spread across his face. "I have an even better idea."

That naughty look was something she definitely recognized. He had a plan, and she didn't know if she should worry or just go along for the ride.

Six

Sweat poured off his head, his muscles burned and he was finally getting that rush he needed.

Kate grunted, sweat rolling off her, and he didn't recall ever seeing her look more beautiful. Of course, he didn't recall much, but right at this moment, she was positively stunning.

"I can't do this anymore," she panted, falling back against the wall.

Luc eased the sledgehammer down to rest, the wood handle falling against his leg. "We can take a break."

"I kind of meant I can't do this anymore…ever."

Luc laughed. They'd just torn out the old vanity in the main bathroom off the hallway, and the scene was a disaster. The construction workers had left the majority of their smaller tools here, so he figured he'd do something useful while he waited for his memory to return. No, he'd never done any home projects before.

He was a prince, for crying out loud. But he knew this bathroom would be gutted and replaced, so he was just blowing off some steam while helping the workers along at the same time.

"What are we going to do with all of this mess?" Kate asked as she glanced around the room.

They stood amid a pile of broken ceramic material, some huge hunks and some shards.

"Leave it," he told her. "When the guys come back to finish this, they can haul it out."

She dropped her hammer on top of the disaster and turned to stare at him. "So we're just causing destruction and closing the door on our way out?"

Luc shrugged. "I'm not really known for my renovating skills. Am I?"

Kate laughed, swiping a hand across her forehead. "No. You're royalty. I don't know of too many blue bloods who go around remodeling."

Stepping over the debris, he made his way to the door. Kate was right behind him. Extending his hand, he helped her over the rubble and out into the hallway.

"How about we take our tools to the kitchen?" he said, smiling when she rolled her eyes. "That room is hideous."

"I'd rather go to the kitchen and make some lunch, because you only had coffee for breakfast and my toast wore off about my fifth swing into that vanity countertop."

Her glistening forehead, the smudge of dirt streaked across one cheek, instantly had Luc recalling a little girl with a lopsided ponytail chasing a dog through a yard.

"You used to play with Booker," he muttered, speaking before he fully finished assessing the image. "At my family's vacation house in the US."

Kate's eyes widened. "That's right. I did. Did you have a memory?"

Rubbing his forehead, Luc cursed beneath his breath when the flash was gone. "Yeah. I've known you a long time, then."

Kate nodded, studying him. "I've known you since I was six."

"I'm a lot older than you."

A smile spread across her face. "Ten years."

"How long have we been together?"

Kate glanced away, biting her lip and focusing on anything but him.

"I know the doctor said to let me remember on my own. But I want to know."

Those doe eyes came back up to meet his gaze. "I started working for you a year ago."

Shock registered first. "You work for me?"

He tried to remember, tried to think of her in a professional atmosphere. Nothing. He'd actually rather remember her in an intimate setting, because that was what crushed him the most. They were engaged, they were obviously in love and he couldn't recall anything about the deep bond of their relationship.

"What do you do for me?" he asked. "Besides get me hot and make me want you. And how did we manage to get around the family rule about not mixing business with pleasure?"

Pink tinged her tanned face as she reached out, cupping her hand over his cheek. "I'm your assistant. I'm not telling you anything else. All right?"

Sliding his hand over hers, he squeezed it, then brought her palm to his mouth. "All right," he said, kissing her. "But I can't believe I let my fiancée work."

Her lips quirked. "Let me? Oh, honey. You've never let me do anything."

Laughing, he tugged her against him. "I have a feeling we do a lot of verbal sparring."

A lopsided grin greeted him. "You have no idea."

When he started to nuzzle the side of her neck, she eased back. "I'm sweaty and smelly, Luc. I don't think you want to bury your nose anywhere near my skin right now."

He slid his tongue along that delicate spot just below her ear. "I plan on having you sweaty later anyway, Kate."

Her body trembled. He didn't need to spell out how their day would end. Sleeping next to her last night had been sweet torture, but seeing her come apart at his touch had been so erotic, so sexy.

He couldn't wait to have her. Couldn't wait to explore her, get to know her body all over again.

"Has it always been this intense between us?" he asked, still gripping her hand and staring into those eyes any man could get lost in.

"Everything about our relationship is intense," she murmured, staring at his mouth. "I never know if I want to kiss you or strangle you."

"Kissing," he whispered against her mouth. "Always choose kissing, my *doce anjo*."

Sweet angel. Had he always called her that? When her lips parted beneath his, he knew the term was accurate. She tasted so sweet each time he kissed her. Wrapping one arm around her waist, he slid his palm over her backside. She still wore that short little sundress she'd had on all morning. She hadn't changed when they'd done the bathroom demolition, and seeing her bent over, catching a glimpse of her creamy thighs, had nearly driven him crazy.

Gathering the material beneath his hand, he cupped her bottom. "I've wanted you since last night," he muttered against her mouth. "The need for you hasn't lessened, and I may not remember our intimacy before, but something tells me I've been infatuated with you for a long time. This ache inside me isn't new."

A shaky sigh escaped her. "That's something I can't attest to. I don't know how long you've wanted me."

Luc eased back, still holding on to her backside. "Forever, Kate. I refuse to believe anything else."

Moisture gathered in her eyes. "You might end up remembering differently."

Then she stepped away, leaving him cold and confused. What did that mean? Did they not have a solid relationship, a deep love, as he'd thought?

Luc let her go. Apparently, they both had emotional demons to work through. Regardless of his temporary amnesia, he wouldn't let her go through this alone. They both needed each other, that was obvious, and even if she tried to push him away, she'd soon find out he wasn't going anywhere.

They were in this together no matter how he'd been before. She was his and he would be strong for her. He would not let this memory loss rob him of his life or his woman.

Kate threw on her suit and headed down to the beach. Luc might have been content with busting things up as a stress reliever, but she needed a good workout. There was nothing like a swim to really get the muscles burning and endorphins kicking in.

She hadn't lied when she'd told him their relationship had always been intense. And she hadn't lied when she'd said she had no clue how long he'd been infatuated with her.

But he was right about one thing. The emotions he was feeling, his actions toward her, weren't new. All that desire, that passion, had been lying dormant for some time now, and she'd wondered if it would ever break the surface. Never in her wildest dreams had she imagined it would take a major injury to further exacerbate this chemistry.

The question now was were these feelings truly directed toward her, or were they left over from his ex? A year ago he'd admitted to an attraction, but had put the brakes on it because of their professional relationship and her parents working so closely with his family. And it was then that he'd explained in great detail why members of his family never dated or got involved with an employee. The list of reasons was lengthy: reputations on the line, the employee could turn and go to the media with a fabricated story... There was too much at stake—even Luc's crown in this case—to let staff in on their personal lives. Kate didn't have a clue how Luc and his ex had been in private. She actually tried to never think of that. But now she couldn't stop herself.

Did Luc really have such strong emotions for her? If so, how had he kept it bottled up all this time?

Kate loosened the knot on her wrap, letting the sheer material fall onto the sand. Running straight into the ocean, the world at her back, she wished she could run from this whole ordeal and stop lying to Luc. She wished she could kiss him and sleep in his bed and have him know it was her and not the fake fiancée he'd conjured up.

He'd said they would be sleeping together later. Dodging that was going to be nearly impossible.

She was in desperate need of advice. She'd wanted to phone her mother earlier, but the call hadn't been able to go through. She would try again later. More than anything Kate needed her mother's guidance. Holding back from Luc was pure torture. How could she say no to the one thing she'd fantasized about for so long?

The warm water slid over her body as she sliced her arms through the gentle waves. The hot sun beat down on her back and her muscles were already screaming from the quick workout.

Kate pushed herself further, breaking the surface to take another deep breath and catch her bearings. Panting heavily, she dived back in for more. She'd not fully worked through her angst just yet.

Before she knew it, she'd gone so far up the coastline she couldn't see Luc's home anymore. She swam to the shore, trudged through the sand and sank down onto dry land. Pulling her legs up against her chest, Kate wrapped her arms around her knees and caught her breath, willing the answers to come.

One thing was clear. She and Luc needed to stay away from the house as much as possible. With just the two of them alone, there was no chaperone, nobody else to offer a buffer. At least back at the palace there was a full staff of butlers, maids, drivers, assistants to the assistants, guards, his parents, her parents, the cooks... the list was almost endless.

Perhaps an outing to the small village was in order. Anything to hold off the inevitable. The hungry look in Luc's eyes, the way he constantly kept touching her, were all indications that the moment was fast approaching. And yes, she wanted that moment to happen more than she wanted her next breath, but she didn't want it to be built on desperation and lies.

Pushing herself up off the sand, Kate stretched out her muscles. She'd never been a fan of running, but she wasn't done exorcising those demons. She headed back toward Luc's home, passing other pristine beach houses. Some were larger, some smaller, but they all had the same Mediterranean charm, and their own docks, with boats bobbing against the wood planks.

The island was a perfect getaway for a prince. Under normal circumstances, he could hide away here without the media hounding him, without the distractions of the internet and the outside world.

This place would be heaven on earth for any couple wanting a romantic escape.

Too bad she was only a figment of Luc's imagination.

As Kate ran, she kept to the packed sand that the waves had flattened. Her thigh muscles burned and sweat poured off her as the sun beat against her back. This felt good, liberating. She would go back to the house and go over Luc's schedule for when they returned to Ilha Beleza. Looking at all his duties and responsibilities would surely help jog something in his mind.

And the memories were returning. Apparently, her dirty state earlier had shot him back to the moments when she'd been a little girl and had gone to work with her parents. She'd loved the Silvas' old sheepdog, Booker. She used to play with him, roll around in the yard with him and be completely filthy by the time she left.

Luc's parents would just laugh, saying how they missed having a little one around. They'd gotten Booker when Luc was eight, so by the time he was a teen, he wasn't so much into running through yards and spending hours playing with a dog.

Kate was all about it. When Booker had passed away, she had taken the news harder than Luc had. Of course, he'd had his women "friends" to occupy his time and keep his thoughts focused elsewhere.

Finding her discarded wrap in the sand where she'd dropped it, Kate scooped it up and quickly adjusted it around her torso. At the base of the steps leading up to Luc's home, she rested her hands on her knees and pulled in a deep gulp of air. She was going in as professional Kate. Keeping her hands and mind off Luc was the only way to proceed. Flirty, dreamy Kate had no place here. They hadn't made love yet, so she could still turn this around, and pray Luc wasn't totally furious once he remembered what her role in his life actually was.

Seven

Luc's phone bounced on the couch cushion when he tossed it aside. Useless. He recognized his parents' names, his best friend, Mikos, and Kate. Other than that, nothing.

Raking a hand down his face, Luc got to his feet and crossed to the patio doors. Kate had been gone awhile and he knew her frustrations had driven her out the door. He'd like to run from his problems, too; unfortunately, they lived inside his head. Still, he couldn't fault her for needing some time alone.

He stepped out onto the patio, his gaze immediately darting down to the dock. As he stared at the Jet Ski on one side and his boat on the other, he wondered what he'd been doing before he fell. Was he about to go out on the water so late in the evening? Was Kate coming with him? Everything before the fall was a complete blank to him. He had no idea what they'd been doing prior to his accident.

Hell, he couldn't even recall how he and Kate had started working together. And some family rule about not getting personal with staff members kept ringing in his head. He reached into his mind, knowing this was a real memory. The Silva family didn't get intimate with employees. So had Kate come to work for him after they'd become a couple? Had she been so invaluable in his life that he'd wanted her to be his right-hand woman in his professional world, as well?

The questions weren't slowing down; they were slamming into his head faster than he could comprehend them. He'd go mad if he didn't get his memory back soon, or if he kept dwelling on something that was out of his control.

Damn it. Of one thing he was certain. Losing control of anything was pure hell, and right now he'd spiraled so far he hoped and prayed he could pull back the reins on his life before this amnesia drove a wedge between him and Kate.

Luc straightened as the idea slammed into him, pushing through the uncertainty he'd been battling. All that mattered was him and Kate. This was their time away, so all he had to do was enjoy being with her. How hard could that be? A private getaway with one sexy fiancée would surely be just what he needed.

A shrill ring came from the living room. Luc ran in and found Kate's cell phone on one of the end tables. His mother's name was on the screen. Odd that she would be calling Kate.

Without giving it another thought, he answered. "Hello."

"Lucas? Darling, how are you feeling?"

His mother's worried tone came over the line. Her

familiar voice had him relieved that his mind hadn't robbed him of that connection.

"Frustrated," he admitted, sinking onto the worn accent chair. "I have a hell of a headache, but other than that I feel fine. Why did you call Kate's phone?"

"I didn't want to bother you if you weren't feeling good, or if you were resting. I spoke with Kate last night, but I needed to check on you today."

"There's no need to worry, Mom. Kate is taking good care of me and the doctor was thorough. I just need to relax, and this is the best place for me to do that."

His mother made a noise, something akin to disapproval. "Well, you call the doctor first thing if you start having other symptoms. I'm still not happy you're not home. I worry, but you're stubborn like your father, so I'm used to it."

Luc smiled, just as Kate stepped through the door. A sheen of sweat covered her. Or maybe that was water from the ocean. Regardless, she looked sexy, all wet and winded. Would his need for her ever lessen? Each time he saw her he instantly went into primal mode and wanted to carry her back to bed.

"Nothing to worry about," he said, keeping his eyes locked on Kate's. "I'm in good hands. I'll phone you later."

He ended the call and rose to his feet. Kate's eyes widened as he moved closer to where she'd stopped in the doorway.

"Were you on my phone?" she asked, tipping her head back to hold his gaze.

"My mom called to check on me. She tried your cell in case I was resting."

Kate's eyes darted around. "Um…is that all she said?"

Reaching out to stroke a fingertip along her collarbone, Luc watched the moisture disappear beneath his touch. "Yes. Why?"

"Just curious." She trembled beneath his touch as her eyes locked back onto his. "I need to go shower. Then we need to discuss your schedule and upcoming events."

Heat surged through him as he slid his mouth over hers. "Go use my shower. We can work later."

She leaned into him just slightly, then quickly pulled back. Something passed through her eyes before she glanced away. As she started to move around him, he grabbed her elbow.

"You okay?"

She offered a tight, fake smile. "Fine. Just tired from my swim and run."

The shadows beneath her eyes silently told him she hadn't slept as well as she'd claimed. He nodded, releasing her arm, and listened as she padded through the hall and into the master suite.

Waiting until he was sure she was in the shower, Luc jerked his shirt over his head and tossed it, not caring where it landed. By the time he reached his bedroom, his clothes were gone, left in a trail leading to the bedroom door.

The steady hum of the water had Luc imagining all kinds of possibilities. And all of them involved a wet, naked Kate.

When he reached the spacious, open shower, surrounded by lush plants for added privacy, he took in the entire scene. Kate with water sluicing down her curves, her wet hair clinging to her back as she tipped her face up to the rainfall showerhead. She was a vision...and she was his.

Luc crossed the room and stepped onto the wet, gritty

tile. In an instant he had his arms wrapped around her, molding her back against him.

Kate's audible gasp filled the room, and her body tensed beneath his. "Luc—"

He spun her around, cutting off anything she was about to say. He needed her, needed to get back to something normal in his life. Kate was his rock, his foundation, and he wanted to connect with her again in the most primal, natural way possible.

"Luc," she muttered against his mouth. "We shouldn't."

Her words died as he kissed his way down her neck. "We should."

That silky skin of hers was driving him insane. Kate arched into him, gripping his shoulders as if holding on.

"You're injured," she panted.

He jerked his head up to meet her gaze. "The day I can't make love to my fiancée is the day I die."

Luc hauled her up against him, an arm banded around her lower back to pull her in nice and snug, as his mouth claimed hers once again. There was a hesitancy to her response. Luc slowed his actions, not wanting her to feel she needed to protect him.

But this all-consuming need to claim her, to have her right now, had his control slipping.

"I want you, Kate," he whispered against her mouth. "Now."

Nipping at her lips, he slid his palms over her round hips, to the dip in her waist and up to her chest, which was made for a man's hands...his hands. She was perfect for him in every way. How had he gotten so lucky to have her in his life?

As he massaged her, she dropped her head back, exposing that creamy skin on her neck. Luc smoothed his tongue over her, pulling a soft moan from her lips.

After backing her up, he lifted her. "Wrap your legs around me."

Her eyes went wide. "I... Luc..."

"Now, Kate."

Just as her legs encircled his waist, he grabbed her hands and held them above her head. Sliding into her, he stilled when she gasped.

"You okay?"

Eyes closed, biting down on her lip, she nodded. Luc gripped her wrists in one hand and used his other to skim his thumb across the lip she'd been worrying with her teeth.

"Look at me," he demanded. "I want to see those eyes."

Droplets sprinkled her lashes as she blinked up at him. He moved against her, watching her reaction, wanting to see every bit of her arousal, her excitement. He might not remember their past encounters, but he damn well was going to make new memories with her, starting right now.

Kate's hips rocked with his; her body arched as he increased his speed.

"Luc," she panted. "Please..."

Gripping her waist, he trailed his mouth up her neck to her ear. "Anything," he whispered. "I'll give you anything. Just let go."

Her body tensed, shuddering all around him. As she cried out in release, Luc followed her.

Wrapping her in his arms, he couldn't help but wonder if each time they were together felt like the first time, or if this particular moment was just so powerfully intense and all-consuming. This woman had the ability to bring him to his knees in all the right ways.

So why was his beautiful fiancée—who'd just come apart in his arms—sobbing against his shoulder?

* * *

Oh, no. No, no, no.

Kate couldn't stop the tears from coming, just as she couldn't stop Luc from making love to her.

No. Not making love. They'd had sex. He didn't love her, and once his memory returned, he wouldn't even like her anymore. She'd been worried about tonight, about going to sleep. She'd truly never thought he would join her in the shower. The sex just now with Luc was unlike any encounter she'd ever had. Nothing could have prepared her for the intensity of his passion.

How had this entire situation gotten even more out of control? The reality of being with Luc had far exceeded the fantasy. And now that she had a taste of what it could be like, she wanted more.

"Kate?"

She gripped his biceps, keeping her face turned into his chest. She couldn't face him, couldn't look him in the eyes. Not after what she'd done. He would never understand.

Was this how he'd treat her if he loved her? Would he surprise her in the shower and demand so much of her body? Part of her wanted to bask in the glorious aftermath of everything intimacy should be. But she knew it couldn't last.

Luc shut off the water behind her, and in one swift move, he shifted, lifting her in his arms.

"Talk to me, baby." He stepped out of the shower and eased her down onto the cushioned bench. Grabbing a towel from the heated bar, he wrapped it around her before securing one around his waist.

Kate stared down at her unpainted nails. Focusing on her lack of manicure would not help her out of this situation. Luc gripped her hands as he crouched before her.

"Look at me."

Those words, said only moments ago under extremely different circumstances, pulled her gaze away from their joined hands and up into his dark eyes. Worry stared back at her. Didn't he know she was lying? Didn't he know he should be worried about himself?

She could come clean. She could tell him right now that she wasn't his fiancée, that she'd been dying for him to make a move on her for years. But all that sounded even more pathetic than the truth, which was that she'd gotten caught up in this spiral of lies. In an attempt to protect him, she'd deceived him. There was no turning back, and if she was honest with herself, she couldn't deny how right they'd felt together.

"Did I hurt you?" he asked.

Swiping the moisture from her cheeks, Kate shook her head. "No. You could never hurt me."

"What is it? Did you not want to make love with me?"

A vise around her heart squeezed.

She shook her head. Eventually she was going to strangle herself with this string of lies.

"I'm just overwhelmed," she admitted. "We hadn't been together before."

Luc studied her a moment before his brows rose. "You mean to tell me we hadn't made love before?"

Shame filled her. She couldn't speak, so simply nodded.

Luc muttered a slang Portuguese term that no member of the royal family should be heard saying.

"How is that possible?" he asked. "You said we've been working together for nearly a year."

"Your family has a rule about staff and royal members not being intimate. We've been professional for so long, we both just waited. Then we ended up here on this getaway and…"

She couldn't finish. She couldn't lie anymore. The emotions were too overwhelming and her body was still reeling from their passion.

Luc came to his feet, cursing enough to have her cringing. He was beating himself up over something that was 100 percent her fault.

Unable to stand the tension, the heavy weight of the guilt, she jumped to her feet. "Luc, I need to tell you—"

"No." He turned, facing her with his hands on his narrow hips. "I took advantage of you. Kate, I am so, so sorry. I had no clue. I got caught up in the moment and wanted to forget this memory loss and just be with you."

"No. This is not your fault in any way." Holding on to the knot on her towel, Kate shivered. "Let's get dressed. We need to talk."

Eight

Luc grabbed his clothes from the bedroom and went to the spare room to get dressed. Of all the plans he'd had for Kate, taking her when she wasn't mentally prepared for it sure as hell wasn't one of them.

Their history explained why she'd tensed when he'd come up behind her in the shower, explained the onslaught of tears afterward. Not to mention the way she'd stiffened against him in bed last night.

Luc cursed himself once again for losing control. He'd thought he was doing the right thing, thought he was getting them both back to where they'd been just before his ridiculous accident.

Heading back down the hallway, he spotted his clothes. Looking at them now he felt only disgust, as opposed to the excitement and anticipation he'd felt when he'd left them behind without a care.

He grabbed each article of clothing and flung them

and his towel into the laundry area. He'd worry about that mess later. Right now he had another, more important mess to clean up, and he only hoped Kate would forgive him.

Guilt literally ate at him, killing the hope he'd had of making this day less about his amnesia and more about them.

By the time she came out, she'd piled her hair atop her head and sported another one of those little sundresses that showcased her tanned shoulders and sexy legs. The legs he'd demanded she wrap around him.

Kate took a seat on the sofa and patted the cushion beside her. "Just relax. Okay?"

Relax? How could he when this entire mess had started with him forgetting every single damn thing about the woman he supposedly loved?

Wait, he *did* love her. When he looked at her and saw how amazing and patient she was with him, and damn it, how she'd let him take her in the shower, and didn't stop him, how could he not love her? When he looked at her, his heart beat a bit faster. When he touched her, his world seemed to be a better place.

He just wished he could remember actually falling in love with her, because all he could recall was this all-consuming, aching need that was only stronger now that he'd had her.

"Luc." Kate held out her hand. "Come on."

He crossed to her, took her hand and sank onto the couch beside her.

"Tell me you're okay," he started, holding her gaze. "Tell me I didn't hurt you physically or emotionally."

A soft smile spread across her face. "I already told you, I'm fine. You were perfect, Luc."

She held on to him, her eyes darting down to where their hands joined.

"Before you fell, we were fighting," she told him. "I take full responsibility for everything that's happened to you, so don't beat yourself up over the shower."

Luc squeezed her hand. "The shower was all on me. If we were fighting before my fall, then that took two, so don't place all of that blame on yourself."

Kate smiled. Her eyes lifted to his. "We could play this game all day," she told him, her smile dimming a bit. "But I need to talk to you."

"What's wrong?"

Her tone, the worry in her eyes, told him something major was keeping her on edge.

"There are so many things that you need to know, but I've been holding back because I don't want to affect your healing process."

Luc edged closer, wrapping an arm around her shoulders and pulling her to his side. Easing back against the cushions, he kept her tucked against him. "If something is worrying you, tell me. I want to be here for you. I want to be strong for you."

Kate's delicate hand rested on his thigh. She took a deep breath in, then let it out with a shudder.

"I was adopted."

Her voice was so soft, he wondered if she actually meant to say it out loud.

"Did I already know this about you?" he asked.

"No. The only people who know are my parents."

His mind started turning. Her parents worked for his parents. Memories of them in his house flashed for an instant.

"Scott and Maria, right?"

"Yes." Kate tilted her head up to meet his gaze. "You're remembering."

"Not fast enough," he muttered. "Go on."

Settling her head back against his chest, Luc wondered if it was easier for her to talk if she wasn't looking right at him.

"I was born in the States," she went on. "Georgia, to be exact. My parents adopted me when I was six. I only have vague memories of being there, but it's always held a special place in my heart."

Luc listened, wondering where she was going with this and how it all tied back into what was happening between them now.

"My parents ended up moving to Ilha Beleza to work full-time at the palace. They used to just work at the vacation home back in Georgia. Your family has one off the coast."

Closing his eyes, he saw a white house with thick pillars extended to the second story. A wraparound porch on the ground floor had hanging swings that swayed in the breeze. Booker and a young Kate running in the yard...

Yes, he remembered that house fondly.

"Since I've been your assistant, I've wanted you to visit that orphanage, the one I came from, but we've butted heads over it."

Luc jerked, forcing Kate to shift and look up at him.

"Why were we fighting over an orphanage?" he asked.

She shrugged. "I have no idea why you won't go. To be honest, I just think you don't want to, or you didn't want to take the time. You've offered to write a check, but I never can get you to go there. I just felt a visit from a real member of royalty would be something cool for those kids. They don't have much and some of them have been there awhile, because most people only want to adopt babies."

Luc glanced around the sparsely furnished room, hoping for another flash of something to enter his mind. Hoping for some minuscule image that would help him piece it all together.

"Is this why we were arguing before I fell?" he asked, focusing back on her.

"Not really. I tried bringing it up again, but you blew it off." She let go of his hand and got to her feet, pacing to the open patio doors. "We were arguing because we're both stubborn, and sometimes we do and say things before we can fully think them through."

He could see that. Without a doubt he knew he was quite a hardhead, and Kate had a stubborn streak he couldn't help but find intriguing and attractive.

"When your memory comes back, I want you to know that everything I've ever done or said has been to protect you." Her shoulders straightened as she kept her back to him and stared out the doors. "I care about you, Luc. I need you to know that above all else."

The heartfelt words, the plea in her tone, had Luc rising to his feet and crossing to her. Placing his hands on her shoulders, he kissed the top of her head.

"I know how you feel about me, Kate. You proved it to me when you let me make love to you, when you put my needs ahead of any doubts you had."

She eased back against him. "I hope you always feel that way."

The intensity of the moment had him worried they were getting swept into something so consuming, they'd never get back to the couple they used to be. Even though he didn't remember that couple, he had to assume they weren't always this intense.

"What do you say we take the boat and go into town?" he asked. "Surely there's a market or shops or restaurants to occupy our time. We need to have some fun."

She turned in his arms, a genuine smile spreading across her face. "I was going to suggest that myself. I haven't shopped in forever. I'm always working."

She cringed, as if she just realized what had come out of her mouth.

"It's okay," he told her, kissing the tip of her nose. "I'll make sure your boss gives you the rest of the day off. You deserve it."

That talk didn't go nearly the way she'd rehearsed it in her head. Coming off the euphoria of having mind-blowing sex with Luc in the shower had seriously clouded her judgment, and obviously sucked out all her common sense.

So now here she was, wearing her favorite blue halter dress, letting the wind blow her hair around her shoulders and face while Luc steered his boat to the main dock of the island's small town. Most people traveled by boat to the village, where scooters were the preferred mode of transportation. The marina was lined with crafts of various sizes and colors. As they'd made their way toward the waterfront, they'd passed by other boaters and waved. Kate really liked this area. Too bad she'd probably never be back after the mess she'd created came crashing down on her.

Through her research she knew the locals would line up along the narrow streets, set up makeshift booths and sell their goods. From what she'd seen online, she might find anything from handmade jewelry and pottery to flowers and vegetables. She was excited to see what caught her fancy, perhaps taking her mind off the fact her body was still tingling from Luc's touch.

She'd never be able to shower again—especially in that master bath—without feeling his body against hers, his breath on her shoulders. Without hearing his demanding words in her ear as he fully claimed her.

Then he'd let his guard down and opened up to her about his feelings. Slowly, she was falling in love with the man she'd been lying to, the man who was off-limits in reality. She'd opened up about her past, wanting to be as honest as she could in an area that had nothing to do with what was happening right now.

Luc secured the boat to the dock, then extended his hand to help her out. With a glance or simple touch, the man had the ability to make her stomach quiver, her heart quicken and her mind wander off into a fantasy world. Still, that was no excuse to have let the charade go this far.

There was no going back now, though. The charade may be all a farce, but her emotions were all too real.

Kate knew she should've told Luc about the false engagement when he'd hinted that he wanted to make love to her. She should've told him right that moment, but she hadn't, and now here she was on the other side of a monumental milestone they would both have to live with.

She was falling for him; there was no denying the truth to herself. What had started as physical attraction long ago had morphed into more because of his untimely incident.

How did she keep her heart protected, make sure Luc stayed safe until he remembered the truth on his own and keep hold of the man she'd come to feel a deeper bond for? There was no good way this scenario would play out. Someone was going to get hurt.

"You okay?" Luc asked, hauling her onto the dock beside him.

Pasting on a smile, Kate squeezed his hand. "Fine. Let's see what this island has to offer."

Other boats bobbed up and down in the water on either side of the long dock. Luc led her up the steps to the street. Once they reached the top, Kate gasped. It was like a mini festival, but from all she'd heard about this quaint place, the streets were always this lively.

Brightly colored umbrellas shaded each vendor. A small band played live music in an alcove of one of the ancient buildings. People were laughing, dancing, and nearly every stand had a child behind the table, working alongside an adult. Obviously, this was a family affair.

Kate tamped down that inner voice that mocked her. Her dream was to raise a family, to have a husband who loved her, to watch their babies grow. Maybe someday she'd have that opportunity. Unfortunately, with the way her life was going now, she'd be looking for a new job as opposed to a spouse.

Suddenly, one of the stands caught her eye. "Oh, Luc." She tugged on his hand. "I have to get a closer look."

She practically dragged him down the brick street to the jewelry booth. The bright colors were striking with the sun beating down on them just so. It was as if the rays were sliding beneath the umbrella shading the area. The purple amethyst, the green jade, the yellow citrine—they were all so gorgeous. Kate didn't know which piece she wanted to touch first.

"Good afternoon."

The vendor greeted her in Portuguese. Kate easily

slid into the language as she asked about the wares. Apparently, the woman was a widow and the little girl sidling up against her was her only child. They made the jewelry together and the girl was homeschooled, oftentimes doing lessons right there at the booth.

Kate opened her small clutch to pull out her money. There was no way she could walk away and not buy something from this family.

Before she could count her cash, Luc placed a hand over hers and shook his head. He asked the lady how much Kate owed for the necklace and earrings she'd chosen. Once he paid and the items were carefully wrapped in red tissue paper, they went on their way to another booth.

"You didn't have to pay," she told him. "I don't expect you to get all of the things I want, Luc."

He shrugged, taking her hand and looping it through his elbow as they strolled down the street. "I want to buy you things, Kate."

"Well, I picked these out for my mother," she said with a laugh.

Luc smiled. "I don't mind buying things for my future mother-in-law, either. Really, think nothing of it."

What had been a beautiful, relaxing moment instantly turned and smacked Kate in the face with a dose of reality. A heavy ball of dread settled in her belly. This was getting all too real. Kate's parents had been inadvertently pulled into this lie. They would never be Luc's in-laws, and once he discovered the truth, they might not even be employees of his family.

They moved to another stand, where the pottery was unique, yet simple. Kate eyed a tall, slender vase, running her hand over the smooth edge. Before she knew it, Luc had paid for it and the vendor was bagging it and wrapping it in several layers of tissue for protection.

"You don't have to buy everything I look at," she informed Luc.

"Did you like the piece?" he asked.

"I love it, but I was wondering what it would look like in your new house."

Luc kissed her softly on the lips before picking up the bag and moving away. "Our house, Kate. If you like it, then it's fine with me. I'm not much of a decorator."

"No, you prefer to demolish things."

Luc laughed. "Actually, our little project was my first experiment in destruction, but I did rather enjoy myself. I really think I'll tackle that kitchen before we leave, and give the contractors a head start."

They moved from place to place, eyeing various trinkets. Kate ended up buying a wind chime and fresh flowers while Luc was busy talking to another merchant. She wanted to liven up the dining area in the house, especially since the room was in desperate need of paint. The lavender flowers would look perfect in that new yellow vase.

Once they had all their bags, they loaded up the boat and headed home.

Home. As if this was a normal evening and they were settled in some married-couple routine. Kate shouldn't think of Luc's house as her home. She'd started getting too settled in, too comfortable with this whole lifestyle, and in the end, when her lie was exposed and his inevitable rejection sliced her in two, she would have nobody to blame but herself.

These past few hours with Luc had been amazing, but her fantasy life wouldn't last forever.

Nine

Sometime during the past hour, Kate had fully detached herself. She'd been quiet on the boat, quiet when they came into the house. She'd arranged fresh flowers in that beautiful yellow vase and placed them on the hideous dining room table without saying a word.

She'd made dinner, and the only sound he'd heard was her soft humming as she stirred the rice. Now they'd finished eating, and Luc couldn't handle the silence anymore.

He had something to say.

"Kate."

She stepped from the kitchen, wiping her hands down her dress. Luc remained standing, waited for her to cross to him.

"I know you've got a lot on your mind right now," he started. "But there's something I need to tell you."

"Wait." She held up a palm. "I need to go first. I've

been trying to figure out a way to talk to you about your amnesia."

She sighed, shaking her head. "I don't even know how to start," she muttered. "I've racked my brain, but nothing sounds right."

"The doctor said not to prompt me." Luc reached into his pocket and pulled out a small, velvet pouch. "While you're thinking about the right words, why don't you take this?"

She jerked her gaze up to his, then stared down at the present in his hand. "What is it?"

"Open it."

Her fingers shook as she took the pouch and tugged on the gathered opening. With a soft gasp, she reached in and pulled out an emerald-cut amethyst ring.

"Luc." She held the ring up, stared at it, then looked to him. "What's this for?"

"Because you don't have a ring on your finger. It hit me today, and I don't know why you don't, but I didn't want to wait and find out. I saw this and I knew you'd love it."

When she didn't say anything or put the ring on, his nerves spiked. Strange, since he'd obviously already popped the question. Unless she just didn't like it.

"If you'd rather have something else, I can take it back to the lady and exchange it. When I saw that stone, I remembered something else about you."

Her eyes widened. "You did?"

A tear slipped down her cheek as she blinked. Luc swiped it away, resting his hand on the side of her face. "I remembered your birthday is in February and that's your birthstone. I remembered you have this amethyst pendant you've worn with gowns to parties at the palace. That pendant would nestle right above your breasts. I used to be jealous of that stone."

Kate sucked in a breath as another tear fell down her face. "You say things like that to me and I feel like you've had feelings for me for longer than I ever imagined."

Taking the ring from her hand, he slid it onto her left ring finger. "There are many things I don't remember, but I know this—I've wanted you forever, Kate."

He didn't give her a chance to respond. Luc enveloped her in his arms, pulled her against him and claimed her mouth. He loved kissing her, loved feeling her lush body against his. Nothing had ever felt this perfect, as far as he could recall. And he was pretty sure if anything had ever felt this good, he'd remember.

Kate's hands pushed against his shoulders as she broke the kiss. "Wait."

She turned, coming free from his hold. With her rigid back to him, Luc's nerves ramped up a level. "Kate, what's wrong?"

"I want to tell you," she whispered. "I need to tell you, but I don't know how much I can safely say without affecting your memory."

Taking a step toward her, he cupped his hands over her shoulders. "Then don't say anything. Can't we just enjoy this moment?"

She turned in his arms, stared up at him and smiled. "I've never been happier than I am right now. I just worry what will happen once you remember everything."

His lips slid across hers. "I'm not thinking of my memory. I only want to make up for what we did this morning."

A catch in her breath had him pausing. Her eyes locked onto his.

"I want to make love to you properly, Kate."

Her body shuddered beneath his hands. "I've wanted you for so long, Luc."

Something primal ripped through him at the same time he saw a flash of Kate wearing a fitted skirt suit, bending over her desk to reach papers. He shook off the image. She'd already said she was his assistant, so that flash wasn't adding anything new to the mix.

Right now he had more pressing matters involving his beautiful fiancée.

"I want you wearing my ring, the weight of my body and nothing else."

Luc gave the halter tie on her neck a tug, stepping back just enough to have the material floating down over her bare breasts. With a quick yank, he pulled the dress and sent it swishing to the floor around her feet. Next he rid her of her silky pink panties.

With her hair tossed around her shoulders, her mouth swollen from his kisses, Luc simply stared at her, as if taking all this in for the first time.

"Perfect," he muttered, gliding his hands over her hips and around her waist. "Absolutely perfect and totally mine."

The breeze from the open patio doors enveloped them. The sunset just on the horizon created an ambience even he couldn't have bought. And everything about this moment overshadowed all that was wrong in his mind with the amnesia.

Guiding Kate backward, he led her to a chaise. When her legs bumped against the edge, Luc pressed on her shoulders, silently easing her down. Once she lay all spread out for his appreciation, he started tugging off his own clothes. The way her eyes traveled over his body, studying him, did something to his ego he couldn't explain. He found himself wanting to know what she thought when she looked at him, what she felt. All this was still new to him and he wanted to savor every single moment of their lovemaking.

"I've dreamed of this," he murmured.

Her brows quirked. "Seriously? You don't think it was a memory of something?"

Luc rested one hand on the back of the chaise, another on the cushion at her hip. As he loomed over her, his body barely brushed the tips of her breasts.

"I'm sure," he whispered. "You were on my balcony, naked, smiling. Ready for me."

A cloud of passion filled her eyes as she continued to stare up at him.

"Maybe I had that fantasy when I first looked at this place, or maybe I had that vision since we've been here." He nipped at her collarbone, gliding up her exposed throat. "Either way, you were meant to be here. With me. Only me."

Kate's body arched into his as her fingertips trailed up his biceps and rested at his shoulders. "Only you," she muttered.

Luc eased down, settling between her legs. The moment his lips touched hers, he joined them, slowly taking everything she was willing to give. This all-consuming need he had for her only grew with each passing moment. Kate was in his blood, in his heart. Was it any wonder he wanted to marry her and spend his life with her?

Kate's fingertips dug into his skin as she rested her forehead against his shoulder. Luc knew from the little pants, the soft moans, that she was on the brink of release.

He kissed her neck, working his way up to that spot

behind her ear he already knew was a trigger. Her body clenched around him as she cried out his name. Before she stopped trembling, he was falling over the edge, too, wrapped in the arms of the woman he loved, surrounded by a haze of euphoria that kept away all the ugly worries and doubts.

All that mattered was Kate and their beautiful life together.

His hand slid over her flat stomach. There was a baby, his baby, growing inside her. He hadn't thought much about being a father, but the idea warmed something within him.

Dropping to his knees, he kissed her bare stomach. "I love you already," he whispered.

Luc jerked awake, staring into the darkness. What the hell was that? A memory? Just a random dream? His heart beat so fast, so hard against the wall of his chest. That had been real. The emotions, the feel of her abdomen beneath his palm, had all been real.

Luc wasn't one to believe in coincidences. That was a memory, but how could it be? Kate wasn't pregnant. She'd said they hadn't made love before the shower, so what the hell was that dream about?

Glancing at the woman beside him, Luc rubbed a hand over his face. The sheet was twisted around her bare body, and her hair was spread over the pillow. Luc placed a hand on her midsection and closed his eyes. That dream was so real he'd actually felt it.

Surely it wasn't just a fantasy of the day he and Kate would be expecting in real life.

He fell back against his pillow, laced his hands behind his head and blinked to adjust his eyesight to the darkened room. No way could he go back to sleep now.

There was too much on his mind, too many unanswered questions.

Something involving a baby had happened to cause such a strong flashback, for the second time now. It just didn't make sense. His mind was obviously the enemy at the moment.

"Luc…"

He turned toward her, only to find her eyes were still closed. She was dreaming, too. Her hand shifted over the sheets as if seeking him out. Instantly, he took hold of her hand and clasped it against his chest. Tomorrow he would have to seek some answers. This waiting around was killing him, because tidbits of his life weren't enough. He wanted the whole damn picture and he wanted it now.

Maybe if Kate talked about herself, her personal life, that would trigger more memories for him. He was done waiting, done putting his life in this mental prison.

How could he move on with Kate when he couldn't even remember their lives before a few days ago?

Ten

She should've told him. No matter what the doctor said, she should have just told Luc that they weren't engaged. Everything else he could remember on his own, but the biggest lie of all needed to be brought out into the open.

Of course, now they'd slept together twice, and she still hadn't said a word.

The heaviness of the ring on her hand wasn't helping the guilt weighing on her heart, either. Instead of trying to make this right, she'd let every single aspect spin even more out of control.

Stepping from the bathroom, Kate tied the short, silky robe around her waist. As soon as she glanced up, she spotted Luc sitting up in bed, the stark white sheet settled low around his hips. All those tanned, toned muscles, the dark ink scrolling over one shoulder, the dark hair splattering over his pecs. The man exuded sex appeal and authority.

"You needn't have bothered with that robe if you're going to keep looking at me like that," he told her, his voice husky from sleep.

Kate leaned against the door frame to the bathroom. "Did you know you never wanted to marry?" she asked, crossing her arms over her chest.

Luc laughed, leaning back against the quilted headboard. "That's a bit off topic, but no. I didn't know that."

Swallowing, Kate pushed forward. "You had no intention of taking a wife, but Ilha Beleza has some ridiculously archaic law that states you must be married by your thirty-fifth birthday in order to succeed to the throne."

"My birthday is coming up," he muttered, as if that tidbit just hit him. Luc's brows drew together as he laced his fingers over his abdomen. "Are you saying I'm not entitled to the throne if we aren't married by then?"

This was the tricky part. "You aren't crowned until you're married."

"That's ridiculous." He laughed. "I'll change that law, first thing. What if my son doesn't want to marry? Who says you have to be married by thirty-five?"

Kate smiled. "That's exactly what you said before you fell. You were dead set on having that law rewritten."

His eyes held hers another moment, but before she could go on, he said, "I had a dream last night. It was real. I know it was a memory, but I can't figure it out."

Kate's heart beat faster in her chest. Was their time over? Was the beautiful fantasy they'd been living about to come to a crashing halt?

"What was the dream?" she asked, gripping her arms with anticipation.

"I had a dream you were pregnant. That image in my

head has hit more than once." His eyes drilled into her. "Why would I keep dreaming that, Kate?"

"Did you see me in the dream?" she asked, knowing she was treading on very shaky ground.

He shook his head. "No. I had my hands on your bare stomach and I was so happy. Nervous, but excited."

"I've never been pregnant," she told him softly. "Do you think maybe you're just thinking ahead?"

Kate glanced away, unable to look him in the eyes and see him struggle with this entire situation. Why couldn't this be real? He'd told her more than once that he loved her, but that was just what he thought he was supposed to say...wasn't it? Still, what if he was speaking from his heart? What if that fall had actually pulled out his true feelings? But even if she stood a chance with the man she'd fallen in love with, Kate had lied and deceived him. He would never forgive her.

She just wanted today, just one more night with him. She was being selfish, yes, but she couldn't let go just yet. Not when everything right at this moment was beautiful and perfect.

"Do you want children?" he asked. "I assume we've discussed this."

Kate pushed herself off the door frame and smoothed her hair back from her face. "I do want kids. It's always been my dream to have a husband who loves me and a houseful of children."

He offered her a wide, sexy smile. "We will have the most beautiful children."

Oh, when he said things like that she wanted to get swept away and believe every word. Yet again, Luc had been weaved so tightly into this web of lies she'd inadvertently created. Her heart had been in the right place. She only hoped Luc saw that once all was said and done.

"I think any child with the Silva genes would be beautiful," she countered. "Even though you're an only child, your father has a long line of exotic beauties on his side. Your mother is a natural beauty, as well."

Luc tossed his sheet aside and came to his feet. Padding across the floor wearing only a tattoo and a grin, he kept his gaze on hers.

"As much as I'd love to work on those babies, I think I'd like to do something that will help get my memory back sooner rather than later."

Kate forced her gaze up… Well, she made it to his chest and figured that was a good compromise. "What's that?"

"Maybe we should tackle that work schedule you'd mentioned." His smile kicked up higher on one side of that kissable mouth. "You know, before we got sidetracked with being naked."

Kate laughed. "Yes. Work. That's where we need to focus."

Finally. Something they could do that actually needed to be done. She could breathe a bit now.

"I'll go get my laptop," she told him. "I've got a spreadsheet there of your tentative schedule, and I have a speech written out for you that you need to look over."

As she started to walk by, he reached out, snaking an arm around her waist. "You write my speeches?"

"For the past year I have."

His eyes roamed over her face, settled on her lips, then came back up to meet her gaze. "You really are perfect for me."

Kate swallowed. "Better put some clothes on. You can't work in your birthday suit."

His laughter followed her from the room, mocking her. She wasn't perfect for him. She wanted to be. Oh, mercy, how she wanted to be. She'd give him everything, but this dream romance was about to come to an end. His memories were coming back a little each day. Time was not on her side.

Maybe by focusing on work, he'd start to piece more things together. Perhaps then she wouldn't have to worry about saying anything. Honestly, she didn't know what scenario would be worse, her telling him the truth or him figuring it out on his own.

Was she a coward for not wanting to tell him? Absolutely. Not only did she not want to see that hurt—and quite possibly hatred—in his eyes, she didn't want that confrontation. There were no right words to say, no good way to come out and tell him he'd been living a complete lie for these past few days.

The end result would be the same, though, no matter how he found out. He would be disgusted with her. Suddenly, losing her job, or even her parents' positions, wasn't the main problem. After this time away from their ordinary lives, she couldn't imagine life without Luc.

And every bit of this scenario made her seem foolish, selfish and desperate.

When had she become that woman? When had she become the woman Luc had actually been engaged to? Because Kate was no better than his lying, scheming ex.

Luc glanced over Kate's shoulder as she sat in a patio chair with her laptop on the mosaic-tiled table. They'd opted to work outside to enjoy the bright sunshine and soft ocean breeze.

Resting his hands on the back of the chair, Luc leaned in to read over the tentative spreadsheet, but he was finding it impossible to focus. Kate's floral scent kept hitting him with each passing drift of wind.

"I can move these engagements around," Kate told him, pointing to the two green lines on the screen. "Both appointments are flexible. I scheduled them like this because I thought it would save time."

"Fine. You know more about this than I do," he told her.

She shifted, peeking at him over her shoulder. "I know about scheduling, but this is your life, Luc. Give me some input here. I can add or take away time. Usually, when you don't want to stay at an event too long, I make an excuse and cut the time back."

His brows quirked. "Seriously?"

"Well, yeah. How else would you escape and still look like the charming prince?" She laughed.

"Wow, you really do everything for me." With a sigh, he straightened. "What you have works for me. You've done this for a year, so you obviously know what you're talking about."

Kate turned fully in her chair and narrowed her eyes. "That's the Luc I used to work with. You never wanted to help with the schedule. You always trusted me to make it work."

Another flash of Kate in a snug suit, black this time, filled his mind. A dark-haired woman stood next to her. Luc closed his eyes, wanting to hold on to the image, needing to see who it was. Who was this woman?

Alana.

The image was gone as fast as it entered his mind, but he had a name.

"Luc?"

He opened his eyes, meeting Kate's worried gaze. She'd come to her feet and stood directly in front of him.

"Who's Alana?" he asked.

Kate jerked as if he'd slapped her. "Do you remember her?"

"I had a flash of you and her talking, but I couldn't tell what you guys were saying. It's like a damn movie that plays in my head with no sound."

He raked a hand down his face, meeting her eyes once more. "Who is she?" he repeated.

"She was a woman you used to date."

Luc tried to remember more, but nothing came to mind. Only that the woman's name stirred emotions of anger and hurt within him.

"Were we serious?" he asked.

Kate crossed her arms and nodded. "You were."

She was really sticking to the doctor's orders and not feeding him anything more than he was asking. Damn it, he wished she'd just tell him.

Pacing across the patio, Luc came to a stop at the edge by the infinity pool and stared out at the ocean. With the world at his back, he wished he could turn away from his problems so easily.

Alana Ferella. The name slid easily into his mind as he watched the waves roll onto the shore. His heart hardened, though. What kind of relationship had they had together? Obviously, not a compatible one or he'd still be with her. Something akin to rage settled in him. She hadn't been a nice woman, that much he knew.

He didn't want to keep asking Kate about an ex-girlfriend, and most likely Alana didn't matter, anyway. He just wished he could remember more about Kate, more about the plans they'd made.

"Are we getting married soon?" he asked, turning back to face her.

She blinked a few times, as if his question had thrown

her off. Hell, it probably had. He'd just gone from quizzing her on his ex to discussing their own nuptials.

"There's no set date," she told him.

That was weird. Once they'd announced their engagement, wouldn't the proper protocol have been to set a date? "Why not?" he asked. "With my birthday approaching, the throne in question and being a member of a royal family, I'm shocked we don't have something set."

Biting on her lip, Kate shrugged. "We can discuss the details in a bit. Can we finalize this schedule first? I'd like to make some calls later, if the cell service is working, to confirm your visit. I also need to let my dad know, so security can be arranged."

She was dodging his question for a reason. Did she simply not want to discuss things because of his memory loss, or was there something more to it? She'd admitted they'd argued before his fall. Had they been arguing over the wedding? Had they been arguing over...what? Damn it.

Smacking his palm on the table hard enough to make it rattle, Luc cursed, then balled his hands into fists. Kate jumped, taking a step back.

Kate started to step forward, but he held up a hand.

"No," he ordered. "Don't say anything. There's nothing you can do unless you want to tell me everything, which goes against the doctor's orders."

The hurt look on her face had him cursing. She was just as much a victim in this as he was.

"Kate, I didn't mean to lash out at you."

She shook her head, waving a hand. "It's okay."

"No, it's not." Closing the gap between them, he pulled her into his arms. "You've been here for me, you've done so much and I'm taking out my anger and

frustrations on you when you're only trying to protect me."

Kate wrapped her arms around his waist. "I can handle it, Luc. It's partially my fault you're in this position,
anyway. If we hadn't been arguing, if I hadn't made you
so angry you went down to that wet dock, none of this
would be happening."

Luc eased back. "None of this is your fault. At least
pieces of my life are finally revealing themselves, and
I'm sure it won't be long before the rest of the puzzle
is filled in."

Kate had sacrificed so much for him. Yet he hadn't
heard her tell him once that she loved him. Luc eased
back, looking her in the eyes.

"Why are you marrying me?" he asked, stroking her
jawline with his thumbs.

Her body tensed against his as her eyes widened.
"What do you mean?"

"Do you love me?" he asked, tipping his head down
a touch to hold her gaze.

Instantly, her eyes filled. Kate's hands came up,
framed his face. "More than you'll ever know," she
whispered.

Relief coursed through him. He didn't know why, but
it was imperative to know her true feelings.

"I want to do something for you." She placed a light,
simple kiss on his lips. "Tonight I'm going to make your
favorite dinner. We're going to have a romantic evening
and there will be no talk of the amnesia, the wedding,
the work. Tonight will just be about Kate and Luc."

Wasn't that the whole point of this getaway? She
cleverly circled them back around to the purpose of
this trip. One of the many reasons he assumed he'd

fallen in love with her. She kept him grounded, kept him on track.

Tugging her closer to him, he nuzzled her neck. "Then I expect one hell of a dessert," he growled into her ear.

Eleven

She had to tell him. There was no more stalling. The anguish, the rage that was brewing deep within Luc was more than she could bear. No matter what the doctor said, she had to come clean, because Luc getting so torn up had to be more damaging than just learning the truth.

And the truth beyond this whole messed-up situation was that she loved him. She hadn't lied when he'd asked. Kate had fallen completely in love with Luc and to keep this secret another day just wasn't acceptable.

She put on her favorite strapless green dress and her gold sandals. With her hair piled atop her head, she added a pair of gold-and-amethyst earrings.

A glance down at her hand had her heart clenching. He'd given her a ring. She wore a ring from a man she loved, yet he truly had no idea who she was.

At this point, she didn't recognize herself. She'd never been a liar or a manipulator. Yet here she was, doing a bang-up job of both.

Even with the patio doors open, the house smelled amazing with their dinner of fish and veggies baking in the oven. No matter how the evening ended, Kate wanted one last perfect moment with Luc.

Her mother would be relieved that Kate was finally telling the truth. What would Luc's parents say? Would they insist she be fired? Would they dismiss her parents from their duties as well, as she'd feared all along?

No matter the ramifications, Kate had to do the right thing here.

She headed to the kitchen to check the progress of dinner. When she glanced out toward the ocean, she noticed the darkening skies. Another storm rolling in. How apropos. Hadn't this entire nightmare started with a storm? For once in her life she wasn't looking forward to the added turmoil from Mother Nature.

Luc stood on the patio with his phone. Kate had no idea who he was talking to, but whoever it was, their call would be cut off soon due to this crazy weather.

Nerves settled deep in Kate's stomach. She wanted nothing more than to go back in time and have a redo of the night Luc fell. First of all, she never would've argued with him. If he didn't want to do the orphanage visit, fine. She'd been beating her head against that proverbial wall for nearly a year and he'd never given in. Why had she assumed he'd grow a heart all of a sudden and go?

Of course, now that he was drawing a blank on certain aspects of his life, he seemed to have forgotten how cold he used to be. Kate truly wished this Luc, the one she'd spent the past few days with, the one who had made love to her as if he truly loved her, was the Luc who would emerge after all the dust settled.

The worry eating at her would not help her be strong when she most needed to be. Everything that Luc threw at her would be justified, and right now she just needed to figure out the best way to come clean, because she truly didn't want to harm him any more than she had to.

After checking the dinner, she pulled the pan from the oven. Once she had their plates made, she started to call him, but realized he was still on the phone. The electricity flickered as rumbles of thunder resounded outside. Kate quickly searched for candles, because inevitably the lights were going to go. Perfect. It seemed Mother Nature was on her side. With the lights off, Kate wouldn't have to see the hatred on Luc's face when she told him that everything he knew about her, about them, was a lie.

"Darling, did you hear what I said?"

Luc concentrated on his mother's voice, the words she was saying, but something still didn't fit.

"You said Alana contacted you because she wants to see me," he repeated slowly, still trying to process all this.

Kate had told him Alana was an ex, but why would she be contacting him if he was engaged to Kate?

"Yes," his mother confirmed. "She's called me twice and she's very adamant that she wants to see you. I'm not going to stick my nose in this—you can respond however you want—but I don't think it's a good idea."

Luc's eyes locked onto the orange horizon. This view alone was reason enough to buy this property, no matter how many upgrades he wished to have inside. But right now, his head was pounding as if memories were rushing to the surface, waiting to get out all at once.

"Why would she contact you at all?" he asked. Resting one hand on the rail, he clutched the phone with his other, struggling to hear through the static. "Alana is in my past."

"So you remember her? Good. Then you don't need me to say how ridiculous this notion is that she can just come back into our lives after the entire baby scandal…"

His mother's voice cut out, but in the midst of her talking Luc did catch the word *baby*.

He rubbed his forehead. A flash of a diamond ring, a snippet of Alana in tears saying something about a pregnancy…

"To think she could trick you into marriage simply by saying she's pregnant was absurd," his mother went on, oblivious to his inner turmoil. "The timing of you purchasing this getaway house was perfect. Alana has no idea where you are."

The timing?

Luc spun around, glancing in through the open doors. Beyond the living area was the kitchen, where Kate stood preparing dinner. Instantly, he saw it all. His mother's single, damning word *timing* had triggered an avalanche of memories.

Kate was his assistant. No doubt about that, but they weren't engaged. They were strictly employee-employer, and that had been the extent of their relationship…until just a few days ago.

He felt sick to his stomach as he reached out, seeking the edge of a wrought-iron chair. He needed support, and right now all he could call upon was an inanimate object.

"Alana has no place in this family, Lucas."

Luc swallowed, his eyes remaining locked on Kate. Obviously, he'd been played by two women in his life— two women he'd trusted and let in intimately—on so many levels.

No wonder she was always so hesitant to let him in on his past. Kate's silence probably had little to do with the doctor's warnings and everything to do with her own agenda.

How could he have been so blind? How the hell could Kate have taken advantage of his vulnerability like that? Being manipulative wasn't like her, or at least not like the Kate he'd known. What had changed? Why had she felt it necessary to lie to his face, to go along with this charade that they were engaged?

Luc closed his eyes, gritting his teeth. "Mom, I'll call you back later. The connection is bad with the weather."

The call was cut off before he could finish. This storm was going to be a big one and he didn't just mean the one brewing outside.

Luc held the phone down at his side, dropped his head and tried like hell to forget the images, the emotions that went along with the fact he'd slept with Kate. He'd had sex with his assistant. He'd thought himself in love with her, believed that he'd be marrying her, making her the next queen.

She knew full well he didn't step over the line of professional boundaries. He'd outlined that fact for her a year ago when their attraction had crept to the surface, and he'd wanted to nip it in the bud. Kate knew every single thing about him and she'd used that to her advantage. She knew of the real fiancée, the fake pregnancy, and even after he'd brought up having visions of a baby, she'd said nothing.

How far would she have let this farce go? How long was she intending to lie straight to his face? Earlier she'd claimed she loved him.

Luc's heart clenched. Love had no place in the midst of lies and deceit.

Bringing his eyes back up, he caught her gaze across the open space. She smiled, a smile that he'd once trusted, and Luc felt absolutely nothing but disgust.

He knew exactly what he had to do.

When he hadn't returned her smile, Kate worried. Again she wondered who he'd been talking to on the phone. Something or someone had upset him.

Well, whatever it was, she couldn't let that hold her back. She couldn't keep finding excuses to put this discussion off.

"Dinner is ready," she called, setting the plates on the old, scarred table.

She glanced at the bouquet she'd purchased just the other day at the street market. She and Luc had shared so many amazing memories in such a short time, but she couldn't even relish them because they were built upon the lies she'd created using the feeble excuse that it was for his benefit. No, it would be to his benefit to know exactly what was going on in his life.

Nervousness spiked through her, settling deep. Kate smoothed a hand down her knee-length halter dress and took a deep breath as she stood beside her chair and waited for him to come in. Luc entered through the patio doors, closed them, set his phone on the coffee table and crossed to her.

"Smells great," he told her, offering a wide smile.

When he leaned down to kiss her cheek, Kate closed her eyes for the briefest of moments. Getting wrapped up in this entire scenario of playing house would only hurt her more. She wished more than anything that every bit of this scene playing out were true. Wished Luc would always look at her as if he loved her, as if he wanted to spend his life with her.

"My mother called," he told her after a long moment of silence. "She asked how everything was."

Kate moved the fish around on her plate, too nervous to actually eat. "I'm sure she's worried about you."

"She cares about me. I assume anyone who cares for me would be worried."

Kate's eyes slid up to his, a knot in her throat forming when she saw him staring back at her. "Yes. You have a great many people who love you."

"And what about you, Kate?" He held her gaze another moment before looking back to his plate. "Do you love me?"

Kate set her fork down, reached over to take his hand and squeezed. "I have so much in my heart for you, Luc."

When he said nothing, they finished eating, picked up the dishes and set them on the counter.

"Leave them," Luc told her, taking her hand. "Come with me."

When he led her toward the bedroom, Kate's heart started beating harder in her chest. She couldn't let him start kissing her, undressing her or even touching more than just her hand, because she'd melt instantly and not be able to follow through with her plan to spill her guts.

She trailed into the room after him. The bed in the center of the floor mocked her. Never again would they lie there in a tangle of arms and legs.

They never should have.

"Luc." She pulled her hand from his. "We can't."

He turned, quirking a brow. "Can't what?"

Kate shook her head, glancing away. She couldn't look him in the eyes. She didn't want to see his face when she revealed the truth.

"You can't make love to me?" He stepped closer, resting his hands on her shoulders. "Or you can't continue to play the role of doting fiancée? Because I have to tell you, you did a remarkable job of lying to my face."

Kate jerked her head up, meeting his cold, hard stare. All breath whooshed out of her lungs as fear gripped her heart like a vise.

"Apparently my real fiancée has been trying to get in touch with me," he went on, dropping his hands and stepping back as if he couldn't stand to touch Kate anymore. "After I heard my mother say that, the pieces started clicking into place."

Kate wrapped her arms around her waist. "You remember everything?"

"I know you're my assistant and you lied, manipulated and schemed to get into my bed." Luc laughed, the sound mocking. "Now I know why we never slept together before."

The pain in his voice sliced her heart open. Words died in her throat. Any defense she had was moot at this point.

"How far would you have gone, Kate? Would you have walked down the aisle and pretended to love me forever?"

She did love him. She'd chosen the absolute worst way to show him, but she truly did love the man. Kate pressed her lips together and remained still, waiting for the continuation of her punishment.

"Would you have gone so far as to have my kids?"

He took a step forward, but Kate squared her shoulders. She wasn't afraid of him and she wasn't going to turn and run, no matter how much she wanted to. Right now, he was entitled to lash out at her, and she had to take it.

"How could you do this to me?" His voice was low,

calm, cold. "Now I know why you cried after we had sex in the shower. Apparently, the guilt got to you, but only for a short time, because you were quick to get back in my bed."

Kate squeezed her arms tighter, as if to keep his hurtful words from seeping in. She glanced away, out the glass doors toward the sun, which had all but set.

"Look at me," he demanded. "You don't get to drift away. You started this and you're damn well going to face reality and give me the answers I want. Are you even going to say anything?"

Kate shook her head. "Anything I say won't change the fact that I lied to you, and you won't believe any defense I have."

Luc threw his arms out. "What was your motivation, Kate? Did you think I'd fall in love with you? Did you think you'd play with my mind for a bit?"

"No," she whispered through the tears clogging her throat. "Hurting you was the last thing I wanted to do."

"Oh, you didn't hurt me," he retorted, his face reddening. "I can't be hurt by someone I don't love. Didn't you know that? I'm furious I ever trusted you."

Kate nodded. "When we made love—"

"We didn't make love," he spat. Luc took a step closer, so close she could see the whiskey-colored flecks in his eyes. "We had sex. Meaningless sex that never should've happened."

Kate looked into his eyes, hoping to see a flicker of that emotion she'd seen during their days together, or when they'd been intimate. But all that stared back at her was hatred. Anything he thought he'd felt days ago, even hours ago, was false. The old Luc was back and harsher than ever.

"I'll call for someone to come pick me up," she told

him. "I'll be at the cottage until then. Anything I have here I can send for later."

Kate walked out of the room, surprised he didn't call her back so he could finish her off.

Mercifully, he let her go. She couldn't cry in front of him, didn't want him to think she was using tears as a defense. Her tears were a product of her own self-ishness. She'd lived it up for a few days, had had the man she loved in her arms and had even worn his ring.

Kate stepped out onto the patio and glanced down at the gem on her finger. Thunder rolled, lightning streaked in the not so distant sky as fat drops of rain pelted her.

"Kate," Luc called from behind her.

She froze.

"What the hell are you doing, just standing in the storm?"

Kate turned, blinking the rain out of her eyes. At this point she couldn't honestly tell what was rain and what were tears.

"Do you care?" she asked.

"I'm angry, but I don't want to see anyone struck by lightning."

Luc stood in the doorway, his broad frame filling the open space. The lights behind him flickered and then everything went black, save for the candles she'd lit on the dining room table and the fat pillar on the coffee table.

Cursing under his breath, Luc stepped back. "Get in here."

Slowly, Kate crossed the wet patio, hugging her mid-section against the cool drops. She brushed by him, shivering from the brief contact and cringing the second he stepped back and broke the touch.

"I just—"

"I'll be in my room." He cut her off with a wave of his hand as if she was nothing more than a nuisance. "Don't take this as a sign that I care. You can stay in here until the storm passes, and that's all."

Luc went to the dining room table, picked up a candle and walked away, leaving her shivering in the darkened living room. The pillar on the coffee table flickered, but she couldn't see much beyond the sofa. Kate sank down, pulling her feet up onto the cushion, hugging her knees to her chest.

Closing her eyes, she dropped her head forward and sighed. For the first time in her life she prayed the storm would stop. She had to get to her cottage, pack her things and call for someone to come and get her.

The hurt that had settled into this house was more than she could handle, and she didn't want to be here when Luc came out of his room. She didn't want to see that anger, that wounded look in his eyes again, knowing she'd put it there.

Whatever they'd had, be it their professional relationship or this fake engagement, she'd ruined any chance of ever having Luc in her life again. She'd taken what didn't belong to her, and she had no choice now but to live with the consequences.

Twelve

Luc must be insane. That was the only explanation for why he found himself crossing the path between the main house and the cottage so early in the morning. He hadn't slept all night. Every moment since his fall kept playing out in his mind like a movie, only he couldn't stop this one.

Kate's rigidity when he would initially touch her, her hesitancy to make love to him, why she was so adamant about him not buying her things at the market. The signs were there, but he'd assumed she was his fiancée, and she'd never said any differently. She'd had time, plenty of time, to tell him the truth. Even if the doctor hadn't given the order to not feed him any information, Luc was pretty sure she still would've kept up the charade.

Now that he'd had time to think, he'd fully processed how deeply her betrayal had sliced him. How could someone get so far into his life, work with him every single day, and manage to take advantage of him like that? Had he been that easy to manipulate? More important, how far would she have been willing to take that twisted game she'd played?

He wanted answers and he wanted them five minutes ago. He wasn't waiting another second to find out what the hell she'd been thinking to even contemplate getting away with such a potentially life-altering, monumental lie.

The anger raging inside him didn't stem just from her deception, but from the fact he'd fallen for her; making her betrayal even worse, Kate knew the emotional state he was in, just coming off a major breakup. Not only that, she knew he didn't date, much less sleep, with staff. How could she claim to care about him and then betray him in the next breath?

Even now that he knew everything, he still cared. He still ached for her, because with his old memories, he also had fresh ones. Memories he'd made with Kate, now tarnished by lies.

As Luc stepped into a clearing of lush plants, he glanced down to the dock. He froze when he spotted Kate standing by the water, two suitcases at her feet. She was not leaving without telling him why the hell she'd done this to him. She didn't get to escape that easily.

Marching toward the steps leading down to the beach, Luc had no clue what he'd say to her. She had plenty of explaining to do, but there was so much inside his mind, so much he wanted to say, he didn't even know where to start. He figured once he opened his mouth, things would start pouring out, most likely hurtful things. He couldn't care about her feelings just yet… if ever.

Kate jerked around as he approached. The dark circles beneath her eyes, the red rims, indicated she'd slept about as well as he had. The storm had lasted most of the night and he truly had no clue when she'd ended up leaving the main house. He'd closed the bedroom door, wanting to shut her out. Unfortunately, his bedroom was filled with visions of Kate.

The shower, the bed, her pair of flip-flops by the closet door, her robe draped across the foot of the bed. She was everywhere, and she'd wedged herself so intimately into his life, as no other woman had.

She'd had so much control over the situation and she'd used that power to consume him. Now he had to figure out how the hell to get out from under her spell, because even seeing her right now, with all his bubbling rage, he found his body still responded to her.

Damn it. How could he still want her? Anything that had happened between them was dead to him. He couldn't think back on those times, because just like this "engagement," they meant nothing.

Her eyes widened as he came to stand within inches of her. "I'm waiting for a boat. My father is sending one of the guards to pick me up."

"Why?" Luc asked, clenching his fists at his sides. "Before you leave, tell me why you lied to me."

Her head tipped slightly as she studied him. "Would it matter?"

Strands of her long, dark hair had slipped loose from her knot and were dancing about her shoulders. She had on another of those little strapless sundresses, this one black. Appropriately matching the color of his mood.

"Maybe not, but I deserve to know why you would betray my trust and think it was okay."

Dark eyes held his. Part of him wanted to admire her

for not backing away, not playing the victim or defending herself. The other part wished she'd defend herself and say something, so they could argue about it and get everything out in the open. He needed a good outlet, someone to yell at, and the perfect target stood directly in front of him.

"I was shocked at first that you thought I was your fiancée," she told him, her pink tongue darting out to lick her lips. She shoved a wayward strand of hair behind her ear and shrugged. "Then I wanted to see what the doctor would say before I told you otherwise. He said not to give you any information, so I didn't. I didn't want to lie to you, Luc. I was in a tough spot and everything blew out of my control before I knew what was happening. I tried to keep my distance, but once we had sex, I wanted more. I took what I shouldn't have. Nothing I can say can change that fact, but I am sorry I hurt you."

Luc propped his hands on his hips, waiting to hear more, but she remained silent and continued to hold his gaze. "There has to be another reason, a deeper motivation than you simply being afraid to tell me."

Kate's eyes darted away as she turned her back to him and focused on the water again. Not a boat in sight. He still had time to get answers from her before she left.

"My reasons are irrelevant."

He almost didn't hear her whispered answer over the ocean breeze. With her back to him, Luc wasn't sure what was worse, looking her in the eyes or looking at that exposed, creamy neck he could practically taste. He would never taste that skin again.

He cursed beneath his breath, raked a hand down his face and sighed. "What were you trying to gain?" he demanded. "I'm giving you the opportunity to say something here, Kate. Tell me why I shouldn't fire you, why I shouldn't remove you from every aspect of my life."

The low hum of a motor jerked his attention in the direction of the royal yacht moving toward them. Kate said nothing as she turned, picking up her suitcases.

Here he was gearing up for a good fight, and she couldn't even afford him that? Did she feel nothing at all? How had he misread her all these years?

If she wasn't going to talk now, then fine. He wasn't done with her, but if she needed to go, he'd let her. She could stew and worry back in Ilha Beleza. Luc actually wanted her uncomfortable, contemplating his next move. She deserved to be miserable, and he had to steel himself against any remorse.

His mother had always taught him to respect women, which he did, but right now that didn't mean he had to make her life all rainbows and sunshine, either.

"Go back to the palace," he told her, hating how she refused to look at him. "I'll be home in a few days and we'll add on to that schedule we finalized the other night."

Kate threw him a glance over her shoulder. "What?"

Luc stepped around her, blocking her view of the incoming boat. He waited until her eyes locked onto his. "You're not quitting. You're going to be with me until I know what game you're playing. And don't try to get sneaky once you're back. I have eyes and ears everywhere."

Her chin tipped up in defiance…a quality he'd once admired when she was speaking with the media or other pushy individuals. "I think it's best if I resign."

Luc gripped her shoulders, cursing himself for having a weakness where she was concerned, considering all she'd done. "I don't care what you think is best.

You're mine until I say otherwise. You started this game, Kate. You're going to see it through to the end."

Pushing away from her, he stalked toward the main house. Not once did he consider glancing back. He was finished looking over his shoulder to see if anyone was stabbing him in the back or betraying him. From here on out, he was regaining control, and he was damn well going to come out on top.

Luc stared at the area he used to call his kitchen. If this royalty thing didn't work out, he was seriously getting a job with a contractor. Demolishing things was an excellent outlet for his anger.

Wiping his forearm across his forehead, he sank down onto a dining room chair and surveyed his destruction. The cabinets were torn out; the countertop lay beneath the rubble. He'd pulled the fridge out enough that he could get to the food, but other than that, he'd completely torn up the space.

Kate had been gone a week. Two weeks had passed since he'd arrived here, and he was heading home tomorrow. In these past seven days alone, he'd had more than enough time to reflect on everything, and he still had no clue what he was going to do once he saw her again.

He'd had to sleep in the guest room on a lumpy old mattress because he couldn't lie in his master suite without smelling her, seeing her…feeling her at his side. The shower he'd so loved when the renovations started was now tainted, because all he could see was Kate's wet body as he claimed her with the false knowledge they were a real couple. They'd been damn good together, but he would never, ever admit that to her or anybody else.

Luc's cell chimed. He thought about ignoring it, but figured he'd at least see who wanted to talk to him.

Crossing the open room, he glanced at his phone on the coffee table. Mikos, his best friend.

Considering he had called Mikos three days ago and spilled his guts like some whiny high school girl with sad love songs playing in the background, Luc assumed his friend was calling to check on him.

"Hey, man," he answered with a sigh.

"You still sound like hell."

Luc laughed, sinking onto the sofa, resting his elbow on the arm. "Yeah, well, I feel like it. What's up?"

"Just checking in."

"Shouldn't you be planning the wedding of the century?" Luc asked, feeling a slight pang of envy.

Envy? Why the hell would he be envious? Sure, he needed to be married because of the throne, but he didn't want to be tied to one woman. No, Mikos had found the perfect woman for him, and Luc was happy for both of them.

There was no perfect woman for Luc. Hadn't he proved that by getting too close to two very convincing liars?

"The wedding is planned down to the last petal and place card," Mikos stated. "Are you still in?"

Luc was supposed to stand up with Mikos, right next to Mikos's brother, Stefan. An honor Luc wasn't letting Kate's untimely backstabbing steal from him.

"I'm in. I'm not letting my disaster ruin your day."

"Have you talked to Kate?"

Luc closed his eyes. Even hearing her name elicited a mixture of feelings, a myriad of emotions. Beyond the hurt, the anger and the bitterness there was still that underlying fact that he wanted the hell out of her. How twisted was that?

"No. I'm heading back tomorrow," Luc answered.

"What are you going to do?"

"I have no clue, man."

Mikos sighed. "Want my advice?"

"You're going to give it anyway, so why ask?"

"I am," Mikos agreed with a laugh. "Figure out why she lied. You told me once you had a thing for her. Maybe she was acting on her own feelings and taking a cue from yours before the accident."

"Are you defending her actions?" The last thing Luc wanted to hear was a justifiable cause. Damn it, he wanted to be angry, wanted to place all the blame on her.

"Hell, no. I'm saying love is a strong emotion."

"You're too blinded by this wedding," Luc replied. "Kate doesn't love me. You don't lie and scheme with those you love, no matter the circumstances."

"I did to Darcy," Mikos reminded him. "She had no idea who I was, and I was totally in love with her. I nearly lost her, but she forgave me. You know how things can get mixed up, Luc."

Luc recalled that time when Mikos's nanny had first been hired. She'd had no clue Mikos was a widowed prince. The two had fallen in love before Mikos could fully explain the truth.

"Our situations are completely different," Luc muttered. "I'm not forgiving her. No matter what."

"Just make sure you really think this through before you go off on her once you get home," Mikos warned. "What she did was wrong, no doubt about it. But she's not like Alana. I know that's something you'll never forget or get over, but Alana had an ulterior motive from the start. You've known Kate for years and she's never once done you wrong."

Luc finished the call, unable to think of anything else but the truth Mikos had laid out before him. No, Kate had never deceived him in any way before. She'd been the best assistant he'd ever had. To be honest, the only reason he hadn't pursued her before was because of their working relationship and possible repercussions to his ascension to the throne. With the mess he'd gotten himself into lately, it would be a miracle if the press didn't rip his family's reputation to shreds if the truth came out.

Once he returned to Ilha Beleza, he and Kate would have a one-on-one chat, now that they'd both had time to absorb all that had happened. They needed to talk. He couldn't keep her around if he didn't trust her. And that was the problem. When it came to his professional life, he trusted no one else.

Unfortunately, when it came to his personal life, he didn't trust her one bit…but that didn't stop him from wanting her. Even this week apart hadn't dimmed his attraction toward her. Which begged the question: What the hell was going to happen once he got home? And would he be able to control himself?

Thirteen

His desk was exactly how he always kept it—neat, tidy and organized, with his schedule in hard copies just as he wanted it. He knew there would also be emails on his computer with the same information.

Kate had kept up her end of the bargain and continued working just as if she hadn't torn their entire lives to shreds. He didn't know whether to be relieved or angry that she was still here, still within reaching distance... not that he was going to reach out to her. He had more pride than that.

Luc flipped through the papers, even though he'd looked through his email earlier and knew what he had coming up. Mikos's wedding was only two weeks away, and other than that, there were a handful of meetings and social events at which he was expected to make an appearance. He'd been knocked down so many times in the past few months he didn't know if he had the energy to put forth for anyone outside his immediate family and staff. He was so exhausted, spent and depleted from trying to perform damage control on his personal life, there was no way he could keep up with his royal obligations, too.

Thankfully, from the looks of his schedule, Kate had helped him dodge any media interviews over the next few months. For that he was grateful, but not enough to seek her out and thank her. He wasn't ready to thank her for anything…and he might never be.

"Oh, sweetheart. You're back."

Luc glanced toward the high, arched doorway as his mother breezed in. The woman possessed more elegance and grace than anyone he'd ever known. With her polished style and loving grin, she made the perfect queen, but her reign was soon coming to an end. Well, it would be if he managed to find a way to secure his title before his birthday, and without a wife.

Luc crossed the room and relished her embrace. Even though he'd always been close with his parents, he didn't have it in him to discuss all the ways he was struggling right now.

"How are you?" she asked, pulling back to assess him. Clutching his arms, she studied his face. "No more symptoms? You remember everything now?"

Luc nodded. "I'm perfectly fine."

She held on to him another moment, then broke the contact. "We need to talk."

He crossed his arms as his mother shut the double doors, giving them complete privacy.

"Have you seen Kate since you've been back?" she asked.

Luc shook his head. "No."

"Darling, she told me what happened." His mother

reached out, took one of his hands in hers and squeezed. "I'm sure she left out some details, but I know you believed she was your fiancée, and she went along with it."

Luc gritted his teeth. Seriously? Kate went to his mom?

"I wished I'd learned this from you," she went on. "I can't imagine how angry you must be, and I know you're feeling betrayed—"

"Don't defend her," Luc growled. "I'm not near that point."

"I'm not defending her actions." His mother smiled, tipping her head. "I just want you to really think about how you're going to handle this. Kate is a wonderful woman and I've always been so fond of her. I know we have a rule about remaining distant from employees, but she and her parents have been around so long, they're like family."

His feelings for Kate were far from family-like, and he sure as hell hadn't been feeling brotherly in that shower.

"I will admit I'm surprised you didn't fire her," his mother added. "She's good for you, Luc. She's the best assistant you've ever had. I'm proud of you for not blowing up."

"It was tempting."

Temptation. The word seemed to go hand in hand with Kate's name.

"I still don't know what to do, but for now, she's going to be working for me like always. I don't have time to find a new assistant, and I sure as hell don't want to have to get to know someone new. I've got enough of a mess to deal with."

"We do need to figure out what's going to happen on your birthday." His mother pursed her lips, as if in deep thought. "Your father would change the law if he could, but the truth is, we never dreamed…"

Luc laughed, the sound void of all humor. "I know. You never thought a child of yours would still be single at thirty-five. It's okay to say it."

She squeezed his arm. "We'll figure something out. We have to."

Luc nodded, unable to speak past the lump of worry in his throat. Failure was not an option. Ever. He was the next leader, for crying out loud. Why couldn't he figure out a way around this ridiculous issue?

"I'll let you get settled back in, then." His mother reached up, kissed him on the cheek. "Glad you're back home and safe. And I'm glad you didn't fire Kate. She means more to this family than you may realize."

What did that mean? Did his mother actually think he and Kate…

No. That was ridiculous. As torn as he was, he couldn't entertain the idea that Kate could remain in his life as anything other than his assistant…and even that role was still up in the air. He'd have to worry about that later. At this point, time was against him, and finding another assistant before finding a wife—or before the coronation—was impossible.

Once he was alone again, Luc turned and went to his desk. Bracing his palms on its glossy top, he leaned forward and closed his eyes. He would do a great job ruling this country, as his father had before him. Luc just needed a chance to prove he could do so without a wife.

The echo of soft footsteps hit him and he knew instantly who would be behind him. He didn't turn, though. He wasn't quite ready to take in the sight of Kate with all her beauty and sexiness.

The click of the heels stopped, Luc's heart beat faster

than he liked. Damn it, he hadn't even turned to look at her, hadn't said a word, yet she had already sent his body into overdrive.

"I'll come back."

Her soft words washed over him as he turned to face her.

"No." He spoke to her retreating back, and she froze in the doorway. "Come in and close the door."

She stood still so long, he thought for sure she wasn't going to stay. After a moment, she stepped back, closed the door and whipped around to face him.

Luc hadn't thought it possible, but he still found her breathtakingly gorgeous and arousing. Seeing Kate in a dark blue suit, with a fitted jacket that hugged her waist and accentuated her breasts, and her snug skirt made it hard for him to form words right now. As her heels clicked across the floor, his eyes were drawn to her open-toed, animal-print pumps. Damn, she looked like a woman who was ready to be stripped and laid out on his desk.

What was worse, now that he'd had her wrapped all around him, he knew exactly how amazing they were together. Why was he paying a penance in all this? He was the victim.

She stopped well out of his reach, clasped her hands in front of her and met his gaze. "I didn't know you were back," she said. "I was just coming in to make sure your computer was ready to go when you needed it."

Luc tore his gaze from her painted red lips and glanced at his desk. He hadn't even noticed the new computer. Hell, he hadn't even asked for one. Once again, she stayed on top of things and kept his life running smoothly.

"Where's my old one?" he asked.

"All of the palace computers have been upgraded, and they put yours in while you were gone. I made sure the security on yours was set up the same as your old one, and I also made sure your old files were transferred. Everything is on there under the same names, just how they always were."

When he glanced back at her, there wasn't a hint of any emotion on her face. Not a twinge of a smile, no dark circles under her eyes to indicate she'd been losing sleep. Absolutely nothing.

Which pissed him off even more.

"Is this how it's going to be?" he asked, gritting his teeth. "With you pretending you didn't change the dynamics between us?"

Kate blinked, pulled in a deep breath and shook her head. "I don't know what you want from me. I can't erase what happened, yet you still want me to work for you, so I'm doing what I can under the circumstances. I can't tell you what you want to know, because—"

She spun around. Luc waited for her to finish, but she kept her back to him as silence settled heavily between them. There was no easy way, no secret formula for them to get beyond this. He wasn't all that convinced they could move on, despite what his mother and Mikos had said during their pep talks.

"Because why?" he pressed, when she remained quiet. "Why can't you tell me your reasons? I'm ready to hear it. I *need* to hear it, Kate."

Still nothing. Luc stepped forward, closing the space between them. "Damn it, I deserve more than your silence. You can't hide like this. You don't get that right. Tell me what prompted you to not only lie, but keep up the charade and play me so perfectly that you ended up in my bed."

"Don't," she whispered. "Don't make me say it."

Luc grabbed her arm, spun her around and forced himself to hold her watery gaze. "I refuse to let you out of this scot-free."

Squaring her shoulders, tipping her chin up and swiping a hand beneath her eye as one lone tear streaked out, Kate nodded. "Fine. You want to know why I did it? Why I lied to you so easily? Besides the doctor's orders of not saying anything more, besides the fact that the deception just got out of control, I knew it was the only time in my life you'd ever look at me like you cared for me. Like you actually wanted me. I knew it was wrong. I never justified my actions, and I won't defend them, because there's no way to make any of it okay. But don't make me tell you more. I can't, Luc."

Her voice cracked on his name. Luc kept his hand on her arm as he took a half step closer, nearly towering over her. "You can," he murmured. "Tell me the rest. Now."

He was so torn between arousal and anger. He'd always heard there was a fine line between hatred and passion. No truer words were ever spoken.

"I fell in love with you," she whispered, her eyes locking onto his. "Is that what you wanted to hear? Do you hate me so much that humiliating me is the only way to make yourself get past the anger? Well, now you know. I've bared my soul to you, Luc. You know about my adoption, which few people do. You know my secret fantasies—you're the only one in that category—and that I'm in love with a man who'd rather belittle me than ever forgive me, let alone love me back. My fault, I know, but that doesn't stop the hurt."

A viselike grip squeezed his heart at her declaration. Why did he feel anything akin to sympathy toward her? She'd done every bit of this to herself, pulling him along for the ride.

"You don't love me." He dropped his hand and stepped back. "You don't lie to someone and manipulate them, taking advantage of their weaknesses, when you love them."

"I never lied to you before this and I won't lie to you again," she vowed, crossing her arms over her chest. "So when I tell you I love you, I'm being honest. I know my word means nothing to you, and I know I went about everything the wrong way. There is no excuse for my behavior, so I'm not going to stand here and try to make one."

Luc watched as she pulled herself together, patting her damp cheeks, smoothing her hair behind her shoulders and standing tall.

Even through all this, she remained strong. He wanted to hate her, because that would be so much easier than to stand here and be torn in two. She'd betrayed the trust they had built, yet at the same time she had tried to keep her distance. He'd been the one to pursue the intimacy. He could look at this situation from so many angles, but none of them gave him the answer or made things any easier.

"You have every right to fire me—I deserve it. But if you insist on keeping me, I think it's best if we keep our relationship professional and try to move on. That means no rehashing the mistakes I made. I can't have you throwing them in my face."

The longer she spoke, the stronger her voice got. The woman who'd emotionally professed her love for him just moments earlier had transformed back into the businesslike assistant he'd always known. Who was the real Kate?

Was she the loving, passionate woman back at the beach house? Was she the take-charge assistant, or was she the conniving woman who'd ruthlessly insinuated herself into his life when he'd been weak?

"I agree that from here on out, we'll keep our relationship strictly professional."

Luc prayed like hell he was telling the truth. He needed to keep his head on straight, focus on securing the title and not think about how much he'd fallen for his assistant.

Well, that plan to keep things professional was about to get blown apart.

Kate closed her eyes, gripped the stick and willed the results to be different.

Peeking through one eyelid, she still saw the two pink lines glaring back at her. If they had been on a billboard or neon sign they couldn't have been any more eye-catching... She couldn't look anywhere else.

And no matter how long she stared at it, the results were still going to be the same. Positive.

Something between a moan and a cry escaped her as she came to her feet. Staring at herself in the vanity mirror, Kate didn't know what she expected to see. She didn't look any different, but in the past three minutes the course of her entire life had been altered.

Now what should she do? She was pregnant with Luc's baby and the man practically loathed her, unless she was writing a speech for him or running interference for some engagement he didn't want to attend.

There was no getting around this. She'd been on the pill since she was a teen, to keep her cycle regular, but they hadn't used a condom the times they'd been intimate, and birth control wasn't fail-safe...obviously.

There was only one answer. She'd promised Luc she'd never lie to him again, and she certainly wasn't going to start off by keeping this baby a secret.

Laying the test stick on the back of the vanity, Kate washed her hands and stepped out of the restroom. She wanted to find Luc now. This couldn't wait, because the nerves in her stomach were threatening to overtake her. She had to find him.

At this point in the day, she honestly had no idea what he was doing, but she did know he was working from home. If she stopped to think, she could figure out his schedule—she had created it. But her mind wasn't in work mode right now and she couldn't process anything other than the fact she was having a baby with a man she loved…a man who could hardly look at her. She was on the verge of freaking out.

Her lies had not only killed the trust Luc had for her, now the whirlwind of secrets had formed a new life…literally.

Kate's hand slid over her stomach as she made her way out of her office and into the wide hallway. She smiled as she passed one of the maids, but her smile faded the second she reached Luc's office door. In just moments, both their lives and the future of this country would be changed forever.

She was carrying an heir.

Kate rested her forehead against the smooth wood and closed her eyes. The sooner she told Luc, the sooner they could start figuring out what to do. Summoning all the strength she possessed, she tapped on his office door, cursing her shaking hands. She heard familiar voices on the other side. Apparently, he was having a private meeting with his parents. Still, this couldn't wait.

Yes, they were the king and queen. Yes, Kate was being rude by interrupting. But she didn't care.

Fisting her hand, she knocked louder and longer, until the door jerked open to an angry-looking Luc. His jaw clenched, his lips thinned, and once he saw her, his eyes narrowed.

"Kate? We're in the middle of something."

Pushing by him, she offered a shaky smile to his parents, who sat with their eyes locked on her. "I'm sorry, but this can't wait."

Ana Silva rose to her feet and crossed the room. Kate swallowed as her heart started beating faster. She was going to be sick. The overwhelming urge to pass out or throw up all over the Persian rug had nothing to do with the pregnancy.

"Darling, you're trembling," Ana said. "Come, sit down."

"We're in the middle of something," Luc repeated.

Luc's father stood, gesturing toward the chair he'd just vacated. "Here, Kate."

Luc muttered a string of Portuguese slang.

"I'm sorry," Kate muttered. "I didn't mean to cause a scene. I just need a few minutes with Luc."

His parents exchanged a look and Kate noticed Luc standing off to the side, arms crossed, jaw still clenched. He wasn't happy. Too bad she was about to drop another bomb on his life. Would he be even angrier at her? Most likely, but hiding the pregnancy wasn't an option.

Kate closed her eyes as she rested her elbows on her knees and dropped her head into her hands. Luc's parents muttered something to him and moments later Kate heard the office door click shut.

"What the hell is this all about?" Luc demanded.

Kate pushed her hair away from her face as she looked up. He was leaning against the edge of his desk, ankles crossed, palms resting on either side of his slim hips. Wearing dark designer jeans and a fitted black T-shirt, he didn't look like a member of the royal family, but he still exuded power. It was the stare, the unyielding body language, that told her she needed to get on with her speech…one she hadn't rehearsed at all.

"I…" Kate shook her head, came to her feet. No way could she remain still; her body was too shaky, too wound up to stay seated.

"Just say it."

Luc's harsh words cut through her. Kate stopped pacing, turned and gazed at him. "I'm pregnant."

He stared at her for several moments without saying a word. Then suddenly, he burst out laughing, and straightened.

"Nice try, Kate." His expression sobered. "That's already been used on me."

"What?"

His words took a moment to sink in. He didn't believe her. Of course he wouldn't. Why should he? He'd been played for a fool by his ex-fiancée, who tried the pregnancy trap, and Kate had also lied to him.

"Luc, I'm not lying," she reiterated. "I have the test in my office bathroom. I need to call Dr. Couchot to confirm with a blood test, though."

Something dark clouded Luc's eyes. "You did this on purpose."

Fury rose to the surface, pushing through the nerves. No matter how much she loved him, no matter how much she wished he would see her as a woman worthy of his love and trust, Kate refused to stand here and be degraded and blamed for something they'd both taken part in.

"I think it was you who came to me," she retorted,

crossing her arms over her chest. "You think I wanted a child with a man who doesn't love me? I made a mistake by lying to you, but I'm not pathetic and I'm not trying to trap you. I promised I would always be honest with you, and I just found out about this myself ten minutes ago. So lose the ego. I don't want to snag you that much."

Kate turned to go and managed to get across the room with her hand on the doorknob before Luc grabbed her arm and spun her back around. Leaning flat against the door, trapped between the wood and Luc's hard body, she stared up into those eyes that could make a woman forget all her problems…almost. Even the great Prince Lucas Silva wasn't that powerful.

"You think you can drop that bomb and then just walk out?" he demanded. "We're not done here."

"We both need to process this before we say anything we might regret." Though they'd already said plenty to cause damaging scars. "I just need… I need to think this through, Luc."

His eyes widened. "What's there to think through? You're having my child. I will be part of his or her life."

A sliver of relief coursed through her. "I would never deny you the chance to be with your child."

Tears welled up, the familiar burn in her throat formed and Kate cursed herself. She absolutely hated crying, hated the predicament she was in, but hated even more that she was pulling in an innocent child.

"I'm scared," she whispered, closing her eyes.

She jerked when Luc's hand slid over her cheek. Focusing back on him, she saw something in his eyes she hadn't expected…fear. Obviously, she wasn't the only one with insecurities.

"No matter what happened prior to this moment,

I won't leave you alone with a baby." He dropped his hand, but didn't step back. "Our baby."

When he stood so close, smelling so amazingly familiar and feeling so sexy against her, Kate couldn't think straight. She wished she didn't still want him, wished she'd never lied to him to begin with. And she truly wished something as beautiful as creating a life with the man she loved hadn't been tainted because of her lies.

"I don't want our baby to suffer from my actions," she told him. "I want to be able to work with you on this, and I know the timing—"

She cut herself off with a sad laugh. "Sorry. There would be no good timing," she corrected. "I just meant with the throne, your birthday and all of that on your mind, I didn't mean to add to your stress, but you needed to know."

When he said nothing, Kate carefully turned. There was no way to avoid rubbing up against him, because he'd barely moved since he'd trapped her against the door.

Luc's hands came up to cup her shoulders as he moved in behind her.

"Who are you, Kate?" he whispered.

Her head dropped against the wood as she tried to ignore all of the ways her body responded to his. Tried and failed miserably.

"Are you the efficient assistant? The woman who stands up for me to the public? Are you the woman who lied to me for selfish reasons? Or are you the woman who claims to love me and who's now carrying my child?"

Drawing in a shaky breath, Kate glanced over her shoulder just enough to catch his gaze. "I'm all of them."

"Part of me hates you for what you did." Luc's eyes darted down to her lips. "I wish I still didn't want you so damn much."

Breath caught in Kate's throat as Luc pushed away and stalked back to his desk. He kept his back to her, as if that revelation had cost him dearly. She had no doubt he hadn't meant to let that slip, and as much as she wanted to revel in his obvious discomfort over the fact that he wanted her, Kate had to put this baby first, above all else.

Even the fact that her own heart was still beating for only one man.

Fourteen

He hadn't planned on taking Kate to Greece for his best friend's wedding, but once she had opened her heart to him and bared her soul, Luc wasn't able to deny the fact that he still wanted her.

Plans were taking root in his mind and he was going to have to take action. Perhaps he could have Kate, the crown and his child without ever putting his heart on the line where she was concerned. Surely she'd stay for the sake of their child. Why not make it official, so he could keep the title that was rightfully his?

But if he wanted to sway her into marriage, he needed to start convincing her, or she'd never say yes.

No, he hadn't forgiven her for lying, but she was pregnant, confirmed by Dr. Couchot, and Luc knew the child was his. The plan forming in his mind was anything but nice, but he couldn't back down. Too much was at stake.

Luc glanced across the aisle to where Kate had reclined her seat and was curled onto her side, with her hand beneath her cheek. She'd been exhausted when they'd left that morning, and he'd nearly told her to stay behind, but he knew she was just as stubborn as him and wouldn't listen. Either the baby was making her more tired than usual or she wasn't sleeping because of the stress. Knowing her, it was probably both.

He'd cursed himself every which way after she'd left his office a few days ago. He'd hated how his heart had flipped when she'd whispered her fears. Damn it, he didn't want his heart to be affected by this woman. There was no space in his life for such things. He had a title to secure, and now he had an heir to think about. Kate couldn't fall under the category of things he cared about, because if he allowed that, then she would have the upper hand. Wanting her physically was difficult enough to have to deal with each time she was near.

His mind kept wandering back to how right it had felt when they'd been playing house. He'd gladly dismissed his family's rule about fraternizing with staff. He would have done anything for her. He'd never felt so connected to a woman in all his life.

Kate embodied sex appeal, that was a given. It had been what had drawn him to her when she'd first come to work for him. He vaguely recalled the little girl, and later on the teen, who used to hang around the palace with her parents.

Then when the time came that he'd needed an assistant and Kate had been recommended, he'd jumped at the chance, because her family knew his so well and he knew she'd be a trustworthy candidate. Plus her references and academics had been superb.

Yet somehow, over the course of a professional relationship that had started out with an attraction, and involved his messy engagement to another woman, Luc's life had spiraled spectacularly out of control.

The irony that he'd gone from a fiancée with a fake pregnancy to a poser fiancée with a real pregnancy was not lost on him. He was a walking tabloid and fodder for the press. Thankfully, Kate was in charge of press releases, and no doubt she'd come up with something amazingly brilliant once they were ready to go public.

Kate stirred in her sleep, letting out a soft moan. The simple sound hit his gut with a swift punch of lust he couldn't ignore. He'd heard those moans in his ear as she'd wrapped her body around his. He'd felt the whisper of breath on his skin that accompanied her sighs.

But no matter how compatible they were in the bedroom, no matter how much he still ached for her on a level he'd never admit aloud, Luc wouldn't, couldn't, allow himself to be pulled into whatever spell Kate had over him.

Even if he would let his guard down and shove the royal rule aside and see a staff member personally, Kate had killed any chance of him ever trusting her fully. So she could sit across from him and make all the noises she wanted; he was ignoring them.

Too bad his body hadn't received that memo, because certain parts of him couldn't forget the intimacy they'd shared.

Luc needed to focus on the brilliant plot he'd started forming. Would she be angry when he approached her with the solution? Yes. Did he care? No. He was plenty angry still, but he wanted her, wanted the crown and refused to allow his heart to become vulnerable again.

The phone near Luc's seat rang and the pilot informed him they'd be landing within a half hour. Once

Luc hung up, he crossed the space and sank down in the plush white leather chair next to Kate. He hated waking her up. Not that he was worried about disturbing her sleep; he was more concerned with the fact he'd have to touch her, have to see her blinking back to reality as she sat there, looking all rumpled and sexy.

As if she was ever *not* appealing. But he couldn't be blinded by lust and sexual chemistry. He didn't need a bed partner, no matter what his body told him. Making love with her was how he'd gotten entangled in this web to begin with.

"Kate."

He purposely said her name loudly, so she'd wake without him having to lay a hand on her. She let out a soft snore and Luc gritted his teeth and called her name again.

Still nothing.

Who was he kidding? It didn't matter if he touched her or not. He wanted her, his body responded to her as it had to no other woman and she was carrying his child. As if he needed another reason to be physically pulled toward her. Knowing she was carrying his child was beyond sexy. There was something so primal about knowing Kate sat there with their baby safely inside her body.

Even when Alana had said she was expecting, Luc hadn't felt this much of a tug on his heart. He'd had an instant protective instinct toward the child, but he'd never felt a bond with Alana.

Damn it, he couldn't afford a tug on his heart or some invisible bond. Kate wasn't trustworthy. Regardless, he didn't need her trust for his plan to work. He didn't need anything from her, because he wouldn't take no for an answer.

Marrying Kate was the only solution. As much as he hated to give in to his country's archaic rule, it was the only way to come out of this situation on top. Some marriages were based on far less than sexual chemistry and they worked just fine.

The fact remained that he still wanted her something fierce. He wanted her with an intensity that scared him, but he had to risk his heart, his sanity, in order to get what he wanted.

Luc reached around, pulled on her seat belt and fastened it with a click. Just as he was about to move away and fasten his own, Kate jerked awake. Sleepy eyes locked onto his and he realized his mistake. He'd leaned in too close, so close he was only inches from her face, and his hand hovered over her abdomen.

"What are you doing?" she asked, her voice husky from sleep.

"Preparing you for landing."

Why hadn't he eased back, and why was he staring at her lips?

"You can't look at me like that, Luc," she whispered. "You don't even like me."

Something clenched in his gut. Something harsher, more intense than lust.

He was a damn *tolo*. Fool. That was the only explanation for having these reactions after what she'd done to him. He needed to focus on the plan, the throne, the baby. Everything else—including his lustful feelings—would have to be put aside.

"I don't trust you," he countered. "There's a difference."

Those heavy lids shielded her dark eyes for a moment as she stared down to where his hands lay on her stomach.

"I didn't trap you," she whispered as her eyes drifted back up to his. "No matter what you think of me, I'd never do that to you or an innocent child."

Luc swallowed as her hand settled over his. There was so much emotion in her eyes, so much he was too afraid to identify, because if he did, he'd start feeling more for her, and he refused to be played like a *fantouche*, a puppet, for a third time.

Pride and ego fueled his decisions. Power and control ran a close second. And all those things combined would get him everything he'd ever wanted…everything he was entitled to.

Luc shifted to sit up, but didn't remove his hand, and for some asinine reason he didn't break eye contact, either. Obviously, he was a glutton for punishment.

"I want you to move into the palace."

Of course, he had bigger plans, but he had to ease her into this. She wasn't the only one skilled at manipulation.

"I'm not sure that's a good idea."

She removed her hand from his, a silent plea for him to move, so he pulled back. The first slight dip in the plane's decent reminded Luc he hadn't fastened his seat belt because he'd been worried for her. He quickly buckled it, then turned his attention back to Kate.

"Why not?" he asked. "Moving into the palace is the ideal solution. We'll be sharing responsibilities. I know we'll hire a nanny, but I plan on being a hands-on dad."

Kate shoved her hair away from her face. A thin sleep mark ran down her cheek. It made her seem so vulnerable, and it was all he could do not to touch her again. "What will happen when you want to actually marry someone? Are you going to explain to your bride that your baby mama is living there, too?"

Luc laughed. "That's a pretty crass way to put it."

Kate shrugged, lacing her fingers together as she glanced out the window. "I'm not sugarcoating this situation and neither should you."

Luc didn't say anything else. He would sway her with his actions, not his words. She would come to see that living with him, ultimately marrying him, would be the best way to approach their predicament. And when they married, she would be sleeping in his bed again. He'd make sure of it.

Now he just needed to get his hormones under control, because he was physically aching for her. Being near her now that he'd had her was pure hell. The woman was made for him. Nobody had ever matched him in the bedroom—or shower—the way she did.

Yet Kate was so much more than a sex partner. He'd discovered an emptiness in him now that they were back to keeping things professional. No matter the circumstances surrounding the false engagement, Luc couldn't help but think back and realize those days spent on the island were some of the happiest of his life.

Kate had been to many royal events over the past year as an official employee of the Silva family. Before that, she'd seen enough to know that royalty never did anything halfway, especially when it came to weddings.

The ceremony uniting Darcy and Mikos Alexander had taken place earlier in the day, and now only the couple's closest family and guests, of which there appeared to be several hundred, remained for the reception.

No expense had been spared for the event taking place both in the ballroom and out in the courtyard at the palace on Galini Isle, off the coast of Greece. Every stationary item was draped with something crystal, shimmering or sheer.

As she watched the bride and groom dance, Kate couldn't help but smile. Mikos had lost his first wife suddenly, leaving him to care for their infant daughter alone. Needing a break, he'd gone to Los Angeles to get away and think. He'd hired Darcy to be his daughter's nanny, and before long the two had fallen in love…even though Mikos had slightly deceived Darcy, because she'd had no idea he was royalty. Of course, none of that had made it to the press, but Kate knew the whole story from Luc.

Luc and Mikos had been best friends forever. Kate was quite familiar with Mikos and his brother, Stefan, who was also in attendance, with his stunning wife, Victoria.

Even if the crystal chandeliers, flawless ice sculptures, millions of clear twinkling lights and yards upon yards of sheer draping hadn't screamed elegance and beauty, the gorgeous people milling about certainly would have.

This was definitely one of those times she was thankful her mother was the royal seamstress. By the time Luc had sprung the trip on her, Kate hadn't had time to go shopping. So her mom had taken an old gown and made enough modifications to transform it into something lovely and totally unique. What had once been a simple, fitted silver dress was now unrecognizable. The sleeves had been removed and the top had been cut into a sweetheart neckline to give the allure of sexiness with a slight show of cleavage. Her mother had then had the brilliant idea of taking strands of clear beads and sewing them so they would drape across Kate's arms, as if her straps had fallen and settled just above her biceps.

Kate actually felt beautiful in this dress, and judging from the way Luc had stared at her without saying a word when he'd come to get her for the wedding, she had to assume he thought she looked nice, as well.

She still couldn't get the image out of her mind of him waking her for the landing. He'd been so close, staring at her as if he wanted to touch her, kiss her. Their chemistry wasn't in question, that was obvious, but he clearly battled whether or not to act on it.

Maybe their time apart would have him coming around, to see that she truly wasn't aiming for the crown. She sure as hell wasn't Alana.

Nervously glancing around the room, Kate toyed with the amethyst pendant that hung just above her breasts. She hadn't worn the ring Luc had bought her; that would've just felt wrong. She'd actually placed it in his desk drawer days ago, though she had no clue if he'd found it.

Since Luc had started his best-man duties, she'd pretty much been on her own. That was fine, actually. The more she was around Luc, the harder she was finding it to face the reality that while she was having his baby, he'd never see her as more than a speech writer who happened to be giving him an heir.

Once the evening wound down, perhaps they could talk. She held out hope that he would remember the woman she was before his accident, not the liar she'd turned into for a few short days.

"Champagne, ma'am?"

The waiter, balancing a tray full of flutes of the bubbly drink, smiled at her. Kate shook her head.

"No, thank you."

As soon as he moved on another man approached her. He'd been only a few feet away and she'd seen him a few times during the evening. The tall stranger with tanned skin and black hair was hard to miss, especially when she'd caught him eyeing her more than once. He'd been smiling her way for a while, and now he was closing the gap between them.

"You turned down champagne and you're not dancing," he said in lieu of hello. "One would think you're not having a good time."

Kate smiled, trying to place his accent. Not Greek. Mikos had friends and acquaintances all over the world, so who knew where he was from?

"I'm having a great time," she told him. "It's so beautiful, I'm just taking in all the scenery."

"I've been taking in the scenery, too."

His eyes held hers, and the implication was not lost on her. At one time that line may have worked on her, but she felt absolutely no tingling or giddiness in her stomach when this man approached, blatantly hitting on her. Good thing, because she was certain she didn't have the strength to be tied up with more than one man.

"Would you care to dance?"

Kate glanced around. She hadn't seen Luc for a while, and more than likely he was schmoozing with people he rarely got to see. Besides, it wasn't as if he had a claim on her. He'd pretty much brought her here for one of two reasons: as a lame plan B or to keep an eye on her. Either way, he'd ignored her most of the evening, and she was entitled to some fun, too.

"I'd love to."

Kate slid her hand through the stranger's arm and held on to the crook of his elbow as he led her to the dance floor. When he found an opening, he spun her around until she was in his arms. Kate purposely kept her body from lining up against his as she placed her hand on his shoulder and curled her fingers around his outstretched hand.

"I'm Kate, by the way."

A smile kicked up at the corner of his mouth. "I'm Lars."

"Pleasure to meet you," she said as he turned her in a wide circle. "You're a great dancer."

"I'm actually a professional ballroom dancer." He laughed as he led her into a slower dance when the song changed. "Stick with me tonight and we'll be the envy of all the other couples."

Kate couldn't help but laugh at his blatant ego. "I should tell you, I'm taken."

Well, she wasn't exactly taken, but she was having another man's child, and she was in love with said man, even though he didn't return the feelings. So she felt it necessary to let Lars know he stood no chance with her.

He leaned in closer to whisper into her ear. "Yet he's not here and I am." When he leaned back, his smile remained in place. "Don't worry. I just wanted to dance with the most stunning woman in the room."

"I think that honor goes to the bride," Kate corrected.

Darcy had looked magnificent in a fitted ivory dress with an elegant lace overlay, complete with a lace train that would make any princess envious. Darcy had looked like a character from a fairy-tale romance, and her Prince Charming at the end of the aisle had had nothing but love on his face for his bride.

Would Kate ever find that? Would she ever find a man who looked at her as though there was nothing greater in the world than the fact she lived in it?

"Uh-oh. I'm going to start questioning my skills if you keep frowning."

Kate shook the thoughts away. "Your dance skills

are perfect, though I'm sure you already knew that. I think the jet lag is getting to me."

Not to mention the pregnancy...which she and Luc still hadn't discussed announcing. So for now, she was keeping it to herself. Granted, not many people knew who she was, but the same could not be said for Luc.

Lars opened his mouth to say something, but his eyes darted over Kate's shoulder as he came to a stop.

"It's time to go, Kate."

Turning, she saw Luc standing less than a foot away.

"I'm dancing right now," she commented, not letting go of her partner's hand. "I can find my way back. You go on."

Luc pasted on a deadly smile and glanced at Lars. "I'm sure he will understand. Won't you, Lars?"

The other man merely nodded and stepped back, but not before kissing Kate's hand. "It was truly my pleasure."

Then he disappeared in the crowd of dancers, most likely heading to find another partner. Kate jerked around, clenching her teeth.

"Watch what you say," Luc warned as he took her arm and led her away. "I've got plenty to tell you, too, so save it until we're alone."

"What makes you think I'm going anywhere with you?" she said through gritted teeth. "You can't tell me who to spend time with."

Luc's fingers tightened around her arm as he leaned in closer to her side. "Oh, we're going to be alone, and I'm going to explain to you exactly why that little scene will never happen again."

Fifteen

Luc was seething. He hated like hell that his emotions had overridden common sense, but the second he'd seen Kate dancing with Lars, all rational thoughts had vanished.

The palace was big enough to house the special guests of the bride and groom, so Luc was glad he didn't have to drag Kate too far before he lit into her.

He'd purposely avoided her as much as he could because of her body-hugging dress. That damn gown nearly had him babbling like some horny teen, but he'd somehow managed to keep his tongue in his mouth when he first saw her. Luc knew if he'd stayed too close to Kate this evening, there would be no way to hide his obvious attraction.

And he couldn't let the attraction show, because Kate might try to use that...for what? Wasn't he set on using her?

Only now that he'd seen her in the arms of another man, the game had just changed. Luc wanted her. Right now.

He reached the second floor and headed down the hall to his suite. He had no clue if Kate was deliberately toying with him, but she had him tied in knots he'd never be able to untangle thanks to that little stunt with Lars...a man Luc despised.

"I want to go to my room," she demanded, yanking from his hold as soon as he stopped in front of a set of double doors. "I'm not going in there with you."

Resting his hand on the knob, Luc threw a smirk over his shoulder. "You are."

Kate's eyes narrowed. "No, my room is down the hall."

Before he realized his intentions, he'd pulled her around, wedging her body between his and the door. "Your room is right here until I'm done with you."

"Well, I'm already done talking. You were completely rude down there. You can't just—"

His mouth covered hers. If she was done talking, then he'd find better use for that mouth and ignore all the damn red flags waving around in his mind. He didn't care about all the reasons this was wrong, didn't care that moments ago she'd been in another man's arms. Right now she was in *his* arms, and he was taking full advantage of that lush, curvy body.

Kate's hands came up to his shoulders to push at him, but Luc settled his palms on her hips and pressed against her. Suddenly, her fingertips were curling into his tuxedo jacket.

The feel of her rounded hips beneath her killer dress was just as potent as this steamy kiss. Kate tipped her head slightly, but the silent invitation was all he needed to trace a path with his tongue down the column of her throat.

"Luc," she panted in a whisper. "We're in the hallway."

Gripping her hips, Luc rested his forehead against her collarbone. "You make me crazy, Kate. Out of my mind crazy."

Reaching around her, he opened the door. As soon as they were inside, he closed it, flicked the lock and leaned back against it.

"Did you bring me to your suite to talk or to have sex?" she asked, her arms folded across her beautifully displayed chest. "Because I know what you said, but that episode in the hall has me confused."

Luc remained where he was as he raked a hand down his face. "Lars isn't a good idea." He ignored her narrowed gaze. "Seeing you in his arms… He's a player, Kate."

She held Luc's eyes for a moment before she burst out laughing. "You're kidding me. You interrupt my dance, you manhandle me out of the ballroom and up the steps, and then you attempt to make out with me in the hallway because you're jealous? And you're calling someone else a player?"

"First of all, I'm not jealous." Wow, that almost sounded convincing. "Second, I never manhandled you, and third, you were completely on board with what was going on in the hallway. You moaned."

Kate rolled her eyes and turned to stalk across the open suite. "I did not moan."

Luc didn't know which view was better, the front of Kate's gown with the glimpse of her breasts or the back, where he could fully focus on the perfection of her shape. She stood at the desk, her hands resting on it, her head dropped forward.

"I don't know what you want from me." Her voice was so low he had to move closer to hear. "I won't allow you to pull me all these directions because of your out-of-control emotions, Luc. You know how strongly I feel for you, and yet you continue to torture me."

He was counting on those feelings to get him what he wanted. As much as he hated to admit it, he needed Kate in every way.

Before Luc realized it, he'd completely closed the distance between them. Sliding his hands around her waist, he pressed his palms against her still-flat stomach and jerked her body against his.

"You think you don't torture me?" he asked, his lips brushing the side of her ear. She shivered against him. "You think seeing you dressed like this, moving your body against another man's, isn't pure hell?"

"Why do you care?"

"Because just the thought of you turns me inside out. Because knowing how sexy you are wearing only a smile that I put on your lips turns me on faster than anything."

Luc eased her around and framed her face with his hands. "Because I'm so torn up over what to do about you, all I can think of is getting you out of this damn dress and seeing if this chemistry is real or if it only existed when I thought we were engaged."

Kate's breath caught in her throat as she stared back at him. "I can't sleep with you as an experiment, Luc. I love you." Her voice cracked and her eyes filled with tears. "I'm not hiding how I feel. I can't. But I also can't be used on a whim, whenever you get an itch you need to scratch."

"You're more than an itch."

"What am I?" she whispered.

Luc couldn't put a label to this madness that had become his life. He'd planned on seduction, but he hadn't planned on the jealousy that had speared through him moments ago. Kate was his.

"You're the woman I'm about to put on this desk and strip until she's wearing nothing but that pendant. You're the woman who is going to forget everything else but what's happening right here, right now."

"Sex won't solve anything."

"No, but it will take the edge off for both of us."

Luc leaned closer, rubbing his lips across hers, so slowly. He reached around, found the zipper and eased it down. When the material parted in the back, he splayed his hand across her bare skin, relishing the way she trembled against him.

"Tell me you don't want this," he murmured against her mouth. "Tell me you don't want to see what happens right now between us, and you can walk out that door before we get too far to turn back."

Luc started to peel her dress away from her body. He stepped back just enough for the gown to ease down and puddle at her feet, leaving her standing in a strapless bra and matching panties, and that purple stone that rested against her flawless skin. Trailing his fingertips over the swell of her breasts, Luc smiled when she arched against his touch.

"Say the word, Kate, and I'll stop."

Her eyes closed as she dipped her head back. "You don't play fair."

"Oh, baby, I haven't even begun to play."

She was going to put a stop to this…then Luc had to go and say those words dripping in seduction while he tempted her with just the tips of his fingers. The man was potent. He knew exactly what to do to get her aroused, to get her wanting more.

Why was she letting this happen? He had no intention of professing his love. He wouldn't even give her a straight answer earlier when she'd asked who she was to him.

Yet here she stood, in her heels, her underwear and goose bumps from his touch.

How could she deny him? How could she deny herself? All she wanted was this man, and here he was. If she had even a glimmer of a chance to get him to see how good they were together, she'd take it. Her heart couldn't break any more…could it?

Luc's mouth followed the trail of his fingertips along the tops of her breasts, just over the lacy bra cups. "I'll take your silence as a go-ahead."

Kate slid her fingers into his inky-black hair as she looked down at him. "I can't say no to you."

"I didn't intend to let you."

He crushed her body to his as his mouth claimed hers. Kate shoved his tux jacket off and to the floor. Without breaking contact, she started unbuttoning his shirt. The need to feel his skin next to hers was all-consuming.

Luc wrapped his hands around her waist and lifted her onto the desk. He jerked his shirt off, sending the rest of the buttons popping and scattering across the hardwood floor. The sight of that bare chest, the familiar tattoo and a smattering of chest hair had her heart beating in double time and her body aching.

He stepped between her thighs, encircled her torso with his arms and jerked her to the edge.

"Wrap your legs around me."

His husky demand had her obeying in an instant.

What was it about this man that could have her throwing all common sense aside and practically bowing to his every wish?

Love. That's all it boiled down to. If she didn't love him, if she hadn't been in love with him for some time, she never would've allowed herself to be put in this vulnerable position.

Luc managed to work off her bra and panties with a quick, clever snap and torn material. The fact he was so eager sent warmth spreading through her. She'd made him this reckless, this out of control.

And that right there told her she had the upper hand.

Squeezing her legs tighter against his narrow hips, Kate gripped his head and pulled him down to her mouth. Instantly, he opened, groaning against her. His hands seemed to be everywhere at once. How else could she explain all the shivers, the rippling, the tingling?

"Lean back," he muttered against her lips.

Kate leaned back on the smooth desk, resting her weight on her elbows. When his eyes locked onto hers, the moment he joined them, Kate couldn't help the burn in her throat, the instant tears pricking her eyes. Even though their bond may have started off with a lie, it didn't diminish the fact she loved him. He cared for her more than he let on, too, or they wouldn't be here right now.

Kate shoved aside all worry, all thoughts, and reveled in the moment. Luc was here, with her. He was making love to her in a slow, passionate way that was polar opposite to the frantic way he'd stripped them both moments ago. Did she dare hope he wanted more from her?

Luc leaned over her, kissed her softly and rested his forehead against hers. With Luc's hands gripping her waist, she held on to his shoulders and kept her gaze on him.

Within moments, her body climbed, tightened. Luc muttered something she didn't quite understand. Between the Portuguese and the low whisper, his words were lost. But then his own body stiffened against hers as he squeezed his eyes shut.

Once the tremors ceased, Luc picked her up and carried her to his bed, draped in gold-and-white sheers. He laid her down and slid in beside her, pulling her body against his.

"Sleep." His hands immediately went to her stomach. "Rest for our baby."

Kate closed her eyes, wondering if this blossom of hope in her chest would still be there come morning. Wondering if the man she'd fallen in love with was actually starting to love her back.

Sixteen

Nausea hit her hard. Kate prayed that if she just lay still the queasiness would pass. Until now, she'd had no symptoms of pregnancy, save for the missed period and being tired. Those things she could handle.

As for the man who had put her in this situation in the first place, well, that was another story.

Kate tried to focus on the fact she'd spent the night in Luc's bed, this time with him fully aware of who she was and why she was there. Surely that meant something. Surely they'd crossed some major barrier and things would only get better from here.

Kate wasn't naive, but she was hopeful. She had to be.

But the bed next to her was empty, cool. She sat up, clutching the sheet to her chest. That abrupt movement had her stomach roiling. Bad idea. She closed her eyes and waited for the dizziness to pass before she risked scanning the oversize bedroom for Luc.

He stood near the floor-to-ceiling window, sipping a cup of coffee. His bare back, with bronze skin and dark ink, stared back at her. She didn't want this to be awkward, but she had no idea what to say, how to act. She'd selfishly given in to her desires last night, not thinking of consequences. Well, she had thought of them, but she'd chosen to weigh heavily on the side of optimism.

Her legs shifted beneath the warm satin sheets. Luc glanced over his shoulder at the sound, then focused his attention back on the sunrise. She had to admit the orange sky glowing with radiant beauty was a sight to behold, but was he not going to say anything?

Please, please don't let this be awkward.

Kate eased back against the headboard and tucked the sheet beneath her arms to stay fully covered. Not that he hadn't seen all of her multiple times, but she was getting a vibe that this wasn't going to be a good morning, and the last thing she wanted to do was go into battle fully naked.

"I've been trying to figure out what the hell to do here."

His words sliced right through the beauty of the morning, killing any hope she'd built. His tone wasn't promising. If anything, it was angry, confused.

"I watched you sleep," he went on, still not looking at her. Damn it, why wouldn't he turn around? "I even tried to rest, but there are so many thoughts going around in my mind that I don't even know where to start or what's real."

"Everything that happened in this room last night was real." If nothing else, she wanted, needed, him to realize that. "Did you only bring me here for sex, Luc?"

Speaking her fear aloud had her heart cracking. She

wanted to be strong, she truly did, but there was only so much a woman could take.

"I wanted you." Luc turned to face her, but made no move to cross the room. "I've fought this urge since you came to work for me. I got engaged to another woman knowing full well I wanted you physically. Even after that engagement ended, I still had this ache for you, even though I knew I couldn't act on it."

Kate clutched the sheet as he went on.

"I wasn't in a good spot when we were at the beach house," he continued. "I was an emotional wreck, and I never should've had you come with me, not when I knew just how much I wanted you."

Her eyes darted back to his. "You were angry with me," she reminded him. "Before the accident, you kissed me—"

"I kissed you because I couldn't keep fighting the attraction. I kissed you out of anger toward myself, and then I was even angrier. I was rough with you, so I stomped off like a child."

And then he'd been injured and forgotten everything.

Kate licked her dry lips. "I don't know what to say."

"Honestly, I don't, either." Luc slowly walked toward the bed, coming to stand at the end of it and holding her gaze. "There's part of me that wants to be able to trust you again, but you hurt me, Kate. I never thought that was possible. And that's what had me up all night."

Kate cringed at his harsh words. What could she say? He was right.

"I thought we were going to move past that," she stated, praying the possibility even existed. "You said we'd move on, that we'd have a professional relationship."

Luc's arms stretched wide as he eyed the bed. "Is

this professional? I sure as hell don't feel like your boss right now, Kate. You're having my child, the next heir to the throne after me."

"And is that all I am, then? The mother to the next heir?" She needed more. Even after her lies, she deserved to know. "Are you using my feelings against me? You know how I feel, and you got so jealous last night. Was that all to stroke your ego or to puff your chest out because you're in control?"

Luc propped his hands on his narrow hips as he stared down at her. He'd put on his black tuxedo pants, but hadn't buttoned them. It was hard to sit here and discuss all of this with him half-dressed and her wearing a sheet, but Kate had her pride, and she refused to give in to her body's needs. She didn't need Luc; she wanted him. Yes, it hurt to know he didn't feel the same, but she wasn't going to beg…ever.

His silence was deafening. Kate shook her hair away from her face. The nausea hadn't lessened; if anything, she felt worse. She placed a hand beside her hip on the bed, closed her eyes and took a deep breath.

"Kate?"

The mattress dipped beside her. When Luc grabbed her hand, she pulled back. "No." She met his worried gaze. "I'm not playing the pregnancy card for your sympathy and attention. You don't get to pick and choose when it's convenient to show affection."

"You're pale. Are you all right?"

If only he would have cared first thing this morning instead of starting this day with voicing his doubts and crushing her hopes.

"I'm dizzy. It's to be expected." She shifted, scooting a bit farther away from him. "I'm not going to be pulled in different directions depending on your moods, either. You either want me, on a personal level and not just for sex, or you don't. If my dancing with some guy bothers you, then maybe you need to reevaluate your feelings. But don't come to me again unless you're sure I'm more than just a warm body to you."

Slowly, Luc came to his feet and nodded. "I plan on having you, Kate. I plan on marrying you, actually. You'll become my wife before my birthday. I'll secure the title and you'll get to live out whatever fantasy you had when you wanted to play the engaged couple."

"What?" Shock replaced her nausea instantly. "I'm not marrying you just so you can get a title. I want to marry for love."

Luc's eyes narrowed. "You say you love me, so why not marry me?"

"Because you don't love me. I won't be used as a pawn in your royal quest."

Air whooshed from her lungs. She'd never thought herself naive, but that's exactly what she was. She should've gone into this with eyes wide-open and seen his motivations for what they were…lust and greed. Any love between them was absolutely one-sided, and she had no one to blame but herself…yet again.

She should've seen this coming, should've known nothing would ever get in the way of the great Luc Silva and his crown. The man she'd grown to love from the island was just as fake as their engagement. Then, he'd been warm, open. Now he was all business.

"I'm going back to the palace as soon as I get my stuff together," she told him. "I'll have the pilot come back whenever you want to leave, but I won't be flying with you. I also won't be working for you. I'll finish out my duties for the next couple of weeks, but after that, I'm done."

"As my wife, I wouldn't expect you to work for me."

Kate clenched her teeth, praying she didn't burst into angry tears. "I won't be your wife."

Luc shoved his hands in his pockets, hesitated, then made his way to the door. "Don't make any hasty decisions. I'll leave you to get your dress back on."

Then he was gone, leaving only the deafening sound of the door clicking shut as she sat there in the rumpled sheets.

That was it? Luc may have walked out of this conversation, but he wasn't going to back down on this ridiculous notion of them getting married. Kate needed to prepare herself, because this fight was just getting started.

She tossed back the sheet and was thankful she wasn't dizzy when she got to her feet. At least she had one thing going for her this morning.

Of course, now she had to put on her dress from last night and do the walk of shame down the wide, long hallway to her own suite, to change and pack. Which was fine, because she wasn't staying any longer. If he planned on using her, using her feelings against her in some ploy to get ahead, then maybe he wasn't the man she loved at all. Maybe she'd been living a lie this entire time…

There was no way she could continue working for Luc indefinitely. No way she could look at him every single day and know she was good enough for sex, but not good enough to build a life with if the throne wasn't at stake. They'd made a baby and he still was only looking out for his title. Well, she sure as hell wasn't sticking around to see him parade his possible future wives in and out of his life.

Kate had been a fool to think their intimacy had

changed Luc's mind. The struggle of seeing him every day, knowing he didn't return her love, would be just too hurtful.

When she returned to the palace, she would call her parents and make plans. She would finish up the projects she and Luc had begun, and then she needed to get away. She needed to focus on what was truly important in her life.

Luc brought the sledgehammer up and swung it through the partial non-load-bearing wall. Busting this drywall to expand the living space with the kitchen wasn't even remotely helping to quell his frustration and anger. All he was doing was working up a good sweat and a bit of nostalgia from when he and Kate had torn into the bathroom.

When Luc had gotten back to the palace, he'd taken his boat—sans guards, much to Kate's father's disapproval—and headed to his beach house. Luc knew the workers would be done for the day, and since the house was only an hour from the palace, he needed time to think, to reflect on what an insufferable jerk he'd been in that bedroom three days ago.

His intention had been to get Kate to agree to marry him. He hadn't cared about her feelings. But the way she'd sat there, all rumpled in a mess of satin sheets, as she'd stared up at him with hurt in her eyes, had seriously gotten to him. He hadn't expected to feel anything beyond want and need for her. Yet it was hard to ignore the constant lump of guilt that kept creeping up when he thought of how he'd broken her so fast, with so few words.

Luc eased the sledgehammer down on the rubble and wiped his arm across his forehead. His mother would probably die if she saw he had blisters on his hands from manual labor, but he needed the outlet. Unfortunately, it wasn't doing the job.

And it didn't help that Kate was everywhere in this house. The empty yellow vase on the scarred dining table mocked him. He couldn't even look at the damn shower in his master suite. The balcony, the chaise in the living room, the bed, the beach… The memories flooded his mind. She'd touched literally every surface here.

Just as she'd touched every part of him.

Luc reached behind his neck and yanked his T-shirt over his head. His cell vibrated in his pocket and he thought about ignoring it, but with Kate being pregnant, he had to be on full alert.

Pulling the cell out, he glanced at the screen. Swallowing a curse, he let out a sigh and answered.

"Yes?"

"You rushed out of here and didn't take a guard?"

His mother's question didn't require an answer, because she already knew. "I needed to be alone."

"That's not smart. You can't be taking off like this, Lucas. You know your birthday is less than two months away. You need to be home so we can figure out what we're going to do."

Luc raked a hand over his damp face and stared out at the sun, which was starting to dip toward the horizon.

"I just needed a few days to myself."

"Is this about Kate? Darling, I know she hurt you, but that poor girl is miserable. I didn't want to say anything, but since the wedding she's been looking pale and drained."

Luc straightened. "Is she sick?"

"I'd guess she's pregnant."

Silence filled the line and Luc's heart sank. They hadn't said a word to anybody, and the pain in his mother's tone came through loud and clear.

"We haven't told anyone," Luc stated in a low voice, suddenly feeling like a kid again for lying to his mother. "She just found out before the wedding, and we had a bit of a fight. Is she okay?"

"A fight?" Of course his mom honed in on that and not his question. "Lucas, the woman is carrying your child and you argue with her? No wonder she looks exhausted. She's been working like a dog since she got back. That's why I wanted to know why you left the palace so suddenly."

Luc gripped the phone. "It's best if I'm not there right now."

"I think you two need to talk. If you're worried about the no-fraternizing rule, I think we can make an exception for Kate. Maybe she's the answer to—"

"I've already thought of that," he interrupted, cutting her off. "Kate doesn't want to marry me."

"Why don't you come home," his mother stated. "We can't solve any problems with you brooding alone."

He glanced at the mess he'd made. It wasn't as if he knew what to do next, but the contractors had done an amazing job of renovating the bathroom he and Kate had torn into. They'd come to finish the kitchen once Luc gave the go-ahead after this wall was gone.

"I'm leaving now," he told his mother. "Tell Kate I want to see her."

"I'll see what I can do, but she may have left for the day."

If she'd left, he'd go to her place. She didn't live too far from the palace, and if he had any say, she'd be inside that palace by the time their baby came.

Anything else was unacceptable.

Having her that last time had changed something in him, and nearly changed his marriage plan. That's why he'd been up all night, second-guessing his motives. He'd thought he could check out emotionally, but he felt too much—guilt, desire...more.

He'd hurt her in ways he'd never, ever imagined he could. Yet she still did her job. She'd still come with him to the wedding. She still supported him.

And he loved her. His feelings were as simple and as complicated as that. He loved Kate with everything he had and he'd messed up—man, had he messed up.

Luc needed to tell her how he felt. More important, he needed to show her. Saying the words was easy; proving to Kate how much she meant to him would be the hurdle. But he hadn't gone through all of this to give up now. Kate was his and he damn well wasn't going to let her go.

Seventeen

It had been nearly a week since he'd last talked to Kate, and he was going out of his mind.

He'd come back to his office and found a letter of resignation on his desk. She'd left a message through her mother that she was fine and the baby was fine, but she wanted to be on her own for a bit.

A bit was longer than he could stand.

He'd lived without this woman for too long and refused to live that way another second.

His birthday was fast approaching, but even the looming date hadn't entered his mind. For the past few days all that had played over and over was how stupid he'd been, how heartless and crass he'd been with his words, his actions. No wonder Kate wanted to leave, to steer clear of him. She loved him and he'd proposed to her with the pretense that he was doing so only to climb higher on the royal ladder.

He hadn't needed much time after their last night together to realize walking away had been a mistake. Letting her believe he wanted her only for the crown was wrong.

Luc wanted Kate because she made him whole.

It had taken him some time to get the information on her whereabouts from her parents, and to have the construction crew finish some of the renovations on his beach home. He'd pulled some strings to get her here, but he wanted this to be perfect when he finally revealed the house and his true feelings. Nothing but the best for Kate from here on out.

He'd taken that extra time to find out more about the woman he loved. And he hoped the surprise he'd planned would help her understand just how much he wanted her in his life.

Luc stood in the living room watching the water, waiting for that familiar boat to dock. He'd recruited the help of Kate's parents. Of course, in order to do that, he'd had to pull out all the stops and really grovel to them. If everything worked out the way he'd hoped, every ego-bursting, pride-crushing moment would be worth it.

When the boat finally came into view, Luc's nerves really kicked into gear. He might have planned every bit of this evening, but Kate ultimately held all the power and control.

Her father helped her up onto the dock, leaned forward for a hug and watched as Kate mounted the steps. Luc moved to the doorway and waved as the man began to pull the boat away from the berth.

By the time Kate got to the top of the steps, Luc's heart was beating faster than ever. She lifted her head, pushing her windblown hair away from her face. The second her eyes locked onto his, Luc felt that familiar punch to his gut. The punch that said if she turned him down he would be absolutely crushed and broken.

"I was hoping you wouldn't put up a fight," he told her, remaining in the doorway.

"I was tempted to jump overboard a couple of times, but I knew my dad would only go in after me." She clasped her hands together and remained still. "What am I doing here, Luc, and why am I being held hostage?"

"You're not a hostage," he countered.

She glanced over her shoulder before looking back. "My father left with the boat and the only other one here is yours. By my accounts, I'm here with no way out except with your permission."

"Come inside."

Her brow quirked as she crossed her arms over her chest...a chest that was more voluptuous than when he'd seen her last.

"Please," he added, when she didn't move. "Please come inside so we can talk."

Finally, she moved forward, and Luc let her pass him and enter first. The familiar, floral scent teased his senses and mocked him. He'd lain awake at night imagining that scent, pretending she was by his side.

"Oh, Luc."

Her gasp was enough to have him smiling. "Looks a little different, doesn't it?"

He watched her survey the newly designed, open floor plan. Thick columns stood as support beams, but they didn't take away from the romantic ambience, they merely added to it. He'd left the back wall of patio doors open, to put the Mediterranean on full display.

"It's gorgeous," she exclaimed, running her hand along the marble-topped table behind the sofa. "This was all done so fast."

"I wanted it done before I invited you back." He remained in the doorway, but kept his eyes on her as she walked through the living area and kitchen. "I even helped the contractors and learned how to do more than tear things down."

She stopped by the old dining table and her eyes landed on the yellow vase, then darted across the room to him.

"I couldn't get rid of either of those," he told her. "We shared too many meals at that table, and even though it's not new, it reminds me of you. Every time I see that vase I think of how excited you were that day at the market."

She picked up the vase, running her hands around it. For a moment Luc worried she might launch it at his head, but she finally set it down and turned back to face him. With her arms crossed over her midsection, she let out a sigh.

"What do you want, Luc?"

Her eyes held his. Now that they were face-to-face, he couldn't deny the force that hovered between them.

"Are you feeling okay?" he asked, taking slow, cautious steps toward her. "Everything all right with our baby?"

"We're both doing great," she informed him. "And you could've texted or called or replied to the emails I sent."

"You sent final work emails through your father."

She nodded. "That's because I quit, remember? I've outlined your next year of engagements. I'm assuming you came up with a way to secure your title? Is that why you can bother with me now?"

"No. I didn't secure the title."

Kate gasped. "Your birthday is only weeks away."

"I'm aware of that." He stood directly in front of her, so close she had to tip her head up to look him in the eyes. "That's why you're here."

Her lips thinned as she narrowed her gaze at him. "You've got to be kidding me. You brought me here to use me? You still think I'm going to swoon, fall at your feet and marry you so you can get a shiny new crown?"

Just as she started to push past him, Luc grabbed her arm and halted her escape. "No. I think you're going to listen to me and look in my eyes when I tell you how much I love you."

Those dark eyes held his, but he saw no emotion there. "Did you hear me?"

"I hear you just fine," she said through clenched teeth. "How convenient that you love me right before you're set to lose it all if you don't have a wife."

He turned to face her fully as he gripped both her bare shoulders. "You and these damn sexy strapless dresses," he muttered, stroking her skin with his thumbs. "Cause me to forget the powerful speech I was about to make. I'm pretty proud, considering it's the first one I've had to write for myself."

"I don't want to hear your speech and I don't want you touching me."

Luc smiled. "Then why is the pulse at the base of your neck pounding as fast as my heart? You may lie to yourself, Kate, but your body is telling me the truth."

Her eyes widened. "Oh, no. You brought me here for sex? You think I'll fall back into bed with you and then, in the throes of passion, agree to a marriage?"

Luc laughed, then kissed her full on the mouth before easing back. "Your imagination is running away with you and I'm royally screwing this up."

"That's the only thing that's getting screwed tonight."

His heart was so full, he couldn't help but keep smiling. "I've missed that smart mouth."

Kate didn't say a word, didn't move and didn't make any attempt to touch him.

"Tell me I didn't mess things up so badly that I've lost you forever."

"You never fully had me," she told him. "I wanted everything with you, but went about it the wrong way. Then you decided to use my love and try to force me into marriage. That's no foundation to build a relationship on."

"We both messed up," he agreed. "I never meant to hurt you, but I was so confused. I wanted to trust my feelings, but how could I when I couldn't even trust you? I thought if you wanted me so badly, you'd marry me and I'd get the title. I didn't realize you truly had no ulterior motive."

"I understand why you couldn't trust me." She reached up, wrapped her hands around his wrists and pulled his hands off her shoulders. "What I can't understand is why you used my feelings against me, why you made love to me at Mikos's wedding and then acted like you had no clue where to slot me in your life."

Luc shoved his hands in his pockets. She didn't want to be touched, and right now he was dying to have her in his arms. This was going to be trickier than he'd thought, but he wasn't giving up. She'd come, she was talking to him and that had to mean a lot.

"I have something to show you."

He walked to the desk tucked in the corner of the room and grabbed the email he'd printed out. When he handed it to her, she didn't take it.

"Please?"

Kate slid the paper from his grasp. Luc watched her face as she read. When her eyes filled with tears, her hand came up to cover her quivering chin and her lips, Luc knew she wasn't completely lost to him.

She clutched the letter to her chest. "You went to the orphanage?"

"I did." And he'd loved every minute of it. "I met Carly and Thomas. I was told they were friends of yours."

Kate nodded, the jerky movement causing a tear to spill. "I love those two so much. They are such sweet kids, but most people want to adopt new babies. The twins are nine, but they have such big hearts and they say they want the babies to go to new homes. Still, I know they long for a set of parents to love them."

"I was told it's hard, too, because most people are only looking to adopt one," he added.

"I try to get there to visit them as often as I can," she said, swiping at her eyes. "I call them if I get too busy working and can't make it."

"They're at the orphanage you were living in as a baby." Luc cupped her damp face. "And that's why they are so important to you. I can completely see why you wanted me to go visit. Those little kids thought talking to a real prince was so neat. I didn't talk much about the royalty side of my life with Carly and Thomas, but we did discuss Portuguese culture, and they were so fascinated."

"I can't believe you went and didn't tell me," she exclaimed.

"Actually, we just missed each other. When I arrived, I was told you had left the day before."

Kate's eyes widened. "I wish I'd known."

"Why, Kate? Would you have stayed there? Would you have waited for me?"

She shook her head. "I—I don't know."

"I want to start over with you." That sounded so

lame he laughed. "I've been miserable without you and I went to that orphanage not because you kept asking me to, but because I wanted to know more about you. I wanted to know more about the woman I had fallen in love with. I love you, Kate. I want a life with you, a life just like the one we had when we were all alone here."

Kate closed her eyes as her body fell into his. Her forehead rested against his chest. "You don't mean all of that," she whispered. "Because if you even think I can just try this out, or be with you because of some tradition, you're wrong."

When she lifted her head, Luc smoothed her hair away from her damp cheeks. "I don't want to try it, Kate. I want to do it. My calling you here has nothing to do with the throne, my birthday or the baby. I mean, I want to build a family with you, but I'm not using the baby to do so. I want you for you. The days we spent here were some of the best of my life. I want more days like that, and nobody else will do. You're it for me, Kate."

When her mouth parted in another gasp, he kissed her. Luc nipped at her lips and nearly cried when she responded and opened for him.

The gentle, tender kiss had that sliver of hope in his chest practically exploding now.

"I missed you," he murmured against her lips. "I missed holding you, I missed watching you cook, I missed seeing you smile, and even arguing with you over stupid things like my schedule. I missed seeing you wearing my ring."

Her brows drew in as Luc pulled the amethyst ring from his pocket.

"Você vai casar comigo?" he asked.

Will you marry me?

"Not because of the throne, not because of anything else but us," he quickly said, before she got the wrong idea of his intentions. "I can feel utter fullness and love only with you, Kate. You're the only one who can make me complete."

Without waiting for her reply, he slid the ring onto her finger and gripped her hand in his. "This is where the ring belongs, until I can get you a diamond or whatever you want."

Kate stared down at her hand and said nothing. She studied the ring, even toyed with it before she smiled up at him. "I don't want another ring. I want this one. It's exactly what I would have chosen, and I don't need anything more."

"Does this mean you'll marry me?" he asked.

Kate threw her arms around his neck, buried her face against his skin and squeezed him tight. "I'll marry you, Luc. I'll raise babies with you and grow old with you."

Luc crushed her body to his and let out the first good breath he'd had since she stepped into his house. No, their house.

Kate jerked back. "Wait. We need to marry soon. Your birthday—"

"It will be fine. My father may have rigged the law a tad to buy us a few extra weeks. I want to give you the wedding you deserve."

"I don't want a huge, highly publicized wedding. Is that okay?"

Luc framed her face, sliding his thumb across her full bottom lip. "Perfectly fine with me. But right now I'd rather have you in my shower, where I can properly show you how much I've missed you."

"I do love that shower of yours."

He kissed her smile. "After I make love to you, we

can discuss the wedding. Oh, and the fact I'd like to adopt Carly and Thomas. I wanted to talk to you first. With the new baby and all I wasn't sure—"

Kate's mouth cut him off as she rained kisses all over his lips, his chin, his cheeks. "Yes, yes, yes. I'd love to have them with me. I love those two so much. I just felt such a connection the first time I saw them."

"I did, too, honey." Luc picked her up and headed toward the master suite. "We'll discuss that later, too."

"You can't carry me," she cried. "I've gained weight."

His eyes dipped to her chest. "I've noticed, and I'm certainly not complaining."

She slapped his shoulder. "That's so typical of a man, to say that when bigger boobs are involved."

"There better never be another man eyeing your boobs," he scolded. "That's my job."

Kate's head fell against his shoulder as she laced her fingers together behind his neck. "Always, Luc. You're the only man for me."

* * * * *

LET'S TALK
Romance

For exclusive extracts, competitions
and special offers, find us online: